APPLE
BROWN
Betty

Phillip Thomas Duck

Apple Brown Betty

sepia™

APPLE BROWN BETTY

A Sepia Novel

ISBN-13: 978-0-373-83041-1
ISBN-10:   0-373-83041-6

www.kimanipress.com

Printed in U.S.A.

We wear the mask that grins and lies,
It hides our cheeks and shades our eyes....

—Paul Laurence Dunbar

ACKNOWLEDGMENTS

These thoughts were supposed to have been in my last year's release, *Grown and Sexy,* but due to unforeseen events didn't make it. Funny thing, I touched it up a bit but little has changed. The same people are in my corner that was present with *Playing with Destiny* through *Whispers Between the Sheets,* the aforementioned *Grown and Sexy* and now this joint. So to all that were disappointed by last year's omission, this is long overdue....

Writing a book is often described as a solitary accomplishment, but no endeavor truly is accomplished without the hands of others. First and foremost, I give honor and thanks to the Creator, from whom all blessings flow, the alpha and omega, the beginning and the end. Known around my home as God, I thank Him for the drive, talent and window of opportunity He cracked open on my behalf.

To my wife, affectionately known as Jay, the hours in my office writing and not by your side are forever lost. Thank you, despite this, for your constant encouragement and never-diminishing love.

To Ariana, you inspired me while working on *Playing with Destiny.* I'm forever grateful for "Daddy's Little Girl." In many ways I was lost until you came along on December 9. Happily, from the 10th on, my way has been clear and focused.

To my mother, my greatest desire is to buy you a house, pay your bills, attend to your every need and whim, satisfy all your wants and desires...and even then it would just be the interest on your loan of love. I think Tupac put it best: "Even though I act crazy, I gotta thank the Lord that you made me." Thank you.

To my brother, Michael, I know it's a lot to ask for you to read this entire book. (Smile). I should have named it *50 Cent* or *Playstation.* (LOL) I know you can get through these Acks though, right? You make me proud. Make yourself proud, as well. Good things soon come.

ACKNOWLEDGMENTS—CONTINUED

To Uncle Joe, for all intents and purposes you have been my father, because my biological one wouldn't bother. The mark of a man is in his words and work. You speak well and labor long. Thanks.

Aunt Ruth and Uncle Eddie, you're gone in the physical, pictures on my wall and memories in my heart now. But both of you added tremendously to my essence. Love y'all. RIP.

Family, on my side and in-laws, I thank you all for your support and love. That means the Duck family, the Hughes family, the Acal family, the Jaggassar family. I can't count you each by number, but you all hold a special place in my heart.

My aunts: Dorothy, Jackie and Janice, much love.

My uncle Pat, much love.

My cousin Vern (my twin) and his lovely wife, Vanessa, much love.

GGB (Gary Garfield Birch) and Pook (Wendell Logan), my brothers from a different mother. Your friendships are greatly appreciated. And yeah, we need to hang more, I know.

My goddaughter, Elania, the only little girl as beautiful as my own.

My entire HealthSouth family, especially my comrades-in-arms: Adrienne Dangler, Maggie Sessoms, Maureen Pressley, Ginny Dimmick, Becky Manning and Micha (finally somebody spelled your name correct!!!!). What we do is "underappreciated" by man, but smiled upon by God. Remember that.

My agent, Sara Camilli. Knew I wanted to do this after reading *Milk in My Coffee* by that other writer you represent. (Smile) It's still a trip to me that all these years later you are my literary guardian, and a darn good one too. Thanks.

Speaking of that other writer, Eric Jerome Dickey, thanks for that early inspiration. I swear I ain't know brothers wrote books. Thought it had to be some classic stuff, my beloved James Baldwin, Richard Wright, Chester Himes, or somebody. Thank you for the remix.

My editor, Glenda Howard. I've brought you wet clay three times so far; you've rolled up your sleeves every time and helped mold it. Thanks.

Linda Gill, for the opportunities and belief. Thanks.

ACKNOWLEDGMENTS—CONTINUED

My writer family.

Starting first with my "Literary Momma,"
Margaret Johnson-Hodge. You were the light when my
writing life was utter darkness. The only thing that trumps
your kind heart is your mighty pen. You write like the devil,
Momma.

Timmothy B. McCann. Miss you much.
"The game needs you."

Keith Lee Johnson. You are my writer-buddy for real.
And for the record, Cool Keith, so many "situations are
critical" concerning this biz, but we got this. It's been a
ride since the ATL, ain't it? And look how many fell off the
roller coaster. (Smile) Keep reaching for those heights.
See ya at the top.

Monica McKayhan, TaRessa Stovall, Philana Marie Boles,
Eric Pete, Victor McGlothin, Earl Sewell, Brandon Massey,
Karyn Langhorne, Marcus Major, Tracy Price-Thompson,
George Pelecanos, Franklin White, Trisha R. Thomas,
Joel McIver, Gregory Townes, Robert Fleming,
Cydney Rax, Victoria Christopher Murray, Brian Egeston,
Vincent Alexandria...and all my brethren crafting stories.
One love.

Tee Cee Royal and RawSistaz. Book-remarks. SistahCircle
Book Club. Avid-Readers. The Romer Review. The Backlist.
Thumper and the aalbc.com fam. APOOO. The Essence
board. Gilda Rogers at The Beyond Group. And everyone
who supports not just me but African-American
fiction as a whole. One love.

Pilgrim Baptist Church; Reverend Terrence K. Porter.

I know I've missed someone. Charge it to my
head and not my heart.

Lastly, but certainly not least...my readers.

Dear Reader,

I toil long hours for you. Write with my heart for you. Cook up stories for you. Hope you appreciate my efforts. I appreciate your support. Reach out anytime: hillwrite@aol.com, or by mail at P.O. BOX 207, Oakhurst, NJ 07755.

One,

Phillip Thomas Duck

APPLE BROWN BETTY

1/4 cup butter, melted
1 1/2 cups dry bread crumbs
4 or 5 tart apples, peeled and sliced
3/4 cup brown sugar
1 tsp cinnamon
Dash of salt
2 tbsp lemon juice
1/3 cup water

Mix melted butter and dry bread crumbs. Combine apples, sugar, cinnamon and salt. Put part of bread crumbs on bottom of greased casserole. Add layer of apples with bread crumbs, alternately, crumbs on top. Pour combined lemon juice and water over all. Cover and bake at 350°F for 1 hour. Uncover and bake half hour to brown. Makes 5 generous servings. Rhubarb or berries can be substituted for apples.

CHAPTER ZERO

"I know, Nan. Hot."

George Williams stuck his tough-as-worn-leather fingers under the bathtub spigot, recoiled them just as quickly. The flowing water was plenty hot, and yet, for Nan, it probably still wouldn't chase away the chill deep in her bones.

Nancy, George's wife, rocked on the toilet seat, an oversize blue terry-cloth robe hanging off her bony frame. She shivered despite the heat rising from the floor vent. George had been pumping her full of Cup o' Noodles for the past few weeks but her eyeballs continued slowly receding into her face. Her lips were dark, like overripe plums, getting darker and more chapped by the day. But George still found warmth in those lips.

"Code," Nancy slurred, bunching her shoulders together and fumbling to close the robe tighter around her body, a body covered with marks and goose bumps. Within the hour, knowing her, she'd be sweating, complaining about how hot it was. Her body temperature, like most everything else, was shot.

George studied the rising water level in the tub. "You cold, baby? I got the heat way up. It'll just be a couple more minutes, Nan. Okay?"

Nancy rocked forward again, snuck a peek in the tub and flared her nostrils in disgust. She looked away and shook her head.

The phone ringing from the living room crawled into the bathroom. George bit into his lip and then rose with expectation. He brushed his hand over Nancy's shoulder as he passed her.

He cleared his throat. His voice was tinged with nerves and regret as he answered the phone. "Hello, Williams' residence."

"Holla," a young male voice said.

"Excuse me?"

"Someone called me."

"I a—" George struggled to form the words.

"You sound like an oldie but goodie, player. You need a blessing, Pops?"

"Got your name off my son," George said. "I need some... stuff."

"Who's your son, Pops?"

"Shammond Slay."

"Slay." The young man's tone changed. "Slay never mentioned any father to me. Matter of fact, I'm lying, he did once. Said dude was dead."

George cleared his throat again; nerves and regret nonetheless remained. "I'm Shammond's stepfather." George closed his eyes, hoping and praying that this was and wasn't a roadblock. He did and didn't want this to go through smoothly. Complex.

"Aiight, Pops. I'll hook you up. What you need?"

"Crack," George said shamefully.

"Da rock...da da da rock," the young boy bellowed. "A blessing, like I said, right?"

George ground his teeth. There wasn't any blessing in this. "You can get it for me?"

"You live in the Beach Arms with Slay's moms?"

"She lives with me, yes."

"Meet me down at the beachfront by your apartment tower, past that shitty-ass bulldozer. I'll be down by where the streetlights are blown out."

"How do I—?"

Dial tone rudely ended George's query.

How do I know you? How much for the product?

Questions swirled through George's head as he placed the phone back in the cradle. It wasn't like he was experienced at this. He sighed and moved back toward the bathroom.

Nancy's blue terry-cloth robe lay in a puddle on the floor. She was submerged in the steaming-hot bathwater, still shivering. Her glassy gaze was off in the distance. She was oblivious of her husband standing nearby. George peered down at her, studying her nude form. Spindly arms, dark marks over her once-perfect maple skin, an unruly thatch of hair, flaked with dandruff, sprouting from between her bony thighs. Almost all of the beauty she once had, gone.

"I'll be back with something to hold you over," George whispered. A tear threatened his eye and he cleared his throat yet again and moved before the tear overtook him, before he changed his mind.

Despite his troubling task, he moved from his apartment tower with a spark in his step. The cold chill of the air hit him as soon as he exited the lobby. To make matters even worse, there was a strong wind blowing. He looked up at the flagpole by the streetlamp. The red, white and blue American flag and the black POW-MIA flag below it violently flapped in the wind. He rubbed his hands together and blew on them for warmth. The gesture was futile. There would be no warmth tonight. He looked both ways as he crossed the trash-strewn lot for the gate leading to the forgotten beach. He thought about years ago—close to twenty now he guessed—when Asbury Park thrived. The carnival rides, the exuberant boardwalk. All of it gone now. Back then he had a different wife and two little girls. Enduring the heartache of a woman that he didn't love and that didn't love him. Then he left it all for real love, for Nancy, Nan. Heartache was still a close friend, but love was a powerful salve. Love, he kept reminding himself in these dark hours, love.

Moving through the gate toward the sand of the beach, George kept his eyes on his feet as he walked through the patchy grass. He didn't want to step on those black bird droppings that dotted the ground like land mines. Reaching the sand of the forgotten beach, he looked back at the apartment tower, shook his head. The things one does in the name of love.

A rusted bulldozer spray painted with graffiti rested in the middle of the sandy plot of beach. He passed by it as he'd been instructed to do and moved down by the water so he could see up the other end of beach. The cold was really pressing upon him now, so he tightened the collar of his plaid hunting jacket and hunched his shoulders in to his ears. He hadn't even had time to change out of his maintenance clothes. He still wore the army-green khaki pants and long-sleeved corduroy shirt. He still had on those cheap and dangerous Honchos boots from Payless without a built-in steel toe. He continued to rub his hands together. Bouncing in place like a man who needed to urinate.

A figure moved from the shadows to his left. Tense and nervous, George jumped. It was an old bum, his pants dirty with what looked like oil stains but wasn't. The old man murmured something as he passed by, carrying a lone tire like a sack of groceries. George looked back to make sure the man had, in fact, moved on. He didn't want to get caught with his guard down and catch a screwdriver to the shoulder blade. The old man with his tire stumbled across the lot and disappeared into the alley next to George's apartment tower.

George looked at his watch, decided he might as well walk up the other end. He headed up the beach toward the non-lighted section, regret peppering his steps.

There were assorted brown and green bottles lying partially covered by sand. Crumpled cans of forty-ounce beers, too. Cigarette butts. Used crack vials. The sight of these things made George's stomach do funny things, made his insides rise and fall.

He noticed an outline move onto the beach ahead. It appeared to be a young man, smoking a cigarette or perhaps something else, so arrogant and hardened that the cold of the night didn't make him shiver or shake. George moved toward the shadow.

George came upon the young man and stood there silently, unsure, waiting on the youngster to speak first.

The young kid blew out a plume of smoke and then dropped his cigarette and stamped it into the sand. He wore a wool FUBU scully, a FUBU sweatshirt, baggy black FUBU jeans, Timberland boots and a black FUBU jean jacket—a walking billboard for FUBU. Even in the darkness of the night you could see the lack of care or worry in his eyes. He stood there looking at the ocean waves, George next to him, waiting.

"You brought some coin right?" FUBU asked after a moment.

George's posture changed. This was the moment. "Yeah, I got your money," he said. The words left a bitter taste in his mouth.

"Got some of my best shit in…you gonna love this, Pops."

"Not me, this is for someone else," George told him.

FUBU turned and looked at George. "That's one I never heard before."

"It's real."

"You probably wishing it so, Pops."

For some reason, George felt impelled to explain. "It's for my lady…she's got a bit of a problem. I'm just trying to help her out until we can figure out how to get her set right."

FUBU smirked. "I feel you, Pops. Screw rehab, right?"

George grimaced from the cut of judgment in FUBU's voice. Of course the kid was right, but life sometimes wasn't as simple as it should be; sometimes it was way too complex. George cleared his throat. "Not to rush you or anything," he said, "but it's cold out. My lady is waiting, this ain't exactly real estate we transacting here. I'd like to get on my way."

"Pass off the coin, then," FUBU said. "Twenty beans for two pops." He was trained to keep it cryptic so he'd never find himself pinned against a fence, his hands pulled painfully behind his back while he was read his Miranda rights.

Twenty beans. Twenty dollars, right?

Embarrassed to ask, George reached into his pocket, pulled out a crumpled twenty and handed it to FUBU. Overtime money, flushed down the drain. FUBU took the bill and placed it in the side pocket of his jacket. He lowered his head as if in thought, reached into his pocket again and pulled out a Newport. Pulled his lighter and deliberately lit the Newport. Shook his head and dragged on the cigarette.

"Aren't you forgetting something?" George asked.

"You got any other children than Slay, Pops?"

"I told you I wanted to move this along. You got my money. Can we finish up here?"

"You got any children other than Slay, Pops?" FUBU repeated.

"Look, youngster—"

FUBU cut him off. "Simple thing to ask, Pops. Answer the question. You got any other children?"

George sighed. "Two daughters from my first wife," he said. "My lady now has Shammond and his sister, Cydney. I consider them mines. I'm all they known since they was young. They daddy, Dare, um Darius, was a friend of mine and I—I kinda stepped in when he passed on."

"Is that so?" FUBU said. He took another drag on his cigarette. "You sound like a for-real cat, Pops. Banging your boy's old lady, claiming his seeds and making sure his old lady don't have to come out in the cold and suck some nigga's dick to get her fix on."

George's chest tightened. He pointed a crooked finger at FUBU's chest. "This is bullshit. Give me my stuff, boy."

FUBU dropped his cigarette, stamped it into the sand like

the previous one. He didn't acknowledge George's anger, didn't appear to fear it. Turning away, he started to walk off.

"Hey. Where are you going?" George called.

FUBU kept his step without looking back or answering.

George rushed him and grabbed ahold of his shoulder. FUBU wheeled around at the touch, something black, cold, steel, in his hand. He pressed that black finger of judgment into George's chest. Released that white heat into George; the shot lifted George up like a boxer's uppercut punch. Two more pops and George slumped down to his knees. FUBU stepped back and let George tumble face-first into the sand with the green and brown bottles, the crumpled forty-ounce beer cans, the crack vials.

"Sucka nigga," FUBU said as he spit on George and walked off with a strut of arrogance. The gunplay hadn't been a part of the job but he figured it wouldn't be frowned upon. He'd more than earned his money.

George moaned in pain for a moment, his eyelids heavy. He wondered how long it would be before he was found. His breaths came slower, just a drip of life left in him. Farther up the beach, in the other direction, was the rusted bulldozer spray painted with graffiti. Just beyond that was the bare grass with all those little black droplets of bird feces. Then there was the trash-strewn lot. The red, white and blue American flag and the black POW-MIA flag blowing violently against the flagpole. Then, at the end, the apartment tower, twenty-five floors in all. George wondered, as his last breath came, if Nancy, on the thirteenth floor, knew how much he truly loved her.

GEORGE

"*Curb. Step up, Dare,*" I say.

Darius Slay been my partner forever, so it pains me to see him like this. You can smell the whiskey without him even opening his mouth, just seeping out his skin I guess. His unlaced, no-name brand sneaker falls off his right foot as he tries to make the six-inch step up on the curb. His tube sock is dingy and has a big hole by the toe. One toe sticks out and I can see that it was recently cut and filed. His wife Nancy's still giving him them foot mani-cures, but I can see she no longer picks out his socks and clothes. She probably stopped because of Dare's lack of appreciation. Me personally, I'd love to have her doing my feet, especially that part toward the end where she rubs lotion on them. I've sat in Dare's living room more than once and watched Nancy tending to his crusty feet while I pretended the television had my interest.

I bend down and pick up the stray sneaker and then ease it back on Dare's foot. He doesn't seem aware that he came out of it in the first place or that I put it back on.

"*Riley had them Lakers boys running,*" *he slurs.* "*Philly ain't know what hit 'em, did they, G?*"

I shake my head and place a steady hand under his arm so as to help him climb this small mountain of a curb. Anything is a mountain when you drink booze like he does. "*You've got to slow down with the drinking, Dare. Doctors done warned you about your liver,*" *I caution him.*

"*Liver smiver.*" *He waves his loosey-goosey arm at me like I'm a Philly Sixer and he's an L.A. Laker.*

"You want to see your little angel walk down the aisle and little knucklehead fight for the heavyweight title, you'll straighten up," I add. He's got two little ones, Cydney and Shammond. I've got two of my own, Georgette and Georgia. I made sure my wife, Mildred, got my name in there for each of them, figuring if they ended up like me, and not Mildred, the world would be all the better for it. All you need to know about Mildred is that she spends all her time singing gospel songs that nobody else ever heard of. Been that way since her mama died. Since she said she lost the only person in the world she could talk to. I've felt like Dare's sock, dingy and full of holes, since my wife told me, in a roundabout way, I wasn't someone she could talk to. We haven't been much as a couple ever since.

Darius giggles now and salutes me as if he's a private in the army. "Yessuh, Dr. J., I'ma lick the liquor as you prescribe."

"I'm serious, Dare," I say.

"Damn, G, relax your mind. Thank God my old lady gives it up on the regular," he answers, "else I'd be uptight all the time like you is."

Funny how his speech clears up the minute he starts in on ragging me.

We reach his little bungalow and I help him up his front porch without another word. Dare knows how sensitive I am about the relations I got at home. Why'd he have to go and make light of it like that? Good a friend as I am to him. I fight the urge to let him fall on his stoop, for his two children and wonderful wife to pick up like garbage. "Nancy left the porch light on for you, Dare, and the door open," I say to chase away my evil thoughts.

"She'd better," Dare answers. "I ain't trying to be outside my own home screaming for that woman to let me in like I'm Freddie Flintstone...or George Aloysius Williams." He starts a laugh that breaks off into a full-fledged cough.

I tighten my jaw and make a mental note not to share my low moments with Dare anymore, lessen they'll come back to bite me.

Sweet-as-brown-sugar Nancy appears in the open doorway. I crinkle my nose. I swear you can catch the heaven scent of that woman from two blocks away. She looks out and around the area for nosy neighbors. I remove my cap and hold it against my chest. Dare will have to take the rail for himself and climb these few steps. Nancy looks past her drunken husband to me. I smile her way, and she doesn't smile back, but she caught my smile; she caught it gladly. I couldn't tell you the last time Mildred smiled at me. She grunts, shakes her head, sings those awful songs to drown out my talking, but never, ever, a smile.

Nancy props open the screen door and Dare passes through without speaking. He raises his hand and waves bye to me before disappearing into the darkness of his house.

Nancy steps outside because I'm lingering like her scent in my nostrils. "Thanks for seeing him home," she says. "You must get tired of this."

"Watching the games without him wouldn't be the same," I reason. "I take the good with the bad. I like to thank I keep his drinking down a bit, too. No telling how much he'd put down if I wasn't in his ear all night."

"Well, thanks," she says. I can tell she's embarrassed. I want to do something to set her mind at ease, let her know that embarrassment has no place between us.

"I think you know that I really bring him home just so I can see you," I say. I'm like the man who has been told he has twenty-four hours to live and throws caution to the wind. My own death is just around the block. The redbrick house on the corner with the porch light out and the door closed and locked.

Nancy grips the collar of her shirt, the night air suddenly chilling her. "He might hear you. That doesn't bother you?"

"You know he's dead to the world by now, Nan," I say.

Nancy shakes her head. "I told you that Nan mess is too comfortable, Mr. Williams."

"Want to get even more comfortable, Nan?" I say back to her. I'm taunting that coming death.

Nancy sighs in despair. She can't take her eyes off me and her legs are being downright stubborn, refusing her brain's instructions to turn and head on back inside. I know all this 'cause I know this woman. Been studying her like a test. Dare'd have to look at my notes to know his wife's favorite color. Blue—everything from her clothes to her mood. I plan on changing that though.

"You're crazy," she says.

"Run away with me," I respond. "You and Cydney."

"And Shammond?" she says, and then shakes her head. I imagine she realizes asking this question of me is improper, that she should be saying, "Good night, Mr. Williams" by now.

Ain't no way I would really want any part of that boy. Hard to even believe he came up out of Nan.

"He's a five-year-old carbon copy of his old man. Shame I can tell it so early, but I can. Let him stay right here and he and Dare can take turns beating up on each other," I tell her.

"George I—" The creak of the screen door behind Nancy steals her thought. Shammond's head barely clears the door. "Go back to bed," Nancy snaps. He glares at me before disappearing into the darkness of the house that welcomed his father just moments before.

Nancy turns back to me. I know our time is coming to a close and that a living death awaits me at home. "I've got to go," she says.

I smile and nod. "You might want to change Dare's shirt, he puked on it earlier."

Nancy purses her lips, goes inside without a further word, turns off the porch light and closes the door.

I smile all the way home. Smile until I place my key in the lock of my front door and realize Mildred placed the dead bolt—for which she refuses to give me a key—on. Death, I think to myself, as I rap my knuckles hard against the door, nothing but death.

CHAPTER 1

They stood eyeing one another. She was on the inside of her apartment, the door slightly cracked, latch still on, he on the outside looking in. It was late, too late for a personal visit, but here he was just the same. Instinctively, she looked down to see that no weapon was in his hand. Then she glanced at his chest to see if he was breathing heavy, just come from some nighttime mayhem seeking the safety of her place. No weapon, she noticed. He appeared to be breathing smoothly.

"You gonna let your brother in, or what?" he asked.

She sighed but undid the latch just the same. He passed inside and went directly to her living room.

"I usually have folks take off their shoes before they walk my carpets," she said to him.

He nodded but kept his shoes on, sat in a heavy clump on her sofa.

She sighed again, crossed over to him and sat on her love seat.

"So, Cydney, how you been doing?" he asked. "You look good."

"I've been well, thanks. You look good, too, Shammond."

He smiled, appreciative of the way she said his name, the only person in his life that didn't call him Slay, the only person he allowed to call him by his first name. She'd earned the right, just by being his loving sister.

"Up and about kind of late," she noted.

He nodded, strained his eyes as he looked around. "You got all new stuff up in here, what you do with the old furniture?"

"Curbed it," Cydney said.

"You bought this with the money I hit you off with?"

Cydney nodded reluctantly. "The old furniture didn't even make it until sanitation could pick it up, though. Some woman and two teenage boys snatched it up. I watched them out of my window. They looked like they had hit the lottery, getting someone else's furniture with stranger's stank soaked into the cushions."

Slay shook his head. "Not too long ago you were sleeping on a pissy mattress, don't forget that shit."

Cydney rolled her eyes.

"But that's kinda why I'm here," Slay said. "I need to forget the pissy mattresses, too. I need your help, Cydney. I need you to get me like you."

Cydney frowned. "Like me?"

Slay nodded, placed his feet on the coffee table, leaned back real comfortably. Cydney eyed his feet but said nothing.

"Yeah, you know, kind of stuck up and shit—" Slay raised his hands "—no disrespect intended. Better than the average nigga out here. I gotta be able to talk and act like some Will Smith-type nigga. By like, Friday."

Etiquette 101, the crib notes version.

Cydney frowned. "That's a difficult thing to ask, by Friday." She sort of laughed. "I don't know what to say, Shammond."

Was she making fun? His feelings for her shifted a bit, about as much as they could ever shift for his beloved Cydney. "Slay," he corrected bitterly. It was his last name, his street name.

"*Shammond,*" Cydney said. "You can start your rebirth by using your correct name."

"Slay *is* my correct name. My government name. It's on my birth certificate and everything. You were a Slay one time, too, before King George came and adopted you...but left me hanging."

Cydney ignored his rant. Same bitter, woe-is-me tale she'd

been hearing from Shammond for years. How their stepfather had done Shammond dirty by not legally adopting him. "So why do you need this transformation, Shammond?"

A gleam came to Slay's eye. "There's this shorty I got my eye on. Let's just say she's on a higher level than the chicks I usually deal with. Theresa. She pronounces it Tear-ess-a. Honey got a good head on her shoulders. Thick-assed chick, got a badoonka donk and one of them Pamela Anderson chests." He eyed Cydney. "You and Theresa could be twins. Both of y'all got that sophisticated-ladies shit going on."

Cydney hunched her shoulders and rubbed her arms; goose pimples waddled from her wrists to her shoulders. It was a bit cold. She rose and adjusted the heat. She could feel Slay's eyes on her as she moved through the apartment.

"You can help?" Slay asked.

"Where did you meet this Theresa?"

"She goes to MU."

Cydney frowned. "You're using college girls now, huh? An expensive private school, too."

"You can help?"

"I don't know what you want."

"Start with books, name me some of them joints you read. I know Theresa is into books. I think she might like that dude you were always reading."

Cydney regained her position on the love seat. "Eric Jerome Dickey? This Theresa is a black girl?"

"Mixed," Slay said. "Black and someshit."

This was a serious departure for Slay; his usual girls had skin that pinked to the touch, and deferential personas. Gullible-ass white girls he called them. Easier to manipulate. "I don't feel comfortable helping you corrupt a black woman," Cydney said.

Slay moved to his sister, grabbed her hands. "Come on,

baby. This shit is on the up-and-up. I like this chick. I ain't planning on using her for that other shit. I wouldn't get her caught up in that stuff." He crossed his heart with one hand, the other holding on to Cydney. "You got to trust your baby brother on this one."

Cydney sighed. "Shammond, I swear—"

"On the up-and-up, on daddy's life," he said, looking upward.

"You know that 'daddy's life' stuff doesn't sway me," Cydney said.

"That's still our blood, Cydney, no matter how you see it."

Cydney eased from his grasp. "You have a beautiful smile," she began slowly. "Get rid of that bling-bling stuff on your teeth. Get yourself a nice V-neck sweater and some khaki pants. What are you driving these days?"

"A BMW quarter to eight." Slay turned his lips up in a mischievous smile. "The lease papers, the registration, the insurance cards...all that shit looks realer than a mug, legit. Authentic, the dude that fixed it up for me said."

Cydney shook her head. She hated hearing him talk of that life, that dangerous world her brother moved through with ease and comfort. "This isn't going to be easy."

"Few things are. I'm used to *not easy*."

Cydney looked off to some faraway place. "How is Mama doing, and Pop G?"

Slay let out a sigh, crinkled his brow. "Mama, she's burned out bad."

Cydney didn't reply; she expected as much. "Pop G?"

"Eff that nigga," Slay barked.

"He's our father, don't talk like that."

"Don't even get me started on that shit. That nigga is not my father. Yours maybe, but not mine, Cydney. I ain't a Williams. I'm a Slay."

"You have to stop romanticizing our birth father. You barely even remember him, Shammond. I don't either, too much. We're lucky George came along or we would have been two more statistics."

"Whatever. All I know is a dude that would run up into his partner's lady soon as his partner died…ain't about jackshit."

Cydney moved on. "So Mama's still using?"

"She's the Jordan of crack, keeps coming back."

"Sad," Cydney said.

"You should come by the crib sometime, let Mama know you ain't totally shut her out. It might do her some good. I was by there yesterday." Slay smiled. "I left a few of my things."

Cydney said nothing. That was the thing—she had shut her mother totally out. She wished she could do the same with her brother, but he had the staying power of a roach. "I'm so busy with college, writing the music and restaurant reviews for the magazine, and my little part-time job at Macy's."

"No gentleman to keep you warm at night?" Slay asked.

"No." She was happy her word was the truth. Even though he asked her with nonchalance, she knew Slay had a greater interest. They had a weird relationship like that; he couldn't stand the thought of her that way, his sister with some man. It was just another reason why she worked so hard at distancing herself from him. Why she kept the few men she encountered at arm's length.

"So," he said, "you think you can hook me up, bring out the white boy in me?"

Cydney sighed. "I'll try."

Cydney sat in the chair across from her couch watching the rise and fall of her brother's chest. She couldn't bring herself to close her own eyes. Not with him here. Her feelings for Shammond were an unhealthy mix of contempt and love. To the outsider, the two emotions seemed implausible, but to Cydney they made perfect sense. Her brother, after all, was two very different people: Shammond and Slay.

Shammond was a protector, a provider, a giver.

Slay was a destroyer, a neglector, a taker.

As Cydney continued to watch him sleep, his baggy jeans hanging below his waist and showing off his boxers, a copy of *Essence* about to fall from his fingers onto the carpet, Cydney wondered which of the two, Shammond or Slay, was stronger.

The phone rang and interrupted Cydney's thoughts. She glanced at the time stamp on her digital cable box. It was well past midnight. She knew without checking the caller ID where the call had originated from. She eased to her feet and tiptoed across the carpet to the kitchen. She checked to make sure her brother didn't stir and then removed her cordless phone from the base. She pressed the talk button on the phone's face.

"Hold on," she said into the receiver and then she placed the phone to her chest and tiptoed into her bedroom, closed the door behind her and locked it. She took a deep breath and sat down on the bed. "Hello."

The voice on the other end was deep, sexy. "Am I interrupting something?"

"No, Stephon," Cydney said. Stephon James, her editor-in-chief at *Urban Styles* magazine, until recently the sometimes, late-night warmth that she lied to her brother about not having. "Why are you calling me this late?" And she added sarcastically, "Your wife away or something?"

"I was just checking on a fellow night owl. I couldn't sleep," Stephon offered. "And my wife's with the painkillers again. She won't be awakening anytime soon."

"I don't know why you think you can bring your drama into my life whenever you want to," Cydney said. "I don't appreciate your calling me this time of night."

Stephon sounded wounded. "I'm sorry—I—just wanted to

talk to you. You're whispering. I imagine that must mean someone's there with you."

"I'm not whispering," Cydney corrected, though she was. "And no one is here with me."

Stephon sucked his teeth like an adolescent boy. "Yell out my name then."

"You must be crazy. It's almost one in the morning."

"I was joking," Stephon said, even though he wasn't.

Cydney could hear the loneliness and longing in Stephon's voice. She recognized the timbre from her own experiences. She knew how it felt to be trapped in darkness with no light apparent anywhere. "Tell me about your wife," she told him.

Stephon sighed. "She's at it again. Been taking Vicodin, Percocet, Advil. Claims none of them work, though I know the dosages she takes are strong enough to down a horse."

"I know the Advil's over-the-counter, but how does she get ahold of that other stuff?"

"Don't know. She hid them from me this time. I found the bottles inside a can of bread crumbs."

"What were you doing looking through a can of bread crumbs?"

Stephon laughed for the first time since he'd gotten on the phone, for the first time really in the past few days since his discovery of the painkiller medicine. It felt good to laugh, take his mind off the worries, the blues setting in on him. "That's a long story."

"Something freaky I bet," Cydney teased.

"Come on now," Stephon objected, "you know me better than that."

"Exactly," Cydney answered. "So what where you planning to do with bread crumbs? You got me interested now. I know about that thing you do with chocolate." She sucked her teeth. "Oh, and that other thing you do with whipped cream."

Stephon's boom of a laugh prodded her on. "Ditto for cherries," she continued. "But bread crumbs? I can't imagine."

"You are something, Cydney Williams," Stephon said, his voice rich with desire. "Why can't we be together?"

Cydney clutched the fluffiest pillow on the bed close to her chest, wrapped her arms around it as she would a lover's waist. "I got two reasons for you," she answered. "Your daughter and your wife. I'm ashamed I let our thing go on as long as I did." She didn't mention her lunatic brother as a reason, but she thought it.

"You know there's no love in this house," Stephon reasoned.

"Don't do that, Stephon. You dishonor your wife and daughter by saying that. When your wife isn't popping those pills, when she's sober and attending to you and your child, there is plenty of love in that house."

"I'm unhappy," Stephon said. "That's all I was trying to say."

"So get happy. Confront your wife again. Let her know what you're feeling, and open yourself to what she's feeling. Obviously she's unhappy, too."

"I wish I'd met you first," Stephon mused, "before I got married, before I got myself in this mess."

Cydney smirk-laughed. "That's what makes life so interesting. You can't go back, and you can't change what has already been done. You can wish 'til the cows come home..." She looked toward the living room of her apartment. Even through the closed and locked bedroom door she could feel the presence of her brother, could feel the presence of her mother. She wished she couldn't, wished she could completely rid herself of them both. Wished.

"I love you," Stephon blurted.

"Yes, I suppose in your own way you do," Cydney said. "At least as best you can under your circumstances."

His voice registered hurt. "Are you not returning the emotion?"

"I can't do that, Stephon. You know that."

"You can, you just won't."

"Correct again, boss." She might as well put it out there and let him know what he was instead of dwelling on what he wasn't. *Boss* and not lover, at least not anymore.

"This is some hurtful shit," Stephon said.

"You haven't given me my restaurant assignment for this month," Cydney said, moving on.

"How can you so easily just brush past the issue of us?"

"No one said it was easy, but it is necessary. Far as I'm concerned, there is no us."

"We shared a lot."

"And still do."

"Not the same."

"Good thing for the both of us it isn't."

"What if I just left my wife?"

"That would show me that when my imperfections became clear to you, you'd be predisposed to calling up some other chick in the early morning and confessing undying love to her. Not exactly what I'm looking for in a life partner."

"You've got to have an answer for everything."

"Not everything." Cydney placed the pillow she'd been clutching back neatly in its spot on her bed. "But look, like I said, you haven't given me my restaurant assignment for the month."

Stephon sighed. "I want you to do a review of that new soul food spot that opened in Asbury Park."

Cydney's posture straightened, buoyed by interest. A new restaurant opened in the bleak city of her birth? "What's that? I hadn't heard about any new soul food place."

"It's on a…hold on." Cydney could hear Stephon sifting through papers. "This downstairs office comes in handy when I want to just get away from it all," he said when he came back on line.

"Yeah, I bet."

Stephon ignored her. "Cookman Avenue. Name of the place is Cush. You know the area?"

I grew up around the corner, Cydney wanted to say but didn't. "I'll find it. Cush? What kind of name is that for a restaurant?" She crinkled her nose. "Sounds too much like mush."

Stephon managed a laugh. "The cat that owns it named it after some ancient African city."

Cydney was impressed. "Deep."

"Yeah, this is an accomplished brother we're talking about. Desmond Rucker. His family owned a chain of restaurants in Pennsylvania. Maybe we'll even look to do a feature on him at some point…" Stephon's voice trailed off; he stopped himself from waxing too poetic about Desmond in Cydney's presence.

"Well, I look forward to this."

"Don't go falling in love with him now," Stephon joked.

"It's all about the food, Stephon, the food."

Her words were reassurance to Stephon's ears. "I'm going to go and try to get some sleep. Thanks, Cydney."

She loved how he always said her name in full; didn't break it down and call her Cyd or something along those lines. She closed her eyelids and gripped the phone receiver firmly as she thought about the inequity of life. How could his wife sleep away these precious moments when she could be snuggling with her handsome husband, cuddling with her beautiful daughter or further decorating her majestic home?

"Peace and blessings, Stephon."

"Same to you, Cydney."

She clicked the phone off and sat on the bed for a moment, composing herself. After a while, she rose to go put the phone back on the charger stand. She attempted to turn the bedroom doorknob and then remembered she'd placed the lock on. She opened the lock and moved through the doorway with her head down and her shoulders devoid of their usual upright strength. Talking with Stephon nowadays always took something out of her. She had moved only a few steps when she bumped into something. She looked up, startled, her brother standing in her way, his eyes dull like a butter knife, but still capable of cutting.

"Who were you in there talking to? And why did you lock the door?" he demanded.

Cydney swallowed hard and tried to smile.

CHAPTER 2

Desmond Rucker leaned against the wall in the large industrial kitchen, next to the swinging doors that led out to the dining area. He could hear the mill of voices from outside. He smiled as he considered this smashing success. Opening night of his restaurant, Cush, and they were teetering on full capacity. Desmond hadn't expected anything less, even though the naysayers questioned the wisdom of opening a restaurant among the ruins of Asbury Park. The block he chose to plant seed was a thoroughfare of abandoned and boarded-up buildings. Only three other entrepreneurs had had the courage to attempt commerce on this block: an antiques dealer, a sneakers retailer and a Chinese food take-out spot. None of it mattered. Desmond could feel a certain soul in the broken city, a certain soul that his restaurant could nourish and help in bringing the city back to the strength of its heyday. He remembered coming over with his parents from Pennsylvania when he was younger. He fondly recalled those stolen weekends like memories of a lost love. They were so few and far between. His parents spent so much time cultivating their business—a chain of Rucker Restaurants—that there was little time for anything else.

"What are you standing there grinning like that for?" Karen, Desmond's handpicked hostess, asked. It was so busy she was moonlighting as a waitress.

"Success, sweetheart," Desmond answered as Karen disappeared through the doors with a platter of hot food in hand.

A moment later, Karen came scuttling back through those same doors, stepping with energy. As she passed by, Desmond couldn't help but notice the cling of her skirt to those luscious hips and that round ass. He blinked his eyes. She's married, Desmond. Married with a capital M.

"Damn right this is success," Karen said to Desmond as she passed him again to go back outside. "I'm going to have to soak my feet in Epsom salts when I get home tonight."

"Get your man to massage them for you." Desmond couldn't help himself; in his life of restraint and refinement, he had but one weakness—fine women. They made him feel whole in ways he couldn't fully explain.

Karen stopped long enough to wink at Desmond and then moved through the door.

"I hope her husband is appreciating that," Desmond said aloud, shaking his head as Karen disappeared through the swinging doors.

The chirp of Desmond's cell phone cut through his carnal thoughts.

He opened the flip of his StarTAC. "Desmond Rucker." He rarely got personal calls so he always answered as if it were a business line.

Desmond was greeted by his younger sister Felicia's voice. "Hey, baby brother."

"I'm older by nine years and a few months," Desmond said, smiling.

"Dang, somebody was shooting blanks for a long time... nine years."

"Workaholics," Desmond said. "The first child was planned. The second was a pleasant surprise."

"Is that it?"

"Yes, it is. Where are they? They haven't picked you up yet?"

Felicia sucked in some of the cool night air. "I love your awning...what color is this, burgundy?"

Desmond's voice plummeted. "You're here?"

"Walking up to your door," Felicia said.

"Man!" Desmond slapped the flip of his cell shut and moved through the swinging doors of the kitchen. One of these days he was going to kill Felicia. She had clear instructions to call him as soon as their parents picked her up from the train station. That would give him half an hour or so to make sure everything was as close to perfect as he could get it. Half an hour to get his nerves under control. Half an hour to prepare for his father.

"Place is hopping," Karen said as Desmond took a spot next to her at the hostess podium.

"My parents are here," Desmond informed Karen. "My fool-ass sister just called."

"Really?" Karen swung her head, swept her long hair off her shoulders. Her skin was the color of fresh-roasted peanuts, her teeth white like copy paper. She brushed the lapel of her jacket and straightened her shoulders. "Nervous?" she asked.

"Nope," Desmond lied through clenched teeth. His heart was threatening to cut through the strong fabric of his suit. "The crowd helps. My father is bound to be impressed. I don't ever remember his restaurants being this crowded, and we have more square footage here."

"Thought your mother ran them with him," Karen said.

"She did."

"You only mentioned your father, Desmond."

"Did I?"

"Yep, you did. Is that a bit of male chauvinism showing its face?"

"Not at all," Desmond said. "My father is the more opinionated of my parents, that's all." An understatement if there ever was one. "Just want to do well," Desmond reasoned. "The culinary business is in the Rucker blood." He looked at her and returned a smile. "You know what I'm saying, baby?"

Karen could feel herself drowning in Desmond's eyes. Before she could compose herself enough to answer his question, the front door opened.

Barbara Rucker, Desmond's mother, stepped in first. She was a striking woman, her black hair highlighted by elegant strands of silver. The perfection of her skin, the absence of wrinkles, made her appear a decade younger than she actually was. Like all the Ruckers, she had a good amount of height on her, close to six feet even without her high-heeled pumps. She wore a burgundy pantsuit that brought out the deep mocha hue of her skin.

Frank Rucker was an older version of his son. Broad through the shoulders. Large hands with thick cords of veins running over the top to give a clue as to their true strength. Same deep mocha color as his wife, an oddity among black couples; usually one partner was shaded differently than the other. He wore a neat, short Afro, salt covering his temples and spraying his crown. His jaw was boxed, chiseled like those of male models, no flab anywhere on his fit frame. His mustard-colored turtleneck sweater and dark brown pants were even more stylish than the cream-colored suit his son wore. He seemed to gain better posture when he spied Desmond at the podium, when the reality set in that his suit was indeed more stylish than his son's.

Felicia, at eighteen, was budding into more of a womanly flower with each passing day. It bothered Desmond that she favored close-fitting blouses that showed her full bosom, not that they could be hidden under a baggy shirt, and pants and skirts that showed off the bubble of her behind. Unlike the other Ruckers, Felicia was a shade lighter. She had large, oval eyes, a thin nose and full lips. She was a touch taller than her mother and had broken all of their hearts by moving to New York City in September to accept a modeling contract. She relished the role of heartbreaker.

Desmond was about to greet his family but then a fourth person stepped forward. Desmond's tongue froze and a mystified look held his face captive. Nora Claxton came in on the heels of his parents and sister. Nora's skin was the color of caramel, her eyes a grayish, bluish, greenish conglomeration. She didn't have Mrs. Rucker's height, but carried the same dignity and straight posture. In a past-gone lifetime, she was Desmond's wife-to-be. She smiled at him now, warmed by his surprised look, his gaping mouth.

While the Ruckers scoped the restaurant, Nora was the first one of the group to speak. "Beautiful place you have here, Des."

"Thanks," he managed to say.

The trio of blood relatives then engulfed Desmond. His mother placed a tattoo of red lips on his cheek; his father offered a firm handshake, seemingly trying to crush Desmond's hand in his grip, and his sister served up a coy smile as she wrapped him quickly in her arms and then stood just a few feet back from the others.

Desmond stood watching them and so Karen pushed forward and extended her hand. "I'm Karen, the hostess," she said. "I've heard so much about all of you." She scanned Nora and tried unsuccessfully not to crinkle her nose. "Most of you," she added.

Desmond sprung to life. "Um, Karen, would you show my family to their seats? I'll join you all in a minute." He looked at his sister. "Felicia, may I speak with you a moment?"

Karen ushered them to a reserved table in the back of the restaurant. On the way, she stopped one of the waitresses and subtly asked her to add another place setting at the Rucker table.

"What's going on?" Desmond asked Felicia, back at the front.

"We're here to get our eat on," Felicia said.

"You know what I mean," Desmond answered. "With Nora?"

Felicia looked in the direction of her seated family and the sister-in-law that wouldn't be. "Oh, her? I honestly couldn't tell you. From what I gather, she was speaking to Mommy and sort of invited herself when she found out they were coming. You know she really must have wanted to see you if she'd put up with Daddy for an entire car ride."

"Figures," Desmond sighed. "This is uncomfortable."

"Why?" Felicia scanned the restaurant with the flair of a soap opera actress. "You got some other hoochie up in here waiting on you?"

"I don't do the hoochies," Desmond said, "and you know it. It's uncomfortable, considering the circumstances of my relationship with Nora and how it ended."

"Oh, you mean the canceled wedding. Daddy was the only person happy about your failed nuptials if I recall."

"It was for the best," Desmond defended.

"No argument from me on it being the best for Nora," Felicia said, "but you might want to send Ms. Nora another candygram. I don't think the sistah got the message. She was Des-this-ing and Des-that-ing the entire car ride here. I'm glad I just had to deal with it from the train station to here. I couldn't have stood all that syrup the entire ride from Pennsy. That chick was about to make me diabetic."

"She wants to remain close," Desmond said, sighing.

Felicia smiled. "She must not know about the legend of Desmond Rucker. No one, regardless of how beautiful, intelligent or whatever, can get close to the black Clark Gable. No one can tame you...not counting Daddy, of course. See you at the table, Romeo." She tapped Desmond playfully and walked to join the others. Desmond stood in his place, looking like he was searching for his car in a crowded mall parking lot.

Karen returned to the podium and loudly shuffled the appointment book across the podium surface. "How come you never told me about your pretty friend?" she asked. There was a definite edge in her voice.

Desmond turned quickly. "What?"

"Miss America over there," Karen said, nodding her head in Nora's direction. "How come you never told me about her?"

"Nothing to tell really," Desmond said.

"You could fool me. You looked like you saw a ghost when she walked in. She had stars in her eyes. There's definitely history between you two."

Desmond tapped the podium and smiled. "Yeah, history, as in of the past, over and done with." He reached up and touched Karen's cheek as he left to join his family.

It was a large crowd at Cush that first night, but sadly, the majority of the patrons were Caucasians. The blacks in the community were not at all supportive, even though the place served food targeted to their taste buds.

One table had an older white gentleman, gravelly-throated like Redd Foxx, wearing a black mock turtleneck, a tweed jacket and purplish tinted shades. He was entertaining a brunette too young to realize she resembled Raquel Welch. Mr. White Foxx kept the waitresses busy, ordering multiple glasses of the most expensive champagne. One of the waitresses suggested he purchase a bottle, but he brushed her off, telling her neither he nor his date were big drinkers.

At another table, the mayor of a nearby municipality entertained a party of seven—all of them big-time political movers and shakers. Loud raucous laughter emanated from the table every few seconds. For serious-minded folks, they surely were having themselves a blast.

Off in the romantic corner of the restaurant, a young man with reddened cheeks kept peering over his shoulder as his giggly girlfriend continued to ask him why he was acting so funny. After much prodding, he reached in his side pocket, pulled out a velvet-covered jewelry box and dropped to his knee. Her giggles stopped, replaced by the heavy fanning of her hands and a high-pitched squeal.

"You must be mighty proud of this turnout, baby," Desmond's mother called to him from across the table. Desmond nodded, looking at Nora out of the corner of his eye.

"Looks almost as good as our first place on opening night," Desmond's father added.

Nora leaned in, a slice of cleavage appearing, and reached across Desmond to retrieve a pat of butter from the butter bowl. "Excuse me," she said in that breathy soft tone that she knew made Desmond wild with heat. Desmond shot a glance at his sister across the table; she looked away and smiled.

"Build this up the right way," Frank Rucker offered, "before you start going and thinking about expanding or opening up another one. Too many restaurants fail because the owners move so fast. I can already see from looking at your menu that you've got quite a bit of a learning curve. Some of these entrées and appetizers seem out of place in here." Desmond nodded, thankful for the advice. He scanned his mother and father. Over thirty years they'd been married. Just another reminder of his father's immense success, another yardstick that Desmond was afraid he'd never measure up to.

"So what do you think, Felicia?" Desmond asked his sister.

"Bangin' like I thought it would be," she said.

"Bangin'?" Mrs. Rucker asked. "I suppose you're not

looking to be a contestant on *Wheel of Fortune*. Or ever get yourself a decent job."

"Come on, Mommy," Felicia said, leaning her head on her mother's shoulder. "That's just the youth vernacular of the times. I'm sure if I went back to like '67, '68, when you and Daddy were young and carefree, I'd find you guys in bell-bottoms with big Afros, talking jive and doing God knows what."

Mrs. Rucker looked at her husband. "You remember that old Volkswagen with the broken passenger-side door?"

Frank smiled. "I would always get in first and make you climb over me."

Mrs. Rucker's eyes glazed over in remembrance. "Yeah," she said, nodding. "And you'd always cop a feel, too." They broke off into a soul-shaking kiss, oblivious to the others at the table.

"Get a room," Felicia said, breaking them apart. She looked over toward Nora. "I apologize that you had to witness this."

Nora waved her hand. "I think it's nice, your parents still in love after all these years. All the memories…"

"We weren't in that broken Volkswagen for long though," Mr. Rucker added, breaking from his wife's warmth. "Our next car was a top-of-the-line Lincoln, been in luxury vehicles ever since." He looked directly at Desmond as he said this.

Desmond cleared his throat, nodded toward the jazz band. "What do you guys think of the live music?"

Everyone turned to the ensemble on the platform at the back of the restaurant.

"Loud and a bit off-tune," Mr. Rucker said.

"I might want to get up and dance to that loud, off-tune swing," Barbara Rucker added, pinching her lips together seductively as she looked at her husband out of the corner of her eye.

"Nice," Nora said. She looked over at Desmond. "Just the thought, dancing cheek to cheek to a slow, romantic song, is…nice."

CHAPTER 3

Slay pulled his BMW 745 up to the curb and idled. The burgundy exterior and gray leather interior held not one trace of dirt. He turned the volume up a decibel when his CD went to track six on Nas's *The Lost Tapes* album. "Blaze A 50"—a banging morality tale about the downside of violence and greed oozed through Slay's state-of-the-art stereo system. Slay nodded his head to the bass and prodigious drums. That Nas sure had a way with words.

Slay looked in his rearview mirror and noticed a police patrol car approaching. He blinked hard to see if they were one of his own and smiled when he realized they were. The patrol car slowed as it passed and the officer gave Slay a slight head nod. Slay nodded in return.

Waiting for this fool, Gabriel "Tuffy" Gibson, was working on Slay's last nerve. Didn't this young cat know making your boss wait set a bad impression? Slay tapped the steering wheel, thinking back on his sister's behavior the night before. Off in her bedroom, whispering on the phone to someone—she wouldn't tell who. He'd have to keep a closer watch on Cydney, not let so much time pass between visits. It was obvious she needed his guidance and direction, even though she was older. Up in that apartment acting like she didn't know the streets. Acting like she didn't grow up in the 'hood. Trying to block out any and everything that reminded her of how it was, coming up. Some things just wouldn't go away that easily. He looked at himself in the rearview mirror.

Slay thought about Theresa. He'd hit her with some of the

shit he'd picked up reading through Cydney's *Essence* magazines. And now that Cydney had given him some quick pointers on making himself more presentable to that caliber of female, he'd do more than just watch Theresa walk from her car to Patterson Auditorium at Mainland University. He'd place himself strategically by those large bushes right outside the entrance and when she moved to pass, he'd strike up a conversation. Dazzle her by mentioning the title of that book his sister told him about. Hopefully, Theresa wouldn't press him about the book, because he couldn't remember how Cydney said it ended. Maybe he'd give Cydney a call later and have her run through it one more time.

Out of the shadows from across the street, Slay spied Tuffy headed his way, smoking on a cancer stick as usual. He had to admit that was one brash shorty. That's why Slay used him for more and more of his side projects. It took serious guts to keep Slay waiting like this and Tuffy didn't appear to have any hurry in his step.

Tuffy came to the passenger side of the vehicle and opened the door. Slay turned down the volume on his stereo. "Hey, yo," Slay said as Tuffy moved to get in. "Hold up, shorty. You can't be tracking that dirt in my shit. And kill the smokes."

Tuffy looked down at his Timberlands. They were caked with grass, mud and sand.

Slay clicked a button on his key chain; his trunk lid rose. "I got shopping bags back there, double something up to free a bag and put your boots in there. You can hold them on your lap."

Tuffy seemed irked, but wisely said nothing. Slay had to smile as he took in the look the boy gave him before he walked to the back of the car.

Tuffy scanned the bags in the trunk: Victoria's Secret; Macy's; Bed, Bath & Beyond—everything all frilly and sweet scented. Dang if this Slay wasn't a player. Tuffy pulled a lingerie set from the Vicki's Secret bag, put it down with the lingerie set in the Macy's bag and pulled off his unlaced Timberlands. He dropped his boots in the bag. He carefully closed the trunk and moved to get in the BMW, tossing his cigarette to the curb as he grabbed the door handle.

"You should have sat down in the car with your feet out, took off your boots, then bagged them," Slay told him. "Your socks got a little dirt on them now. You still tracked some shit in here."

"My bad," Tuffy replied.

Slay shook his head. "You're late, too." He knew Tuffy's reply before it even came—My bad.

Tuffy held up the shopping bag holding his Timbs. "You sure got a lotta stuff back there for the females."

Slay nodded. "Ladies like to look and smell nice. They like the feel of silk, and the smell of flowers on their skin," Slay schooled him. "And more importantly, men like seeing them in that stuff. It makes them more willing to part with their hard-earned money."

"Well, you in, then," Tuffy said. "S'like a mall back there."

True. But Slay had other business to attend to; he'd expound on the ladies some other time. He nodded to his dashboard. An early edition of the *Asbury Park Press* sat on the edge, folded back, a portion of the newspaper's text highlighted in yellow. Tuffy picked up the paper and looked over the text.

The Monmouth County Prosecutor's Office and the Asbury Park Police Department are requesting any assistance and information concerning the investigation into the murder of George A. Williams. On Saturday, October 3, 2002, George Williams, 56 years old and a longtime resident of Asbury Park, was discovered murdered along the boardwalk on Ocean Avenue, victim of three gunshots.

George Williams. Slay's stepfather. Not that Slay actually considered the man to be his stepfather. Just some dude that stole his mother's and sister's hearts.

Tuffy placed the paper back on the dash, turned to Slay. "My condolences," he said with no irony in his voice.

"You wanna tell me what happened?" Slay asked.

"George got himself dead," Tuffy said.

"I told you to 'hem' him up, Tuffy. Not kill him."

"I meant to just 'buck fifty' his face like you had said," Tuffy said, "but I reached in the wrong pocket. My heat is in my right and my blade is in my left." *Buck fifty* was street slang for a vicious slash that required one hundred and fifty stitches to mend. "I got crossed and reached in my right instead of my left."

"Dang, Tuff."

"You mad?"

Slay sighed. Took the newspaper and folded it away from the article about George. "He give you any problems?"

Tuffy shook his head, his eyes wide in remembrance. "Nah, when I moved to bounce on him, he rushed me like you said he would. That old school pride. That's when I deaded him. Spit on him for good measure."

Slay nodded. "Right, right." Kept nodding, trying to calm his churning stomach. He was losing the edge needed for this tough, brutal, unkind world.

"How ya moms takin' it?"

Wrinkles moved to the edges of Slay's eyes as he narrowed them. "Hard, but she'll pull through, she's been through this before."

"Sister?"

"Doesn't know yet," Slay said. "My good old sister is about as removed from this neighborhood as she can be. Lives less than fifteen minutes away and won't darken our mama's doorstep. She doesn't keep up on anything to do with Asbury

Park." Slay changed the tone of his voice, mocking, "She reads the *New York Times*. Wouldn't think of opening the *Asbury Park Press*."

"Oh, word," Tuffy said. "I feel her. Me neither."

Slay reached into his pocket, pulled a thick wad of bills and placed them on the dash in front of Tuffy. Tuffy reached up, took the bills, placed the money in the inside pocket of his black FUBU jean jacket.

"You sure no one saw you?" Slay asked.

"Nada soul, it was just me and poor Georgie. I did okay with this, Slay?"

"Yeah," Slay said hesitantly.

"Kewl. I hope you can use me for some more stuff."

Slay nodded.

Tuffy extended his hand and they tapped fists. He opened the door, tapped the rolled-up window as he moved to part and bopped up the street. Slay watched Tuffy walk into the Chinese Jade take-out restaurant and then he moved to drive off. He did an illegal U-turn and headed off in the other direction, his Nas CD turned way up again.

No.

How many times did Desmond say it before it morphed to yes? Not enough times, he thought now as he stood naked over his bed and watched Nora sleeping beneath his covers. This was a major step backward for him. What's done is supposed to stay done. But Nora, like most women, had a finger pressed to his pulse. She was beautiful, sophisticated, had a wicked sense of humor and a puppy dog's loyalty. Anything she put her mind to, Desmond was sure she could achieve. Everything, that is, except taking Rucker as her last name.

Regret sat heavy in Desmond's stomach as he considered this grave mistake. It wasn't in his nature to bring muddy footsteps onto anyone else's polished floors. Yet, here he had trampled through Nora's house again, leaving his tracks everywhere, pained in the knowledge that she wouldn't be able to remove these tracks for a long time, and worse yet, the walls of her home would come tumbling down.

He thought back to the evening prior. He was exhausted from his opening night, exhilarated by the presence of his family, broken down by Nora's incessant plea for a "crumb of his time" when his parents prepared to drop Felicia back at the train station for her hop to New York and then leave for the drive back to Pennsylvania.

"I can get a way back," Nora insisted. "I'd just like to spend this special night with you, talk over some of the things we never did get settled. Can't you give me that much?"

Could he give her that much?

No.

"That's awful harsh of you" was her response.

No.

She didn't stop. "I never did you any harm."

No.

"I treated you like a man deserved to be treated."

No.

"I gave you my heart and my soul and now you dare to devalue that, tell me it doesn't equal a few hours of your time in return?"

Next thing he knew, they were headed to his home. He drove his Range Rover in silence. She looked out the window at the central New Jersey landscape in awe.

"I must say I didn't get the full impression of how beautiful New Jersey is from that area around your restaurant. Your place is *it* on that strip. But, this...this is all absolutely beautiful."

They were traveling down Ocean Avenue, the homes of IT

wizards, stock-market geeks and other white-collar benefactors whirring by as Desmond drove.

"These houses are showy," Desmond offered.

"What about your place?" Nora asked.

Desmond smiled for the first time since he'd been alone in her presence. "Showy."

"So your place is all that?" she asked.

"And some," he said. He was disappointed and relieved that his parents didn't have the time to check it out on this trip.

"I would have loved to help you decorate."

He let the comment drift to that place where uncomfortable thoughts went. Let it settle beside all the other things she'd said to him tonight that he had no reply for.

"So, have you met anyone since you've been here?" Nora asked.

"I've met a lot of folks."

"Women?" Nora asked.

"Men and children, too."

"You know what I mean, Des."

He looked to her, one of the few times he gave her the benefit of his gaze. "No, I haven't."

She seemed pleased, eased her taut body back in her seat. Turned and looked out the window again at the passing castles. About a mile farther in their travel, she turned to him again. "You're not going to ask me if I've met anyone since our…?" She couldn't finish it, hoping it wasn't finished.

He shook his head. She felt her eyes tearing, breaking the promise she'd made them commit to. No crying. She touched his hand on the steering wheel. "What could I do better, Des? What is it about me that I could improve?"

Desmond didn't take long to answer. "Nothing, Nora. You're as close to perfect as they come."

"That means—"

"That means you need to move on with your life and find someone who can appreciate all that you are," he said, cutting her off.

"I still think you can be that someone," she replied, defiant.

He smiled, not really a smile, though. "Okay, I found your one flaw."

"And it is?" she asked, her shoulders bunched in tight, posture pulling her forward in anticipation.

"You're naive."

Naive. Wasn't what she'd expected. She sat back and remained quiet the rest of the ride.

"What town is this?" she asked some time later when they pulled into his driveway.

"Deal," he told her.

They entered through the front. Nora lingered in Desmond's living room, amazed by the rustic wood beams and wrought-iron chandeliers about the ceiling. She was ready to get on her hands and knees and run her fingers over the glistening hardwood floors. She couldn't help imagining a wonderful night of lovemaking by the warmth of his rugged stone fireplace. She couldn't believe he had the taste and ability to set the room off so wonderfully with the light purple chenille sofa and the gooseneck accent chair.

"That's a Sam Moore," Desmond told her as she ran her fingers over the soft upholstery of his sofa. "Ultrasuede…has the look and feel of suede."

"All that," Nora said, repeating the phrase over and over as he showed her through the rest of the house.

"And you did this all by yourself?" she asked.

"Yes."

"You should have insisted your parents see this, Desmond. They'd be so impressed. Why have you shut yourself off, become so withdrawn and secretive?"

He didn't answer. She didn't press.

Somehow they ended up in the bedroom last. Somehow clothes were shed. Somehow their warm tongues were shared. Desmond wanted Nora up until the moment he climaxed; then, like men often do, he didn't want her anymore. She was expendable. A short-term fix. He needed a long-term answer that could outlast the longevity of even his parents' union. The dim prospect of finding such an answer left him gun-shy in the commitment department.

He moved to Nora now, sleeping so peacefully, and shook her shoulder. "Nora…Nora."

She opened her eyes, momentarily thrown by the strange surroundings. She yawned, stretched. "What?"

"You know what we agreed to. You have to go. I want you to call your friend to pick you up."

She blinked her eyes; the reality that her plan didn't work hit her like a ton of bricks. She started to whimper. She reached out for him but he turned to retrieve her neatly folded clothes from the chair behind him. He brought them to her and placed them on her lap.

"Go ahead and take your time," he offered.

She looked at him, her eyes moist.

"It's me, Nora," he said, shaking his head. "It's me. I'm sorry. I couldn't and can't chance failing at another relationship. I'd rather not even try." He thought about his mother, his father. Thirty years, after all, was a long and elusive ghost to chase.

He turned and left the room.

"Cydney, I been trying to reach you all day."

"I was at the library doing some research for a paper." She could hear something in her brother's voice. "Why? Something happen, Shammond?"

"You spoke with anyone from the county prosecutor's office or Asbury Police Department yet?"

She'd just walked in the door, had her heels in her hands. She dropped them to the floor, bypassing the stand in her living-room closet where she neatly kept her shoes. County prosecutor's office? Asbury Park police? "Shammond, tell me what's going on. Are you in trouble?" She could hear a tear in her brother's voice, though she was oddly sure it was manufactured.

"George."

"Pop G, what about him?" Her heart started to race. He was the one member of the family who actually accounted for something, worked hard, worked within the parameters of the law and didn't have any damning vices.

"You sitting down?" Slay asked. "I know how you feel about George."

"Oh, my God!"

"They found him down by the boardwalk. Shot dead."

"Pop G?" The words hurt as they left her mouth.

"Yeah, couple gunshots."

"How could something like this happen? When?"

"They found him the other night. A drug deal gone bad, they're guessing."

"Pop G wouldn't…" She couldn't continue, felt her head spinning, the ground leaving her. She dropped to the spot where she stood, leaned her back against the island separating her kitchen and living room.

"Wouldn't what?" Slay asked.

"Drugs," she whispered.

"You don't know?"

"Don't try and tell me—"

"Not for himself…for Mama. Been copping her shit for a while now, since she got beat up that time."

"No!"

"You sit up in your little pretend palace acting like the earth stopped spinning over here where you grew up, but it hasn't. Some bad shit goes down over here. Your wonderful stepfather couldn't figure out how to change Mama any more than you could. You just ran away from it—he chose to give in to it. He died a coward's death for it, too. Mama will be next, thanks to him."

"This is too much," Cydney cried.

"Yeah, well, I just wanted to let you know. I can come by later if you want."

"No, no, no. Let me handle this by myself. I'll call you if I need you."

"Aiight," Slay said, disappointed.

"Bye."

She sat there for a while, crying, hugging herself in grief. Then she wiped her face with the back of her hand, slipped her feet into her shoes and grabbed her car keys. She didn't know where she planned on going, what she planned on doing, but she knew she had to get out of her apartment.

Before she knew it, she was traveling around the Asbury Park circle, coming down Asbury Avenue headed into the broken city. How long had it been since she had come here? She came to Main Street, turned right instead of going left, toward where her mother stayed on First Avenue. She drove a few streets, then made the left on Cookman. Most of the businesses were boarded up. The sight of the decaying Steinbach Building jolted her. She noticed the lineup of cars just across the way. The glowing banner emblazoned with the name Cush outside the new restaurant. A line of white couples waited by the door to the restaurant, a half dozen or so other people making their way up the sidewalk toward the entrance. Cydney drove past.

Farther up the road, by the bridge, the weeping willow tree

bent to a lean that placed it almost perpendicular to the ground; still stood strong. The tree had been like that for a long time and she wondered what act of God it would take to make it finally fall. She continued on.

A small posse of kids, none of them older than ten, darted by in front of her. She slammed on the brakes and laid into her horn. They didn't even look in her direction. One of the kids threw his basketball high in the air, aiming it at the electrical wires above, trying to dislodge a pair of worn sneakers hanging by their laces over the wire. Cydney continued on.

She came to the end of Cookman, with Heaven on Earth dance club in front of her. She turned left. Passed by that horrible go-go bar, Hot Tails. Passed an abandoned lot with weeds growing heavy from cracks in the pavement. Passed by what at one time was a parking garage. Now the entire facility was abandoned, the metal skeleton of the parking structure rusted brown, slabs of concrete angled up against the side of the ground-floor building. She continued on.

A boarded-up building ahead had an elaborate NJ Lottery logo spray painted in graffiti on the one free window. There was raw talent in this jungle, but seldom was it used for any good; seldom did it garner any value. Cydney continued on.

She passed another one of the endless paved lots. This lot had a rusted crane sitting along the edge, up on its haunches as if it had decided to sputter out halfway through its work. Farther up the road was the Berkeley Carteret—a lavish hotel—which somehow still thrived, still had business in the midst of all this poverty and neglect. It made her think of her brother. Slay— because that's who he was when he spoke of the hotel—always referred to the Berkeley as his corporate offices. Cydney came to a stop at the lake that separated the squalor of Asbury Park from the richness of Deal. She started to drive around the lake on the circular road and ride through Deal back to her home in

West Long Branch, but she didn't. She stopped the car, cut the engine and sat looking at the ripples of water in the lake. She wasn't sure where exactly, but she knew not too far from here Pop G had faced his end. As she considered all she had seen on her way to this spot, she couldn't help but think he was all the better for getting out of this when he did, morbid as that seemed.

SLAY

"Where the backyard?" I ask my sister.

Cydney taps me on the back. "There isn't a backyard, stupid. This is an apartment tower." Cydney always has been one for telling me stuff she thinks I don't know.

The building is tall and not too wide. Sign out front says, B…h A…s. George told us proudly when we pulled up in his getaway car that it would spell out Beach Arms if all the letters were there. Whatever. I don't like him and I don't trust him. To me he looks like the dudes that kill Bruce Lee's master in the movies I watch on Saturday afternoons. 'Cept George ain't Chinese and he doesn't talk so fast his mouth can't keep up. I walk inside the building and Cydney follows.

"He dragged us out our house to come to this," I say to Cydney. The light thing above in the lobby is broke, hanging, wires and whatnot sticking out. "Ain't fair, I want a backyard."

"He didn't drag us out our house," Cydney corrects me. She gets that look grown folks get when they tell us kids to leave the room. "Mama lost the place 'cause Daddy didn't pay the bills right and he didn't leave no money to bury him."

I swing back around facing her. "You shut up," I tell her. I change what I said about George not talking fast before. He is a fast talker; he started spreading that lie before my daddy was dead hardly a month. I ain't liked George since before my daddy died. He used to bring Daddy home after getting him sick watching basketball and then stand out on the porch whis-

pering stuff to Mama. He'd take off his cap, too, and something ain't right about that 'cause he won't come inside or nothing.

"Will not, it's the truth," Cydney says.

I raise my hand to pass her a lick like my daddy did to Mama when she told lies, but I look up and see Mama coming through the lobby door. George is behind her, boxes in hand, wobbling along. I don't know how you can go from one house with two little girls and a Missus George to another house with somebody else's kids as easily as George did, but I'm sure Bruce Lee would frown on it.

"You two cutting up?" Mama asks.

"No," I say. Cydney shuts down when grown folks question her. I know grown-ups ain't nothing but little kids that done got big, so they don't scare me as much as they do Cydney.

"Shammond, why don't you help your Poppa George carry some of the boxes in."

"He ain't none of my poppa," I say. I can feel Cydney shutting down beside me. I hold my chin up.

"You watch your mouth, Shammond," Mama says to me.

George puts his hand on Mama's shoulder and smiles that smile them dudes give to Bruce Lee when they get off their first licks. Bruce wipes them smiles off their faces soon after. I wish I knew some of that hand-chop and foot-kick stuff for myself. I'd use it on George. "Let the boy go ahead and get used to the new place, run around and explore. I can handle these boxes," George tells Mama.

Mama looks at me. "Thank Poppa George for letting you play instead of work," she says.

I don't thank him. Instead, I take Cydney by the wrist and walk her with me through the lobby and down the hall. Cydney's older by two years but I'm more headstrong according to Mama. Headstrong—I think that means I'm smarter than Cydney.

"You've got to stop being like that with Pop G," Cydney says. "He's our daddy now."

I heard George tell Mama I was a thief last week when he noticed a few dollars missing from his wallet. Takes one to know one is all I can say to that. He stole Mama after all. "He ain't our daddy," I tell Cydney. Bruce Lee and Daddy both would be proud of me.

CHAPTER 4

Slay curbed his BMW outside his mother's apartment tower. He stayed with her from time to time, but not often. He couldn't stomach George, but now that he was dead, Slay would probably spend more time at his mother's. Most nights, Slay worked into the morning and then dropped his head wherever, usually some fine young thing's Section 8 apartment.

Slay nodded to the young boys playing kickball with a deflated soccer ball on the sidewalk in front of the apartment tower. The boys scurried over to him like rats to cheese. Slay peeled off a couple bills, gave each of them one. They knew the routine. Anyone even think about going near Slay's car, the boys were to chase them off with rocks or the ragged pieces of red brick that fell from the front of the building and collected on the lawn where flowers should have been planted. The boys, all in the eleven- to thirteen-year-old range, thanked him and watched with adoration as Slay moved into the building.

Slay stood by the elevator waiting for that slow bucket to come carry him up his mother's apartment on the thirteenth floor. He looked down the hall at the apartments on the ground level, looked over by the stairwell and considered climbing the stairs for a fleeting second. The ding of the elevator saved him from having to move up those steps.

The elevator door opened and he was about to step on when the door of the nearest apartment swung open. Kenya, who had Pam Grier's nose and bosom, but was darker than the night in skin tone, peeked her head out. Slay held his hand in the elevator opening.

"I could feel you out here, Slay. I had to stick my head out," Kenya said. "Sorry about Mr. George."

Slay smiled at her. "What's going on, baby?"

"Nuttin' much. You know Boom got locked up again?" Boom was her on-again, off-again boyfriend. When Boom was off, Slay usually was on.

"Nah, word?"

"Yup." She stepped out a little farther; a man's dress shirt with the buttons opened from her navel up hung off her slender frame. She bent down and picked up a half-full bottle of beer someone had left in the hall by her apartment.

"When he coming home?" Slay asked, peeking at Kenya's breasts.

Kenya held the bottle to her leg, swirled the butter-brown liquid inside the bottle around. "Not sure this time. His moms said she ain't bailing his black ass out no more."

"You and the kids cool?" Slay asked. "Y'all got food and everything you need?"

Kenya's eyes dropped as she thought about her two little boys. "We tryin'."

Slay moved his hand from the elevator, let the doors close on him, walked to Kenya. He'd pulled out a wad of bills by the time he reached her, placed them in her free hand. Kenya leaned into him. He hugged her with just his one arm.

"I'd be willin' to do work for you," she said, her voice dropping. "You think I fit the bill, I bet I could make you some money."

Slay had grown up with Kenya; had seen her through much. She'd seen him through even more. She was the one constant in his life. No way was he getting her involved in *that* life. He shook his head. "Take care those kids, you need anything, hit me off. I got the same celly number. Aiight?"

She nodded, grateful. " 'Preciate it, Slay."

He smiled. "Right, right."

"You goin' up to see Miss Nancy?"

"Yeah."

"How she doin'?"

Slay managed a smile. "Mama? She doing good."

Kenya nodded. She knew it wasn't so from what she'd heard from others in the building. She looked down at her feet again. "You can come down, hang out after you done upstairs..."

Slay touched her shoulder. "Got some things to attend to. You just take care of yourself and them kids. And hit me on the celly like I said, you need anything." He was back at the elevator when he remembered something. Kenya still stood in her doorway watching him. "Hey, yo," he said. "What's up with those dogs? Your uncle got 'em for me?"

"Oh, yeah, true. He said he had two pits you'd probably like. Come check him at the spot whenever you get the chance."

"You weren't even going to tell me," Slay playfully admonished her, shaking his head.

"I'm sorry. I got so much on my mind. And it's been awhile since you had asked me."

The elevator dinged again. Slay nodded to Kenya, waited for the doors to open, and then got on. He pressed for the thirteenth floor and leaned against the side wall as the elevator moved up. It was a wobbly ride, like riding a bicycle with no air in the front tire. Bumper stickers for old rap album releases covered the majority of the wall.

On the thirteenth floor, Slay moved to his mother's door, paused, then pulled out his key and stuck it in the lock. He closed the door behind him and walked into the darkened apartment. George's extra pair of work boots and a broken television stand with an empty fish tank on top lined the hall. Slay scooted past the hall clutter, moved through the living room and came to his mother's doorway. He could hear the radio playing, heard the announcer say, "That was The Standells and 'Dirty Water.'" Slay tapped on the door. He opened it wider and walked right in instead of knocking a second time. Her body lay in a clump beneath the covers. Slay pulled them back. What he'd taken as his mother was actually a pile of dirty clothes, arranged neatly beneath the covers. It broke his heart to see those wrinkled clothes because he knew where his mother was. He wheeled and rushed from the apartment.

Her favorite spot was just around the corner, behind the basketball courts where no one played anymore because the rims had been torn down and never replaced. Slay parked the BMW and trotted across the asphalt, afraid of what he'd find.

Behind the court, he found her splayed across the dirt and grass like a neglected leather jacket. A busted Ziploc bag with water spilling from the slit and a goldfish that had taken its last gasp moments before rested in her lap. Her mouth was broken, bleeding.

Her dark skin was rough and ashy. The braided twists of her hair were coming loose at the ends. Slay slowed his trot, moved beside her, bent down over her. It felt as if he were peering at her in a coffin.

"Mama," he called out. She didn't stir. He touched her shoulder and she jumped. "Mama?"

She grumbled and looked up at him.

"Mama," he repeated.

"Georgie, baby, that you?" she asked, her voice distorted by her heavy tongue inching in the gaps where her teeth used to be.

"Nah, Mama, it's me."

"Georgie, baby, pleeease. I been waitin' on you."

"It's me, Mama."

"You get it, Georgie, baby? Please tell me you got it, Georgie, baby. I cain't hole on much more. Come on, Georgie, baby, give it to me…"

"He's gone, Mama, it's me," Slay said softly.

Nancy seemed to realize where she was. She looked around and crinkled her forehead. "Tole this fool my husband was gone and I needed help," she said. She grabbed ahold of the Ziploc. "Offered him my fish…offered him my wet tongue and these juicy-fruit lips…" She was speaking of the one-named youngster—Larry—who conducted his business behind the courts. Larry was nowhere to be seen now.

"He hurt you, Mama?" Slay asked.

Nancy nodded her head. "Punched me in the mouth and tole me to get on."

"Again," Slay sighed. He hated this cycle. His hands were tied behind his back because he didn't like to acknowledge the place his mother was in, and if he came back here and got revenge off that poor sucker Larry who held down this plot of land like he was Donald Trump, then Slay would be admitting something he didn't even like to acknowledge in the solitude of his thoughts—his beautiful mother was a junkie. Slay looked around, over his shoulders. The night was still and quiet. They were alone. "Come on, Mama," he said, placing his hands under her arms for support. "We need to get you home and cleaned up."

"What about my goldfishy?" Nancy asked.

"He's gone," Slay said. "I'll get you another one, but you got to promise to keep him in the tank."

Earlier, Cydney had a difficult time getting up for work. She'd thought a steaming-hot shower would loosen the tension in her shoulders but the water just seemed to bounce off her skin. She'd spent the night reworking the last pages of a paper for her Critical Thought class; then, unable to sleep, she combed through her dozens of movie videos searching for something to settle her down and possibly ease her into the bliss of her dreams. She picked *While You Were Sleeping,* ironically enough, always having loved the wonder of the romantic comedy. She wondered if she, like Sandra Bullock in the movie, would ever get her Mr. Right.

Unfortunately, the movie made her even wider awake. She thought about her girlfriends from the old neighborhood. Chamique, Wanda and Miah. She wondered how many children they each had by now. She was glad, despite how hard it was, that she finally had the chance to pursue her college degree. She'd quickly stopped thinking of the old days. That life was firmly behind her. Her new life was college, the magazine, her new girlfriends Faith and Victoria. Changes for the better.

She'd ended up calling Slay, catching him on his cell phone, some girl in the background talking all loud to let whoever was calling know that she had him for the night.

"Cyd-a-knee," Shammond had said, slurring his words. "I was thinking about you."

Cydney was surprised to hear her brother sounding drunk. He despised alcohol and drugs. "Hey."

"I wanted to call you but I got tied up." He giggled like a fool into the phone. "Wanted to let you know there's going to be a memorial for George this weekend at the funeral home."

"Chapman's?"

"Come on, Cyd-a-knee. You know ain't nobody else to fix up niggas around here but Chapman."

"Yes, I suppose."

"I'm handling all the arrangements—getting him cremated."

"Cremated?"

"Yeah," Shammond said. "It'll be nice."

"What about his other children and his ex-wife, they in on it?"

"Sheeit," Slay said, "they could care less. I did talk to his one daughter, though. She wanted to know if he had a policy or anything."

"Did he?"

"Got some associates of mine looking into all that," Slay said.

Cydney never liked to think about that portion of Slay's life, the portion where he had associates available to him. "Saturday?" she said.

"Yeah, around noon." He giggled again.

"You been drinking, Shammond?"

"Little."

"Why? Thought you didn't drink."

"Taking my mind off things, is all," he said. His mama, broken, beaten, addicted to that shit.

"Saturday," Cydney said. "Okay, I'll be there. Bye."

"Hey, yo, holeup," he cut in. "What were you calling for?"

"Just couldn't sleep," she told him.

"Ahhh, you learning to lean on me again, that's good."

She smirked. Was it? "Bye."

"Right, right...and wear something nice to the memorial."

Now, at the Elizabeth Arden fragrance counter for work, Cydney was fighting the ill effects of that sleepless night. She yawned into her heavily scented wrist between stopping potential consumers so she could spray their wrists and make them smell like her own. She was dealing with such a woman now, an older white woman who appeared to have benefited from quite a bit of plastic surgery. The woman wore expensive sunglasses and an elegant scarf.

"This is devilish, sugar," the woman said. "What is it called again?"

"Green tea..." Cydney's voice trailed off as she noticed a

familiar face in the distance. She always caught a sense when he was near. He stood by a rack of jewelry, waiting for this woman to leave so he could come forward. He smiled when Cydney's eyes caught a glimpse of him. Cydney looked away, gave her attention to the starlet in front of her. "Smells wonderful on your skin, too," Cydney told her. Then she whispered conspiratorially, "You know, every perfume isn't for every woman. It has to blend correctly with the natural oils and scent of the person. I've got a feeling, though, that everything smells good on you."

The woman nodded in agreement. "I do have a devilish relationship with fragrance. I'll definitely take this."

Cydney smiled. The commission from this sale was a week's worth of cable.

Cydney processed the sale, plus a few other accessories the woman noticed on her way to the checkout counter, and looked up as Stephon approached. She didn't want to see him but had to admit he looked mighty fine in that pink-striped shirt with the white collar, his tie loosened, his coat hanging cockily over his shoulder. His hair was cut low, his beard looking as if he'd recently had it touched up and trimmed, forming a perfect black border around the jawline of his face.

She looked down as he neared her, fumbled with a calculator, tallying her commission thus far today. She could feel his shadow looming over her. Then his voice lowered upon her. "Hello, Cydney." It was so rich with feeling, so hefty in its masculinity. Cydney lost her place on the calculator keys, closed her eyes to gather her calm. "Cydney," Stephon repeated. She slammed her fingers into the calculator, pushed it aside and looked up at him. His even-teethed, perfectly white smile made her abandon her attempt to ignore him further.

"What are you doing here, Stephon?" she asked, her heart

pressing against her chest where she secretly wished his hands were.

"I left the office and decided to take a drive down this way. I wanted to see if you had done that restaurant review yet for Cush."

"My deadline is weeks away," Cydney said.

"You get off soon, don't you?" Stephon asked.

"Yes, but I'm dead tired. I've got to get myself some sleep."

"No classes tonight?"

"No," she said, "and I think you know that. Don't you have every detail surrounding my life filed in your PalmPilot?"

He laughed. "What do you say we go check out Cush together?"

"I told you, I'm bone tired. And I also told you we had to stop doing this."

"I didn't ask that we do our usual," he defended, his arms outstretched, pleading his case. "You're my drug, Cydney. You have to let me ease off of you. A meal, that's it. I promise."

"I don't know, Stephon. This doesn't make it any easier."

He batted his eyes. "One meal, that's it. Please, Cydney."

She glanced at her watch. "I'll be done in about twenty minutes, okay?"

Stephon clasped his hands together. "I'll go look around while I wait." He started to move away, then turned back. "Where is the intimate apparel in here?" he asked, a twinkle in his eye.

Cydney didn't miss a beat. "Your wife's a what—large? I believe that section is upstairs. I'm not sure, though. The petites—where I get my things—that's on the next level to the right after you get off the escalator. Check next to there."

Stephon looked at her, smiled. She looked down, fumbled with the calculator again.

CHAPTER 5

The restaurant was full once again, a cause of celebration for Desmond. Even though this had become the norm, Desmond always worried about the day it wouldn't be the norm. The day he would find himself, sleeves rolled up, walking around from one empty table to the next adjusting the flower centerpieces and pulling wrinkles from the table linens to keep his body and mind occupied. Conventional wisdom said that no business stayed hot from its birth onward, but his parents' restaurants had, and it would leave serious discord in Desmond's stomach if his couldn't match that success. It wasn't something he needed to do, or simply wanted to do, it was something he had to do. Drive, ambition, those were admirable qualities, but for Desmond this was something far greater. This was about leaving his father speechless and in awe.

Desmond walked toward the front of the restaurant, stopping to shake a few hands as he traveled through the maze of aisles. Karen was still acting funny toward him, still cool. It was high time he thawed her a bit, let her know she was important to him, professionally, and remind her that she did have that big diamond rock on her ring finger since it appeared she didn't remember.

Karen was on the phone when he reached her, appointment book opened, pencil in hand. She turned slightly as Desmond approached, gave him a bit of shoulder.

"Yes, seven-thirty is fine," she said in that voice that was so sexy. "We look forward to serving you, Mrs. Buchanan.

Goodbye." She hung up and took her time writing down the Buchanans' reservation, spending more time with each letter than a calligraphist.

"Why are you so upset with me?" Desmond asked.

Karen didn't look up, but answered, "Not upset with you, you're a grown man, entitled to do as you please. I have no claims to you and if you want to go around—" She caught herself. "I'm not upset with you, Desmond."

Desmond put his hand to her wrist, stopped her furious writing. "The only way I'll know what's bothering you is if you come out and say it. I thought we were close."

Karen looked up, those eyes boring into him. "We are."

"Then?"

"It's just that I don't get you sometimes," she said.

"How so?"

"You're contradictory."

Desmond crinkled his forehead. "Me?"

Karen closed her reservations book, placed the pencil against the catch plate of the hostess podium. "The times you've talked about your family, it has become obvious to me that you adore them, yet you've made it clear that the last thing in the world you wanted to do was run their chain of restaurants."

"That's correct," Desmond said, "and I didn't. So where's the contradiction?"

"But you still chose to follow behind them into the business. Maybe not the family business, but you're in the business."

"I grew up around restaurants," Desmond defended. "It's in my blood. I just said I didn't want to find myself as district manager of the Ruckers' chain."

Karen shook off his answer. "What about that woman, Nora, who came with your family on opening night?"

Desmond grunted. That's what this was all about. Now they were getting to the heart of the matter.

Karen dodged his look of judgment. "I asked your sister about her. You were engaged to marry, but you broke off the marriage."

"I know this," Desmond said. "I'm the one who did it."

"You know that woman still loves you…anyone could see it in her eyes. I looked in yours and all I could gather was a twinge of regret. Yet, you took her home with you." Desmond's gaze shifted to his feet. Karen softened her voice. "I think very highly of you, Desmond. I have no qualms about admitting that my husband is less than perfect and that I sometimes think about…" Her voice dissipated as Desmond looked up again. "Sometimes I think about how different my life would be if I had married someone with a stronger purpose, someone like you. In many ways, me coming to work, flirting with you, makes going home more bearable."

"I didn't know your marriage—"

She shook him off. "I hate to think that the man I think so highly of would cause the kind of harm that I know you've caused that Nora woman. You were the typical guy when you took her home that night, and I like to think that you aren't typical."

Desmond eyed her, his expression serious. "I try not to be."

"Have you ever been in love?" Karen asked him.

"I don't even like to think about that question," Desmond said. He shifted his weight from left leg to right, wrung his hands.

"Too many of our men have that same problem," Karen said sadly. "And too many of our women suffer because of it. It'll hit you one day, Desmond. When it does, do what feels right in your heart—because I know you have a good heart—and you'll never go wrong."

"The talk shows condemn thinking with just your heart," Desmond said. "Sometimes you have to use your head."

"What you have to do is make sure your heart and mind are on one accord, that they're both clear—like they say at the end of church service. In your heart you knew you would never marry Nora, I bet. I also would wager my salary—" she smiled to let him know she meant figuratively "—that you knew it in your mind before you even proposed."

Desmond nodded. Karen was alright. Where was she when he was growing up?

"Turn left up here," Cydney said.

Stephon put on his blinker, made the turn, slowed about halfway up the block. "Goodness!"

"What is it?"

"I'd heard horror stories about Asbury Park, but this is incredible. Who would dare open up a business around here? Nothing but junkies, dealers, whores and burnt-out buildings."

Cydney said nothing. By condemning the city, Stephon was condemning her. The harshness of his tone, the disgust in his voice made leaving this married man alone a more doable task. She could just picture him with the same upturned nose, the same judgment in his voice, looking at her with disgust. But she'd never give him the opportunity; she'd never let him know that this city of nothing but junkies, dealers, whores and burnt-out buildings had spawned her.

"You believe this," he continued as they passed a young girl with red boots up above her knees, a jean skirt with the hemline up above the top of the boots. "She's peddling her ass in broad daylight."

"She's trying to survive," Cydney shot back.

Stephon smiled. "Well, that's mighty Democratic of you, Cydney. The Republicans will be very upset to have lost you, but they'll recover. I suppose you'd probably like me to offer that young lady a job, something in…customer service." He chuckled. Cydney didn't.

Republican, was that how he saw her?

"Cush is up there on the right" was all Cydney could say.

Stephon curbed his car, moved the transmission arm to Park, but sat with the engine running. "You think my car will be safe here?"

Cydney shrugged. "We'll see when we come back out." She unbuckled her seat belt and waited for him to open her door. He didn't seem certain of his next move. "Stephon, I'm waiting."

He came back from a million miles away, tried to smile with comfort. "Yes, let's go and see what Mr. Desmond Rucker has for us here."

Cush had a deep burgundy awning, an elaborate sign with the cursive Cush insignia that could be lighted at night. A thick carpet, the color of the awning, led up the small slope of sidewalk directly to the front door. The door was some rich heavy wood with a polished brass handle and had a menu screwed to the frame and enclosed in sturdy plastic casing. To the left of the entrance was a little window with a picture of Desmond Rucker and a second picture of his staff displayed like jewelry in some fine jeweler's storefront.

Stephon stopped and looked at the picture. Cydney did as well.

"That's Desmond Rucker?" Cydney said.

Stephon wheeled toward her. "Yes, it is." He clenched his teeth and made his jaw muscles bulge. "Why?"

"Surprised to see he's so young," she said. "I was expecting a much older man."

"You know that cliché about wine getting better over time," Stephon said. He pulled at his necktie, tightened it. He was a handsome, influential man. Just over forty years of age. He wasn't in his late twenties like Desmond and Cydney, though. Looking at how Cydney looked at the picture of Desmond Rucker, Stephon was happy his instincts had forced him to come with her.

"You ready to go in?" Cydney asked.

Stephon hesitated. "Yes, I'm ready." Cydney moved to open

the door. Stephon rushed across her. "Let me get that for you," he said.

Desmond Rucker was standing by the entrance podium engaged in a deep conversation with the hostess. His head was down, looked as if he'd just been scolded. Cydney could feel her pulse in her fingertips as she got a good look at him. He was fine with a capital F. She immediately regretted the decision to come with Stephon.

The woman at the podium with the silky hair and the warm smile greeted Stephon and Cydney. "Welcome to Cush. Party of two?"

"Yes, just the two of us," Stephon said. Cydney did a double take. Was it her or did Stephon's voice deepen even more than usual?

"Smoking or nonsmoking?" the silky-haired woman behind the podium asked.

"Nonsmoking," the suddenly Barry White-esque Stephon answered.

Cydney stood back, trying to keep her eyes from drifting to Desmond Rucker. When he finally did look up, and held his gaze on her, she made sure to scan the restaurant and act nonchalant. Desmond stepped forward.

"I'm Desmond Rucker, the proprietor," he said, extending his hand to Stephon.

"Nice place you have here, Mr. Rucker," Stephon said.

"Thank you," Desmond replied. He looked to Cydney. "I hope your wife agrees." Desmond eased his hand from Stephon's firm grip and extended it to Cydney.

"I most certainly agree," she said. She turned her left hand, held it up. "And wife isn't on my résumé." They held eyes for a moment, a connection taking place. Nothing else needed to be said.

"Your table is right this way," Karen said. She took up two

menus, shot Desmond a stabbing glare as she walked off with Cydney and Stephon.

Stephon pulled out Cydney's chair for her to sit. She never remembered him doing that before. She placed the linen napkin on her lap and opened her menu. She could feel unspoken words hanging over her, Stephon's eyes watching her. It took a great deal for her to keep from smiling.

"I'll be right back," Stephon said after a moment. "I have to make a quick phone call."

"Checking in on the wife?" Cydney asked. Stephon gritted his teeth before walking toward the restroom where the phones were nestled in the hallway.

No sooner had Stephon left than Desmond Rucker took his place. "I hope your boyfriend doesn't mind but—"

"You make a lot of presumptions, don't you? Stephon's not my boyfriend," Cydney corrected. "He's my boss."

Hard as he tried, Desmond couldn't keep his eyes from widening with pleasure. "Oh, okay. In that case, may I ask your name?"

"Sure you can ask." Cydney dropped her head and scanned the menu.

"Well?"

She continued studying the menu. "I didn't say I'd give it." She didn't know why she took this playing-hard-to-get route, but something told her Desmond would appreciate the mystery of her.

Desmond smiled, nodded. "Name isn't important for now."

The confidence in Desmond's voice stirred Cydney's insides. She tossed her hair, looked him eye to eye. "You say *now* as if there will be a later."

"I haven't been more positive of anything in my life, Miss Wonderful," Desmond told her. He nodded. "There will definitely be a later."

Cydney didn't know how to respond. Miss Wonderful. God, it was poetry to her ears.

"You're kind of cocky about yourself, aren't you, Mr. Rucker?"

"I'm trying to be confident," Desmond answered, "while I wonder to myself what kind of man could make you smile just at the thought of him, and if I could ever be that man."

"All you have to do is ask me," Cydney said.

"I haven't had very much success in asking you questions."

Cydney nodded. "This is true."

Desmond tried to mask it but there was desperation in his voice; where it came from and why it was there was a puzzle even to him. "What kind of man could make you smile with just the thought of him, Miss Wonderful?"

Cydney had been asked variations of this same question for as long as she could remember, all women had, but something in Desmond's eyes made her change the answer she normally gave, made her search deep within herself for the answer she didn't even know existed. "A man," she heard her voice say, "that makes me forget about the passage of time. A man that I'll look at forty years after I looked at him for the first time and wonder where the years went and how it was that I lived them with such happiness and joy."

Desmond was as dumbfounded by her answer as she was. Again, as he'd been doing a lot of lately, he thought of his parents, his father. "Thirty years gone like that," he said, his gaze off Cydney, wandering with his thoughts.

"Yes," Cydney said.

"Good answer," Desmond said, nodding.

"I don't know where it came from," Cydney admitted.

"I don't want to cause any problems between you and your *boss*, though," Desmond offered, "so I'm going to go attend to other matters. It's been a pleasure, Miss Wonderful." He turned to leave and then moved back. "I'm here every day except Sundays. I hope you stop in again—without your boss."

Cydney's tongue held in place, her knees shaking below the tablecloth. She nodded. Desmond moved to leave again.

"Desmond—I mean, Mr. Rucker," she summoned the strength to call to him.

"Please, call me Desmond," he said, turning back. He looked at her as if she were a painting in the Metropolitan Museum of Art. "What can I do for you, Miss Wonderful?"

Cydney was thrown and having a difficult time acting as if she weren't. "What do you—what do you—recommend? From the menu, I mean."

Desmond reached over her, his muscular arm brushing against her, and touched a spot on the menu in her hands. His scent of Curve tickled Cydney's flesh. "The honey-fried chicken."

"What about for dessert?" she asked, hypnotized by his voice and scent.

Desmond smiled. "The apple brown betty, it's rich, sweet, a large serving—built for two people to share."

Cydney's eyes glazed over, and the corners of her mouth turned up in a crease at the mention of the dessert.

"You're smiling," Desmond said to her.

"Someone I knew once loved sharing his dessert with the woman he loved," Cydney answered. She steadied her gaze, held it on Desmond despite the trembling of her knees below the table. "He was an older gentleman, though. You young guys don't have that kind of appreciation and romance in your souls."

Desmond nodded at her appraisal, his smile an umbrella against the rain of judgment. His greatest desire was to kiss the soft lips of Miss Wonderful, show her through physical connection the depths of his appreciation and romance, but he held back. "Enjoy your meal, Miss Wonderful."

He turned to leave, and then turned back abruptly. "Hold off on the apple brown betty this time. Okay?"

"Why?" Cydney asked.

"Come alone next time and I'll show you," Desmond said. He added, "Remember, I'm here every day except Sundays."

NANCY

"We have two kinds of cheesecake. Italian ricotta, which, obviously, is made with ricotta cheese. And, Easter cheesecake, which has rich butter-cookie crumbs as the crust, and ground macadamia nuts through the creamy batter," the waiter tells us.

I wouldn't want any even if it was sprinkled in gold dust. I want the better life George has been preaching to me since before Darius passed. I want my son to get himself together, at home with me where he belongs instead of in some juvenile detention center. George bringing us—Cydney, myself and him—on this little family trip up to God knows where in Massachusetts doesn't change anything. We should be at the JDC looking into these new accusations that Shammond started some riot.

"We'll take the cheesecake," George says. "Just one. Two spoons." He looks at Cydney. "You want anything, Cydney Doll?"

She shakes her head. Looks away. She's like me, not in the mood for any dessert, any trip, any more time away from Shammond.

"Make it three spoons," George tells the waiter. The waiter nods and moves away.

George eyes me. I can feel him looking even though my head is down. George is a good man, no doubt about it, and I do love him, but Shammond is my own flesh. I carried him around for all those months. I'm the one he tossed and turned inside.

"You two stop looking so down and out," George says to me and Cydney. "Try and enjoy yourselves."

I want to hug George, not just for the attempt at bringing us joy with this trip, but for everything. For carrying Darius home all those nights. For providing hope I thought was lost way back when Darius started drinking so heavily. "I'm sorry," *I tell George.* "I guess I'm not being appreciative enough."

George pats my hand on the table. "Nonsense, you're very appreciative."

"The nature-trail tour will be good," *I tell him. I know my voice sounds less than sincere, which is upsetting because I really tried to stir up emotion. George, knowing how much I read and how I love learning about new things, planned all this to make me happy. Under normal circumstances, I would be.*

George shakes his head. "Change of plans."

"We're not going to do it?"

"Nope," *George answers.* "After we all eat this cheesecake together, we're gonna head on back home and I'm gonna have a word with my boss, see if that partner of his who works in the court system can do anything to help your boy out." *I wish he'd said* "our boy" *but that's nitpicking.*

I look at George and something happens between us, an unspoken truth. I'm glad he doesn't stumble home on one of his partner's shoulders and he's glad I don't sing obscure gospel songs and lock him out the house.

"Thanks," *I tell him in a near whisper.*

George nods and looks at Cydney, my child, smiling for the first time today. "One thing, though. I get the biggest piece of cheesecake," *he says. Cydney and I agree that is more than a fair exchange.*

CHAPTER 6

Slay knew Theresa's schedule probably better than she knew it herself. Tuesdays she arrived for an early class. Usually late, trotting from her car, her expensive little pocketbook swinging against her leg as she crossed the lot and then the big lawn. He took this to mean she wasn't a morning person. Good, because he wasn't either. Wednesdays she came in later in the afternoon. A late start and a late finish—the sky dark, the lot thinned out by the time she returned to her car. She always came out walking slowly, looking dead to the world. Reminded him of his mother before the drugs, back when she worked all those hours keeping old Mr. Chesterfield's stinky ass cleaned up— so the old man wouldn't get bedsores—and strained her back lifting his heavy ass from the bed to his wheelchair. Thursdays, Theresa arrived early afternoon and was finished in a hot minute. She always seemed so pleased on Thursdays, smiling, taking the time to talk to other students as she moved through the lot to the main campus building. Her conversations were always with other females, too. The girl of his dreams was pure. Fridays was a schedule similar to Thursdays. Fridays were always difficult for Slay because Theresa didn't have classes on the weekend or Mondays. Longest three days in the world.

He'd spotted Theresa over a month ago on what had been a normal day until he pulled his BMW into the Exxon station across from where the Kentucky Fried Chicken used to be at in West Long Branch. Slay took the second pump, a black

Honda Accord at the first fuel pump in front of him. He had
his Nas CD on loud, as usual, was bobbing his head and
thinking about making money as the pump meter spiraled.
Then the driver's door of the Accord opened and she stepped
out. He didn't know her name at the time. Her complexion was
nut brown. She had on some shades tinted the color of Boone's
Strawberry Hill, long brown hair bunched in a ponytail,
hanging down the nape of her neck. Long-sleeved blouse with
a plunging neckline, hardly any cleavage, though. She wore a
jean skirt that complemented her strong, tight legs and round
rump. She walked to the attendant who was standing by the
little brick building of the station, next to a garage with two
bays, smoking a cigarette. Slay turned his Nas CD down way
low, lowered his passenger window and leaned to see if he
could hear anything.

"I'm running late," she said, sweet as molasses. Slay rubbed
his hands together. Damn, she had a beautiful voice. Sounded
like the "what city what state 411 operators."

"It's still pumping," the attendant casually told her.

"Can you stop it?" she asked. "I have enough."

"You said fill up," the attendant said. Slay clutched his hand
in a fist. It took every ounce of willpower and constraint he
had to keep from getting out and smashing this dude in the grill.

"Okay," she said, defeated. "Here's my credit card, then. So
you'll have it to run as soon as the car fills."

The attendant looked at the card, huffed, tossed his spent
cigarette to the ground and stamped on it. "You should have
given me that before I started pumping. I could have run it
through the pump."

"Sorry, I didn't know. I'm a student here now, but I'm from
Chicago. We pump our own gas there."

The attendant eyed her. "You pumped your own gas? That's
a scary thought."

Slay balled his hand in a tighter fist. The girl made a face and strolled back to her car.

The pump clicked for Slay's vehicle and the attendant came and attended to finishing his fueling. He crossed the back of Slay's BMW and came up to the driver window.

"Nice ride," the attendant said.

"Gracias," Slay said, not even sure if this guy had an ounce of Spanish in him. He looked like he did, though.

"That's twenty."

Slay eyed the attendant's greasy hand, the wad of bills in his right, the woman's credit card in his left. "What's the name on that card?" Slay asked. He nodded his head to the car in front. "Shorty over there."

The attendant started to say something to the effect that he couldn't divulge that information, but he saw the seriousness in Slay's eyes and thought about how a young black guy got an expensive car like this. It added up to more than the attendant was willing to confront. He looked down at the card. "Theresa King."

Slay handed him a twenty and a ten, nodded his appreciation. "Go finish her off—and be nice. Show her a little customer service." Slay rolled up his window and pulled from the lot. He parked on the street just outside the gas station, pretending to be going through papers, waiting.

Of course, when she came out, he followed her—to Mainland University about a mile farther up the road. He spent the next few weeks studying her, camping out in the lot to get to know her schedule, getting a connect in the DMV to run her plates. She lived off campus, in Tinton Falls.

Today, he was prepared to finally cross her path, introduce her to his world. He could feel the excitement rushing through him. Seemed like everything he touched sent back a static-electric charge. It was Friday and he couldn't bear the thought of waiting until next week. If this went as well as he suspected, he'd take her to dinner—maybe at Olive Garden or Red Lobster, someplace nice like that—then a movie. He wouldn't even sweat her for that nappy dugout just yet. He could tell she was classier than that. He would even ask her to come with him to Chapman's Funeral Home tomorrow so he could introduce her to his sister. He figured explaining the situation with his mama would endear him to Theresa more, have her rubbing his head before the night ended. He would do right by Theresa, not get her caught up in this other mess that ruled his life and kept money in his pockets. Make sure she kept herself focused on those books.

Now, Slay waited outside the Patterson Auditorium building that he knew she entered on Fridays. He wished he'd taken up smoking so he'd have something to do with his hands. The college kids shot him glances as they moved into the building. Many of the white girls smiled at him or giggled as they passed. He deflected it all; this was about Theresa.

He thought about that one time he had had the courage to call her home.

This is Tear-ess-a. To whom am I speaking?

He'd hung up like a child.

Slay squinted his eyes now, the sun sending a strong glare down. He placed a hand up to shield himself from that deep orange glare and looked up the path. Theresa was headed his way. She had her books pressed against her chest, looking magical and brilliant. Slay could tell by the casual way she walked up the path that her mind was elsewhere. Slay brushed his shirt, closed his eyes to get a clear remembrance of the things he'd read in Cydney's *Essence* magazines, the few things Cydney had told him about this caliber of female.

Theresa was on him before he could calm his nerves. "Excuse me," he said just as she put her hand on the door to walk into the auditorium. "Can I get a word wit' you?"

She hesitated, but lingered. "Me?" she asked, pointing at her chest. There wasn't anyone else in earshot.

"Yeah, true."

She let the door handle loose from her hands, let the door swing shut and came closer to Slay.

"How you doing?" he said.

"Good," she answered coolly, not making this easy for him.

"I been seeing you around, wanted to introduce myself."

She crinkled her nose. Been seeing? "Okay."

He smiled, extended his hand. "I'm Slay."

She crinkled her nose a second time. Slay? She took his hand. "Nice meeting you, Slay. I'm Pamela."

Slay's eyes rose. "Pamela? Thought your name was Theresa."

She eased her hand from him, her body tight, posture leaning away from him. "Theresa's my aunt. Who are you?"

Slay tried to think of something quick; he could tell he'd frightened her. He couldn't come up with anything solid. "I saw you one day and asked this girl if she knew you—she a—she said she thought your name was Theresa."

Pamela didn't seem too convinced.

"What you reading there?" Slay asked, nodding to her books, trying to deflect from his mistake.

"*To Kill a Mockingbird* by Harper Lee," Pamela said.

Slay hadn't heard of that one but he nodded and smiled. "Oh, yeah, that was cool. I liked his other book better, though."

Pamela had had enough. "Well, it was nice meeting you, Slay, but I have to go to class."

"Can I get your math?" he asked.

"Excuse me?"

He shook his head, cleared the cobwebs. "I mean, may I have your number? Give you a call sometime?"

Pamela laughed nervously and shook her head. "I don't think so." She turned to leave. Slay made the mistake of grabbing her shoulder. "What the hell are you doing?!" she barked.

He released his grip, put his hands up. "Sorry 'bout that. I just would like to get to know you a little better."

"I told you good day, Slay."

"What would it hurt," Slay asked, "us talking a little more?"

"Talk?" she said, smirking. "You can't even put one decent sentence together."

Her words made Slay's forehead line.

"You truly need to get yourself some edgu-ma-cation, Slay," Pamela added, teasing him. She turned her mouth up as if he smelled and moved from him.

Slay's eyes dropped down to his feet. Damn, he'd forgotten to lace his Timberland boots, to drop the cuff of his left pant leg, as Cydney told him he must do. He looked to the doors of the auditorium. What was he thinking? No decent woman would ever want anything to do with him. This was sure to be a long weekend, he thought as he started his slow walk, against the glare of the sun, back to his BMW.

Ever since that meal at Cush, all Cydney could think about was Desmond Rucker. Miss Wonderful, he called her. Damn if he wasn't the best thing since…since anything.

Stephon had noticed a change in her when he came back to the table from making his phone call. He wasn't too happy about the smile that crossed Cydney's face every time Desmond walked by. Desmond made it a point to walk past their table at least five or six times, shooting Cydney glances each time, making her cheeks cherry blossom. He was digging her; she was digging him.

But first, she had to get through this day. Had to confront the sorrow of Pop G's death, confront the sorrow of her mother's life. Shammond had said he'd make sure their mother was at the funeral home.

Cydney pocketed her set of keys and moved up the front steps of the funeral parlor. The building was plain, sided with gray shingles, green awning over the brick step area that led through the front door. Green carpet adorned the immediate lobby; an arrowed sign with George Williams written in cursive pointed her in the direction of his service. Cydney made the left turn, her legs shaking, her hands trembling. It had been close to twenty years since she had dealt with a death this close to home—her birth father's funeral. All she really remembered about that day was George getting her pink cotton candy afterward and her making Slay throw a tantrum when she told him she didn't feel like playing catch football with him.

Cydney came to what amounted to a small ballroom. Slay was standing by the door closest to the urn stand at the front. He looked more subdued than she had expected, sad, off someplace else. Cydney's mother sat in the front row. George's supervisor sat behind her mother, a cheap dress jacket that didn't match his pants draped across the back of his chair. One of George's daughters sat on the other side, silent tears streaming down her face. They were arranged to fill the place out a bit. A few of George's coworkers stood in a group along the far wall, talking amongst themselves in whispers. George's ex-wife, Mildred, whom Cydney had only met once or twice, was standing by the urn, an overdone hat on her head, waving a church fan furiously as she sang some tune out loud.

Cydney looked at her mother again.

Slump shouldered, with most of her weight gone, she was wearing a black dress that looked as if she had picked it up from a pile in the corner of her bedroom and stepped into without ironing. Her eyes were closed and she appeared to be sleeping.

Cydney stood in place at the back of the room. Shammond nodded for her to come forward. She took a deep breath and then obeyed his command, taking small steps down the center aisle. She stopped at the end, gazed at the urn with the light shining on it, the picture of George from when he was younger. That picture had to have been thirty years old. Cydney never remembered him looking like that. She looked into the eyes of the enlarged photo, could see the decency in his pupils. She started to sob.

"No use crying, chile," George's ex, Mildred, said.

"He was a good man, a decent man," Cydney told her.

Mildred harrumphed. "I would have agreed with you up until the day he came home and told me he was leaving me, and his two daughters, for some tramp and her snotty-nosed younguns."

Cydney closed her eyes. For a moment she'd forgotten the demons of the past—that George had indeed run out on his first family for a second one. "I'm sorry," she said to the matriarch of that first family as she reopened her eyes.

Mildred waved her off, turned toward Nancy. "A gat-damned toothless crack ho." George's daughter moved forward and tried to gather her mother's arm, which Mildred brushed away. "Get off me, Georgette. I'm speaking the truth up in here."

"No, Mama," Georgette said. "This isn't the time or the place."

Mildred grabbed Cydney's shoulders and wheeled her to face her mother. Nancy rocked back and forth in her chair, her head bowed, unmoved by the commotion happening just feet from her. "Look at her!" Mildred shouted to Cydney. "And tell me you see something other than a toothless crack ho."

Everyone in the room directed their attention to Cydney. Cydney looked at her brother in the far corner, turned and looked at the other folks in the room, and then turned back to Mildred. "You're right," Cydney acknowledged, tears dropping in heavy clumps from her eyes.

Mildred raised her chin high, snorted in a pompous manner and turned back to the urn, singing that unknown tune again. Cydney looked toward Slay; he sighed and looked away.

CHAPTER 7

Cydney walked through the doors of her apartment and immediately fell to the couch. Her brother stepped in behind her, closed the door and latched the locks. He eased his way into the living room, found a spot next to the bookshelf and CD tower.

Cydney was exhausted from the wake. Exhausted from the mental strain of dealing with the loss of the only man she'd ever recognized as a father. Exhausted from the mental strain of dealing with the loss of the woman she called mother.

"I'm tired," she told her brother. He'd been eerily silent.

"Get some rest."

"Are you upset with me?"

He shook his head. "You called it how you see it."

"You think I'm wrong."

"I was ready to hit that lady for what she said about Mama," Slay offered.

"So yes?"

Slay nodded toward the couch. "Get that rest."

Cydney bit into her lip and then settled into a curled-up position on the couch. Before long, she was in the peace only sleep could give her; even her brother's presence in the apartment with her wasn't stopping her from chasing down slumber.

Slay ran his fingers over the spines of the books on Cydney's bookshelf. All of them were hardcover, the majority of them thick. He pried a particularly thick one from the shelf and opened the cover. The photographs inside startled him. Pictures he'd never seen before of Cydney in a bikini. He guessed they were from one of her trips. The trees and the background looked nothing like New Jersey. He flipped through them one by one, spending a considerable amount of time studying her features in each photo. She was beautiful, smart, a Theresa— no, scratch that—*Pamela* type of female. The type of woman who didn't have time for gat-damned toothless crack hoes or the sons those hoes gave birth to. He wondered who took the photos. Some dude Cydney hadn't told him about? Slay bunched the photos back as he'd found them and placed them in the crease of the book, placed the book on the shelf. He shook his head and pawed at his temples with his hands.

He moved from the bookshelf and pulled Cydney's ottoman to the edge of the couch. He sat down on the ottoman and undid the strap of her shoes, slid them off her feet. He took her foot and started massaging the underside, then the top, then the toes. Love coursed through him.

"Hmm," Cydney murmured, breathy, sexy and still fast asleep.

He moved his way up to Cydney's ankles, then her calves, both of his hands working the knots from her muscles. Cydney shuffled her position, turned her head the other way and twisted her torso in the same direction as her head. Slay hiked up her dress and started to massage her thighs.

Cydney's eyes opened at that point. "What are you doing?" she calmly asked, though her heart raced in her chest.

"You were tense and shit. I was giving you a massage," Slay said, pulling her skirt back down.

"I wish you hadn't done that," Cydney told him. She wanted to scream but decided remaining calm was her best option.

Slay stood and moved the ottoman back in place by her chair. "I was thinking… You really feel that way about Mama?" he asked without turning to face Cydney. He spotted some anger in her voice and wanted to move quickly past it by putting guilt in its place.

Cydney pulled her legs up on the couch and crossed them under her.

He turned to her and sat on the chair, his eyes probing her for an answer.

"Hard seeing her like that," Cydney said. "She wasn't even coherent."

"A lot of Nyquil to keep her calm. Only thing I could think of," Slay said.

"Nyquil?"

Slay nodded. "Otherwise she would have been jumpy and out of control the whole time, and right about now, without me watching her like a hawk, she'd be out on the Ave trying to get her fix on."

"Unreal." Cydney sighed.

Slay leaned in. "How it make you feel knowing that's your mother? That her blood runs through you."

Cydney didn't quite know how to respond. Here she was, a college student studying sociology, and her street hoodlum brother was analyzing her. Well, it would take a mind deeper than he possessed to figure out a mind as complex as hers.

"Easier not to answer," Slay said. His mouth turned up in a lopsided smile. "I'm feeling you though. I know what you thinking. Thinking there ain't any of that skuzzy glass dick worshipping shit up in you."

"You read minds now?"

Slay leaned back in the chair, scratched at his scalp, that lopsided smile still on his face. "She shames you—you think you so much better than her."

Cydney got up from the couch, stomped to the kitchen, the carpet swallowing the echo of her footfalls. Slay got up and followed on her heels.

"Always were a runner when the heat was on," he said.

Cydney opened a cabinet above her stove, the door swinging hard against another cabinet. She pulled down a box of hot-chocolate mix, slammed the door shut again and tossed the box of mix on the counter. Then she opened the refrigerator and plucked out a carton of milk.

"You ain't gotta use milk, you can make that cocoa with hot water," Slay told her.

"I like to make it with milk, okay, motherfucker?" Cydney barked.

Slay's tone softened. "You're cursing. Damn, I upset you?"

Cydney huffed, waved the carton of milk at him like a sword as she spoke. "Just because I wanted to better myself and not stay—" She stopped, shook her head, sighed and moved to her lower cabinet to get a boiling pot.

"Not stay what?" Slay asked as she stood upright again, boiling pot in her hand.

Cydney didn't answer.

"Not stay what?" he repeated. He thought back on his experience at Mainland University, stung by the memory, stung by the look of disgust on his sister's face now. It was the same look that stupid trick bitch Pamela shot his way. Seeing it again made his blood boil. "You better answer me, Cydney."

Cydney rinsed the pot, poured the milk in it, ignoring him. She placed the pot of milk on a burner and lit the flame, then turned to grab the cocoa mix. Before he knew he'd done it, Slay had knocked the pot of milk onto the floor. Cydney wheeled on him, started throwing punches into his chest. His muscles easily deflected the punches. He wrapped his arms around his sister and she began to shake in his clutch. He could feel her wet warm tears on him. They felt good, like an unexpected flash rain during the heat of summer. He thought all was recovered between his sister and him. But he was wrong.

Cydney pried herself from his grip. Her eyes were streaked with black smudges, but she was still so beautiful to him. "You are right, you know," Cydney said. "I am ashamed of her— can't even say Mama without my insides churning. I don't want anything to do with her, as awful as that might seem. I want to go on with my new life and pretend you guys don't exist—just erase you away."

Slay laughed nervously. "You said, 'you guys.' You meant Mama, right?"

Cydney shook her head. "You too, *Slay*. That's who you are, you know. You're Slay. I try to make you out to be Shammond, but you're Slay."

He moved a step toward her, but she pointed a knife at him that stopped him in his tracks. Where did that come from? "Watch yourself with that, sis," he said. "Your head ain't clear right about now."

"My head is very clear, *Slay*," she mocked, sounding like Pamela again. "And if you come near me I will cut your sorry ass from ear to ear."

"Oh, I'm sorry now?"

"Always have been," she said matter-of-factly.

Slay sighed, looked around the kitchen as if it were his first time here. "You forget a lot of shit, Cydney. My loot's helping you with college, and this place. I've been good to you."

"Blood money," she said. "I never should have taken it. You think you own me now because of it."

Slay gazed at her again. "We're family. I ain't looking to own you. I love you. Truth is, all we've got is each other."

"I hate you! Do you know what you've done to me? One moment in my life and you've managed to take that and..."

Slay moved forward. She raised the knife again. He stopped. "Look, this is getting out of hand. You don't hate me," he suggested.

Cydney shook her head. "Oh, but I do. I want you out of here, out of my life. Please leave."

"Cydney, come on," Slay begged. "It's been an emotional day for the both of us."

"Leave!"

"Aiight, I'll chill for a moment out in the living room and let you get all this shit out. Then we'll laugh it all off and go on biz as usual."

"Do I have to get someone to get you out?"

Anger returned to Slay. "Who you gonna get, huh? Ol' dude you was locked in your room talking to that night? The motherfucker took them bikini shots you got tucked in that book in there?"

Cydney crinkled her forehead. "I'll get someone," she said, waving the knife. "Go, before I have to do it."

Slay pointed his finger at her, his eyes narrowed. "You making a mistake, sis. Big mistake. I'm already pissed at you for that shit at the funeral home. This is a big mistake."

"Just one in a long line of mistakes," Cydney shot back at him.

Slay's head moved up and down like a bobblehead doll as he sized up the situation, sized up his sister. "Right, right," he said. "And I guess I'm one of those mistakes?"

"The biggest," Cydney said.

He pointed his finger at her again. "Remember this."

And then he left.

Gone in a flash.

Cydney bolted the door behind him, turned and pressed her back against it. Free at last?

Desmond made the familiar turn onto Cookman Avenue but at the last moment bypassed his restaurant and continued driving up the block. He came to the end, the dance club bordering the ocean in front of him, and made a left turn. The go-

go bar, with the silhouette of a curvy beauty on the signage, lured him in. He parked his truck on the street, across from the bar. He rubbed his hands together, thinking of Miss Wonderful, thinking of Nora, thinking of his inadequacies in the romance department. This was so much easier. Instead of flashing his heart, his soul, he would be expected to flash nothing except his dollar bills. He stepped from his truck, engaged the alarm, looked both ways along the mostly abandoned thoroughfare and crossed.

The bar was like a large matchbox, with no windows, and no adornments other than that delicious sign with Hot Tails embroidered below the woman's silhouette. Desmond could only hope the dancers inside had the same dimensions as the woman on the signage.

Desmond walked in. The human wall at the entrance greeted him without a smile.

"Two-drink minimum," the wall informed him. "Make sure you order the first before you get yourself a permanent seat."

Desmond nodded, headed for the bar. The bartender was an attractive young woman dressed in black spandex shorts and a little white shirt, Nasty in black lettering across the front. She had the shirt tied up in a knot that rested just below her small chest.

"Wha'chu having?" the female bartender asked Desmond.

He focused his eyes to get a close look at her name tag. "Screwdriver, Wendy."

She subtly smiled and quickly prepared the drink. "Six," she said, handing him a small glass of mostly orange juice.

Desmond gave her a ten.

"Enjoy…everything." She smiled again, nodded her head to another patron who'd just walked in.

Desmond moved, with drink in hand, to the adjoining room, where the stage and the music were. A woman with deep dark skin was onstage, grinding some imaginary lover. She was pretty about the face, with lips that could swallow even the most endowed of men whole. Her body was her real commodity, though. Desmond did a double take when she turned and bent over. She wiggled that bottom for all she was worth, had a couple of the men in the room gasping for oxygen. Desmond moved closer. She turned around, and in one smooth motion, yanked her top off. The temperature rose as she executed the strip-down. Her breasts were more than a handful, natural, firm against her chest. She tried without success to keep her fingers covering her nipples. Desmond blinked his eyes, thinking that those things could poke out an eyeball. He looked at his watch, sighed, sipped his drink and settled into a seat. The young lady onstage pounced on him like a vulture. Desmond had a few bills in hand almost as quickly.

"Hey, Papi," she cooed, pressing her breasts up to his face. "You like?"

"Yes, I do," Desmond said, struggling to remove the refinement from his voice. He wanted to take it to the gutter with this girl. "No doubt."

"Tell them," she said.

Desmond smiled, played along. He shifted his eyes to her breasts. "I'm feeling you guys."

"You silly," the dancer told him.

Desmond nodded. "Yes. I mean, yeah, I am." He handed her the bills. She shook her head and indicated the soft spot between her breasts. Desmond placed the bills as instructed and she winked and twirled her way to a gentleman farther down the front row.

Desmond sat back in his seat, let out a breath of air. Over the bang of music, he caught the tone of his cell-phone ringer. He got up and went to a far corner to answer.

Desmond covered his ear, flipped the cell open. "Desmond Rucker."

"Desmond?" It was Karen from the restaurant.

"Karen," he said.

"Where are you?" she asked.

"I'll be in shortly. I had to make a quick stop."

"Sounds like booty music in the background."

Desmond laughed. "Don't be ridiculous."

"Well, look," Karen said, "you need to get over here right away. Your sister's here. She was okay when she first came in, but then turned solemn all of a sudden. She's very upset about something, but she won't speak to any of us. She's holed up in the bathroom."

A breath held in Desmond's chest. "On my way," he said, closing the flip in the same motion.

Slay stood in the lot outside his sister's place. He couldn't force himself to leave, couldn't even make himself get inside his car. He kicked his tires, slammed his hand on the hood. Breathing heavily, mouth filling with saliva, he hocked a glob of mucus and spat it against the windshield of the car parked next to his own. He pounded his two fists together, staring with narrowed eyes at his sister's apartment window. As if on cue, her lights turned off. He imagined her in there, in the dark.

Slay turned his back, leaned against his car and fished out his cell phone. He had to think for a moment to remember the number—the last digits were either 06 or 07. He pushed in the digits ended with 06.

"Hullo."

Slay straightened his posture, moved the phone to his right ear. "'Sup, baby?"

"Slay?"

"Yeah, Kenya. What's going on with Boom? He still locked down?"

"Umm-hmm. They saying he might have to stay in past

Thanksgiving, maybe even past Christmas," Kenya said. There was more vibrancy in her voice than one would expect from someone with a loved one in jail. "Why?" she asked, softening her voice. "You wanna swing by?"

Slay turned and looked at the still-dark window of his sister's apartment. He gritted his teeth, looked at the night sky. Something stirred in his groin, a need he had to satisfy. "Yeah, if that's cool with you," he said to Kenya in his sexiest voice.

"I'd like it," Kenya replied.

Damn, he could barely hear her speak. Her voice was getting softer, farther away.

"I'll see you in a minute." Slay closed the flip without waiting for Kenya's reply. He paused for a moment, thinking. He was forgetting something. Damn, it hit him. He had business he hadn't attended to. He opened his cell phone again. Scrolled through his message book and stopped on *William Jeffries, esquire*. He dialed the number.

"Mr. Jeffries, Shammond Slay here. How are you?" Slay asked, struggling to sound professional.

"Good, Slay," Jeffries answered. He put Slay in mind of that cool white dude that wore the dark suits and used to host that who wants to get-a-million show. Jeffries cleared his throat. "You have some good news for me?"

"Yeah, I mean, um, yes," Slay said, really mangling this. "She'll be checking into the Berkeley Carteret tomorrow. Rooms booked under Gabriel Cohen as you asked. She's yours for the weekend."

"Hispanic as I asked?" Jeffries asked.

"What you mean?"

"Puerto Rican, Cuban, something like that?" Jeffries said.

"Oh, yeah…yes, she's Spanish. She'll be real good to you, Mr. Jeffries. She dances at one of the clubs around here."

"Well, thank you, Mr. Slay," Jeffries said. "My associates

have told me you do a wonderful job. If this goes well, I'm sure we'll be in touch again."

That was candy to Slay's ears. He fully understood the impact of repeat business. "Thank you, Mr. Jeffries." He was prepared to hang up, but something ate at him, something he had to ask. "Mr. Jeffries, what's that e, s, q for at the end of your name?"

"I'm an attorney. A lawyer," Jeffries said, and then he hung up.

Slay pocketed his cell phone, nodding in understanding. He'd made himself some cheddar, was about to get some ass. Still, though, his mood wasn't the best. He opened the car door, shot one last quick look at his sister's window. "This ain't over," he said aloud. "This will never be over." He started the engine, gunned it out of the lot without looking back.

Within ten minutes, he was at Kenya's, walking through her small living room. He patted her two boys on their heads as he passed. Neither of them acknowledged him with more than a quick polite nod, busy playing video games on their outdated Nintendo 64 system. Slay made a mental note to get them either an Xbox or a PlayStation 2, possibly both.

Kenya's bedroom was neat like the rest of the apartment, neat, but small and crowded. Her bed and dresser took up all the floor space in the bedroom. She had a little stereo playing—one of Tupac's slower sentimental songs, the ones the media never quoted from, never credited to his mind and pen. Only one of her secondhand speakers actually worked, so the music, which she had turned down low to begin with, wasn't very clear. The room smelled good. She had a burning incense stick lit, jutting out from the surface of her dresser, held in place by a pickle jar weighted down with a fill of pennies.

"You went all out for me, huh?" Slay said to her. He leaned over and inhaled the incense.

Kenya beamed. "That's Jamaican Spice," she said proudly.

"Shit smells real good," Slay said. "I feel like biting off a chunk of that shit and eating it."

"You hungry?" Kenya asked. " 'Cause I got some KFC left over."

Slay shook his head. "I was just joking. Save that for the kids' lunch or something." He moved over to Kenya, sat down next to her on the bed. She pulled his hooded sweatshirt over his head, pulled off his wife-beater undershirt, started to massage his shoulders.

"You been lifting?" she asked. "You're like totally diesel."

"Nah."

"You tense," she continued.

"Sister got me all upset."

"How is she doing? I never see her around anymore."

Slay sighed. If they had to talk, he might as well ask her what he came to find out. "I didn't get a chance to stop by your uncle's and check out those dogs yet," he said, "but, yo, check it out. He not working no job or nothing is he?"

"Nope."

"He still got that truck?"

Kenya nodded. "True."

"Is it running?"

"Yeah," Kenya said. "He runs me places sometimes. Moves shit for people every now and then. Why?"

Slay thought about Cydney. Something or someone had brought out this hatred in her. That wasn't his usual sister, or how she truly felt, he was sure. "I want to see if he'll do something for me," Slay told Kenya. "Follow someone for me. I would do it myself but I got a lot of other shit I have to take care of."

"I'll ask him," Kenya said. "I'm sure he'd do it."

"Cool," Slay said. He kissed Kenya's cheek. "So when is Boom getting out?"

Kenya got up and moved in front of Slay. She eased him back on her mattress by the shoulders. "Don't be worrying 'bout Boom or your sister stressing you. Let me take care of you."

SLAY

"Not much to tell," I say.

In my mind, I'm not even here, lying across my sister's bed, free. I'm still inside juvie. When I close my eyes to try and squeeze away the fucked-up shit that happened in there, something unexplainable happens to me.

I lean over the side of Cydney's bed and rub my fingers over her carpet, but instead, it's the cold concrete floor. Her bed is actually a small cot. The bandages haven't been put on my right hand just yet. I have nicks on the inner and outer part of my hands—from a fight earlier that day with the kid whose last foster mom fed him cat and dog food. A kid that didn't have anyone to go home to, so he talked shit to all the rest of us without caring what happened to him. I may not have liked George, but I had a mama and a sister at home that I couldn't wait to get back with.

I look toward Cydney's door and her Salt N Pepa poster disappears like a shaken Etch A Sketch drawing. "Slay!" One of the guards raps his stick against the wall. I sit still, except for my fingers spiderwalking the cold concrete floor. "Slay," the guard repeats, "your counselor needs to have a word with you."

I rise at my own pace, which angers the guard—Fuck him!— and wipe at the corner of my eyes, expecting them to be moist, but they dry. I stretch my body, then move forward in short, choppy steps. Walking like I did as a little boy when I'd sneak my father's too-big shoes, put them on and step around the house in them. I didn't care that they weren't Adidas or Chuck Taylors, they were my father's.

The guard opens the gate and offers me an escape from the loneliness of these four walls.

"Take the lead, Slay, stop at the door!" the guard says. This toy cop motherfucker don't seem to realize that he don't need to waste all his energy barking out shit all the time.

As I work my short but stocky body down the narrow hallway, the other youth offenders yell out stupid shit, trying to punk me down, but I keep moving forward without even a blink.

"Pussy-ass nigga!" one of them yells. "You soft punk." I keep moving, don't look in the direction of the voices. I know later on, when we're congregated together, that a few of them will do their best to "punish me" for not acknowledging them, but I'll deal with that when the time comes.

As I come upon the conference room they have set aside for me, I notice someone waiting other than my faggot-ass counselor. Cydney!

"What you doing here?" I ask her.

"What?" she says.

I blink my eyes. I'm in Cydney's bedroom again. I'm draped across her bed. The conference room is gone. "I'm home?" I ask her.

"Yes," she tells me, touching my wrist. I look down and touch her hand. I'm not dreaming.

"Were you scared inside there?" she asks.

I start to smirk, smile, brush aside any thought of fear, but with Cydney I can't be anything but what I am. "Yeah, plenty of times," I tell her.

She sucks in air and rubs her hand across my head. I'd spent so much of these early years in trouble that I didn't really know the softness of a female's touch. I almost said bitch instead of female, but Cydney ain't no bitch. I like how Cydney's fingers feel on the curve of my head. I'ma close my eyes and when they reopen, she'll be that cute girl from the famous Jackson family that I've been seeing on that show Different Strokes. *The one dating Willis on there.*

"It's been so tough not having you around," Willis's girl tells me as she continues to rub my head. Cydney is gone now.

"Tough not being around," I answer, my eyes still closed. I can practically feel hairs sprouting on my little thirteen-year-old chest as I think about what's gonna happen next. I sit up facing Willis's girl and smile. She smiles back. I'm 'bout to steal her from Willis same as George stole my mama from my daddy. I lean in and kiss her on the mouth, force my tongue inside her lips.

"What are you doing?" she asks me, wide-eyed and pushing me back.

"So many things I don't know about, haven't had a chance to get down wit' 'cause of my problems. Dudes be talking about getting a nut and I have to pretend I'm doing something else so they don't ask me questions about how many girls I done fucked."

"Well, I'm not an Easy-Bake Oven for you to practice on," Willis's girl tells me. "You have to do your cooking in a real oven, with a real girl that isn't me."

I ignore her, reach forward and grab her breasts. She fights me off for a short while and then her muscles and her mind get too tired to fight me any longer. She gives in, let's me do everything I want, short of sticking my shit up in her. I'm satisfied just to suck her titties and run my fingers through that rough hair between her thighs.

I hear something and let up. The door cracks open and I'm expecting Mr. Drummond to step in the room. It's…George? "What's going on?" he asks.

"Nothing," I answer. I notice that I'm breathing heavy and my voice cracked.

George looks at Cydney. I do too. Her hair is all wild and

her eyes got big ol' tears in them just waiting to fall down. "You okay, Cydney Doll?" George asks her.

She nods her head. "He was telling me about how bad it was inside that place," she stutters. Her voice trembles as she answers and I'm surprised because I know how Cydney usually locks up when grown folks question her.

I nod at George, too, though I don't remember talking to Cydney and don't even know how I got here in her bed. "Telling her horror stories 'bout inside the hole," I add.

George turns his gaze back on me. "It's late, why don't you get on in your own room and get some sleep, boy. Try to will yourself a dream where you figure how to keep out of the hole."

I turn and kiss Cydney on the cheek. "Night, thanks for letting me rap with you." She squints slightly, then forces a smile as I rise and brush past George.

George lingers in her doorway. He's good for that shit. I remember him doing the same thing with my mama after he brought my daddy home from watching their games. When I was little, I thought my daddy was sick. I realize now that he was drunk. I wouldn't be surprised to learn that George opened my daddy's mouth and poured a bottle full of shit down it himself. "You sure you all right, Cydney Doll?" I hear George ask Cydney.

I stand on my tiptoes and look into her room. She nods her head and pulls the covers up to her neck.

George turns to hit the light switch and leave.

"Leave the light on, would you, Pop G?" Cydney says. That's right, I think to myself, watch your back. I wouldn't put it past that fool to come in there and get you.

"Sure thing, Cydney Doll," he says.

He turns back into the hall and sees me watching him. "Thought I said get on to bed, boy."

"I'm just watching to make sure you get on, too," I tell him.

I know his game, talking Mama into taking on extra night work so he could have us here alone.

"I can dig that," he says, trying to be cool to me, " 'cause I'm watching you too, boy."

CHAPTER 8

Desmond glided inside Cush, his heart pounding against the fabric of his shirt. Karen sidestepped, barely escaping the swing of the door. She'd been dusting the counter area a few feet inside. Desmond was too occupied with worry to apologize for his careless entry. "Where is she?" he asked. "Where's Felicia?"

Karen frowned. "Where were you? I wasn't expecting you to get here so fast."

Desmond scanned the dining area. "I was on my way. Where's Felicia?"

"She's in the ladies' room."

Desmond turned, looked at Karen for the first time. Fear and doubt clouded his face. "What did she say? You said she was crying?"

"Yes," Karen said.

"No one went in to try and talk with her?"

"Of course we did. A few of us. She wouldn't tell any of us a thing."

"I should go and talk with her," Desmond said.

Karen nodded. "Yes, you should."

Desmond held his spot, though. "I'm not good at this kind of thing." He turned and looked at Karen again, his eyes wide with a deeper fear than she ever remembered seeing in him.

Karen touched his shoulder, eased him forward. "You'll be fine."

"Hope she's not pregnant or something," Desmond said.

He'd stopped again, Karen's gentle push no longer moving him. "You know she's living in New York, modeling. She lives with a couple of other models. That's not the greatest environment for a beautiful young woman."

"I know," Karen said. Her arm was entwined in his and they started walking again.

He stopped again. "My parents were dead set against her doing this modeling thing. They wanted her to go to college. I wish she would have listened to them, but she's headstrong, stubborn, set in her ways."

"Sounds like someone else I know," Karen replied.

"It's different with me, if that's what you mean," Desmond said.

Karen was able to get him to move a few more steps.

"You're a good woman, Karen."

Karen smiled. "This is true. Now come on, your sister is waiting."

Guilt covered Desmond. "I try to do the right thing when it comes to women, but it isn't easy," he offered.

Karen rubbed his back, moved yet a few more steps. "Your sister, Desmond, she needs you."

"I'm just saying…I'm probably not the best person to help her deal with a woman's problem."

They reached the threshold of the ladies' room. Karen released her hold on his arm, stopped rubbing his shoulders, and looked at the restroom doorway. "You can bare your soul to me some other time. Right now—" she nodded her head toward the bathroom "—your sister needs you."

Ten minutes ago, Desmond was lusting over a beautiful young woman, defining her by the sum of her assets, her ass and breasts. Now he was expected to tend to his sister? What in the world could he offer Felicia in comfort and wisdom? He couldn't imagine what would shake Felicia up so much that she would come down here from New York. Teary-eyed no less. He couldn't ever remember Felicia brought to tears in all her eighteen years. She was the little girl who could take lumps better than the boys.

"Go on, Desmond," Karen directed.

He turned to Karen, had forgotten she was still here as his mind ran amok. "I'm going." He clasped his hands together, rubbed them, took a deep breath and went to move forward but then stopped. He turned back to Karen. "Check and make sure no one else is in there."

"I've kept my eye on it, there's no one in there except Felicia."

"You positive?" he asked.

"Go!" Karen barked.

Desmond put his hand up in defense. "I'm going."

He knocked as he entered. Felicia didn't answer. "Felicia, it's me, Desmond." The sound of his voice was followed by an onslaught of his sister's sniffles. He noticed only one of the stalls closed and went to that stall and tapped on the door. "Felicia, sweetheart, you want to open up so we can talk?"

She paused for a moment before unlatching the door. Desmond pushed it open softly. Felicia stood pressed against the wall, a heap of twisted, wet scraps of toilet paper at her feet. Her makeup had run, black mascara showing the trail her tears had taken down her face. She looked up at Desmond. The woman he'd imagined her to be was not present. In the innocence of her eyes and the vulnerability of her posture, he could only see an eighteen-year-old struggling to be older and wiser than her years.

"What's the matter, Felicia?" He found himself rubbing his fingers along her hairline, caressing her face. To Felicia, the touch was as gentle as a breeze. She knew she'd made the right decision to come to Desmond instead of running home to her folks.

"Everything is screwed up," she said.

Desmond desperately wanted to move from the cramped quarters of the stall, grab a seat at one of the tables outside in a quiet corner, but here would have to do. Felicia obviously wasn't up for a move just yet. He asked Felicia, "Screwed up. Why? What's happened?"

"I'm not going to slut my way to success," Felicia said, shaking her head, defiance taking ahold of her. "I'm not sleeping with some slimy old creep to *advance my career.*"

Desmond's voice rose. "Someone propositioned you?"

The tears started to flow again from Felicia's eyes. All she could do was nod.

"Who was it, Felicia?"

"One of the agency photographers...Kenneth," she sneered. "He works with getting our portfolios together to send out for job prospects. He hinted to me that he could increase my chances if I—" She stopped, hung her head for a moment. Wiped her eyes dry with her hands and blew her nose in a wad of toilet paper. Desmond had been awfully quiet, so she looked up at him. "Why are men such pigs?"

Desmond thought about Nora, about Karen, the dancer at the go-go bar with the mouthwatering ass and eye-popping nipples. He thought about the generous deposit he'd given the dancer, in the crease of her breasts, simply because she was built like a prizewinning Thoroughbred and jiggled like a pocket of change. Why were men such pigs?

"I don't know, Felicia," he replied honestly.

"If they're not cheating on you, they're demeaning you," Felicia continued.

Desmond nodded despite himself.

"They make you question yourself," Felicia said. She looked at Desmond, hard. "Nora, she's all caught up with you. I know you probably have, but I have to ask anyway. You ever make her cry? Besides the wedding fiasco, I mean."

Desmond sucked in air. "More times than I care to announce," he admitted.

"How does that make you feel?"

"Ashamed."

Felicia shook her head and looked away, tossing the thought of her brother's issues, most men's issues, aside. "Can I stay with you for a little while?" she asked. "I'm not ready to give up on modeling yet, but I'm not comfortable staying in New York right now, and I can't go home to Mommy and Daddy."

Desmond placed his hand on her shoulder. "What's mine is yours."

"Thanks. You're the best," Felicia said, falling into his arms.

Desmond thought about that go-go bar again, knowing that today was probably just the start of his visits there. Was he the best?

The meltdown with her brother was on Cydney's mind as she sat down, crossed her legs and rummaged through the pile of dusty photo albums she'd just pulled from under her bed. She kept the albums in a cardboard box, next to a plastic box filled with shoes she never wore. As with the shoes, she'd considered trashing the albums several times, but never did. The phone rang as she picked up the first photo album and opened the cover. Cydney reached for the cordless, glad she'd had the foresight to bring it with her so she didn't have to run and grab it.

"Hello?" she said. She eyed a picture of Slay and her running through the water of a fire hydrant when they were younger. She smiled, remembering how Slay had taken the blame for opening the hydrant when the police came down that block. In the picture, Cydney was soaked all the way through; Slay had a bit of water on his pants and shirt. In truth, Cydney had opened the hydrant herself and had been playing in the water for quite some time before her brother joined in.

"Cydney?" Stephon spoke from the phone receiver.

Cydney flipped the page. Ooh, there was a picture of Slay when he was about ten or eleven, in his Pop Warner football uniform. Everyone was just sure he'd at least go to college on a football scholarship. He was magic with a football. Some of the older men in the neighborhood said he had Gale Sayers's moves and Jim Brown's power, whoever those two were.

"Um…yes," Cydney said as she continued turning pages.

"I don't want to do the review for Cush," Stephon said.

That caught Cydney's attention. "What? Why?"

Jealousy or insecurity, take your pick. "I'd rather run a piece on that new restaurant in Atlantic Highlands. The Wharf."

"The seafood place?"

"Yes," he said. "It's been getting tremendous buzz."

"I thought our mission was to keep people of color informed about opportunities for cultural enhancement and entertainment here in New Jersey," Cydney reminded him. "That is *Urban Styles*'s mission statement."

"It is." He cleared his throat. "But come on, you know niggas love theyselves some scrimp," he said, failing to tickle Cydney's funny bone.

"I'm doing Cush," Cydney stated matter-of-factly. "You're being ignorant and you know it."

"This isn't personal."

"Right, Stephon."

"I could make it personal," he said. "I could mention how inappropriate I thought your behavior was that day we dined at Cush."

"Inappropriate?"

"Highly. Making googly eyes at that stuffy Negro like some teenager."

"Desmond Rucker is far from stuffy, Stephon."

"Why you say that so certainly?" He swallowed loud enough for Cydney to hear on her end. "You were in his presence only a short while. Have you been back?"

Cydney started to say yes. "No."

"You're sure?"

"Positive, Stephon."

"I'm divorcing Samantha, Cydney. I'm really going to do it."

"I hope you don't think there's hope for us, that you're thinking of divorcing her with some delusion of us being together."

"Delusion?" His voice softened like a cried out child.

"I'm serious, Stephon. You and I are done."

"You weren't talking this definite before meeting Mr. Restaurateur," Stephon said coldly.

"Thought this wasn't personal," Cydney responded.

"You have been back."

"I haven't."

"I can just tell you have," Stephon said.

"Stephon, you—"

He cut her off with, "So how was it?"

"How was what?"

"That dick, Cydney, don't play coy with me. I just know you fucked him. You never were very discriminating in that department."

Cydney's mouth opened into a capital-size O. "No, you didn't."

"Yes, I did. So tell me. How was it?"

"I'll have the review over to you by the end of the week," Cydney fumed. "Read it and see just how good it was." She clicked the phone off. It rang back almost immediately but she let the voice mail pick up the call.

Okay, Stephon, she thought, you want me to go back so bad. Then I'll go back. She shut the photo album. There was no use in traveling down memory lane any longer. Slay was of the past. Stephon was of the past. Desmond Rucker...he was the future.

Slay pulled up to Kenya's uncle's house. He didn't need directions or a house number because the old man had a front yard full of useless odds and ends. The township inspectors had cited him for zoning violations on quite a few occasions, but as of yet they hadn't followed through with fines or jail time. Slay got out of his BMW, nodded to some people across the way that he knew and walked through the gate toward the house. The right portion of lawn was piled high with tires, hubcaps, and those gaudy Christmas ornaments that some people liked to stamp in their grass—a life-size Santa Claus, a sleigh and three reindeer. The left portion of lawn had a couple of old car engines, stacks and stacks of tied newspaper, a rusted stove, a refrigerator with the door lying on its top and garbage cans filled with leaves. Slay shook his head as he moved up the path to the front door. Kenya's uncle was a regular old Fred Sanford.

Slay opened the screen door and rapped on the main door frame. He rapped again after his first knock went unanswered. He moved to the edge of the porch and leaned over the side. The truck was parked in the narrow drive. Old man had to be home. Slay went back to the door and rapped again. This time he heard footsteps. Somebody fumbled at the lock behind the door and opened it.

A young woman appeared just behind the screen. She was wrinkled from hard living instead of years; she couldn't have been more than thirty-five or thirty-six, Slay estimated. The woman had her hair wrapped in a red bandanna and was missing a few teeth on her upper row. She stood in the screen, guarding the house with the fortitude of a Secret Service agent. "Yeah," she said. Her voice had been deepened by years of smoking Newport cigarettes and worse.

Slay smiled. "Hey, I'm Slay. Kenya called ahead. I'm supposed to speak with her uncle."

"Chuck?" the woman asked.

"Yeah," Slay answered.

Recall flashed through her eyes. "'Bout the dogs, right?"

"Right, right," Slay said.

Ms. Hard-Luck Life moved aside and opened the screen door. "Chuck is down in the basement. End of the hall, door on the right. Ain't no light, so watch your step."

"You his daughter?" Slay asked as he walked in.

The woman laughed. "I've been taking care of him since his wife passed. Not like no daughter, though."

Slay looked at her and she winked. "Right, right," he said. He moved down the hall and came to the door, opened it and walked in a crawl down the steps, making sure to hold to the rail for guidance. At the bottom, he saw that it led to another room, which was lighted. Slay walked through the opening. A large pit bull lurched for him and got pulled back by the chain around its neck. Slay stared at the dog and then turned to a smiling old man. Kenya's Uncle Chuck.

"You the first person didn't jump out they skin when Stinger jumped up like that," the old man said.

"I was about to snap her neck," Slay answered, "but that would be rude."

The old man smiled. "Got a litter of four, you can have two of 'em."

Slay looked over by the adult pit, noticed the four little puppies lying sleep at her underside. "The two black ones," Slay said.

"What's Kenya up to these days?" the old man asked as he moved around Slay.

"Taking care of those kids. Her man is locked up again."

"Same ol'. Same ol'."

"Yup."

The old man turned and looked Slay over. "You a pretty-put together fella. I've been hearing your name since she was little. How you figure in Kenya's life?"

Slay didn't know how to respond. His relationship with her had never been defined even though it spanned the majority of his life. "We close" what he came up with.

The old man looked up, up where the girl with the missing teeth, weathered skin but young backbone and strong thighs was. "Nice to have someone you close to."

Slay studied the old man for a second. He placed him in his early sixties. He was small in stature but had hands the size of baseball mitts. Strong hands. "Did Kenya mention to you I might have some work that'd interest you?"

The old man looked at Slay. "She did."

"I see you have that truck outside. I want you to follow my sister around, just for a week or so, and tell me where she goes, what she does...who she sees."

The old man shook his head. "I don't like the sound of all that. I make it a habit not to be getting up into other folk's business."

"You know my mother," Slay said. "Nancy Williams. She lives in Kenya's building."

The old man nodded.

"You seen her lately?" Slay asked.

Old man nodded again.

Slay forced himself to speak. "You seen what the drugs did to her, then. I'm concerned about my sister, Cydney. I think she might be headed in that same direction. I really need your help on this one. I'd follow her myself but I got a whip that screams out 'look at me.'" Slay puffed his chest out. "A BMW quarter to eight."

The old man nodded, unimpressed.

Slay frowned. "The drug trade ain't no joke, sir. I don't want my sister caught up in it."

The old man looked up at the roof again, thinking of the

young woman with the weathered skin and the missing teeth. "Cydney, you said your sister's name is?"

"Yes, sir, Cydney Williams," Slay said, smiling. Slay always was good at figuring a person's weak spot and exploiting it for his own gain. Kenya's uncle's jaws tightened at the mention of drugs. He'd be Cydney's second skin this next week.

Kenya's Uncle Chuck nodded. "I'll keep a watch on your Cydney."

CHAPTER 9

This particular evening had drained almost all of the energy from Cydney's overworked body. Her feet hurt even though she was wearing her Reebok cross trainers, and her hands were sore from writing. She'd just completed what was perhaps the most difficult test she'd ever taken. Her Critical Thought instructor, Professor Greenwood, pushed her harder than all of her other professors combined. His tests left the body sore and the mind exhausted. It was like some military strike gone bad and Cydney was the POW of his hostile exam.

Cydney settled onto the couch in the lounge and nursed a cold ginger ale and a small bag of honey-roasted peanuts. She was feeling a bit jittery—blood sugar low—and decided a quick snack would be wise before she took that drive on 18 South back home. A woman was on her cell phone across from Cydney, standing against the window of the lounge, whispering microwave-warming instructions to her husband. Cydney eavesdropped on the woman for a moment before a thought hit her. That woman had a husband—children, too, it appeared from what Cydney could make out. When that woman graduated she'd have someone cheering her on, someone to share in the moment with. Cydney had no one, unless you counted Faith and Victoria, and both of them would be reveling in their own graduations, with their own family and loved ones. Cydney had successfully moved from the confines of her old life only to find that her new life had even greater challenges, different challenges to be sure, but still, challenges.

The woman standing by the window closed her cell phone and moved back toward the lounge area. She walked over to the little table where she left her pocketbook and textbooks and placed the cell phone in her purse. The woman, like Cydney, appeared exhausted. She sat down in her seat, closed her eyes and ran her fingers over her temples. Cydney heard the woman mumble, "It's all prepared. Just remove the aluminum foil. Cover the dish with a paper towel. Put it in the microwave. Hit time. Punch in three minutes…voilà." Cydney smiled. Okay, so this woman didn't have the perfect life either, but she had more than Cydney.

Cydney was about to glance at her watch and see what was taking Faith and Victoria—the only friends she had at school or anywhere anymore—so long. But just then they came around the bend of wall. Faith looked as exhausted as Cydney. Victoria looked like she'd just stepped out of a rejuvenating hot shower. Cydney hated Victoria for always having her stuff together.

Faith scooted next to Cydney on the couch and plopped back against the softness of the cushions. "That man should be decertified," Faith said. "That wasn't a test. That was a darn master's thesis."

Cydney nodded in agreement. Faith definitely grew up more privileged than Cydney—father a judge, mother a big-shot accountant—but she had a down-to-earth quality that Cydney appreciated from the first moment they met. Faith had a nutmeg color to her, brown hair and a tight little dancer's body. She'd been destined for ballet stardom until an ankle injury developed a tolerance for ice packs and hot-wrap treatments. After that disappointment, college was the logical option.

"I wish," Victoria chimed in, "in the name of everything just and sacred, that that man would recognize the error of his ways, and cease, effective immediately."

Faith and Cydney laughed. Victoria had a way of putting things that made laughter the only option. She was a diva among divas. On quite a few occasions it had been noted that Victoria bore a striking resemblance to Vanessa Williams. Every time, she waved off the comments. "I think not—isn't she in her forties?" was her usual reply. Victoria had come to college after spending her early twenties traveling the world.

The three of them had been sistahgirlfriends since alternative schedule orientation, over two years prior.

"How did you get finished so darn fast, Cydney?" Faith asked.

"I've been studying for this exam like you wouldn't believe," Cydney said. "I have to raise my scores in this class."

"Your eyes show it, too, honey," Victoria said. "You need to move from the perfume counter at Macy's and go over to the makeup counter."

"Thanks," Cydney said.

Victoria waved her off. "Don't thank me, thank Lancôme."

"I do need something," Cydney admitted.

"I'm off to the Bahamas after the semester ends," Victoria said.

"Sounds like a plan," Faith responded.

Cydney forced a smile.

"So what new music have you discovered for us, Cydney?" Faith asked as Victoria, who had been standing the entire time, settled in the tiny space next to Cydney.

A thought crossed Cydney's mind. "No music this month. But I am doing a feature on this great new soul food restaurant."

Victoria's eyes crested. Even though it was hard to tell by her svelte figure, she was a food connoisseur. "Do tell," she begged of Cydney.

"It's called Cush," Cydney said.

"Oh. That's a name of an African city, from ancient times," Faith said.

"It's a delicacy as well," Victoria chimed in. "A Southern dish, like a cornmeal pancake. Oh, and also a soup made with cornmeal, milk, onion and seasonings."

Cydney looked at the both of them. "Can anyone say, *Jeopardy?* Damn, you two are something."

Victoria smiled. "I told you, anything you ever need to know about food you come to me."

"We've been talking the past few weeks about getting together," Cydney said. "Why don't you come with me to the restaurant. We can't let these books hold us hostage."

"That's a wonderful idea," Faith said. "Where is it?"

Cydney hesitated. "Asbury Park."

Victoria said, "Oh."

"Asbury used to be the happening place in New Jersey," Faith offered. "My parents say it's on the upswing again. They go down there and shop in this one antique place all the time."

Victoria seemed surprised. "Well, let's do it then, once and for all. What day, Cydney?"

"How about Friday?" she asked.

Victoria and Faith both nodded.

"Friday it is, then," Cydney said, beaming.

Desmond was having one of those mornings everyone has from time to time. The kind of morning you wish you could start again from that first glimpse of the sun's orange haze, that bright beginning filled with promise that the rest of the day never lived up to.

Felicia had attempted to be helpful by cooking him breakfast. She wasn't in any danger of being a guest on that cooking show Desmond liked, *Nigella Bites,* that's for sure. She glazed his last frozen waffles in a black-toasted crust. They'd make perfect drink-glass coasters but were totally inedible. She spilled a half carton of orange juice on the floor, startled by the smoke detector going off, she said. So, Desmond, who relied on his breakfast as the fuel for his day, left the house with an empty stomach.

His stomach growling on the way to work, Desmond

stopped at a convenience store to grab a bagel and a small bottle of juice. He walked to the register, smiling, but then a few moments later backed away from that same register, embarrassed, and still with that growling stomach. He'd rushed from the house without his wallet.

When Desmond arrived at the restaurant he received the news that Karen had called in and would be running late, some personal problems. Desmond would have the fine pleasure of meeting, greeting and seating the patrons until Karen arrived. Thank God it was Friday.

Desmond was at the front of the restaurant now, reflecting on his poor day when the promise of that bright early-morning sun walked through the door. Desmond noticed her immediately and couldn't hold in his smile.

"Miss Wonderful," Desmond said to Cydney.

She smiled. "You remembered me."

Desmond looked to her two companions. One looked like Vanessa Williams and the other looked as if she'd work the hell out of some spandex. "I see you brought along much better company this time." He extended a hand to the spandex queen. "Desmond Rucker, I'm the proprietor."

"Faith," she said. "It's nice to meet you, Mr. Rucker. We could smell the food from outside."

Desmond then gave the Vanessa Williams clone his hand.

"Victoria Beauville," she offered. "I'm very much looking forward to this meal, Mr. Rucker. Cydney told us so much about the place."

Desmond's eyes widened, his smile, too. He turned to his Miss Wonderful. "Did you, now...*Cydney?*"

Cydney shot Victoria a scowl. Victoria covered her mouth. "Oops. I meant, *Miss* Williams."

Desmond bore his eyes into Cydney. "Cydney Williams. It has a nice ring to it."

tive man, Victoria. And yes, I would be lying if I said I didn't have any interest—"

Faith reached for Cydney. "Cyd—"

"Hold on a second, Faith," Cydney said, fanning her hand away. "Like I said, Victoria, he's handsome, has style and cool, my type of man. But as of yet it has been nothing but some harmless flirting. I don't know anything about him. Is he married? Does he have a girlfriend? Is he even interested in me?"

A deep voice bellowed, "No. No. Yes, with a capital Y."

Cydney didn't even have to turn to the voice. Embarrassment shot through her. She looked at Victoria, who winked. Faith gave Cydney an I-tried-to-warn-you shrug. Cydney closed her eyes for a moment of composure, and then turned to Desmond, smiling. "Desmond."

"Miss Wonderful, née Cydney Williams."

"Been standing there long?" Cydney asked.

"Long enough to have you make my day. Which I might add is quite an achievement on your part because my day hasn't been going well."

"Sorry to hear that," Cydney said.

"No need to be," Desmond assured her. "You've done more than your share to correct that." He pulled the free seat at the table and looked at Faith and Victoria. "Excuse me a moment, ladies."

"I have to be going anyway, Cydney. I'll see you in class on Wednesday," Faith said, rising from her seat.

"No dessert?" Cydney asked.

Faith grabbed her stomach. "Stuffed—" she looked to Desmond "—everything was wonderful and it was nice to meet you."

Desmond nodded.

"I better head out, too," Victoria said. "I have a hot date with one of my beaus tonight." She looked at Desmond. "A real pleasure, Desmond," she told him. Victoria then looked at Cydney. "One word—camcorder." Cydney smirked, looked down to conceal her smile. Victoria blew Desmond a kiss and sashayed through the aisle and out the front door.

"Your friends are something, Cydney," Desmond said.

"They're the best," Cydney agreed.

"I trust you enjoyed your meal, Miss Wonderful."

Cydney dabbed at her mouth with her napkin, touched her stomach as Faith had done. "Yes, it was very nice."

"Look, I have to watch the front door, I'm a bit shorthanded today, but I'd love to have your phone number."

"Would you?"

"Yes."

"And then what?"

"Then—" Desmond pressed his fingers to his lips "—then I call you, talk your ear off, make you fall in love with me and we live happily ever after."

"That sounds straight up Harry Potter, a fairy tale."

"Try me and see," Desmond said, smiling, his dimples hypnotizing Cydney. "You just might find yourself, forty years down the road, looking over at me and wondering where the years went."

"Wondering why I was foolish to put up with your stuff for all those years, you mean," Cydney shot back.

"I hope that isn't the case, Cydney."

"But you're not saying it definitely won't be," Cydney said, catching that important omission.

"I owe it to you to be real," Desmond countered.

"You barely know me, you don't owe me anything."

"But I *want* to know you, so I do owe you," Desmond said.

"Is it always going to be a dance like this between us if we do get together?" Cydney asked.

"I've got soft shoes on if it is."

"Prepared, huh?"

"Didn't know it…but yes, I guess so," Desmond admitted. His heart was doing things inside his chest he'd never experienced before. He didn't for one second think about his father and how Frank Rucker would view Cydney Williams and Desmond's prospects with her. "So, may I have that number?"

Cydney wrote the numbers on the lunch tab, her hands shaking the entire time. "Hope I'm not making a mistake," she said as she handed the slip of paper to Desmond.

"The gentleman will try and see that Miss Wonderful hasn't," Desmond responded.

"Such a charmer."

"Let me walk you to your car," Desmond said as Cydney rose from her seat.

"You don't have to do that," Cydney said.

"I want to," Desmond told her.

"Okay."

He walked Cydney to her car and stood holding the driver-side door for her. "I'll be giving you a call soon."

"I look forward to that," Cydney told him.

He surprised Cydney and himself, leaning down and kissing her on the mouth. The kiss was long, passionate, a shedding of sorts for the both of them. They both got an inkling their lives wouldn't be the same again after the kiss. They handled it with loud silence. Staring each other in the eyes but saying nothing.

"Well," Desmond said after a moment, "you take care of yourself, Miss Wonderful. Expect my call soon."

Cydney nodded, bit her lip, smiled, got in her car and drove off. Farther up the road she ran her fingers over her lips. She'd never been kissed like that before. Especially this early in the game. And she was always a fast mover, never known to look before she leaped.

Back at the restaurant, standing by the curb, Desmond

touched his fingers to his lips in a similar fashion. Where had that come from? Kissing her like that. It felt so right, though. As did Cydney. Felt very right.

Slay was inside the Dunkin' Donuts on Main Street, flirting with the Mexican girl behind the register, trying to recruit her, when Kenya's uncle pulled up outside.

"Hit me off with another strawberry filled," Slay said to the girl, dabbing his mouth with a little white napkin. "Those shits is tight. Almost as tight as you, *chica.*"

The Mexican girl smiled politely and scooped aside another donut for him.

Slay dropped a single on the counter and moved toward the door to meet Kenya's uncle. The old man's truck coughed a few times as he exited, the engine clearing all that dust from its carburetor. Slay shook his head. Old cat has some nerve driving around in that dusty bucket.

"How do?" the old man said as he came in the doorway.

"Good," Slay responded. "You want something?"

Kenya's uncle squinted at the big menu board. "Get me a coffee, black, no sugar and one of them plain donuts."

Slay nodded to the Mexican cashier girl. "You heard that, *chica?*"

She nodded and went to work preparing the order. Slay directed the old man to a booth in the farthest corner of the shop.

"So what's the word?" Slay asked as they took their seats.

"Mockingbird," Kenya's uncle said, smiling.

"You crazy old school, ain't you?"

"I guess."

"So what you find out so far?" Slay asked, rephrasing the question.

The Mexican girl brought over the donut and black coffee, no sugar. She smiled at Slay after she set it down.

"Throw that thang, *chica,*" Slay said, watching her hips as she moved back behind the counter.

"You like the ladies, I see," Kenya's uncle said.

Slay nodded. "Some would say different. But I think I do." He left it at that. "So...my sister?"

"I've been enjoying this little project," the old man said. "I been using my horse-racing binoculars—" a pained expression crossed his face, like he'd felt a sharp pain in his side all of a sudden "—God knows they ain't never helped me none at the track."

"Right, right," Slay said, wanting this to move along.

"Well, your sister, Cydney, I don't think you have to worry about her with no drugs."

Slay forced a fake bit of glee. "Thank goodness!"

"She drove up to Rutgers that one day—we gonna have to discuss extra monies for that lag. My baby out there almost went into labor out on that highway."

"That's no problem," Slay said.

"Then she went up to the mall the next day. She's got herself a good job at Macy's, you know that?"

"Selling perfume," Slay said. "Right, right."

"She only went out one time," the old man went on. "I mean out-out."

This was interesting. "Where about?" Slay asked.

"Over to that fancy restaurant on Cookman. She was with two other girls—you'd like them for sure."

"Okay."

"Yeah," the old man continued, "they got some good sweet-potato pie in that place, I tell you. And your sister's boyfriend, he seems like a good brother. I think he manages the place or something. He's a big shot over there. That much I know. They were, 'yes, Mr. Rucker-ing' him to death."

Slay shot his eyes at Kenya's uncle. "Boyfriend, you said?"

"Yeah, that Rucker fella. He walked her out after her girlfriends left, gave her a long kiss at her car and then went back inside. I followed your sister back home and then—" the old man stopped, grinned sheepishly "—then I headed on back over to that Cush—funny name for a restaurant, but that don't matter. I headed back over there and got me a rib dinner, and some of that sweet-potato pie."

"And you sure this Rucker cat kissed her?"

"Yeah, why, you haven't met up with him before?"

Slay shook his head. "Not as of yet."

"Well, he's a good fella like I said. I can't see him letting your sister get involved in no drugs."

Just as Slay suspected, his sister had found someone to replace him. That's why she'd been so quick to toss him aside.

"You gotta get over to that Cush and try some of they food," the old man continued.

Slay looked at him, a smile creeping across his face. "Right, right." He would definitely pay this Rucker cat a visit; get himself some eats, too.

CHAPTER 10

Cydney promised herself she wouldn't play the game of sitting by the phone waiting for Desmond to call. However, the only way she could fulfill that promise was by busying herself with whatever task she could find to do around the house. She thoroughly cleaned the place. Only after she turned off the vacuum cleaner did she allow herself a peek at her caller ID box. There wasn't any red flash indicating a call. She stood on the floor looking around her pristine apartment. Without even knowing it, Desmond had already added something to her life; the place had been in need of a thorough cleaning for quite some time.

Next, Cydney drew a hot bath, threw in her flavor crystals like pennies in a mall decorative fountain and eased her weary body into the soothing water. She lay back in the tub and let the water engulf her, let it work into every muscle, let it massage away her tensions like a skilled and diligent lover. The possibilities Desmond offered had her in a spiritual mood, so she'd pulled her Donnie McClurkin *Live in London and More…* CD from the tower beside her television and brought it into the bathroom. She kept her favorite song, "Great Is Your Mercy," on repeat for the entirety of her soaking.

Done in the tub, Cydney toweled off with her softest linen and with a surgeon's care rubbed her skin from crown to heel with baby oil. She wrapped herself in the one silk robe she owned and went to return the CD to the living room. As she passed her kitchen she allowed herself a second peek at the caller ID box. The music and the din of the exhaust fan in her bathroom could have easily drowned out the phone ringer. There wasn't any red flash indicating a call.

Much later, after more useless housework had been done, the phone finally did ring. Cydney took a deep breath and scurried across the carpet on the tips of her toes. Her exhilaration ended as she scanned the caller ID monitor. It was Stephon.

Cydney contemplated not answering for a moment, but then decided against that. Stephon was still her boss. "Hello."

His voice sounded far off, strained and weary, like he needed a hot bath himself. "It's done."

"What's done?"

"I served her with papers."

It was a move he'd talked about many times but one Cydney never thought he'd follow through on. She'd always hoped he would even though she told him contrary. From the first moment she eyed him, walking through Macy's on his wife's heels like a stray puppy, Cydney had desired him all to herself. They locked eyes that first day as his wife moved about in her own world. Cydney didn't look away coyly and neither did Stephon. They had an instant connection. He'd come over to her post a short while later and relayed his entire life story in a rushed few minutes. He told her about his unhappy marriage, his wife's problems with painkiller medicine and his feelings of entrapment. He handed Cydney a business card and asked her to call him at work sometime.

"Wait a minute," she'd said, looking at the card print. "You're the publisher of *Urban Styles?*"

"Yes," he replied.

"You know I'm a subscriber," she said. "Some nights I'm reading that magazine and I should be working on my papers."

"Papers?"

"Yes," she said. "College work. Rutger's University."

His eyes smiled. "I'm a Rutgers alum."

She smiled at him. "Small world."

You could see gears churning in Stephon's head. "Cydney, can you write?"

"Yes, I mean, what do you mean by write?"

"I've been looking for someone to come on staff at the magazine for my restaurant and music criticism columns. I've been writing them myself because we're shorthanded. Would you be interested? It doesn't pay a huge salary or anything, but—"

"I'd love to."

Stephon had smiled at her, so pleased with the burgeoning situation. "Now I need to get my wife a bottle of perfume as explanation for my time away. You collect a commission on sales?"

"Yes," Cydney said.

Stephon had looked at her with those eyes that would eventually invade her dreams, both in sleep and awake. "Give me the most expensive thing you have. Matter fact, give me two."

A business relationship that would evolve into so much more was formed that day. It never moved to the level that Cydney always hoped it would though, and eventually she stopped praying that it ever would. The lonely nights of this past summer when Stephon and his family vacationed in Jamaica had been the moment the prayers stopped. Now their relationship had evolved again—to strictly business. The hope of Desmond gave Cydney the strength not to falter in her conviction to keep Stephon at bay.

"Cydney," Stephon was saying into the phone now, breaking her thoughts. "Did you hear what I said?"

"I heard you."

"You're not going to say anything?"

"What do you want me to say?"

"Ask me how I'm doing," he said. "What my new hopes are. Ask me was it difficult. Ask me if we can meet up at our special little hiding place."

"How are you doing?" Cydney said. "What are your new hopes? Was it difficult?"

"You left out the question I most wanted to hear from you."

"I left in the questions I most wanted to ask," Cydney responded.

"I did this for you—for us," Stephon whined.

Cydney shook her head as if he could see her over the fiber-optic line. "No, no, no. I told you don't make this decision based on you and me."

"Is it because of the other night?" Stephon said. "Because I'm sorry about that."

"That showed me something about you," Cydney answered. "You don't have to be sorry, though, I've moved on."

"I got your e-mail earlier with the review of Cush," Stephon said slowly and softly. "You're really feeling this Desmond Rucker, aren't you? That has a lot to do with you not wanting to try this with me, doesn't it?"

Cydney knew it would hurt him but she had no choice. "Yes, Stephon, you're right. I'm sorry."

He coughed, the revelation making him sick immediately.

"I'm sorry," Cydney repeated.

"Me too," he said. "Goodbye, Cydney."

His voice haunted her as his eyes once had. "Stephon, don't—"

It was too late, the phone clicked in her ear. He'd hung up. Cydney hung up too, pressed the delete key on her caller ID box to erase the number and stop the machine from flashing for a new call. However, the box continued to flash. Cydney picked up her phone again—the special dial tone for new calls buzzed. She'd received a call as she spoke with Stephon and must not have heard the call-waiting beep. Cydney anxiously dialed the voice mail system to retrieve the call.

Cydney Williams, née Miss Wonderful, this is Desmond—Desmond Rucker from Cush. I wanted to tell you that I truly, truly hope we can start something that ends up being special and long lasting. I've never really been the lucky-in-love type, I have to admit, but there is something about you that makes me believe my luck just might be changing.

I'm an honest guy. I work hard. I don't have any major vices. You look like an honest woman. You seem to have a good head on your shoulders. I'm hoping we can create something that— I'm talking too much for a voice mail message. Listen, I'll try you again tomorrow. I just wanted to call and let you know that you're heavily on my mind and that I hope we can do this. Bye for now.

Cydney closed her eyes and held the phone to her chest. That quickly Stephon was forgotten. Desmond was so sweet, so sincere, his words warmer than the bath she'd taken earlier. There was no looking back. Cydney was going forward.

"You're going out?"

Desmond turned to his sister standing in the entrance of the kitchen. She was still dressed in her pajamas—her uniform of late. He swallowed a gulp of orange juice. "Yeah," he said. "I see you aren't though, again."

Felicia moved into the kitchen, wiping the sleep from her eyes as she dragged her slippered feet across the linoleum. "I'm heading back into the city tomorrow to meet with some folks from the agency—discuss my concerns."

Desmond nodded. "That's good to hear. I was afraid you were going to turn into a couch. You shocked me the other day by not taking my offer to rent you a car."

Felicia smiled. "You're going in to the restaurant? I thought you tried to stay away on Sundays?"

"I do," Desmond said. He threw the empty juice carton into the garbage can, brushed the crumbs from his toast onto his paper plate, balled the plate and tossed it into the garbage as well. "I'm just going to drop in for a moment and make sure everything is in order. Then I have to make a couple of stops. We can go to a movie or something if you want to later."

Felicia shook her head. "I'm just going to chill today."

Desmond scooped his keys off the table, walked over and gave his sister a kiss on the cheek. "Suit yourself. I'll be back later."

"Enjoy your day, baby brother," Felicia said as Desmond neared the door. "And tell whoever she is I said hello."

Desmond stopped, half in and half out. "What?"

"Tell this new woman in your life I said hello," Felicia said.

"Who said anything about a new woman in my life?"

"I can see the excitement all over your face," Felicia said. "I imagine she's one of the *stops* you plan on making before coming back."

Desmond eyed his sister. "Smart aleck." He blew her a kiss and shut the door behind him.

Miss Wonderful *was* on Desmond's mind as he approached the turn for his restaurant. He could imagine her smiling as she played back his message. He couldn't wait to talk to her at length, to take her out and show her what a woman of her magnitude deserved, to make love to her for the first time.

Today would be the last time. He swore it to himself.

Desmond made the left turn onto Cookman and slowed as he neared his restaurant just enough so he could peek inside. As usual the crowd was thick, his staff busy attending to them. He drove past without stopping. At the end of the avenue he made that familiar left turn and came to a rest across from Hot Tails go-go. Today would be the last time.

Desmond cracked his knuckles and moved from his truck. He set the alarm and carefully crossed the street, looking both ways as if cars were whizzing by. Besides his truck there were only a few other cars as far as his eyes could see. Desmond walked inside the bar.

The human wall from last time was still manning the door. "Two-drink minimum. Make sure you get the first drink before you get a permanent seat."

Desmond nodded, getting to know the routine. He walked to the bar immediately and leaned against the counter. The bartender today was a guy, not the girl from before with the small chest who wore the T-shirt with Nasty written across the front.

"CanIgetforyou?" the bartender said. He seemed wired on some type of drug, his words coming out in fast speed while he himself moved in slow motion.

"Screwdriver," Desmond told him. Desmond moved from the bar and took a look in the room where the performers danced. A thin white girl with no ass but plenty of fake boob was onstage. Desmond turned back to the bartender.

"Thatabesix," the bartender said.

Desmond reached into his pocket and pulled out two fives. The bartender reached for the money but Desmond held it. "I was here the other day and this one dancer really caught my eye. Dark-skinned girl, real big butt, nipples the size of—"

"Jacinta," the bartender said, not needing to hear any more.

"Is she dancing today?" Desmond asked.

"She's one of the house girls. Jacinta dances almost every day," the bartender said. It was funny how the mention of Jacinta seemed to calm the bartender. Jacinta had that effect on quite a few men.

"When can I expect her?" Desmond said, still holding the money, the bartender still tugging at the bills.

"She's up in about an hour, after the next two or three sets."

Desmond released his grip on the bills. He had time to burn. He'd wait for Jacinta. "Thanks for the info," Desmond told the bartender.

Bartender nodded. "Enjoytheshow."

Slay parked across the street from where Cydney parked and watched as she exited her vehicle. She had on sunglasses and was wearing a long silver coat, flossing like some Hollywood actress, like she was Halle Berry or somebody. Slay pulled out his R. Kelly and Jay-Z CD, *The Best of Both Worlds,* and put it into the CD changer. Slay forwarded the CD to track 8 "Shake Ya Body"—the joint featuring Lil' Kim. R. Kelly, now that was a misunderstood dude, Slay thought. Not many men in his position, with the nappy dugout being thrown their way every five seconds, would avoid the kind of trouble that R. was now enduring. Those fast-assed underage girls probably lied about their age and set Kelly up for the downfall. It was to the point you needed two forms of ID before you slept with these tramps nowadays.

Slay sat with the engine running, the music playing, the heat blasting, and waited as Cydney went into the CVS pharmacy. "Bet her trick ass is going in there to get body spray and condoms," he said aloud, disgusted. He fumbled at the CD player, struggling to move to another track as the current one finished playing. This wasn't his beloved BMW, instead the car of an acquaintance; Slay hadn't wanted to risk Cydney spotting him. The last thing in the world she'd expect was her brother tailing her in a Toyota Camry.

Cydney emerged from the store with a small shopping bag and got into her car. Slay was dying to know what it held. She pulled from the curb and rode on up the block. He followed a few car lengths back. Not too farther up the main stretch she stopped in front of a small record store, Mike's Music, and emerged from her car. She walked into the record store with a purpose. "Hooker is really setting this up nice," Slay fumed. "Bet she's getting some Maxwell, some smooth shit like that. Gonna work this nigga over good today." He pounded his fist on the steering wheel and accidentally hit his horn. He looked to see if she'd noticed. She hadn't. She'd already gone into the store.

Cydney emerged from the store a short while later, another bag under her arm. She got in her car and drove off. Slay continued to follow her. She surprised him by driving back in the direction of her home. He was sure she'd be going to this dude's house. She probably planned to have the guy come over to her place instead. Slay shook his head at her bravery as he continued his tail.

A short while later, she made the turn into her apartment complex and parked in her numbered spot at the front of her building. Slay eased into a spot on the other side of the Dumpster enclosure and parked out of her view. He moved from the car quickly and rushed around to meet her on her way in.

He could see her sitting in the car, appeared as if she was singing to her music, waiting for the song to finish before she got out of the car. Eventually she killed the engine, grabbed her bags and got out. She walked around to the trunk and pulled another bag from there. She sure is spending some cash, Slay thought. Probably some of the money he gave her.

She walked up the sidewalk toward her place, whistling, swinging the bags with her stride. Slay rubbed his hands together in anticipation. He glanced behind him and at all the windows to make sure no one was looking out with their phone propped to their ear, worry on their face as they dialed 911. Everything seemed normal and peaceful. That was the thing about these condominium complexes, they were so quiet.

Cydney was about ten feet from him now. He readied himself. She stopped suddenly. He wondered if she'd spotted him and would try to make a break for it. But no, she dropped her bags and bent down and ran a finger under the sole of her foot. He saw a small pebble fall out, heard her say, "Woo." She picked up the bags and started moving forward again. She was five feet away now.

Showtime.

Slay stepped out in her path.

"Hello there, sis," he said.

Cydney jumped, startled, and dropped one of her CVS bags.

"Here, let me get that for you." Slay moved forward and picked it up for her. It didn't appear she had the capability of moving or speaking. He handed her the bag but her hands didn't, or couldn't, reach for it. "I'll hold on to this for you then," Slay said. He narrowed his eyes. "So, Cydney, tell me something—who's this GQ Smooth dude I hear you been hanging with?"

Her eyes were on him and he could see that she was trembling. That bothered him, she should know she didn't need to fear him; he loved her, he was her brother. The sight of her trembling took some of the hardness from him. "Cydney, come on, don't do this."

"What are you doing here?" she said finally. She had the coldhearted demeanor from their last encounter back. She looked to him like a soldier willing to spill blood right here on the sidewalk for the cause, if need be.

Now he was angry again. This was no way to treat a loving brother. "I'm asking the questions," he barked. "Now, who the fuck is this GQ Smooth dude I hear you been hanging with?"

She smiled. Slay smiled, too. This was more like it.

"None of your damn business," she said with edge, still smiling.

Slay's smile disappeared as Cydney's held.

CHAPTER 11

The DJ interrupted his spin of a club version of one of Whitney Houston's songs to introduce the next performer coming to the stage. Desmond had raised his glass to his lips, but held it without taking a sip, his ears and eyes on the DJ, waiting. Since he'd come in, over an hour before, he'd endured the white girl with the silicone boobs, a clumsy Asian girl who didn't have the sense to get her own boobs inflated and a black girl with overlapping teeth, reddened hair and a trail of brown freckles that traversed her entire body. Still, no Jacinta, though.

"*Muy caliente,*" the DJ said with a hint of excitement and rousing in his voice. "Coming to the stage to shake what her mami and papi gave her...Jacintaaaaaaa."

Desmond took that sip of his drink, actually gulping down the rest of it in one shot. He wiped his mouth with the back side of his hand and moved to the front of the room, directly by the stage. The entire room seemed to perk up. The DJ replaced the revved-up Whitney Houston cut with what he billed "a hot one from Shakira." Desmond nodded his head to the syncopated rhythm, adrenaline shooting through him because of the three drinks he'd downed and the performance he'd come for.

Jacinta came on, spotlighted in the center of the stage, her hair pulled back, dressed in a brassiere with tassels swinging. Desmond's eyes started at her feet and worked their way up. He very much liked what he saw. A strong urge started to pull at him in that place where men's urges began and ended.

Jacinta held to the pole and shimmied around it with the grace and poise of a figure skater or a ballerina. She kicked her legs up, presumably to show her flexibility, and then fell into a split. Two men on the other side of the room who looked as if they were a couple of drinks away from needing CPR applauded Jacinta's moves. She moved in their direction to take advantage of their adoration, and to fill her collection plate.

The Shakira cut ended and an even faster one took its place. On cue Jacinta sped up her moves, thrashing her head and body furiously, that long tail of hair flapping like a "just married" stringer on a car bumper. She moved back to the side of the stage where Desmond sat. He pursed his lips and held a breath in his chest. Jacinta reached behind her and pulled the Velcro bra strap loose. She deftly covered her bosom with her hands as the material fell in a heap on the floor. Desmond released that breath, licked his lips. Jacinta moved over to him.

"Back again," Jacinta said.

Desmond's eyes hunched. "You remember me?"

"Of course," she said, winking.

"How?" Desmond wanted to know. "So many come through here?"

"Majority of 'em horny neighborhood guys or the suit-and-tie types headed home to their wives. They're hard to differentiate. You, you're neither."

"You're pretty smart, Jacinta."

"Why?" she asked, making her voice extra sweet and sexy. "Because I used *differentiate* correctly in a sentence? What's your name, cutie?"

"Desmond."

She leaned in close to him and whispered in his ear, "Life is a stage, Desmond. Everyone is a performer on that stage. Nobody is as they appear."

It took Desmond a moment to recover, her hot breath lingering on his earlobe even after she'd moved back to a more appropriate separating distance. "What happened to that accent you had the other day?" he said after a while.

"Part of the performance," Jacinta admitted. "See, I told you."

"So, you're a philosopher now?" Desmond asked her, smiling.

"How many people from your real life know you're in here today, Desmond? That this is your second time here in a week?"

Desmond was rendered speechless. He thought about the wrinkle that would form on his father's nose if his father knew he was here. The I-told-you-so look in his father's eyes. *I told you that you couldn't measure up to me, son.*

Jacinta smiled, took Desmond's money and wiggled on across the stage.

"What did you say to me?" Slay said, gripping hard to Cydney's bag, leaning into her with a scowl on his face.

"None of your business," she repeated. "Who I spend my time with is of no concern to you."

Slay grinded his teeth, looked around him. "You lucky we all out in the open."

"You're luckier than I am," Cydney responded. She held out her hand. "You can give me my bag now."

Slay looked at the bag—from CVS. "Let's see what kind of freaky shit you planning," he said, opening the bag. His brow furrowed when he saw the contents: a pack of black pens, pack of white lined paper and a Skor candy bar. He looked up at Cydney.

She smiled and shrugged her shoulders. "You can have the candy bar if it's that important to you."

He pushed the bag into her hand and this time she took it. "This ain't no game, sis."

"No, it isn't," Cydney agreed, "and I think it is best you realize and recognize that. I'm done being your chess piece, Slay."

"Don't call me Slay," he said, dropping his head, defeated.

"Why not? That's your name, isn't it?"

He looked up. "Not with you, Cydney."

Cydney sighed, shook her head. "You're just not good for me now."

Slay nodded. The toughness he always projected was gone. His shoulders sagged, his eyes narrowed, not from anger, but to keep him from getting emotional. "You probably right," he said. "*Cydney Williams* has always been about something. No use in *Shammond Slay* pulling her down, keeping her from getting all her goals and shit."

The difference in their last names had been a source of angst for him for a long time.

"Pop G would have adopted you, too," Cydney said, "but everything was so confusing then. He didn't know if they were going to let you out of juvie or what. It looked like that place was going to be your home away from home. Look at how many times you were sent down. He didn't know if you were ever coming home for good and what you'd be like if you did."

Slay forced a smile. "Right, right."

"We're still brother and sister. I just need some time to get my life in order. You should do the same," Cydney said.

"I won't bother you again, Cydney. You should check in on Mama every now and then, she ain't gonna be around forever." He balled a fist and placed it over his heart and moved around Cydney to walk to his car.

"I'm always going to love you," Cydney called to him as he walked down the sidewalk. And despite everything, she would. Truth be told, Shammond was just a damaged soul, same as she was.

Slay didn't respond. He kept his slow bop toward his car. This GQ Smooth dude was the source of all this heartache. Cydney was different than she'd ever been. Slay didn't have any beef with her, but GQ Smooth, that was his newest enemy. That dude had managed to come in and take one of the only good things this world ever gave Slay. For that, GQ Smooth, would pay, in full.

Desmond moved from Hot Tails with a new lease on life. When you started getting mother wit from women who made their money being coy with their breasts it was definitely time to reevaluate the route you traveled. Jacinta, the go-go Aristotle, had hit him over the head. Her words echoed in his ears like the baseline from that Shakira song.

Life is a stage. Everyone is a performer on that stage.

Desmond gripped his keys and pressed the keyless entry button for his truck as he crossed the street. It chirp-chirped like a bird. He looked up at the sky absent of sun as a light breeze from the nearby ocean swept across his face. He got in his truck, turned the ignition, but sat thinking instead of pulling away.

Life is a stage. Everyone is a performer on that stage.

Why? Why was it so difficult to let down our guards and allow people to see inside our hearts and souls? Desmond looked at himself in the rearview mirror. Jacinta had him talking to himself. "I'm a son, a brother, an entrepreneur," he said. "I'm a decent, proud black man. I've never put my hands on a woman with any intent other than tenderness and caring. I've never abused drugs. I'm a careful lover, always use condoms. I'm a romantic. I love women..." He sat back against the plush leather of the truck's interior, closed his eyes and sighed.

He thought about his parents, married all these years. As far as he knew, his father had been faithful the entire time, his mother the same. Desmond wondered if there was any hope of the same for him. He thought about Miss Wonderful, Cydney Williams. She'd come into his restaurant with two other beautiful women, and yet, all he could see, all he desired, was Cydney. She was his hope.

Desmond opened his eyes and looked across the road at the sexy, curvy silhouette of the Hot Tails sign. In there, right now, Jacinta was in the back room fitting her bodacious body into some awe-inspiring outfit. In a short while she'd be back onstage again, gyrating to a club tune. Desmond smiled and fished in his pocket for his cell phone. He had to try his hope again. Hopefully, this time, Miss Wonderful would pick up the other line.

Slay got in his loaner Camry and watched Cydney climb the steps to her apartment. He felt the urge to cry but opened the flip of his cell phone to attend to some business—moneymaking always chased away the fiercest blues. He scrolled through his address book, stopping on J. He selected the option and waited.

It rang three or four times before a soft voice picked up. "Hello." There was loud music in the background and Slay could tell she had the phone cupped to keep out as much of the noise as possible.

"*Hola, Hah-seen-ta,*" he said. "I was going to leave you a voice mail message."

"Slay," she said.

"How did I do with your name, my *español* any better?"

"Getting there," she acknowledged.

"You working?"

"Always," she said. "I just finished my set, preparing for my next one as we speak."

"You killing 'em today, or what?"

"You got something for me, or what?" she shot back.

"You can't even have a word wit' a nigga for a minute. All business and shit."

"Cash rules everything around me," she responded.

Slay laughed. "Cream, dollar dollar bill, y'all. That was the shit, wasn't it? What's going on with Wu Tang now?"

"I look like Ol' Dirty Bastard or something, Slay?"

"You look like new clean pussy, baby, you know that," Slay told her. He thought the comment clever and quick-witted. She seemed unmoved.

"You got something for me?"

Slay shook his head, this was not a good day on the female front. "Dude named William Jeffries, esquire."

"A lawyer…great," she said, sighing.

"What did you say?"

"Nothing. I'm just not looking forward to this guy."

"His pockets are deep," Slay told her.

"Is that a fact," she said. "Good. At the Berkeley?"

"Always. You know I take care of my ladies."

"Don't front on me, Slay. I don't like how that sounds. I'm not one of your ladies."

"I try to broker a good situation," Slay corrected. "That better?"

"Much."

"Same deal as usual. His room is registered to Gabriel Cohen. Your money will be waiting for you at the desk, wrapped up with a bow and the whole nine."

"Pleasure doing business with you again," she told him.

Slay smiled. "Right, right." He closed the flip and pocketed his cell phone. He looked up at Cydney's apartment, toward her window. This was one time moneymaking had failed to chase those fierce blues away. A knot sat heavy in his stomach. He shook his head and pulled from the lot.

Cydney rushed down the hall to the bathroom, used the toilet, missed the flush but didn't turn back, and ran her hands under the water spigot. She wiped her wet hands dry on the extra-long shirt she wore and grabbed a two-liter bottle of Coke from the refrigerator. She scooted across the carpet and plopped down on the couch. A commercial for Tide laundry detergent ran its course and then a silky-smooth woman's voice came on.

We now return to Lifetime's A Vision of Murder: The Story of Donielle.

Cydney closed her eyes and took a breath to steady her heartbeat. She was proud to have accomplished so much in the short ninety-second span the advertisers gave her. Cydney pulled the coffee table closer to the couch, a bowl of micro-wave popcorn—mixed with a bit of butter and a touch of sugar—within reach. She sat crossed-legged, her caramel-colored legs smooth beneath her after a nice shave and the pampering of an earlier bath.

The scene on screen moved to a bar. Then a woman in a tight pink top fell on the floor, choking. Maria Conchita Alonso knelt over the woman, screaming for someone to help. Cydney leaned in, her heart beating fast and in tune with the dramatic music from the movie score.

The phone rang.

Cydney jumped.

She looked across the room toward the kitchen, the phone on the counter, then back at the television. The phone rang a second time. Cydney huffed and got up. She walked across the floor, looking back with every step. She reached the kitchen island and pulled the cordless from the cradle.

"Hello."

"Miss Wonderful, I caught you this time."

It was good to hear his voice but his timing sucked the big one. "Desmond."

"You don't sound that excited to hear from me," he said.

Cydney turned from the view of the television screen. "I'm sorry," she said. "I was watching a movie."

"Oh, I can call you back, then."

"No—" she looked back at the television as if it were a dying loved one "—no. I'd rather talk with you."

"What were you watching?"

"A movie on Lifetime."

"Ooohhhh," Desmond said. "The *shattered* network."

Cydney blinked, eased into a seat far from the trappings of the television. "Come again?"

"Lifetime," Desmond said. "I call it the shattered network."

"And why's that?" Cydney asked, interested.

"Every other movie on there has shattered in the title. Shattered Souls. Shattered Lives. Shattered Lovers. That and betrayal," Desmond said. "Betrayal of Trust. Shattered Betrayal."

Cydney laughed. "You're a fool."

"Go grab your *TV Guide* and look over the next week's programming," Desmond said. "You'll see."

"I believe you, Mr. Rucker. So how goes life?"

Desmond sat back in his truck, surprised at how easy it was to talk to this ray of hope. "Life goes well...now."

"I received your message last evening," Cydney said. "It was nice."

"So much I want to tell you," Desmond said. He stopped and laughed to himself. "I didn't mean to tell it all on your voice mail, though."

"It was cute."

"Uh-oh, cute isn't good for a grown man."

"Cute is veeerrry good for a grown man, who told you otherwise?"

"Oh, is it?"

"Absolutely."

"Cydney Williams?"

She loved the way he said her name, even more so than when Stephon said it. "Yes."

"I would love to see you today," Desmond said. "Would that be a problem?"

"You're not bogged down running that fabulous restaurant of yours?"

"I told you, Sunday is my free day."

"So what did you have in mind for me?" Cydney asked.

"Fly by the seat of my pants," Desmond said. "I'm sure when I see you—if I'm blessed enough to—that I'll come up with something."

"You're quite persuasive, Mr. Rucker."

"At this moment I truly hope so, Miss Williams."

"You know where the Monmouth Mall is?" Cydney asked.

"But of course."

"I have to return something at Macy's. I can meet you there in two hours."

"Consider it done," Desmond said.

"What will you have on?" Cydney asked.

Desmond looked down at himself. "I've got on a mustard turtleneck and black pleated pants. Why?"

"Just gauging what I should wear," Cydney said. "I'll see you in two hours. You can meet me at the food court."

"I can't wait to see you, Miss Wonderful."

Cydney eased the tongue that had crept from the corner of her mouth back in, wiped that lip-cracking smile off her face. "Feeling's mutual."

An hour and forty-five minutes later Cydney was in Macy's. She walked over to the men's cologne section and placed two bottles of Alfred Dunhill's Desire on the counter. She handed the cashier, who she didn't recognize, her receipt.

"Return?" the lady asked, and then looking closer at the receipt. "You work here?"

Cydney nodded. "Part-time."

The woman smiled. "The employee discount is nice. I took the job to save my husband money. I was always in here buying something."

Cydney smiled politely. She was on the clock and wanted to get this transaction completed so she'd be on time for Desmond.

"Do you want a store credit or a refund?" the lady asked her.

Cydney considered the bottles of cologne. Early Christmas gifts she'd picked up for Stephon and Slay. "I'll take the refund."

The woman stepped away and returned a short while later with a refund receipt for Cydney to sign. Cydney hurriedly signed, took her money, thanked the woman and rushed toward the food court.

Cydney caught a glimpse of Desmond as soon as she made the turn around the bend that led to the food court. He caught her at the same time. Man, they had a connection between them. Desmond's eyes brightened and he started in Cydney's direction. She slowed what had been a half trot to a slow sashay. He was wearing the heck out of those clothes, she noticed, his broad shoulders filling out his black leather jacket, his stride confident and sexy.

When they reached each other he leaned down and placed a soft kiss on her cheek. "You look wonderful, Cydney Williams."

What, no lips this time?

"Thanks," she said. She scanned him, head to toe. "You look good, too."

He nodded toward the table closest to them. "I took the liberty of grabbing lemonade for you. I'm not hungry just yet, I really just wanted to see you, but if you want to grab something to eat now that's cool. I'm not skimping on you, either. I plan on taking you to a real restaurant later."

Cydney crinkled her nose. "I ate my fill of popcorn."

Desmond smiled. "That's right. I took you from your movie. I apologize."

Cydney looked up at him. "Words are cheap. Make it up to me."

Desmond rubbed his hands together. "You are so right," he said, taking her arm and wrapping it in his own. "Let's go. I'll bring you back for your car later." He stopped. "Oh, I'm sorry. Didn't you have something you needed to do here?"

"Did it already," Cydney told him, loving the feel of his arm around hers.

"Oh, okay." Desmond scooped up the cup of lemonade and handed it to Cydney.

Cydney took a sip. "Mmm, sweet and cold, just the way I like it."

"I remembered that's what you had at my restaurant the other day," Desmond offered.

Cydney looked him over. "You remembered that?"

Desmond nodded. "Sure did. Lemonade, half a rack of ribs, honey-fried chicken, smothered pork chops—"

Cydney jabbed him in the side. "I wasn't that bad."

Desmond looked her up and down. "It's all good, Cydney Williams. Food does a body good."

"So where we headed?" Cydney asked.

Desmond smiled. "You look like absolute royalty," he said. "Only one place to take a queen around here."

CHAPTER 12

Desmond eased his truck in Reverse and pulled from his parking spot. Cydney sorted through his small pile of CDs and cassettes. She stopped shuffling as she came upon one particular cassette, laughing as she tapped the cassette case with the tip of her fingernail.

"No, you do not have Eddie Murphy, Desmond."

Desmond moved through a turn, his face serious. "What? 'Put Your Mouth On Me' was the joint."

Cydney shook her head. "I've definitely got to help you update your music collection. You don't have anything from the last couple of years."

"I like the classics," Desmond told her.

Cydney picked up a second cassette and waved the hard pure evidence at him. "PM Dawn is not the classics, Desmond."

That cued Desmond to laugh. "I liked that 'Set Adrift on Memory Bliss' or whatever it was called," he said in defense. "Maybe I got caught up in the hype. You know KRS-One rushed them onstage at one of their shows?"

"Oh, so you like hip-hop?" Cydney asked.

That easy smile of Desmond's came like a flash rain. He nodded. "I don't really listen to music too much in the truck. Most of the music I hear is at work, in the kitchen. I know what's hot, though." He smiled, counted off on his fingers, "Jay-Z's Blueprint. India. Arie and Alicia Keys. Oh, and I'm feeling that kid Jaheim."

Cydney drew in her mouth and rainbow curved her eyes. "Well, excuse me."

Desmond moved past the multiplex movie theater on his way from the mall lot. A crowd was gathered on the steps and in the lobby. Desmond nodded toward the large overhead movie billboard. "Speaking of hip-hop...I want to see that *Brown Sugar* movie."

Cydney tapped his arm. "Me too, and I bet I know why you want to see it."

"Why's that?"

"Sanaa Lathan."

Desmond smiled. "I'm sure Taye Diggs isn't informing your desire to see it, right?"

Cydney fanned herself. "Woo, don't go there."

Desmond smirked. "Women." He moved through a light onto Highway 35, took it north. "So what do you do, Cydney?"

"I'm studying for my bachelor's at Rutgers. I work part-time in fragrances at Macy's. And one other thing but that'll have to remain a mystery for a few more days."

"Keeping secrets?"

"No, just holding on to something for a little while longer. You'll find out soon, I promise. I think you'll be pleased. And don't worry, I'm not going to take you on *Jerry Springer* or something and unload my sexy secret job. I'm not some nasty exotic dancer or anything like that."

Considering where he'd been earlier, and how he'd responded to Jacinta, Desmond didn't quite know how to respond, so he shifted gears. "So what is this bachelor's degree at Rutgers preparing you for?"

"Sociology—I either want to teach or work in community development for a corporation, maybe counseling."

"So you're a deep sistah, then, is that it?"

Cydney looked away from him and out the window as they blurred up the highway. "Not as deep as I would like to be. No."

"I know you're not supposed to ask a woman her age, but I'll chance it."

"Twenty-seven," Cydney said. "And you?"

"I've got a year on you."

"I thought I saw some gray in your beard."

Desmond laughed. "What about family?"

Cydney continued to look out the window. "My father is deceased. My mother...she's in a home. My father's passing sent her into a terrible spiral of depression." Having to tell a lie hurt almost as much as the truth did.

"That what got you into wanting to be a counselor?"

Cydney saw an opening. "Yes, it sure did."

Desmond nodded. "Cool. Siblings?"

Cydney shook her head. "Nope, I'm an only."

"You know they say only children tend to be more intelligent, more introspective," Desmond told her.

Cydney turned back to Desmond, smiling, with a devilish look in her eyes. "So you must have a lot of brothers and sisters then."

Desmond let his mouth hang open, and pointed a finger at her. "Now, you know that ain't right."

Cydney laughed. "You know I'm joking."

Desmond shook his head before moving along. "I've got one sister. Felicia. She's staying with me now. She's a model signed to this agency in New York. She had an incident with a photographer last week and came down to my place to do some soul-searching, decide if she wants to continue pursuing the modeling."

"He didn't harm her, did he?" Cydney asked, concerned.

"Physically, no, but he did plenty of emotional damage. Men don't think sometimes." Now it was Desmond's turn to look away. He considered his own demons. Cydney had a father looking down on her, hoping for the best, Desmond didn't want to be the man that didn't think, the man that broke her spirit.

"What about your parents?" Cydney asked. "Are you close to them? I know they owned that chain of restaurants in Pennsylvania, so obviously their influence rubbed off on you."

Desmond nodded. "Yeah, we're close. A tight-knit unit, I guess. You can plan on some big-time eating for Thanksgivings and Christmases."

"Oh, you plan on bringing me home to Mommy?"

Desmond looked at her. "I've got big plans for you. Gonna treat you like the queen you are. Meeting my parents is just the beginning."

Cydney smiled, looked out beyond the windshield, they were still traveling down Highway 35. "Speaking of queens, where exactly do you take a queen around here? I'm too curious now."

Desmond somehow blushed, a severe feat for a chocolate brother such as himself.

"What?" Cydney asked.

Desmond made a face. "I shot off my mouth back at the mall. I didn't really have anything in mind. I just wanted to drive and talk." He shrugged, tossed those dimples at her. "I figured if I was lucky I'd possibly get to wrap my arms around you and give you the world's greatest hug. At any rate, get to know you."

Cydney shook her head, fake huffed. "The world's greatest hug, huh? Well, keep on driving into Red Bank. They've got a beautiful park where we can go watch the sun go down, and then we can walk up Broad Street and pick a restaurant to eat at. Cool?"

Desmond touched her knee. "Right now, everything is so cool."

Slay pulled into the twenty-four-hour FoodMart, his Nas CD cranking from his sound system, the back windshield of his BMW vibrating to the music, sounding as if it might crack into pieces. He located a spot, parked and cut the engine, and then rubbed his hands over the dashboard. It was like coming home after a business trip and finally getting to sleep in your own bed again. In the short time they'd been apart he'd missed his BMW dearly.

There was a crowd milling about in front of the Mart, the same faces as the day before yesterday, and the day before that. Smoking, drinking, talking shit, bopping to the tunes from the stereo plugged in and cribbing juice from the Mart's electrical outlet. Not one of them thought about the future or exercised their voting rights. They were a part of the lost generation, and unfortunately, their greatest affliction wasn't that they were lost—it was that they didn't recognize that they were. As the temperature dipped and spring acquiesced to winter, the crowd would thin but at no time during the year would it disappear completely.

Slay stepped from his car and moved toward the Mart. He stopped and gave a few pounds on his way in.

"Your whip is lookin' tight, son," one of the lost told him. "Them twinkies is glittering, dawg."

Slay nodded and moved inside the store. He headed directly to the back, the beverage cooler, and picked out a carton of orange juice and a carton of milk. He walked the items to the front and sat them on the counter and went back out to the sales floor. He grabbed a loaf of rye bread and was looking over the overpriced cereal for something with high nutritional value and little sugar.

A shadow came up on Slay. "Yo," the shadow called to him.

Slay turned, a box of Cheerios in his hand. "Tuff," Slay said, breaking off into a smile. He placed the cereal box on the shelf, moved to Tuffy and clasped hands with the young boy. He hadn't seen the kid in a while, not since just after he took care of that situation with George for him. "How you been, dawg?"

Tuffy shrugged, chewed up his face. "Chillin'. I was wondering when you might have some more work for me."

Tuffy was about the business. Slay liked that. "Funny you ask. Soon."

Tuffy seemed pleased, let a small smile creep from his lips. "Word?"

"Word is bond," Slay told him.

Tuffy extended his fist for a pound, Slay touched with him. "Holla at me," Tuffy said. He walked off and out of the store. Slay watched as Tuffy moved through the crowd outside and walked across the street, smoking on a cigarette as he disappeared around the corner. Tuff reminded Slay so much of himself when he was younger.

Slay turned back to the shelf, scanned the cereal boxes again, then settled on the Cheerios. He moved to the open-air cooler at the side of the store and grabbed a pack of bologna and walked these last items up to the register. He moved everything to the center of the counter. "Hit me off with one of them three-dollar scratch-offs, too," Slay said to the cashier. "Maybe my luck will change."

Ten minutes later Slay was knocking at Kenya's door. The door opened and her two little boys ushered Slay in; he rubbed their heads as he passed through to the kitchen. He split the tied plastic bags and pulled out the orange juice and milk, placing them on the top shelf of the refrigerator. He put the box of cereal on the counter, out in the open so the kids would see it. He put the luncheon meat in one of the refrigerator compartments and put the bread on the bottom shelf. Kenya strolled into the kitchen as he put the slit plastic bags in the garbage. She had on an oversize pajama shirt and her hair was wrapped in a towel covered by lint.

"Hey," she said. "I was in the shower."

"I picked up a few things for the kids."

Kenya moved to him, wrapped her arms around his waist and leaned her head against his chest.

"You gonna get my Michael Vick jersey wet," Slay scolded her.

Kenya leaned back from him. "I'm sorry."

Slay smiled, pulled her back in, let her lean her head on him again.

"You staying the night?" Kenya asked from the warmth of his embrace.

"Yeah, I'll hang."

Kenya planted a kiss on his chest. He could feel the intensity of her lips even through the fabric. "You gonna take care of me, I hope," he said. "I had a bad day."

"You know I got you, Slay."

Slay tightened his arms around her. "Tomorrow I wanted to take you to this new restaurant over on Cookman. You can get someone to watch the kids?"

Kenya leaned back from him, looked up in his eyes. "Really, Slay?"

He smiled. "Really."

Kenya rushed to the kitchen phone. "Let me call my girl, she owes me a favor." She dialed the numbers as if the digits were 911. "Girl," she said after a beat. "This Kenya. I need you to do me a really big favor…"

Slay moved to the edge of the kitchen, looked out to the living room. The kids were arranged around the set. "Y'all move back from that TV some," Slay said. "You're gonna ruin your eyes." The two boys moved back without looking in his direction.

Kenya came up behind Slay and wrapped her arms around his torso. "It's all set."

Slay nodded. "Right, right."

"Well," Desmond said, pulling into the mall lot, "here we are." He parked in the empty spot next to Cydney's car.

"I hate for the night to end," Cydney said, "but all good things have to eventually."

"There'll be plenty more nights for us." Desmond seemed to be asking more than saying.

Cydney held her ring of keys, jingling them together in anticipation of her exit. "I hope so."

"You're all that and then some, Miss Wonderful," Desmond said. "I thought I might as well put that out on the table."

Cydney leaned in, kissed him on those luscious lips. She pulled back, biting on her bottom lip, her eyelids heavy with desire. "I better go. If I stay much longer we'll end up fogging your windows."

Desmond's eyebrows arched. "Oh, yeah?" He hit the power-locks button, the click echoing through his truck. "In that case I'm going to have to keep you here with me."

Cydney smiled as Desmond hit the lock button again to unlock the doors. He said, "I'll give you a call tomorrow, okay, Cydney?"

Cydney touched his shoulder. "You better."

She opened her door and slid from the truck, moved behind the vehicle in the direction of her car, Desmond's eyes on her every move. She adjusted her seat, fixed her rearview mirror and put on her seat belt. He was still looking at her from the perch of his truck. She waved, started her car, and backed out of the spot. He followed behind her until they got to the main road. She turned left. He went right.

Slay slid on his jeans and then his Michael Vick jersey, and eased his feet into his boots. Kenya stirred behind him just as he placed his hand on her bedroom doorknob. She sat up in bed, the sheet wrapped around her chest like a bra.

"You leaving, Slay?"

He turned to her. "Yeah, just for a minute."

Kenya turned on the lamp next to the bed. The small lamp

shot off a dense bit of light that only lit the half of the room where Kenya lay. She was under her own spotlight like a star. "You going to check on Ms. Nancy, you can stay up there with her tonight, you want. I ain't going nowhere. I'll be here in the morning."

Slay smiled. "I'll see you in the morning. I want to hit the restaurant for lunch, okay?"

Kenya nodded. "Hey, Slay," she said as he turned to leave. Slay turned back to her. "Yeah?"

"Thank you for not gassing me, telling me you loved me and all that stuff niggas be saying. Thanks for showing me that you do care, though. For always looking out for me and the boys."

Slay was about to say something, but Kenya turned off the lamp and settled back under the covers. He stood there for a moment watching her before he turned and left. When he closed the door Kenya shifted in the bed, took the warm pillow Slay had been resting his head on and hugged it tight against her chest.

Slay took the rickety elevator up to the thirteenth floor. He pulled the key as he exited through the doors and went to his mother's apartment. The hall lamp just across from his mother's was busted and so he fumbled in the darkness to get the key in the lock. On the third try he got it in, turned the lock to open and walked in. As usual the apartment was dark, the radio in his mother's bedroom playing. He went in the kitchen and pulled down a glass from the cabinet. Went in the refrigerator and took out the two-liter of Schweppes Ginger Ale and poured a half glass full. He put everything back in place and grabbed the white package of saltine crackers from the countertop, where he'd left them yesterday. He went to his mother's bedroom, tapped as he always did, and went in without getting her approval, as he always did.

Nancy wasn't in the room. The sheets and blankets were off the bed, bare mattress the only thing left. Slay plopped down on the mattress; he was too tired to go searching again. He'd just wait for her to return. He ran his fingers along the surface of the mattress. The only positive thought he had was the reality that some old sheets wouldn't buy anything in the bartering crack game.

Cydney walked in her apartment and went straight to the phone without removing her jacket or shoes. She dialed Faith's number.

"Hello," Faith said.

"You didn't cancel your three-way calling service, did you?"

"I been meaning to. I hardly use the darn thing, but no, not yet—"

"Good," Cydney cut her off. "Get Victoria on the line with us."

"You haven't even said hello yet," Faith said.

"Do you want to know about my date with Desmond Rucker or what?"

"Y'all went out, already?" Faith said, her voice rising with interest. "Hold on, I'll get Victoria."

There was dead air for a few minutes.

"I knew you'd be on him before the weekend let out," a voice cut through the dead air.

Cydney smiled. "Good of you to join us, Victoria."

"Skip the preliminaries and get right to the scoop," Victoria replied.

"Yeah," Faith said. "The complete blow by blow of the good stuff."

"Whoa there, Faith dear," Victoria said. "Cydney is a lady of the highest honor. There's no 'blow' in her repertoire."

"You know what I meant, darn it," Faith said.

"You two finished playing sexual innuendo at my expense?" Cydney asked.

"You are so right, of course," Victoria said. "The floor is yours."

Faith couldn't let that go. "Whoa, there, V. Cydney is a lady of the highest honor...she wouldn't be caught dead doing anything on the floor."

The three of them laughed together.

"I was wondering where that shirt was."

Felicia turned from the running water spigot of the kitchen sink. She had on one of Desmond's shirts and his favorite slippers. "Hey, lover boy," she said to her brother.

Desmond moved closer to her, saw her feet as he came around the rise of the island counter. "Man, you got my slippers, too!"

Felicia looked down, turned off the spigot, and dried her hands on his shirt. Desmond gasped. Felicia smiled. "Manolo Blahniks these slippers are not, but they're comfortable."

"Manolo what?"

"Manolo Blahniks," Felicia said. "They're like the hottest shoes for women right now. You want to impress this new mystery lady, mention the name to her. Manolo—m, a, n, o, l, o. Blahnik—b, l, a, h, n, i, k. If she has any sense of style whatsoever she'll know them."

"You keep assuming there's some new woman in my life," Desmond said.

Felicia placed her hands on her hips. "You telling me there isn't?"

Desmond fought unsuccessfully to keep a smile off his face.

"Thought so." Felicia sat on one of the bar stools that lined the wall next to the kitchen counter. "So what's her name?"

Desmond pulled a bottle of Snapple from the refrigerator, twisted off the cap, sat across from his sister. "Cydney Williams. And she is prime."

Felicia raised one eyebrow. "Oh, is she now?"

Desmond took a long swig from his drink, nodded his head as the iced tea eased down his throat.

"Does she have a brother?" Felicia asked, smiling.

"Hey, now," Desmond said, "you're my baby sister, I don't want to hear that."

"Women have needs, too, you know."

Desmond covered his ears.

"I am young, supple—"

Desmond hummed over the sound of her voice.

"A vine of fresh fruit waiting to be plucked—"

"*Huuuuuuuummmmmmmmmm.*"

"Waiting to have my skin peeled back—"

"*Hummmmmmmmmmmmmmmm.*"

"My ripe flesh—"

Desmond stopped humming. "Enough!"

Felicia laughed. "Don't be a prude, Desmond."

"You not telling me that you—" he chewed up his face "—that you've done the do?"

At that, Felicia covered her ears and hummed.

Desmond shook his head, swallowed the last of his tea. "This is too much for me." He got up and placed the bottle in the recyclables bin. "I have to get into the restaurant. We'll finish this discussion later."

"Whatever, baby brother."

"I'm older by nine years and a few months."

"I'll say," Felicia said, squinting her eyes and leaning forward. "Is it me or is your hair starting to recede?"

"Funny."

"I try my best."

"You decide what you're going to do?" Desmond asked as he retrieved his car keys off the hook by the phone. "Model-ingwise, I mean. Are you going back or are you going to talk with Mom and Dad, maybe do the college thing like they wanted you to?"

Felicia got up off the stool. "I'm definitely not doing the college thing. I was heading to the city today, but they had some kind of something or other, so I set up a meeting with some of the agency folks for tomorrow. I'm not going to let that one asshole, Kenneth, sour me on this. I've been into fashion since I was a little girl. I'm going to keep modeling as long as they'll have me."

Desmond nodded. "You were going through Mom's stuff before you got potty trained. I even let you practice applying makeup on me."

Felicia smiled. "Riiiiigggght."

"Make sure we keep that between us."

"Consider it done."

"On the real, you're a strong young woman," Desmond said. "I'm proud of you."

Felicia smiled. "I'm proud of you, too, baby brother."

Desmond thought about Cydney Williams, the good time he'd had with her, the bright future he knew they could have. He blew Felicia a kiss and walked through the door toward his truck.

Felicia was proud of him. He could take that. Cydney was all he expected and more, he could take that, too. He looked toward the sky as he moved toward his truck, toward Cydney's father looking down. "I'm going to do your daughter proud," he said just before he slid inside the truck.

NANCY

"*Can I come in? I don't have anywhere else to go,*" I say.

I peek through the cracked, chain-locked door with hope. Indecision and lack of get-up-and-go must run in these folks' family, I think as I wait. Finally, the door opens for me. I walk inside. It's more naked than it was the last time I was here, the day of Darius's funeral. The entire apartment carries the smell of burnt eggs.

"*Why ain't you home curled up with your husband?*" Darlene asks. She's Darius's sister, my ex-sister-in-law. Before I answer, Darlene moves toward the kitchen in hyper steps, her back to me, but I can still see the sneer on her face, or at least imagine it.

"*Bit of discord,*" I tell her, following slowly behind.

"*Speak English,*" Darlene prods me. She is sitting in a chair at the corner of the kitchen. The small dinette table that usually centers the room is absent.

"*Got in a fight,*" I retry, scanning the room with my eyes. I just know she's going to eat all this up. She never really forgave me for marrying so quickly after Darius died. I'm not sure I forgave myself, but I know I've come to forget it.

"*About?*" Darlene asks.

"*George is upset at me because he thinks I'm not doing a good enough job mothering my children. Cydney is running around with this bad boy, Byron, and Shammond...*" I don't even want to get into what Shammond is up to.

"*I believe the children are the future,*" Darlene sneers.

I lean against the counter self-consciously. The bare apartment and Darlene's slovenly appearance have me wondering. Darlene's clothes drown her slight frame. She's lost so much weight since I last saw her. "Where are your children?" I ask her, looking around.

"Away?" Darlene answers. The sneer that had been a part of her voice for the past few moments was gone.

"With who?" I press.

"Folks."

I wring my hands, looking toward the refrigerator. "I'm a bit thirsty, Darlene. You mind?"

"Help yourself. There's juice and soda."

I trudge to the refrigerator, open it. Empty except for an extra-large bowl of spaghetti that looked as if Darlene had been pecking at it for over a week. "I'll just grab a glass of water," I tell her, closing the refrigerator. I turn around to find that I'm alone in the kitchen. "Darlene?" I quietly walk from the kitchen, move toward Darlene's bedroom. I knock on the door. I can hear shuffling inside.

Darlene emerges, her head down. "Been looking for something the past hour and can't seem to find it," she says as she scurries by.

I follow her to the living room. We both sit on the couch, the only piece of furniture in the room. Up close I can see discoloration on Darlene's lips. Darlene notices my probing eyes and sits back against the couch cushions.

"So King George has come down off his throne," Darlene says.

"He means well. He still hasn't figured out that nagging me just makes me more resistant. Not that I'd know what to do anyway. Cydney's at the age where she can make her own decisions and Shammond is just stuck in the rough years."

"How old they now?"

"Cydney's seventeen, Shammond is fifteen."

Now Darlene was shaking her head. "Darius would trip out, he could see them practically grown."

"Can I stay with you tonight, just to cool off and not have to hear George's voice for a bit?" *I ask. I don't want to think about Darius. Even though George has been wonderful to me, and I love him, there's still a part of me that wishes Darius had worked out. For our children's sake.*

Darlene looks me over before nodding her head. "Why not."

"Thanks."

Darlene smiles. "You did Darius dirty in death but you never did him dirty in life."

I take that as a compliment and let it ride.

"I need to step out," *Darlene says.* "You can grab some sheets and stuff from my bedroom closet and make up this couch. I'll be back shortly."

"It's late," *I hear myself say. Same thing I used to tell Darius. I feel a need to share the same info with Darlene because she and Darius have similar tendencies. Her bare apartment is all the proof.*

Darlene simply pats my knee before rising and seemingly walking out the door in the same action.

It's her life, I think as I move to the bedroom with George's voice echoing in my head. "That boy's the source of all these problems, Nan. He's mixed up in all kinds of stuff. His sister's unable to get herself back on course 'cause of him. You need to do something."

Didn't the fall of one's children always land on the shoulder of the mother?

"Should have listened to me when I told you that boy did something to Cydney Doll way back when," *George's voice says to me as I step into the bedroom.* "She ain't been the same since."

Blame, blame, blame.

What kind of mother did he think I was? Did he think I'd

stand by and let one of my children hurt the other? I'd questioned Cydney. Cydney said nothing happened.

I move to the closet of Darlene's bedroom.

"I blame you, Nan," George's voice tells me as I open the door. Of course he did. Darius had no ambition and diligence. George had enough for the both of them. He seemed to come to the realization now, after these years of marriage, that I wasn't perfect. The realization seemed to shake him. But it was breaking me because I wanted to be perfect, I wanted him to still look at me like he did those nights he carried Darius to my doorstep. I needed George to stop nagging me and help me, same as he did Darius.

The blankets and sheets are balled in a clump at the base of the closet. I crinkle my nose. Sleeping on them isn't at all appealing. I can hear George tomorrow, once I tell him whose couch I spent the night on. "Hang around Darius's sister long enough and you'll surely be about nothing."

I pick up the ball of sheets and turn to leave, tripping over a sneaker too large to be Darlene's. Something falls from the sneaker. I place the sheets on the edge of the bed and lean to retrieve the sneaker and its contents. A lighter, a few small whitish shavings and some kind of pipelike contraption, a glass bowl fitted with fine mesh, lay next to the sneaker. I hesitate to pick up the contents and return them to the sneaker. For some reason I start to think about the day George caught me in the bathroom, smoking a Newport, washing the ashes down the sink. "Nan," he'd said, shaking his head. "Only trashy women smoke. You're not trashy, now, are you?" I shook my head at the time. No, I wasn't trashy. I was the woman he'd looked on so adoringly when he carried my husband home. All this drama in our lives had chased away that look in his eyes. I wanted it back. I wanted him to take care of me, shield me from the problems of the world, hold me under the arm like he did Darius.

Tears find my eyes, and my hands shake as I pick up the lighter. I fumble to place the shavings in the bowl. Crack. I'd seen Shelby Lewis, who'd lived across the street from Darius and I, smoke it once, after her first child's father got caught with that underage girl, violating his probation. Overnight, Shelby's problems multiplied like roaches. But, for the few moments she sucked in the grayish smoke, she didn't seem to feel the pain anymore.

I spark the flame as tears drip down into my mouth. I'm a sensible woman. I know this is no answer.

"I blame you, Nan." I hear George's voice in my head, clear as day.

I know you do, George. I also know you don't hold me like you used to. Why'd you have to go and stop? Don't you know I came to you because I'd been through a lifetime of not being held? Don't you know I expected you to hold me until the day I died?

I look at the cooked elements in the glass bowl.

Just for this moment I wasn't going to be perfect, wasn't going to strive to meet an ideal I knew was light-years away from me. I place the pipe to my lips. It worked for Shelby Lewis. Maybe it would work for me. Then, tomorrow I'd go and have a long talk with George, let him know how much I love him, and that his constant badgering is tearing me apart. I'm already a broken woman, two kids that I have no idea where and how they're going to turn out. Two kids that have turned a deaf ear to my pleas of concern and worry. All I have right now is George.

"I blame you, Nan."

Oh, George, don't say that. Please don't say that.

"But I do, Nan."

Okay, George, you win.

Put this in your pipe and smoke it, George.

CHAPTER 13

Slay came down from his mother's apartment showered, shaved and well rested. Nancy had stumbled in late last night, shame in her eyes, and curled up with Slay on the bare mattress. They slept in each other's arms, keeping each other warm.

Now Slay wore oversize Rocawear jeans that fell into a bundle on top of his gray Timberland boots. He had on a gray Sean Jean cardigan V-neck sweater with a burgundy stripe shadowing the neckline. He rapped twice on Kenya's door.

Kenya stepped out, backward, and locked her door. She turned around all smiles. "Ready," she said.

Slay couldn't believe his eyes. She wore a two-toned leather jacket over a lace-trimmed top, and black wool trousers.

"You like?" Kenya said, noticing the dumbfounded look on Slay's face.

He nodded.

"Hope so," Kenya offered. "You bought it."

Slay crinkled his forehead. "What you mean?"

Kenya started walking, Slay on her heels. "That money you gave me for my birthday a while back, told me to get something nice for myself."

She stopped at the lobby door, Slay rushed to open it for her. "You did a good job," he said as they stepped outside.

"Thanks," Kenya said. "You look nice, too."

Slay shook his head, his gaze trained on Kenya. "Not like you."

He forgot about the purpose of this outing as he drove to

the restaurant, all shook up by the look and smell of Kenya. "What's that you wearing...that perfume?"

"Waters Sheer Passion," Kenya said, adding, "You got me this, too."

"I ain't never smelled this on you before."

"I was waiting," she told him.

"For?"

She turned away and looked out the window without answering.

As they neared the restaurant Slay remembered his purpose again. GQ Smooth.

"Ooh, this is nice," Kenya said as Slay parked across the street from the restaurant in the metered spots.

Slay nodded. "Right, right."

They walked in, shoulder to shoulder. A pretty woman behind a small podium greeted them.

"Welcome to Cush," she said. "Party of two?"

Kenya nodded.

"Smoking or nonsmoking?"

"No smoking," Kenya told her.

The woman gathered two menus, tapped them on the podium and waved Slay and Kenya toward her. "Follow me this way."

Slay scanned the place, noticed a well-dressed dude walking around making conversation with the people at each table. When Kenya and Slay reached their quaint table, Slay motioned to the hostess. "Who's that?" he asked, nodding his head at the well-dressed gentleman.

The hostess blushed. "That's Desmond Rucker, the proprietor."

"The what?"

"He owns the restaurant."

Slay nodded. "I thought so."

The hostess walked off.

"This is the straight bomb," Kenya said as she looked over the menu.

Slay picked up his menu, squinting his eyes to read the offerings.

"You still need glasses?" Kenya asked.

Slay smiled at her. "Yeah, probably."

Desmond Rucker came to their table. "Hello, folks," he said. "I hope you're enjoying everything so far."

"We just got here," Slay said.

"It's real nice," Kenya added.

"I'm Desmond Rucker, the proprietor," Desmond said. "I'll be right around. Holler if you have any concerns or anything, and I truly hope you enjoy." He turned to leave.

"Yo, Desmond?" Slay called to him.

Desmond turned back. "Yes?"

"Good luck to you with this," Slay said. "This is a tough neighborhood for a business. Most of the places that try get chased away eventually."

Desmond smiled. "I don't give up so easily. I fight to the end."

"It'll be a fight," Slay said.

Desmond smiled again, nodded and walked off.

Slay sat back in his seat, leaned to the side like he did when he drove, rubbed his fingers over his lips and smiled. It was going to be a fight for GQ Smooth for real. Word up.

Cydney was watching the Lifetime Channel again, absorbed in a movie, when the phone rang.

"Dang, you people just don't want me to finish a movie," she said as she moved across the carpet to the phone stand. She looked over the number on the caller ID; it was unfamiliar, but the 973 area code let her know it was from North Jersey. She picked up. "Hello."

"Cydney Williams?"

"Yes," Cydney said to the female on the other end. Immediately she thought about Desmond. Please don't let this be a live-in girlfriend, or worse yet, wife, connecting the dots after finding Cydney's number in Desmond's shirt pocket. "Whom am I speaking with?"

"My name is Villa Moore. I don't believe we've ever spoken before," the woman said. "I'm Mr. James's personal assistant."

What, Stephon had his staff making calls on his behalf now? "What can I do for you, Ms. Moore?" Cydney asked.

"Mrs. James asked me to contact Mr. James's friends and business associates, especially the people from the magazine. I came across your name and number in his PalmPilot."

Cydney swallowed. "Has something happened?"

Villa's pause told it all. "Mr. James has had an unfortunate— Mrs. James would like me to call it an accident, but I know Mr. James wouldn't want me lying to you. It's a very awkward situation. They were divorcing as you probably know."

"Accident?" Cydney took a breath, sat down on the floor where she had stood. "Is he dead?"

"Hospitalized," Villa told her. "He swallowed quite a few prescription pills." Villa seemed to be gathering herself on the other line. "Quite a few."

"Oh, my goodness, are you telling me that Stephon tried to kill himself?"

Villa lowered her voice. "I just thought you should know. I hope you'll keep this quiet. Mrs. James has asked that no one contact her but go through me for the time being. She's trying to get everything sorted out."

"Is he going to make it?" Cydney asked, tears in her eyes now.

"I'm not sure," Villa said, "but I'll personally keep you posted. I—" she hesitated "—I know Mr. James thought very fondly of you. He was shockingly open to those of us he was close to about how he felt about you…"

"You make it sound like he doesn't stand a chance," Cydney said.

"I'll keep you abreast," Villa offered. "I'm sorry."

Villa said her goodbyes and hung up. Cydney slumped against the wall, phone dangling in her hand. The obvious question hung above her head: Was this all her fault?

Desmond slipped into his office for a quick phone call. He dialed the numbers, which he'd memorized overnight, and sat humming to himself as the rings cycled. It picked up on the fourth ring.

"Hey, there," Desmond said. "I've been thinking about you all day and had to call and check in on you. I had a wonderful time yesterday."

"That's good," Cydney said.

Her demeanor was ice cold, to Desmond's dismay.

"Am I catching you at a bad time?"

"No," she lied.

"So what are you up to today?"

"Not much."

"Up for some company?"

"Honestly," Cydney said, "no."

Desmond's face fell. He shifted in his seat. "Oooo-kay."

"Talk with you later?" Cydney asked, in a hurry to hang up.

"Yeah, sure."

"Good."

"Cydney, are you—" His query was halted by the sound of a click, then the dial tone.

She'd hung up.

Desmond stared at the phone for a moment. Eventually he placed it back in the cradle. He sat back in his chair, rocking even though it wasn't a rocker, tapping his fingers together. Once again the gods of romance had thrown him a pitch he had no capability of hitting, one that appeared to come at him straight, but just as he tightened his grip on the bat and prepared to swing it looped beyond his reach.

A knock came to his office door.

"S'open," he said.

Karen poked her head around the door but didn't enter the room. "The performers are here, they're just setting up."

Desmond nodded. "Good."

Karen hung around like a dust cloud. "Everything okay? You look down."

"I get in these thinking moods from time to time," Desmond said. "I'm fine."

"Well, hurry on back out. I miss seeing you milling around talking to the people."

Desmond got up, clasped his hands and flashed Karen a smile. "Coming right now, can't have you missing me."

Karen smiled in return and disappeared from the doorway. Desmond pushed his chair flush against the desk, gave the phone one last hard look and moved from the small office.

Slay drove his BMW up the main thoroughfare of Asbury Park, Kenya beside him, bobbing her head to his Nas CD, turned down quite a few notches below the level he usually played it at. She had her purse in her lap, her hands crossed on top of it, sitting how he imagined that bitch from the college that dissed him—Theresa/Pamela—would sit. It surprised him to see Kenya, so, so…womanly, sophisticated like.

"Had a good time?" he asked Kenya.

She smiled, kept bobbing. "The best."

"What you thinking about now?"

"Thinking about the boys," she said. "It's good to get a break, good to spend some time with you, but I miss they bad asses."

"You a good mother, Kenya, you know that?"

She looked at him, smiled. "I get plenty of help."

Slay tried to smile. Couldn't.

The light ahead turned a shade of orange, Slay could have punched the gas pedal and made it through but he braked to a stop. By the side of the road a couple of white guys, their hair spiked and colored, their dress a collage of army gear, clown suit and white-collar worker, held up large white placards with handwritten Magic Marker messages.

Asbury Park police are bullies who abuse their power

Criminals don't wear black, they wear blue

Slay nodded to the sign, smirked. "Asbury Park cops are expensive, too. Costing me a grip to keep them at bay, let me handle mines without interruptions."

Kenya stopped bopping to the music, turned to Slay. "You ever thought about doing something else?" she asked. "You smart, got all kinds of connections, all kinds of respect. My uncle says you got a good business mind, he could tell."

Slay moved through the green light. "Nah, I like where I'm at with my life."

"Do you?"

He looked at her, started to smile, but the look in her eyes made him hold the smile. "Everything ain't perfect, but yeah, for the most part I like it."

"I don't wanna ever see you go back in, that's all."

"That makes two of us. I can't. I won't."

Kenya pursed her lips, went back to bobbing her head to the music. She didn't say anything for the balance of the five-minute ride and Slay didn't either. He pulled up to the front of the apartment tower and put the transmission arm in park. He seemed nervous, as if he had something to say but didn't have the words clear, as if he wanted to kiss her but was too bashful.

"Best time I think I ever had," Kenya said. "I won't be forgetting this for a long time."

Slay smiled.

Kenya leaned over and kissed his cheek. "Thanks again." She turned and opened her door and was half out when Slay said, "I'll be around to see you soon." Kenya nodded without turning back, eased out of the car and shut the door carefully. She knew how Slay was about his car, the handle-with-care directive that guided anyone lucky enough to get a ride in his whip.

Slay watched her walk up the sidewalk toward the front lobby. She had a strong dignified strut just like his mother had at one time. Kenya looked like a woman from Social Services coming to check on one of the poor families inside, not at all like someone who actually lived here. In all his years of knowing Kenya, today, for the first time, Slay really looked at her. She was beautiful.

Kenya moved through the front door and turned back toward Slay. He was embarrassed that he was still sitting here watching her, until she raised her arm and waved. The embarrassment left him. He waved back, and then when she moved from the entrance, he pulled off from the curb. His stomach was doing funny shit, shit he couldn't explain.

Cydney grabbed her bag of goodies from CVS. Then she commandeered the cordless phone and went into the bathroom. She sat the phone on the countertop and emptied the contents of the CVS bag into the sink. Slay would have blown a gasket if he'd picked this bag instead of the one holding her school supplies, she thought to herself. The candles, rose oil and bathwater colorant inside filled the curve of the porcelain basin. She'd purchased the items as a possible "love kit" for the future; she hadn't expected at the time that the love expressed through the items would be love for self, a means of pampering and revitalizing her own worn body, mind and soul. She'd expected the items to be for her and Desmond.

Cydney turned the spigot of the tub on, drew the water as hot as she could tolerate. She looked over the label for the bottle of rose oil. There wasn't much to it, so she uncapped the bottle and poured a generous amount of the sweet-smelling therapy into the rising water. Next, she tore the plastic covering off her three small candles and tossed the garbage in her small wastebasket. She opened the medicine cabinet, pulled out her Bic SureStart and set flame to the candles. She placed one candle on the lip of the tub, one on the counter, and the other on the wooden toilet seat. She stepped back to admire her placement, and made a motion with her hands for the candles to be easy, don't tumble over and ignite her bathroom in flames.

Cydney then picked up the bottle of bathwater colorant, looked over the label as she'd done with the rose oil. *Doesn't stain skin or tub surface,* the label claimed. Cydney smirked and then poured a modest amount of the colorant into her peaceful stew.

She slid off her silk robe and hung it over the plastic door hook. She grabbed the phone off the counter and put it on the wooden magazine stand with wheels she kept in the bathroom, rolled the stand next to the tub. She stopped and took a deep breath, closed her eyes for a moment. She opened her eyes and stuck a foot in the water. It was hotter than most people could stand but perfect for her. She settled under the water, turned off the spigot and lay back in the tub.

Cydney sat forward, grabbed the phone, dialed the number she'd committed to memory just yesterday.

"Desmond Rucker," a voice said into her ear.

"Desmond, hi, it's Cydney."

"Hey." There was no warmth, no disdain, no excitement and no frustration in his voice. No emotion. Cydney didn't quite know how to proceed.

"You still at the restaurant?" she asked.

"Yeah, I'm in my office closing up shop for the day. I was

just about to walk out the door. I had my cell ringer down low but I heard it anyway."

"What you got planned for the rest of the evening?"

"Nothing much," he said. "Probably head home and lick my wounds." That was his manly way of broaching the subject of their earlier phone call.

"I'm sorry about before," Cydney told him.

"Wasn't anything," he said, still being manly.

"I was a bit short with you. I didn't mean to be."

"Happens."

"I was going through something at the time," Cydney said. "You want to know about it?"

"If you want to tell me," he replied. "If not, that's cool."

"Do you, yes or no?"

Desmond sighed. Cydney could hear the springs of a chair taking on added weight. "Tell me," he said as he settled into his chair.

"Remember the guy I was with the first time I came to your restaurant?"

"Your boss, yes?"

"Boss now," Cydney said, starting slowly. "But at one time we were more."

"I figured as much."

"Was a bad situation," Cydney confided. "He's married—unhappily—but married."

"Really?" There was judgment in Desmond's tone.

"His wife has a nasty addiction to painkiller medicine. Stephon had been talking about leaving her since I first met him."

"We need more men like that," Desmond said tersely.

"You're perfect, I suppose?" Cydney said.

Desmond sighed. He thought about Nora, thought about Jacinta, the go-go dancer. "No, far from it. I'm being stupid, I guess. I know where this is headed."

"I don't think you do."

"You've still got feelings for him. He's probably left the wife now and wants to start over again with you. You're conflicted, or, maybe not conflicted. Either way you slice it, I can tell I'm out in the cold."

Cydney was surprised to hear Desmond sounding like a defeated, wounded boy. "Would that bother you, Desmond?"

"What kind of question is that?"

"Just want to know," Cydney said. She could hear those chair springs again, this time one after another, in a rhythmic drone. Desmond hadn't answered her question. "You there?" she asked, to move him along.

"I'm here," he said.

"Well, would it bother you to be left out in the cold?"

Desmond swallowed. "Yes... It would, very much so."

Cydney smiled. Desmond didn't know it but his admission was a major breakthrough in their early relationship. "I like you very much, Desmond," she said. "I have high hopes for you, for us. I like to think of myself as wholly independent, the anti-needy modern woman, but I know I need you in my life. I hope my saying this doesn't scare you off."

"What about your boss?"

Cydney took in a deep breath, held it for an eternity before she released it. "Stephon swallowed a bunch of his wife's pills. He tried to kill himself."

"What!"

"His assistant phoned me just before you called earlier. I was pretty much in a fog when you called."

"Damn! Are you all right?"

"Feeling a bit guilty," Cydney said. "You're right about one thing. He called me the other day telling me he'd filed for divorce and that he wanted to be with me. I told him I couldn't. I told him I had my eyes on a certain gentleman restaurateur. He didn't take it that well. He threatened not to run the piece on Cush."

"Piece on Cush?"

"I do freelance writing work for *Urban Styles* magazine. Restaurant reviews, music reviews, that sort of thing. I came to Cush because we're doing a feature on your restaurant. At least we were supposed to be. Stephon wasn't too happy about what I wrote about your place. He said it was a love letter to you and not a restaurant review. That was the surprise I had for you."

"You're blowing me away, Cydney."

"This is a lot to process, I know. Look, I need some time to myself today, but tomorrow I'm hoping you can get together with me after I get off my other job at Macy's, so I can hold you and..." Her voice drifted away.

"And what?" Desmond asked.

"I don't know," she said, "continue to grow with you. Build a foundation. All this sound corny?"

"Not at all," Desmond said. "What time do you get off?"

"Around ten, closing, I hope that isn't too late for you. I know you're a hardworking brother."

"I'm going to be tight and sore after a long day," Desmond told her. "Probably need a massage or something. You know how to give massages?"

"I've got magic fingers, baby."

"Ooh, say that again," Desmond implored her. "The *baby* part."

"Baby, I've got magic fingers."

Desmond could feel his manhood coming to life.

"So, tomorrow we're on?" Cydney said.

"Yes, we are. You want me to come to the mall?"

"Yes, baby, and you can follow me home. I'll make up for all this craziness, I promise."

"Are you trying to seduce me, Cydney Williams?"

"How am I doing?"

Desmond touched that stiff part of himself. "I'd say you're doing real well."

Cydney laughed. Just a few hours ago she would have thought the possibility of her laughing didn't exist. "I know it's early in whatever this is we have, but I appreciate you so much already, Desmond."

"Likewise," Desmond said. His hand lingered down below.

Cydney clucked her tongue against the roof of her mouth. "Tomorrow then, okay?"

"I'm really sorry about your boss," Desmond offered before ending the call.

"I know now that I can make it through this," Cydney told him. She blew a kiss in the phone. "Good night."

"Sweet dreams."

Desmond had made a pact that he wouldn't go to Hot Tails go-go again. He left Cush, an unquenched thirst aching in his groin, with the full intent of heading straight home. He turned on his radio, settling on the cool jazz and R&B ruminations of WBLS. He hummed along to the songs, hummed to keep his mind from wandering, hummed and kept his eyes on the road and out of the rearview mirror.

It didn't work.

As he reached an intersection he looked over his shoulder and then turned his truck around, tires squealing, and headed back in the direction from whence he came.

He passed back by Cush, barreling his chest out with pride as he blurred by the awning and neon signage. He rode to the end of the stretch and made that turn that was becoming as second nature as breathing. He parked in his usual spot, directly across the street from the bar. Moving quickly, he was at the door before any second thoughts settled in.

He walked in the door, said, "Getting my first drink before I get a permanent seat," to the bouncer. The bouncer nodded, seemingly pleased for the first time in Desmond's memory.

Desmond walked over to the bar. The pretty bartender from his first visit, Wendy, was back manning the drinks. Her chest was noticeably larger, stretching the material of her T-shirt. She wore a black short-sleeve with Free Iverson etched across the front in white letters.

"Mr. Screwdriver," she said as she came to Desmond.

"What is it with me, I'm that memorable?"

She smiled. "Yes, you are."

"I missed you the other day."

Wendy the bartender cupped her breasts. "Went for my master's," she said. "I'm looking to improve my job prospects in a down economy."

"You're going to start dancing?"

She hesitated. "Yup. Soon as I heal. The implants have to drop first."

"Looking forward to that," Desmond told her.

She let a smile slip from her lips. "Thanks."

Desmond moved to the opening for the performers' room. He just wanted to check and see by any chance if Jacinta was onstage. She wasn't. He moved back by the bar, took his drink, paid the tender and sat on the stool.

God certainly was on his side because it wasn't long before Jacinta walked in the front doorway, dressed in oversize sweatpants and shirt, a large duffel bag draped over her shoulder. She jabbed at the bouncer when she walked in and he leaned over, pretending the punch had hurt his side. This was the first time Desmond saw the guy smile.

Jacinta was headed toward a door at the right of the room when she spotted Desmond. He nodded at her; she nodded back, stopped, and then started walking in his direction. He quickly finished his drink, wiped his mouth and sat up straight in his chair.

"Getting to be a regular," Jacinta said as she approached him.

Desmond smirked. "I like the customer service here. How are you doing today, Ms. Jacinta?"

"I'm doing," she said.

"I been meaning to ask you—"

"My daddy's black, mother is Cuban and Dominican," she said.

"How did you know I was going to ask that?"

"That's the first thing most men want to know about me," Jacinta confessed. "I knew you'd get around to it one day."

"You are something," Desmond said, shaking his head.

Jacinta sat on the stool next to him. "I've been thinking about you."

Desmond crinkled his forehead. "Really?"

Jacinta mouthed something to the bartender before turning her attention back to Desmond. "Yeah. I've been wondering about your life outside this place, wondering what brings you here."

Desmond scanned the rest of the room. "The same thing that brings all these other guys—beautiful women such as yourself."

Jacinta shook her head. "No, I don't think so. Something different about you."

"You have a lot of opinions, you know that?"

The bartender brought over a drink and placed it on a napkin in front of Jacinta. "Thanks, Wendy," Jacinta said. She turned back to Desmond. "Opinionated. I've been told that before."

"Justifiably so."

"Remember what I said about everyone being a performer on a stage?"

Desmond made a face. "You kidding, I had it engraved on a plaque and hung in my office."

Jacinta smiled. "Where might this office be?"

Desmond frowned.

"Come down off the stage," she prodded.

"I own a restaurant…Cush, right around the corner."

"You own that place?" Jacinta's eyes lit. "Every day I drive by there in awe, a place that beautiful in the center of all that ugly." She shook her head, smiling. "I wondered who would have the guts to open a business there. Should have known it would be you. Damn!"

"You're flattering me," Desmond said.

"You should be proud, not flattered."

Desmond ordered another drink. "You sound like my sister."

Jacinta took a swallow of her own drink. "Younger or older?" she asked after the elixir moved down through her throat.

"Younger, she's a model out in New York." Desmond smiled at the vision of Felicia that danced around in his head. "That's my heart there, my sister. Only woman I've ever felt compelled to stick it out with." He laughed to make light of his issues. "She's staying with me now, trying to get some things settled in her life. The world isn't too kind to you beautiful women, is it?"

Jacinta shrugged. "Is what it is." She looked at Desmond. "So, tell me about your woman—your girlfriend, or is it, wife?"

"Who said I've got a woman—" Desmond started, but stopped when Jacinta crooked her head to the side and looked at him with those dark eyes of hers. "I don't know," he said, stopping to sip his second screwdriver. "It's very new. I'm hoping it'll lead to something substantial. I thought we made a breakthrough yesterday but today I'm not so sure anymore. She's having a sort of crisis in her life, says all the right things about needing me, but…"

"That's the one thing about you that fits the profile of the men that come in here," Jacinta told him. "Problems at home with their partner, be it a girlfriend or wife. For some reason men come here to escape the drama of their relationships, but then when they go home the same problems exist. This place is just a temporary diversion. Come down off the stage, Desmond, and get yourself right so you and this woman can go on and make beautiful babies, create a future together." Jacinta downed the last bit of her drink, placed the glass on the counter and moved to get up. Desmond reached for her shoulder and she didn't flinch; the bouncer didn't rush him and put him in a headlock, either.

"Why you take such an interest in me?" Desmond asked.

Jacinta smiled. "You're one handsome brother," she said. "And I love a handsome man, simple as that." She rubbed her hand along his shoulder. "I wish you were available. You're just the kind of man I lay awake in bed dreaming about coming in here and whisking me away from all this." She smiled sadly. "Good luck with your girlfriend...and pray for a sistah, would you?" She grabbed her duffel bag and walked off through that door to the right that led to the bowels of the building.

Desmond swallowed the last of his drink and moved to leave. Tonight he just didn't feel like seeing Jacinta onstage. Pray for a sistah? Pray for a brotha, too.

CHAPTER 14

Desmond pulled his truck into the parking lot at the train station. He looked at his watch. "What time does your train arrive?"

"Seven-sixteen," Felicia said. "We've got a few minutes."

"You know what you're going to say to these people?"

"Keep Kenneth away from me," Felicia said, "and I'll do my best to make the agency and myself some money. If I even get a whiff of his hot garlic breath again, I'm walking...for good."

"You're not going to put up with anyone degrading you," Desmond added.

"Exactly," Felicia said. "I want to make that point perfectly clear. I'll also mention how it would be a shame if the New York papers got wind of a reputable agency, with photographers contracted by that agency, promising young vulnerable girls modeling opportunities in return for sexual favors."

Desmond nodded, impressed. "Well said."

"I got that off of *20/20*," Felicia confessed, smiling. "They ran a story about something like this."

"You're way too beautiful and intelligent for that kind of nonsense."

Felicia nodded. "And this girl can *sashay chante* better than those coked out-looking white girls they had with me that day. I didn't see Kenneth breathing shrimp scampi down their necks."

Desmond smiled. "At-ti-tude."

Felicia snapped her fingers. "Please believe it."

"You're a trip, girl."

Felicia pressed for the clock function on his dashboard. "We've got a couple more minutes, so let me know all about this new mystery woman."

Desmond laughed. "Cydney Williams—"

"I know her name," Felicia cut him off. "I want to know the real details, like, how long you plan on keeping her around?"

"Don't go there."

Felicia rolled her eyes. "Proceed."

"She's sexy, beautiful, smart, strong-minded, easy to talk to, fun to be around."

"Oh, shit, that bests the previous record holder, Nora." Felicia said.

"What are you yapping about now?"

"That was like four adjectives and Nora only got three. This Cydney might just be in there."

"Don't go rushing us to the altar, it's still early. She's got a few issues I think she has to settle."

"Is Cydney Terrific aware of how issue free you are, baby brother?"

"What's that supposed to mean?"

"In other words, does she know your M.O. is stick and move?"

"Is that how you see me?" Desmond asked, his eyes narrowed and shielded by heavy lids.

Felicia smiled and touched his hand. "You show this Cydney Terrific what you show me on a daily basis and she'll be in good hands."

Desmond's posture settled back into the hospitality of his interior leather. "I'm going to try," he said softly.

"Us women have to stick together," Felicia added. "I want to see a good woman get the good man she deserves."

Desmond's eyes came to life. "Which reminds me—we were having a conversation the other day about whether or not a certain young woman did the do or not. What's the deal with that? Please tell me you're still pure."

Felicia was about to respond, but the waiting passengers on the platform in front of them stood up and started making their way forward. She smiled, reached in the backseat and grabbed her bag, then turned and gave her brother a quick kiss. "Saved by the toot-toot, little brother," she exclaimed.

"We'll revisit this again, Felicia."

"But of course."

"You sure you don't want me to meet you here to bring you back tonight?"

"No, no," Felicia said. "I'm not even certain I'm coming right back tonight."

"Well, call me on the cell if you change your mind. I'll be out with Cydney."

"Look at you," Felicia said. "Pushing me aside already."

"I got your back you need me. Be careful."

Felicia blew Desmond a kiss and exited the truck. Desmond watched her walk with attitude toward the train while the other passengers half trotted or outright ran. When she reached the conductor she extended an arm so he could help her onto the raised step of the train. She turned to the conductor and smiled. The conductor's legs looked as if they might fold under him. Desmond shook his head. The power women held over men was one of life's greatest phenomena. He put his truck in drive and drove off thinking about a certain Miss Wonderful, wondering if he had the patience to make it through the day until this evening.

Villa Moore's voice came on the line, cutting through the music that had been playing for close to ten minutes. "Cydney," she said, "I am *sooo* sorry to keep you waiting. I had an important matter I had to attend to."

"That's okay," Cydney said. Her knees were bouncing out of control. "I got your message asking that I call you back. Is there a development?"

"Hold for one moment," Villa said. The sounds of a door closing echoed through the phone line on Villa's end, then the sound of Villa settling into her seat. "Nosy ears," Villa said when she came back on the line.

"I understand."

"To answer your question, yes, Stephon is definitely going to pull through this…physically."

"What does that mean…physically?"

"He's in severe depression," Villa told her. "He's told them in no uncertain terms that he plans to finish what he wasn't able to complete the first time."

"Suicidal."

"Very much so. Mrs. James has elected to have him sedated."

"She would consider that the answer," Cydney huffed. Villa made a sound on the other end, Cydney could tell it as the sound someone made with a smirk.

"The other thing," Villa said, talking deliberately. "Mrs. James has decided to take over the day-to-day duties of running the magazine."

"You've got to be kidding me."

"Afraid so," Villa said.

"I don't think I can deal with that woman," Cydney said.

"That's the thing…" Villa took in a deep breath. "Mrs. James has decided to cut down on freelance pieces and farm out everything to the staff writers."

"I guess she made my decision for me, then," Cydney said.

"I'm sorry," Villa said. "I think the whole thing reeks. She's coming in now acting like the devoted loving wife."

"Thanks for the info, Villa."

"I'll keep you posted, Cydney. You take care of yourself."

"I will, and you do the same."

"And, Cydney?"

"Yes?"

"Don't blame yourself, girl." Villa's voice dropped to a whisper. "That man had nothing but unhappiness. You, the magazine and his child are the only things that made him happy."

Cydney took in a deep breath and let it hold. The words were appreciated but they didn't fill the empty place in her stomach. She couldn't shake the guilt in knowing she'd abandoned Stephon as he embarked on the most crucial change of his life. She'd moved on to someone new so fast it defied logic.

Two other thoughts filled her head as well.

Could logic ever be successfully defied? What were her chances with Desmond?

Slay curbed his BMW outside of Hot Tails and walked inside like he owned the place. He gave the bouncer a pound and walked straight for the bar. Wendy, the bartender, smiled at him as he approached. She mixed some grenadine and a Sprite and brought it right to him, placing the virgin drink down in front of him on a napkin.

"What's going on, stranger?" she said.

"Ain't nothing," Slay said. He studied her a moment, then nodded at her chest. "I see you went ahead and had it done."

Wendy nodded.

"So why you still mixing drinks?"

"My big debut is coming up in a few days," she said.

"You gonna kill them," Slay told her. "Ain't too many of these chicks pretty about the face and body like you is."

Wendy smiled so deeply it looked as if her jaw muscles might cramp up and leave the expression forever on her face.

"Don't go getting all blushy on me," Slay said. "You know it's true."

"You're the sweetest," Wendy told him.

Slay nodded. "Right, right." He looked around. "Where's my girl at?"

"In the back, you know you can go on back there."

Slay took his drink off the counter, took a sip, moved to the door that led to the back. He stopped before reaching for the doorknob and questioned the bouncer with his head and eyes. It was a gesture of respect more than a query. The bouncer nodded. Slay walked through the door. He walked down the narrow corridor to the door marked Premier Talent and rapped his knuckle twice against the wooden frame.

"*A dios mío!* What!"

Slay smirked, shook his head, opened the door and stuck his head in. "You decent?"

"Come on."

Slay walked in. "Damn, Hah-seen-ta, what you call that getup?"

Jacinta wore a purple G-string with a see-through wrap around her waist, and a glittery brassiere. "My uniform," she said.

Slay closed the door behind him, moved into the room, took a seat on the counter in front of her mirror. "Why you always giving me the ice-grill treatment? I've seen your show, so I know you've got a better personality than that."

Jacinta shook her head. "Nothing personal," she said, "you just remind me of all the wrong turns I've taken in my life."

Slay touched his chest, right above his heart, made a motion like he'd been stabbed. "No, nothing personal about that," he said after his quick performance.

"I'm sorry."

"Yeah."

Jacinta put down the makeup brush she'd been using to deftly add a flourish to her face. "So what brings you here? Jeffries, I assume."

Slay nodded. "I was sorry to hear that things didn't go well between you and him the other night."

"He's a creep," Jacinta said. "He wanted to do things that I just..." She shook as if a chill suddenly brushed through.

"You had to knee him so hard?" Slay asked. "He said you caught him in the balls. He sounded like you drove them shits up into his mouth."

"I tried to," Jacinta said.

"In a situation like that you have to run down the options," Slay offered. "And pick the best one."

Jacinta nodded to the table across the room, the long knife lying on her duffel bag. Slay turned and looked, too. "The kneeing in the nuts was the best option," she said.

Slay turned back around, smiling. "Anyway, I fixed it for him. I hooked him up with somebody else."

"White girl?"

"Yeah," Slay said, smiling. "Jeffries doesn't want to ever hear anything about Spanish, Hispanic, Latina, whatever y'all are, ever again. My man probably gets heartburn *just looking* at a can of Goya beans."

"Good."

"Not for business, but what the heck."

"It couldn't be avoided, Slay. Trust me. That Jeffries is a foul creep."

Slay shook it off. "I wanted to check on you, to be honest."

"I'm living."

"I worry about you, believe it or not. That situation messed my day up," Slay said. "Things were going well up until that call from Jeffries. Took my—took this girl to that new restaurant around the corner—"

Jacinta sat up straight. "Cush?"

"Yeah, that place."

"How was the food? The atmosphere?"

Slay made a face. "Food was okay. I can't get with the atmosphere stuff. My—I mean the girl—she was feeling it."

"I knew he'd have a nice place."

"Who?"

"Desmond, the guy that owns it," Jacinta said. She slid back in her chair, her gaze off someplace else.

"You say it like you know him."

Jacinta smiled, her gaze still adrift.

"You know him?" Slay asked.

Jacinta nodded.

"From where?"

"He's come in here a few times."

Slay sat up. "No shit?"

"Yeah, he's different than all these other pigs that come in, though."

"Is that right?" Slay said. "School me."

Jacinta looked at Slay. "He's a gentleman. He has a good head on his shoulders."

"Umm-hmm."

"He's got passion," Jacinta continued. "Cares about his life and the people he loves."

"He loves that ass, is what he loves. GQ Smooth, I know the type."

Jacinta looked ready to lay a right hand on Slay. "Why are you hating on him? We talked. He's got some issues, for sure, but he's trying to resolve them."

"What issues?"

"His sister, she's a model, she's having some problems. She's staying with him. He told me she was his heart. Isn't that something?"

Slay rubbed his chin. "Right, right."

Jacinta waved him off. "Enough about him, though. So,

what do you need from me, a solemn promise not to knee anybody else in the nuts?"

Slay shook his head. "You've given me more than I deserve," he said. "I don't need any promises from you. Just keep yourself safe." He looked over to her knife on the duffel bag, shook his head. "Hah-seen-ta, if you ever come around to your senses I think we could make a beautiful couple."

Slay entered his mother's apartment, venting out loud. "I never liked the idea of this dude. I knew it."

Nancy was sitting on the couch, dressed in her blue terry-cloth robe, having just taken a bath. The reality of George's death had just started setting in, as well as the depths of her struggle with that demon white rock. She'd taken two baths and a shower since waking up this morning.

"What's going on?" Nancy asked Slay.

He stopped sudden, his thoughts swayed by the sight of his mother, bathed and alert. "Hey, Mama," he said, smiling.

"What you yelling about?"

Slay shook his head. "Wasn't nothing."

"Was something," Nancy pressed.

Slay took a spot on the couch next to his mother. "Cydney done went and got herself mixed up with this dude that owns the new restaurant over on Cookman. I got a few problems with how that dude operates, is all."

Nancy looked down at her hands; hearing about her estranged daughter troubled her.

"Enough about Cydney, though," Slay said, jabbing his mother's side and smiling, "look at you with your shit all niced up."

Nancy didn't respond, her thoughts suddenly back to the different items of value in the apartment and how much they could bring her in crack.

* * *

The sun set off an orange glow that came down like pellets of sleet. In place of the chill that had been the norm lately was an Indian summer breeze that had the bums and degenerates near Cush outside of their cardboard homes, walking up and down the block. One such degenerate, pushing a shopping cart holding an old television and a fish tank piled on it was passing by as Desmond went to enter his restaurant.

"Excuse me, brother," the sloppily dressed lady said. "You happen to have the time?"

Desmond stopped, looked closer—from afar he'd thought it was a man but it was in fact a woman—and turned over his wrist. "Quarter after nine." He looked at the woman again. She was dressed in a flowery housedress and wore an ugly blue coat that wouldn't make the clearance rack at the Salvation Army.

Desmond moved to go by, but the woman with the plum-colored lips and rotting teeth, and a face covered in what looked like a shaky-handed application of mascara, reached into her cart and pulled something out for him to see.

Desmond moved closer to the woman, and took the newspaper that she'd lifted up from the shopping cart from her hands. It was a current edition of *USA TODAY*, stained with coffee and what looked like strawberry donut filling. "What am I looking at?" Desmond asked her.

When she opened her mouth the smell of too much mint Listerine rose up like sewer steam. "You see they caught that DC sniper, two of 'em?"

Desmond nodded.

"Shame it was two brothers," she said offhandedly. "But that's the ways it goes sometimes."

"Yeah, real shame," Desmond agreed. "I was definitely expecting some scrawny white guy wearing a plaid shirt, hiking boots and with a bad haircut."

"Right," the woman said, poking out her finger. "They obviously got turned wrong on the road somewhere." She looked off wistfully. "They poor mothers…"

"Well," Desmond said, handing her the paper back, "it's great that whole ordeal is over." He moved to go back inside but the lady stopped him again.

"I heard this place is something," she said.

Desmond stuck his chest out. "Thanks…I own it."

The woman smiled, nodded. "I thought you was the guy from the picture on the door. I guess you got yourself together. Bet your mother's proud."

"My mother?" Desmond asked. "Yes, she is."

"Got yourself a special lady to share it all with?" the woman inquired.

Desmond smiled. "Something like that. It's still very new."

The woman nodded and her eyes seemed to glow. "You know that Chief Moose caught them snipers," she said. "He's my sister's husband's brother's child."

"You don't say," Desmond said. He began to realize it would take finance to rid himself of this nuisance. He reached in his pocket, pulled out his billfold, handed the woman a crisp twenty. "You must be mighty proud."

"Mighty proud," the woman said. She grabbed the money with her shaky hands. A gold name ring with Nancy emblazoned on it in sprinkles of diamond glimmered against the sun.

"Nice ring," Desmond said.

Nancy smiled her rotten-toothed smile at Desmond. Her eyes lingered on him as if she knew him. She seemed to be taking him in, appraising him. "Gift from my husband—may he rest in peace."

"I'm sorry to hear that," Desmond said.

Nancy nodded. "This ring is one of only three things in this life I hold dear."

"What are the other two things?" Desmond asked, immediately regretting it. He was prolonging this exchange instead of moving it along quickly. Something about the woman was comfortable, familiar.

"My two children," she answered.

"Are they doing well?" Desmond asked.

Nancy smiled, nodded. "Particularly my daughter."

"That's good."

"Take care of yourself…and that lady of yours," Nancy said after a moment, moving on.

Desmond turned and watched her continue pushing that shopping cart up the block. He shook his head. When he looked at that thrown-together woman the thought of her reading the daily news was the last thought that would normally cross his mind. Jacinta's philosophy was becoming clearer with each passing day.

Everyone was a performer on a stage.

Desmond walked through the door of his restaurant with a smile on his face. Karen greeted him without smiling in return.

"Thought you were going to stand out there with that bum lady all day," she said. "She came in here earlier, asking about the owner, I sent her away."

"She was kind of cute," Desmond replied. "Something about her I liked. She comes again, give her some food."

Karen nodded. "Hmm… You just can't help yourself with the ladies. Blind, cripple or crazy."

Desmond moved closer to Karen, lowered his voice. "Is there a problem?"

"None whatsoever," Karen said. "You have a package waiting for you in the back office."

"Package? What is it?"

"Hurry on back and see," Karen said. She shut her appointment book, the pages making a louder thud than the closing of a steel door.

Desmond said hello to the few other employees he passed on his way to his office. He reached his hand inside along the wall and hit the light switch, shut the door behind him. On his desk was a delicate display of flowers in an intricately woven wicker basket. Desmond smiled, pulled his chair out from the desk and sat down by the flowers. He leaned in, sniffed the bouquet of pink and yellow roses, and plucked the envelope with his name written in cursive from the clip nestled in the bunch of flowers.

Inside the envelope was a folded sheet, which he unfolded, then he reclined in his chair to read. Across the top was scribbled, *I'm not sure if this will see the light of day, but thought you'd want to know what I thought. I can't wait to see you tonight.* He looked down farther at the center type. Cydney's review of Cush for the magazine piece was included.

The words were poetry to him.

"...a tantalizing array of down-home-variety food."

"...atmosphere that rivals the most celebrated restaurants in the country."

"...a guaranteed enjoyment."

Desmond folded the paper back and placed it in the envelope. He sat back in his chair, smiling off into space. I've met someone, Daddy, and she's prime.

"What do you suggest?"

Cydney glanced at her watch. She didn't have time for a load of questions. She returned her eyes to the kindly middle-aged black woman before her. She smiled at the woman without showing her teeth. "Perfume is such a personal expression," Cydney told her. "I wouldn't want to suggest anything to you.

Do you like sweet fragrances, flowery fragrances? Do you like your perfumes with a subtle or strong scent?"

The woman looked down the counter, examined the bottles displayed. She took in a breath, held it, her jaw twisted to the side. "I don't know," she said finally. "I'm not much of a shopper, and, actually, this is for someone else."

Cydney sighed. "Okay," she began, looking at all the choices. "Tell me a little something about the person you're purchasing this gift for, maybe that'll help."

The woman smiled, put a finger to her lip and turned her head up in thought. Cydney glanced at her watch again. Soon she'd be with Desmond, and this long draining day would end on a worthwhile note. "She's really pretty," the woman said.

"Anything else?" Cydney asked.

"She's worth a lot of trouble," the woman told her.

Cydney clucked her tongue in her mouth, rolled her eyes. "All righty then. That helps oh so much."

"How about I just give her what you like?" the woman said.

Cydney didn't protest. It seemed like the perfect route out of this situation. "I really like the Vivid, by Liz Claiborne."

"Let me try that."

Cydney reached under the counter, pulled out a sampler bottle. "It's a nice floral scent, I believe with a hint of violet and freesia," Cydney said. "I've liked it for a long time. I need to get around to buying it for myself."

The woman's eyes widened. "Oh, you don't have it?"

Cydney smiled, shook her head.

"Perfect," the woman said.

"Excuse me?"

"I'll take it. Do you have gift-wrapping services?"

"You can take it to the customer service area in the corridor just before the food court. Show them your receipt, they'll take care of wrapping it for you."

The woman clasped her hands together. "Great." She crinkled her forehead. "Do they do the gift ID tags, you know with *to* and *from* on them?"

Cydney nodded.

"Great," the woman said. "I want to have it signed to Miss Wonderful, from Desmond."

Cydney nodded, bagged the perfume bottle. "That's very ni—" She stopped short, looked up. The woman giggled so hard it looked as if she were on one of those gigantic bouncy balls toddlers rode on. Cydney's face dropped into a huge smile; she swept the surrounding area with her gaze. Desmond stepped out from behind a large display, his hand upraised in a gesture of guilt. Cydney looked at the woman, pointed a finger at her. "You were good."

"*You* were good," the woman said. "You kept looking at that watch like the battery died or something, yet never lost your patience with me."

"I rolled my eyes," Cydney confessed to the woman as Desmond walked over.

Desmond placed his hand on the woman's shoulder, leaned down and gave her a kiss on the cheek. The woman closed her eyes, accepted the kiss. She opened her eyes and gave him a hug. "Good luck to you, young man—" and turned to Cydney "—hold on to him, young lady."

Cydney eyed Desmond, delight all over her face. "I'm certainly going to try."

CHAPTER 15

Slay shuffled his cell phone to his right ear and said, "William Jeffries, esquire, how goes things?"

"You have a word with that Ja—whatever her name is?" Jeffries asked. "She has a major attitude problem."

"Again, I apologize for that, Mr. Jeffries. I hope Clarissa took care of you."

"She did."

"Good."

"That other one should be put on a leash, though," Jeffries added. "She's really unprofessional. Has a huge chip on her shoulder."

"I had words with her," Slay assured him.

"I'm looking for no-hassle companionship," Jeffries continued. "I'm not some sleazebag disrespecting women in some half-lit back alley for twenty dollars. I show these women respect, treat them to the finer things in life. I bet she'd never see the likes of the Berkeley Carteret if not for me."

"'Course," Slay said. "Jacinta just forgot how good she had it for a moment. She's fine now."

"Let's hope so. If anything like that happens again I'll start to question your abilities, Mr. Slay. My colleagues have been speaking wonderful things about you and your services. I'd hate to see it all dry up for you because you failed to manage your people properly."

"Like I said, I had a word with her."

"I'd expect as much."

"How did your friend's son like those dogs? The pit bulls," Slay asked.

Jeffries growled. "He loved them. Personally I think the boy has problems. He's all into tattoos, body piercing, who knows what else. I think his father and mother are doing him a major disservice by feeding into everything he asks for. They need to be instilling in him the lessons of good clean family values. I do with mine. You won't see my daughters bopping around with their stomachs bared, their pants sagging down to show off their panties, listening to that big-lipped Jay-Z rapper, wanting to date ni—" Jeffries stopped himself, lowered his voice, which had begun to rise. "I'm off the path, the kid liked the dogs."

"Good. Listen," Slay said. "I called also because I wanted to see if you could do me a solid."

"A solid?"

"A favor."

"I hope you're not going to ask me to do anything illegal," Jeffries said.

" 'Course not."

"What is it, then?"

"I need a bit of information on a guy named Desmond Rucker—"

"Desmond Rucker, I know him. He owns that restaurant, Cush," Jeffries said. "Fabulous place, I've been there with some colleagues of mine."

"Right, right. Anyway, I need you to get some information on him and his sister. I don't know much about either of them other than Desmond owns the restaurant and the sister's name is Felicia…and I believe she's a model."

A guttural growl rose from Jeffries. "A model, you say?"

"So I've been told."

"I'm pretty busy, Mr. Slay."

Slay cleared his throat. "Clarissa went on and on to me about the wonderful time she had with you the other night and how she hoped I could set something else up between the two of you," he said. Slay was the grand marshal of pushing the correct buttons.

"Felicia Rucker you think the sister's name is?"

"Yeah."

"Let me check it out for you," Jeffries said. "I'll get back to you sometime tomorrow."

"Aiight, that works...and I'll give a call to Clarissa."

"That'd be great."

Desmond followed Cydney into the condominium complex. After a turn she stuck her arm out the window, waving Desmond forward. He drove up alongside her and rolled down the passenger window.

"I forgot to tell you we have assigned spots," she said. "I'm in fifty-three. You can park in any of the spots you see without numbers."

"I can't squeeze into fifty-three with you?" Desmond asked, smiling.

Cydney waved her hand at him dismissively, rolled her window back up and moved to her spot. Desmond parked in an open spot close by. Cydney was waiting on the sidewalk as he walked up afterward.

"So this is where Miss Wonderful resides," Desmond said, craning his neck, swiveling his head. "Nice."

"Quiet," Cydney said. "Everyone is to themselves, no one bothers you. Just the way I like it."

Desmond rubbed his hands together. "I can't wait to get inside and check out your place. You find out a lot about a person by the home they keep."

Cydney took his arm in hers and began walking down the

narrow sidewalk toward her building. Desmond was the only man she'd ever brought here. It felt good not worrying about her crazy-ass brother, only thinking about herself, her own hopes and desires. She gripped Desmond's arm tighter. "Don't expect much. It's neat, cozy, but far from spacious or luxurious. It fits my needs, though."

"You don't have things scattered all over the place like I do at my place?"

Cydney frowned. "No, I'm very organized. I hope you're not telling me you're junky."

"No, I'm just joking," Desmond admitted. "If anything, I'm a neat freak."

Cydney seemed relieved. "That's a plus. I mean, I have things set a certain way and I like to keep them like that. The drawers in my kitchen are arranged just so." She put her arms out, to demonstrate her point.

Desmond laughed softly.

"What?" Cydney asked him.

He shook his head.

Cydney stopped in her tracks. "Tell me," she demanded.

"I was just thinking that I'm very much looking forward to looking in your drawers."

Cydney's eyebrows arched. "Listen at you," she said, "loosening that collar, huh?"

Desmond smirked. "Loosening the collar, unfastening the buttons…"

Cydney licked her lips. "Mmm." She started walking again, her step a bit faster. She climbed the stairs and came to the second landing. Her unit was the first one on the left. *"Mi casa,"* she said, her hand outstretched in welcome.

They walked in, Cydney slipped her shoes off at the door, Desmond followed suit. The dining area, kitchen and living room were connected, set off by the luminance of an elaborate chandelier. Desmond nodded toward the chandelier. "Beautiful."

"Thanks. Didn't come with the place," Cydney said. "I put it in myself."

She took their jackets and hung them on the jacket tree in the far corner of the living room. Desmond walked over to her bookshelf and stereo entertainment unit. He fingered the books on the shelf. "I see you enjoy Margaret Johnson-Hodge, Cydney."

"Curling up with one of her novels is like taking a Caribbean cruise on the cheap. Log on to Amazon.com and input your credit card info, twenty dollars or whatever, and in a week it's smooth sailing. She's so vivid and such a good storyteller, it's like you're vacationing with the characters on the page. She's one of the few I'll splurge on at hardcover prices. Eric Jerome Dickey is another. My mother was a big reader." Cydney moved closer to Desmond, by his shoulder. "You like to read?"

Desmond shook his head. "I did at one point, but life doesn't afford me the opportunity to sit in one place long enough to finish a book." He picked up a brightly colored, yellow and green novel, flipped it over and read the back flap.

"Timothy McCann," Cydney told him. "Another of my favorites. You want to know about romancing a woman, making her toes curl, her back arch and her heart do flips—" she dipped her chin, nodded toward the book "—read that scene in the beginning of chapter thirteen."

Desmond opened the book, flipped through the pages, looking for chapter thirteen. When he came upon it he read for a moment and then turned to Cydney. "Damn, I have got to start reading again." He looked down at the book once more, scanned the page quickly, his fingers marking the lines as he read. He nodded his head, closed the book and sat it on the lip of the shelf without placing it back in its spot. A mischievous smile crossed his face as he rubbed his hands together, and his eyes drank Cydney up from hairdo to pedicure. Cydney swallowed his admiring stare like some rich Starbucks blend. He pulled her to him, wrapped his arms around her and kissed her gently on the lips. "What do you say we reenact that scene?"

The phone ringer echoed through the condo.

Cydney was going to let it ring and have voice mail pick up the call. "You better get that, it could be someone important," Desmond said.

"Someone important is here with me," she answered back.

"Don't keep me waiting long then." He turned and went to look through her music collection.

Cydney hustled to the kitchen and grabbed the phone off the island. "Hello, this better be good."

"What, I'm cutting into one of your Lifetime movies or something?"

Cydney lowered her voice, cupped the phone with her hands. "Slay?"

"I'm honored. You didn't forget the sound of my voice."

"What do you want?"

"Hello there, brother, how's life treating you, is Mama still among the living?" Slay said in a mocking tone.

"Is our mother okay?" Cydney asked.

"She's living," Slay told her.

"And you?"

"Same."

"Wonderful," Cydney said. "Now, I have to go." She hung up and walked back toward Desmond in the living room. He was bent over looking through the CDs in her stand. "Go ahead and borrow anything you like," Cydney said. "Lord knows you can use some new music."

"I don't see Eddie Murphy here anywhere," Desmond joked. He turned back to her and put his arms around her waist again. "Now, where were we?"

"You were just suggesting we reenact the scene from—"

The phone rang again. Cydney took in a deep breath. "I better get that," she said. "I promise I'll be quick."

Desmond rubbed her cheek. "Do your thing, Miss Wonderful. The night is still in Pampers."

Cydney stomped across the carpet to the phone. "Yes?"

"Hanging up on me like that is some eighth-grade bullshit," Slay said.

Cydney took the phone, moved into the kitchen, sat down on the floor with her back against a cabinet. "I don't want or need to have a conversation with you right now."

"I agreed to stay away," Slay said. "You mean, I can't call and see how you're doing from time to time?"

"I'm doing well. Okay. Can I go now?"

"So what's up with you and Mr. GQ Smooth, y'all still trying to kick it?"

"I'm concentrating on school, work and surviving," Cydney said. She sighed. "Relationships will come later."

"That's good because ol' boy ain't what he—"

"Hey, Cydney," Desmond called out. He was at the threshold of the kitchen. His eyes narrowed a bit when he saw her on the ground whispering into the phone. "Oh, I'm sorry... I lost you for a moment. Where's your bathroom?"

Cydney frowned, pointed down the hall. Desmond observed her for a moment, crouched on the floor, phone pressed against her thigh. He tightened his jaw and nodded, turned from her and went to the bathroom.

Cydney closed her eyes and mouthed a quiet "damn" as she watched Desmond disappear from view. She picked the phone back up. "Slay?"

Slay clucked his tongue. "You lied to me, Cydney, that's not nice. You got company. That wouldn't be GQ Smooth, would it?"

"Yes," Cydney admitted, "I have company."

"You shouldn't have lied," Slay said.

"Listen. Hello. Hello…" She dropped the phone in disgust and then picked it back up and turned off the ringer. Now Slay had hung up on her. She rose to her feet and placed the phone back on the charger stand. Desmond came out of the bathroom as she made sure her dead bolts were locked tight on the front door.

"We won't be getting any more interruptions," she told Desmond.

"What, you turn off the ringer?" he said, the tenderness gone from his tone.

"I'm sorry," Cydney said.

He waved her off. "Forget about it."

"It was rude," she said.

"You're entitled to your phone calls. To your friends, whether they're male or female."

"I know what you're thinking and it's not that," Cydney said.

Desmond's eyes crested. "Oh? I was thinking that was one of your girlfriends calling to check on you. So it was one of your boyfriends then, I take it?"

Cydney moved to him, ran her fingers up his stiff arms. "I have fallen so quickly for you it amazes me," she said. "I have some issues in my life that don't affect you—that I won't allow to affect you. I promise you, though, that I'm an absolutely faithful and committed partner. And I expect that anyone I date seriously is faithful and committed to me in return. I'm hoping that we end up dating seriously, Desmond. I truly do."

Desmond took her hands, interlocked his fingers with hers. "I was tripping," he said. "It's just that I don't want to have to share you with anyone else. I want you all to myself."

"Is that your way of saying that you want to date me seriously?"

"Absolutely," he told her in his sexiest voice.

"You want a committed faithful relationship?"

"Absolutely."

"You want to sweep me off my feet like he did the woman in that book?"

"Absolutely."

"Did you notice my bedroom when you went to the bathroom?"

"I peeked in."

She took his hand, walking him in that direction.

"Are you taking me to show me inside your drawers?" Desmond asked her.

Cydney licked her lips. "Absolutely."

Slay slammed the flip of his cell phone closed and tossed it on the small kitchen table. He pulled on the arm of the refrigerator, the door slamming against the chipped cabinetry behind it. He snatched out the carton of orange juice. Turned the almost empty carton up to his mouth and finished off the last drops, collapsed the box, crumpled it in his fists and tossed it at the garbage can. His hands were balled in a fist as he looked around the place for something to hit. He moved to leave the kitchen and looked through to the living room. Kenya and the kids were on the carpet around the television watching BET's *Comicview*. She had one arm on each of her boys and was giggling just as loudly as them with each joke the comedian on the screen told. Slay stood there for a moment watching Kenya and the boys.

After a while, Slay walked into the living room and stood just behind them. Kenya looked up at Slay standing in place and tapped an empty spot on the floor behind her for him to sit. He sat down with his legs in a V; Kenya filled the gap between his legs and leaned back against his chest. The boys scooted forward, moved closer to the television.

"You gonna check on Ms. Nancy anymore tonight?" Kenya asked Slay.

He scrunched his face. "I should, but I ain't up to seeing her like that again until tomorrow. My brain is got too much going on now."

"You tell me what to do," Kenya said. "I can go check in on her."

"You'd do that for me?"

"Hell, yeah," she said. "You kidding me?"

"You too good to me, girl."

"You're going through a lot," she offered. "Someone has to be good to you. You've always been good to me."

"I just thought about something," Slay said.

"What's that?"

"When I was in juvie you was the only one that wrote."

"I figured you were lonely there, it won't nothing."

Slay rubbed on her shoulders, an act she was usually performing on him. "Was too something. I looked forward to those letters."

"You did?" Kenya said, her voice rising. "You never wrote me back."

Slay sighed. "Yeah, I know..."

"It was a lot," Kenya said. "You've always had a lot on you."

Slay stopped rubbing her shoulders, leaned his head forward and rested it in the nape of her neck and wrapped his arms around her waist. "What we gonna do when Boom gets out?" It was the first time he'd ever said anything of that sort, the first time he acknowledged that what he'd borrowed would have to be returned. He didn't seem ready to let go. He could feel Kenya's posture slump.

"We worry 'bout that when it happens," she said.

Cydney looked at Desmond carefully. "You know if we do this the stakes rise?"

"Yes."

"Are you prepared—are you ready to deal with a relation-ship? Because that's what this will be."

Desmond wanted to be ready, so he nodded to the affirmative.

"I'm expecting a monogamous situation," Cydney continued.

"And I likewise," Desmond added. "The only thing I want boss man touching of yours is your paycheck to sign his name."

"Don't be silly."

"I'm being serious, Cydney. Believe me."

Cydney unlatched the hook of her bra, her plump breasts spilled out. Desmond's eyes registered approval. She pulled down her panties and stepped from them. Desmond instinctively looked down; her pubic area was shaved clean. "I'm usually sensitive about being seen naked," Cydney informed Desmond.

"You shouldn't be," he said without looking up into her eyes.

Cydney stepped back and fell into the give of her mattress. "Come make love to me, Desmond."

Desmond moved toward her with anticipation.

Cydney put up her hand, stopping his forward progress. "No other women or situations I need to be concerned about?" she asked for the final time as he reached arm's length of her.

"None," Desmond said, shaking his head.

Cydney pointed her tender hand of fingers at her shaved pubis. "Take this. It's all yours, Desmond."

Desmond bent to his knees and nuzzled Cydney's pleasure point. He cut her in half with his tongue, made her back arch as he lapped at her juices. Her fingers pressed into his shoulders and his hands gripped her waist. She pushed away as he pulled her in. To Desmond, Cydney tasted like his favorite delicacy in the world, cooked apples and cinnamon.

He moved his hands from her waist to her buttocks, gripping the rounded flesh and bringing her closer, closer. She squirmed in his grip. He varied the pressure of his tongue, moved the location, attempting to find that correct spot. That one spot that every woman had but few men were ever able to find, and fewer still were willing to expend their energy searching for. Cydney started drifting across the mattress, to the left. Desmond chased her mercilessly, that wet hot tongue of his refusing to release its shackle on her.

She grabbed ahold of the canopy bar of her bed. The soft purring she'd been doing was replaced by a moan that rose from deep in her chest. Desmond pulled her closer, closer, and the moan grew louder. He increased the speed and pressure of his mouth on her and the moan grew louder still. He tightened his grip on her firm ass—the moan turned again, now a staccato hiccup sound that made him stiffen with joy.

Cydney screamed. Her body slackened.

Desmond wiped his mouth with the back of his hand and climbed on the bed beside her. He pulled her to him and ran his strong fingers up and down her back, kneading her tightened muscles with the care of a surgeon. She went to speak and he covered her lips with one finger and moved to kiss the underside of her neck, then her shoulders, then her breasts. She shivered as he touched some of her spots, and gently pushed against him as he touched others. Desmond made note of the spots that made Cydney shiver and kept returning to them.

After a while, Cydney gripped Desmond's butt and worked his boxers down an inch or two. The bunch of the material rubbing against his penis made Desmond harden even more. He felt as if he might explode if he didn't get inside Cydney soon.

Cydney reached her hands inside Desmond's lowered boxers and grabbed his wood. She massaged him until he seemed uncomfortable and then she opened her legs and directed him toward her. He scooted closer. She lowered the boxers farther, and he finished off, pushing them to his feet and then kicking them off. She rolled a condom on him and he carefully entered her folds.

Desmond struggled with the rhythm at first and so she took his waist and guided him. The feeling of explosion didn't lessen for him; in fact, with each stroke it worsened. He pumped at her with desperation. As he pumped faster and harder, Cydney's hiccup of a moan returned, "Aw...aw...aw," and prodded him on. That warm heat started to rise from inside his thighs, that hot lava about to bubble to the top.

"Oh," he said, biting into his lip to keep from saying more.

Cydney grabbed at his buttocks, made him push deeper.

"Oh," he said again.

She pulled him deeper still.

"Mmmmm," he growled.

She wrapped her arms around his neck and kissed his chest, let him coast on home.

"Oh...damn."

Cydney could feel the cannonlike blast in her torso, then the slump of Desmond's body against her belly. He moved to turn over so he wouldn't crush her but she craved his weight, the feel of him, so she wouldn't let him go. He settled into her, his chest heaving as her warm breath tickled his scalp.

"That was intense," he said after a few minutes.

"No," Cydney corrected. "That was lovemaking."

The tone on Slay's cell phone startled him awake. He glanced at the digital clock on Kenya's dresser—6:12 a.m. He started to ask Kenya to get the phone for him, but he could smell what he thought might be pancakes and sausage, and could hear Kenya off in the distance, singing in the kitchen. He fumbled to grab his phone and opened the flip.

"Wussup?"

"Mr. Slay?"

Slay yawned, sat up in bed and stretched. "Mr. Jeffries, you up and at 'em mighty early."

"My day begins early and ends late, Mr. Slay. But anyway, I have that information you requested."

"Shoot."

"Can I ask why you need to know about Rucker and his sister?"

"No."

Jeffries hesitated but wisely went on. "Desmond and Felicia are from Lower Merion, Pennsylvania. It's a suburb of Philadelphia. Their parents, Frank and Barbara, owned a chain of restaurants that they sold last year. I think the tally was eleven—in Pennsylvania and Ohio. Desmond graduated from Penn State, toiled for a few years in corporate America. A clean-cut guy."

"Give me more, Jeffries, I need more."

Slay's tone alarmed Jeffries, and so he dug deeper. "He's twenty-eight, no criminal record or anything like that. The local media and the township government loves him…loves what he's trying to do for Asbury Park."

Slay ran his hand over his eyes. "That's it?"

Jeffries's voice cracked. "I'm not sure what you're looking for."

"I want to know what his weaknesses are."

Jeffries was silent for a bit. "Women," he said after a while, "like a lot of us."

"Oh?"

"He has a bit of a reputation as a womanizer."

" 'Kay?"

"He was engaged to a young woman, Nora, but he broke off the marriage."

"This dude is married?"

"No, he broke it off."

"He still tapping this Nora?"

"Tapping?"

"Come on, Jeffries…knocking that, fucking her?" The

pretense Slay usually reserved for Jeffries, when they were doing business, was absent today.

"Oh?" Jeffries responded. "I couldn't say. I don't believe so."

Slay sighed. His runaway imagination placed Cydney heart-broken instead of the Nora woman. He couldn't allow Mr. GQ Smooth to exact that kind of humiliation on Cydney, and yet, in his heart he figured that's exactly where their relationship was headed. Cydney was so quick to fall in love, so reckless when it came to matters of the heart. GQ Smooth would eat her alive. "Where does Desmond live, you get that?" Slay asked.

"I do have that with me," Jeffries said. "Hold on one second, I'm driving." He fumbled through some papers then came back on line. "His address is 5454 Ocean Boulevard. Over in Deal."

"Holeup." Slay reached over to the nightstand and took up one of Kenya's *Jet* magazines and a pen. Kenya would kill him for writing over Morris Chestnut's face, but oh well. "Aiight, tell me again."

"It's 5454 Ocean Boulevard. Right along that stretch you take when you leave Asbury Park, past the lake. All those fine houses."

"Right, right," Slay said. He put the magazine and pen down beside him. "So Desmond likes pussy. What else?"

"What do you mean?"

"I need something else, Jeffries. I could have told you the dude liked pussy. What about the sister, what you get on her?"

"Now, *she's* interesting," Jeffries said. "She's a definite nonconformist."

"A non-what?"

"A rebel. Whatever is expected of her—she does the exact opposite."

"Really?"

"And she and Desmond are very close."

"Right, right."

Jeffries cleared his throat. "If I might offer, Mr. Slay. If I had a problem with Desmond Rucker—" he paused "—I'd go for the sister."

Slay smiled. "Would you now?"

"Yes."

"Appreciate the info."

"You're quite welcome," Jeffries said. He paused again, hung on line a moment before adding, "My lovely wife is going to be out of state all of next week for a medical conference."

"Gabriel Cohen wants the Berkeley for the week, I take it?"

Jeffries panted. "That would be lovely."

"Clarissa would like that. I suppose you want her the entire time?"

"You read minds, Mr. Slay."

"Yours ain't too hard to read," Slay said, laughing. "Clarissa. You got it, and again, good looking on the hookup."

"What's that?"

"Thanks for the information."

"Oh. Not a problem. I guess that's it, then?"

"For you, yes," Slay said. "For me, the fun is just about to begin."

NANCY

"Byron Bodeen?" I say to the police officer outside my door.

I pretend the officer asked me about a James Muhler or some other name I truly had never heard of before. I pretend he hadn't asked me about Byron Bodeen, who unfortunately I know of all too well. I stand with the door propped open, George next to me. I'm squeezing George's hand to let him know that he never heard the name Byron Bodeen either.

"Yes, that's right, Mrs. Williams," the Asbury Park police officer answers. "He claims to be involved with your daughter. Says your son was the one stabbed him."

"This is all so..." I feign not having the words to finish. Next to me, George's jaw muscles tense and now he squeezes my hand harder than I'd been squeezing his.

"I'd like to have a word with your son, Mrs. Williams," the officer continues. "Would he happen to be in?"

"No," I say. I'm thankful this is the truth, so I can stop with the pretending. Been doing too much pretending lately, it sickens me.

"Would you know where I could find him, Mrs. Williams?" the officer asks.

I'm back to pretending much quicker than I'd hoped. "No," I assure him, shaking my head to double up the point.

George clears his throat. "Could I have a word with you?" he says to the officer.

George breaks free from my grip before I can squeeze the

*blood out of his fingertips, before I can damn near break his
knuckles and mangle his fingers. I look at him but he ignores
my eyes and steps down the hall with the officer. I come out
into the corridor and watch the two men speaking in hushed
tones by the elevator. The officer nods solemnly after a moment
and touches George on the shoulder. He then presses the
elevator for down and a short moment later disappears inside,
the door closing him in. George turns, stops when he catches
my piercing eyes, then steps toward me with his head held
high. I know he's punishing me for the bit of a problem I've
been having since that night I stayed at Darlene's, but this is
oh so wrong.*

*"What did you tell him?" I ask as George brushes past me
and heads inside.*

*"The truth," he says as I follow on his heels. I slam the door
shut behind us and take a couple of hard steps in his direction.*

"Why?" I demand.

*George shrugs. He goes and ruins my life and the best he
can do is shrug. Now I'm really mad. He eyes me. I can tell
he's appraising me, down about ten pounds these last few
months, spending more time than anyone ever needed to spend
at the grocery store, though the cupboards and the refrigerator don't seem to carry any more food than normal. The super-
market is my cover, you see, when I go hunting for salvation
in those little rocks.*

"Stop looking at me like that," I snap.

*"Can't," he says, shaking his head. That one word and how
he said it almost make me forget the betrayal with the police
officer, almost make me take him in my arms and beg him to
place his hand under my arm and carry me to joy. Almost.*

*Sweat beads dribble down my forehead like big clear
marbles rolling across a maple-wood tabletop. "Why,
George?" I repeat.*

"That boy needs help," George tells me. "He's headed for an early grave."

My nostrils flare. "And who are you? You're not his father. You never did give him a chance, never tried to guide him. You always treated him and Cydney different." I want to place some of the guilt George has been placing on me back onto his shoulders, see how he deals with it. Who ever heard of adopting one of a woman's children and not the other? That'd mess up any child.

"I did give him plenty of chances," George disagrees.

Not the answer I was looking for. "Like I said, who are you?" I ask him. My voice is thick and I can barely see through my squinted eyes.

George sits on the couch, away from my wild eyes. "I don't know who I am anymore, Nan. But I'm starting to think maybe God put me here to save all of you. And that's what I'm gonna do, if it kills me."

CHAPTER 16

Desmond stepped from Cydney's bathroom fully dressed and groomed for work. Cydney was in the kitchen, still in her robe, her back to him. Desmond tiptoed to her and wrapped his arms around her waist. She inhaled in surprise and then settled back into the warmth of his embrace. He kissed her neck and then rested his chin on her shoulder. "What you doing?" he asked in a child's drone.

"Fixing you a little something," she said.

"What you fixing?" he asked. Still talking like a curious little boy.

"Toaster strudels, I hope you like apple."

"I love apples," he said.

"Apple juice, too?"

He nibbled on her ear. "Mmm-hmm."

She closed her eyes; let her head cock back as he ran his fingers through her hair and kissed the spot behind her ears. Her ears had always been a ticklish point, an area she didn't like men to touch, but Desmond's lips there now didn't make her giggle or move away. It took her breath away. Desmond turned her toward him and reached inside the flaps of her robe, cupping her breasts in his hands. He could feel himself stiffening and he pressed her close to him so she could feel what he felt.

She opened her eyes. "Whoa, we better chill or you'll never get to work and I'll never get my chores finished before class tonight."

"You have to give me a rain check, then," he said.

"You got it."

He shook his head. "Uh-uh, I want it in writing."

Cydney pursed her lips and ran her hands up the curve of Desmond's biceps. She batted her eyes at him and ran one of her fingers over her lips. She then took that finger and drew an R on his chest, then an A, then an I—

"Rain check," she said, plucking her luscious lips and staring at Desmond with a sexy smirk as she finished spelling it out on his chest.

"I was thinking of a simple note on a scrap of paper," he said. "But I'll definitely take that."

"I figured you would." A bell dinged and his strudels popped up from the heat of the toaster. She turned and pulled the pastries and dropped them onto a paper plate, blowing on her fingers afterward to cool the heat.

"You didn't burn yourself on my account, I hope," Desmond said.

She shook her head and poured him a long glass of apple juice. She sat the quick breakfast on the small kitchen table, pulled a chair across from his and sat down herself.

"This is a real treat having someone cook me breakfast," Desmond told Cydney.

She studied him like the morning newspaper as he took bites of his food, sips of his juice.

"What?" he asked.

"You have nice lips."

"Smacking lips," he said.

"You eat nice," she replied.

"You think?" He licked his lips, put a finger in his mouth and sucked on it.

"See, now you had to go and be nasty," she chided.

"You bring it out of me." He took his last bites, swallowed

the last drops of apple juice and pushed back from the table. "That was great, now I have to get going."

She rose and came around the table to meet him. "I'll call you as soon as I get in from class tonight, okay?"

"You better." He leaned down and took her in a hug, running his fingers through her hair again. "I can't tell you how much I enjoyed last evening."

"I don't want you to tell me anyway," she said. "Show me. Actions speak louder than words."

He nodded, kissed her forehead. "I'll be counting the minutes to tonight."

"Me too."

He held her hand as he took a step back and took one last look at her. "Okay, I'll see you."

She walked him to the door, where he gave her one more knee-shaking kiss. She bolted the locks behind him and went to the bathroom to take a shower.

"Yes?"

Slay was thrown for a loop by Felicia Rucker when she answered the doorbell. Her skin was bronze colored, her facial features carved in deep angles, her legs longer than his drive over here.

Slay had an associate of his, Ryan, who worked for the local telecommunications company, look up Desmond's telephone number from the address and call the house earlier, pretending to be a telemarketer. To his surprise, instead of Desmond, Felicia answered the phone. She immediately shot down the pitch of Slay's friend but she seemed to want to talk to the guy anyway. She went on and on about staying with her brother for a little while, how unexciting it was for her out in the middle of nowhere. Her flirting voice oozed through the phone lines like blood through veins.

Nonconformist.

Slay had slowed and passed by the house once, making sure there wasn't a car in the driveway and then came up and parked his BMW in the circular driveway, the music turned low, the car running, his driver-side door ajar. It had all been part of his ruse to make this seem to be a random visit. He'd made sure his right pant leg was rolled down, that his Timberland bootlaces were tied, that he had on his good watch. He'd run through his little routine a thousand times on the way over, but now, seeing Felicia up close, the script was lost. She was that stunning.

Felicia smiled as Slay took her in like a Blockbuster movie rental. She grabbed the zipper of her outfit. "Zipper-front jumpsuit," she said, "in an eye-catching, patchwork mix of indigo blue denim and white cotton twill." She ran her slender fingers down her stomach to her waist. "Plus a wide hipster belt—all by House of Field." Slay still hadn't spoken a word. Felicia pointed one of those luscious fingers at his chest. "Okay, your turn," she said. "I see the sweater's Enyce. What're the jeans, Ecko?"

"Excuse me?" Slay finally managed to say.

"You were looking me over so damn hard I figured you wanted a rundown of what I'm wearing," Felicia said.

Slay smiled. "I apologize. You caught me off guard. I wasn't expecting a Nubian queen, such as you, to answer the door—" he turned and looked over his shoulder "—out here."

Felicia had her hands on her hips. "Well, isn't today your lucky day."

Slay smiled again. "It just might be."

Felicia looked past his shoulder. "Nice car...how many keys did you have to move to get that?"

Slay turned and looked at his vehicle as if he'd never seen it before. He turned back to Felicia, his eyebrows furrowed. "Say what?"

"I listen to rap," she informed him. "I know about moving keys—kilos of cocaine. I know about holding heat, popping collars—all that stuff. I know a drug dealer's car when I see one." She narrowed her eyes. "A drug dealer, too, when I see one…"

"That's a dis," Slay said.

"Oh, I'm wrong. Don't tell me." She left the one hand on her hip and the other she dramatically tapped against her chin. "You got in on the dot-com boom and made a killing. You're like the ghetto Bill Gates or something."

Slay pointed a finger at her. "You got a sharp tongue, shorty."

Felicia smiled. "Shorty? See, I knew it would come out of you eventually. That's rap vernacular 101."

Slay shook his head, damn, this chick was about to make him nut his jeans. She had sass.

"I'm fooling," Felicia said. "I don't mean to give you such a hard time. I'm bored as hell out here in Vanillaville." She batted her eyes. "What can I do for you, cutie?"

Showtime, Slay thought.

"Actually, you were right in a way. I do some work with a rap group out of Asbury Park," he said. "And they got me out scouting locations to possibly shoot a video. I was passing by your place and it caught my eye." Slay had seen a scene like this in a movie once, but if Felicia asked him anything whatsoever about the specifics of "scouting locations" he'd be up shit creek. The point was to get himself into her presence and then, once there, move past this rap-video scouting nonsense and never return to it again.

"You'd have to talk to my brother on that," Felicia said.

Slay looked over her shoulder into the house. "Is he in?"

"He's working," she said.

Slay made a point of having his face drop in a display of disappointment.

"Don't do that," Felicia said. "That puppy-dog thing gets me every time."

She's a nonconformist.

Would a nonconformist go out with a complete stranger who showed up at their doorstep?

Slay looked up, smiling. "Enough to convince you to come with me for a ride, maybe get some lunch or something?"

"I don't know you from a can of paint."

Slay extended his hand. "Shammond Slay." Felicia took his hand and he pulled her hand to his lips and kissed it. She pulled it from him and rubbed where he kissed as if it were sore.

"You're a player, I can tell," she said.

"Far from it," Slay said. "If anything, you are. What's your name, player?"

"Felicia Rucker."

"Felicia. That's definitely a player's name."

"What about Shammond? And Slay as a last name?"

Slay shrugged.

"Got kids?" Felicia asked.

Slay shook his head. "Not me. What about you?"

"I'm asking the questions."

Slay raised both his hands, made a play of taking a step back. Felicia smiled. He moved forward again, this time closer to her. "By the way, you're wearing that indigo-blue denim and white… What did you call it?"

"White cotton twill."

"Yeah, that. They must have designed it specifically for you. You're looking like a model and shit."

Felicia smiled. "Actually, I am a model." Her heart was racing. "Thanks."

"I thought you might be. Who've you done work with?" Slay asked.

"Still getting my feet wet," Felicia admitted, embarrassed.

Slay narrowed his eyes. "You wet…now, that's an image I like."

Felicia blushed.

"You have to pardon me," Slay said, "but I've also got this image in my head of me kissing those beautiful lips of yours."

"Maybe by the time we finish lunch," Felicia said.

Slay's eyebrows arched, a smile crossed his face. "You're down, then?"

"I probably shouldn't," Felicia said. "After all, you could be some dangerous psycho, but something about potentially dangerous psychos excites me. Give me a minute, I'll be right out."

Nonconformist, for sure.

"Don't keep me waiting too long," Slay said.

"I won't," Felicia said. "I'm just going to write my brother a note and grab my Mace and a steak knife." She looked Slay up and down. "Just in case."

Slay smiled, turned and walked back to the BMW.

Slay turned down his Nas CD for the fifth time. Felicia immediately turned it up to the highest level for the sixth time. Frustrated with the tug-of-war, Slay hit the power button on his stereo. "I can listen to Nas anytime, can we talk?"

Felicia frowned. "Whatever."

"So how old are you?"

"Nineteen in a couple weeks," she said. "You?"

"Twenty-five."

"So how did you come upon such an expensive car at such an early age? And don't give me that BS about working with a rap group."

Slay looked at her. "That wasn't BS, you thought that was BS?"

Felicia held her stare.

"I broker things," Slay admitted, wondering why he was opening himself up to this girl like this. "Them suit-and-tie types that want certain things but don't know how to go about getting it. I hook them up, for a fee, of course."

"Illegal things?"

"Sometimes," Slay said honestly. "Things their, what's the word—colleagues—would be surprised to see them wanting. Things they can't shop for online or at their little strip malls."

"This pays well, I take it," Felicia said, tapping his dashboard.

"Sometimes," Slay said.

"Particularly when it's illegal items, right?"

Slay simply smiled.

"So why did you come by my brother's place? I know it wasn't to scout for any rap video."

Slay had to think quickly. "I did some business with a gentleman—I'll call him a gentleman—up that way about a month ago. Let's just say he owes me some money. I messed up, though. I'm not sure which one of those houses he lives in."

"They do all look similar," Felicia agreed.

Slay took a deep breath; he'd moved through that smooth enough.

"So where do you stay?" Felicia asked.

Slay was telling her a bit too much but he couldn't seem to bite his tongue with this girl. "My mama's place, here and there, wherever."

"I get the feeling you like it like that," Felicia said. "That you've had opportunities to settle somewhere but prefer to keep it moving."

Slay thought about his sweet Kenya and her boys for the first time this day. "You probably right."

"So where we headed?"

"I know a shorty like you is probably used to the finer things in life, fancy-ass restaurants and whatnot," Slay said, "but I want to hook you up with something different, something that you'll straight up get addicted to."

"Ooh, are we going to smoke weed?" Felicia said, bouncing around all giddy.

"Italian hot dogs," Slay said.

Felicia stopped bouncing. "That's cool, too, I guess." She burst out laughing. "You must think I'm crazy."

"Thought has crossed my mind."

"Don't pay attention to the stuff I say. It's mostly for shock value. I started doing it a few years ago to throw off my parents and upset my perfect brother."

"Perfect brother?"

"Desmond," Felicia said, crinkling her nose. "He went to college, got good grades, served his time on Wall Street, yadayadaya. Now he owns a restaurant. I love him, though." A smile of remembrance darted across Felicia's face. "You should have been a fly on the wall when I informed my parents and my brother I was going to model."

"Bet they was tripping."

"Oh, hell yeah. My father was like, 'What kind of model?', and I made a big play out of it. Told him *Playboy.*"

"Your pops didn't like that, did he?"

Felicia shook her head. "It was a riot. Once they found out I was going to be represented by a legitimate agency, doing tasteful-type modeling, they actually started to be a bit proud, just a little bit, but enough to piss me off."

"You like modeling?"

Felicia nodded. "I've been into fashion for as long as I can remember. It is hard work. You have to deal with creepy photographers, long shoots, being picked and touched over."

"So what does this brother of yours think about it?"

"Desmond? He's cool."

"That's good."

"He's been questioning me about whether I'm still chaste, though," Felicia said.

"Chaste?"

She looked down at her crotch. "Whether anybody has run up in this."

Slay smiled. "Has anyone?"

"Not yet, but my prospects are increasing."

"Oh, yeah?"

Felicia nodded. "Yeah."

"Your Mr. Perfect brother won't like that."

"This is my pussy."

Slay shook his head. "You've got a gutter mouth."

"I bet I can make you like my gutter mouth."

Slay nodded. "I bet you could."

Felicia stopped. She was taking this too far. Kenneth's words had her all twisted up. Maybe using her obvious sexual appeal wasn't all that bad. The agency representatives hadn't thought too much of Felicia's concerns when she met with them. She didn't know what to believe anymore. She did know, though, that this Thug Lover sitting next to her stirred something inside of her. The realization was both scary and exciting. Felicia looked out the window. "When are we getting to this place? I'm starving."

"Soon. It's over in Red Bank."

"What's an Italian hot dog, by the way?"

Slay closed his eyes for a brief moment. "It's a long beef dog on a bun, with French fries—the round ones—red sauce, onions and peppers. This place in Red Bank, Mr. Pizza Slice, makes the best ones."

"Damn, sounds good," Felicia said. "I'm glad I lowered my zipper before I opened the door."

"You did what?"

"I looked out the door and saw you standing there," she said, "and I liked what I saw, so I lowered my top zipper a tad to show off my boobs. I think it worked."

Slay looked over at her, licked his lips. "Right, right."

* * *

Paperwork sat in a pile on Desmond's desk but he decided to leave it for later, take a walk outside and see how things were progressing with the lunch crowd. Truth of the matter was, he never took too much to the business aspects of this entrepreneur thing; he liked mingling with the people, liked joking with his staff. The day-to-day nuts and bolts operational matters, that was his father's cup of tea.

Desmond opened his office door, shut off the light as he exited, a sure sign he wouldn't be coming back in for a while, and headed out to the dining area. Karen was making heavy-footed strides toward him, a couple menus pressed against her chest, a young couple following behind her, her eyes on Desmond as if he'd harmed someone close to her, someone she loved. Desmond stopped so she could make her way by with the young couple. He smiled as the patrons crossed his path. Karen quickly seated them and came back toward Desmond. He stood waiting for her.

"What now?" Desmond asked.

"Another of your groupies, table eight," Karen said as she swept by like a breeze.

"Who?" Desmond asked Karen, but she kept on trucking up the aisle, back toward her post at the front of the restaurant.

Desmond shrugged and walked over to the area of the restaurant where table eight was. From a distance Desmond could see an attractive woman looking over a menu. She wore tinted shades and had on a fitted gray turtleneck sweater. Desmond moved closer. The woman saw him coming and put down the menu, a smile on her face. As Desmond drew nearer he recognized the form of her nipples pressed against the material of her sweater, the deep richness of her dark skin, the full lips of her mouth. There was a slight hitch in his step but he kept moving toward her. She looked so different from how he usually saw her, so different than she did under the lights at Hot Tails. Desmond reached her table and stood there.

"Well, hello, Mr. Rucker," Jacinta said to him.

"Jacinta," he said, nodding, keeping his smile a thought.

Jacinta curved her mouth upward. "Mona, actually, but you can keep calling me Jacinta, if you want to," she said. "I know old habits die hard."

"Come again?"

She smiled at Desmond. "My given name is Mona. Jacinta's my stage name."

Desmond nodded and let a return smile slip loose. "Life's a stage, right?"

"You're such a quick study."

Desmond pulled out a seat and sat with her. "So what brings you in?"

Jacinta looked around her, looked down at the menu. "You're asking what brought me into a restaurant? I would think that's obvious—I was hungry."

Desmond smirked.

"Are you uncomfortable because of your girlfriend over there?" Jacinta said, nodding her head toward the front of the restaurant.

Desmond followed her nod, his gaze falling at the podium up front. "Karen? She's not my girlfriend. She's my hostess, my right arm."

"She's got the girlfriend attitude to her," Jacinta said. "She was pleasant until I asked if you were in."

"She's a bit protective of me," Desmond said.

Jacinta drew her mouth to one side. "Hmm, I wonder what happened to make her think she needed to be your protector."

"So, how do you like the place?" Desmond said, redirecting the conversation.

"All I've had so far are these honey and butter-topped rolls,"

Jacinta said, "and they are unbelievable. I imagine everything else will be good as well." She looked around, nodding her head repeatedly, her lips tight, impressed. "The way it's designed is nice, too. I think you've definitely got something here."

"Thanks," Desmond said. "Strangely, your opinion matters."

"Why *strangely?*" Jacinta asked. "Because I'm just a go-go slut?"

"No, God no," Desmond said, "I wasn't implying—"

Jacinta raised her hand. "It's okay, really. Men only seem to fully appreciate me when I'm in a G-string, I'm used to it."

"That's not right," Desmond said.

"Not right," Jacinta said, "but a fact."

"I'm a little deeper than that," Desmond told her.

"That why you looked like you swallowed a horse tablet when you saw me sitting here?" Jacinta asked.

"I was surprised to see you. That's all."

Before he knew what he was doing, Desmond reached over and covered her hand with his own. "Believe me, I'm glad you came. Glad to get to see you like this. You look just as I pictured you would offstage." What was he saying? Worse yet, what in the world was he doing? What about Cydney? Just last evening he and Cydney had taken their relationship to the next level. That next level left no room for even harmless flirting with the likes of Jacinta.

Jacinta studied him for a moment, shook her head. "Never know what to expect from you, Desmond."

Desmond smiled despite himself. He ignored his father's voice, ringing in his ears. *That's right, son, show your true colors.* "Expect the unexpected."

Slay pulled his BMW into Desmond's circular driveway. Felicia bopped her head to the low music coming through his state-of-the-art speakers. Slay put the transmission in Park and sat watching her as she mouthed the words to the song with her eyes closed. He liked her, liked her a lot, but the fact remained that she was on the wrong side of the line, she was on the enemy's side, he had to stay mindful of that.

Felicia opened her eyes, saw Slay just staring at her, so she stopped singing. "What?"

"You be wildin'," he said.

"Do I be?" she said, then went right back to singing her song, wiggling, leaning in and making a real play of this.

Slay sat there as her cleavage waved in front of him, as her scent kept passing by his nose.

"Oh," she said as the song finished, "Heather Headley is the shit." She eased back in her seat, let out a deep breath and folded her hands in her lap. "So, are you coming in?"

Slay shook his head. "I better not."

"Why? You have erectile dysfunction or something?"

He crinkled his brow. "Say what?"

Felicia waved him off. "Nothing."

"So you got my number, you gonna call, right?" Slay asked.

"If I stay around here much longer, yeah," Felicia said. "I'm going haywire out here in the boonies."

"I'd really like you to get down with this weekend's party," Slay pushed.

Felicia nodded. "Berkeley Carteret, yeah, yeah, I got it."

"It's gonna be off the hook."

"I hope I'll get more than an Italian hot dog and—" she looked down at the bunch of his jeans, the swell by his zipper "—a tease."

Slay followed her gaze. "You truly ain't ready for this yet."

Felicia licked her lips. "Oh, I truly am."

Slay smiled. "Stick around to the weekend then. I got something for that ass."

Felicia leaned over, went to kiss his cheek but ended up

licking his earlobe. "We'll see," she said as she opened the door and moved from the car.

"Berkeley Carteret, Saturday," he yelled to her. She walked toward the house, throwing all kinds of twists in her step. Slay fingered his chin, smiling. "Yeah, boy, I got something for that ass, Felicia *Rucker.*"

Desmond walked with Jacinta from her table. He stopped at the front of the restaurant.

"I'll be back shortly," he told Karen.

"That's on you," Karen said. She shot Jacinta an ice-melting stare. Jacinta smiled and looked away.

"Come on," Desmond said to Jacinta. "Let me see you out."
They moved through the door to the nip outside. Jacinta hunched her shoulders together and Desmond placed an arm around her as she moved toward her bright red sports car.

"This is you?" he asked.

"Yeah, you like?"

Desmond nodded.

"I keep it clean, too."

"I bet you do."

Jacinta walked around to the driver-side door, cracked it and stood. "Well…"

"It was good of you to come," Desmond said. He wrung his hands, looked over toward the restaurant to see if anyone was looking out. He could imagine Karen away from her podium, her face pressed to the glass in the walk-in lobby.

"So," Jacinta said, "you were right about that apple brown betty. I can't believe I managed to finish it on my own. I'm stuffed. I need to go work this all off now."

"You work out?"

Jacinta smiled slyly. "I like to keep my heart pumping any way I can—work that cardiovascular."

"Ha." A peek of Desmond's tongue crept from between his lips.

"You must work out, too," Jacinta said and she reached for his biceps. "You're pretty hard."

"Am I?"

Jacinta's eyes widened, she covered her mouth in embarrassment. "I didn't mean it like that."

Desmond smiled. "So where to now, work?"

Jacinta looked at her watch. "I've got a little over an hour before I head in."

Desmond tapped her car. "You want to go for a ride?"

Jacinta nodded her head toward Cush. "Don't you have to get back inside? I imagine Glenn Close in there is probably boiling rabbit in the kitchen by now."

Desmond laughed. "It's going to be a long day for me," he told Jacinta. "I can use some time away."

Jacinta pulled her keys from her side pocket, tapped the low hood of her car. "Hop in then."

Desmond moved around the back of the car to the other side, glanced once more at his restaurant and hopped in. He knew it was a mistake.

Cydney dialed the numbers and sat waiting. After a few rings the voice mail greeting came on.

Hi, you've reached the voice mail of Desmond Rucker. I'm unable to answer your call right now, but leave a message and I'll get back to you as soon as possible.

Cydney sighed and waited for the beep. "Hey, Desmond, this is Cydney. Just wanted to let you know I'm thinking about you and I can't wait to talk with you after class tonight. Okay, lo...bye." She hung her cordless back on the charger stand. Damn, she thought, did she almost say that she loved him? Slow down, girl.

CHAPTER 17

Jacinta let up off the gas and let the car slow to a near stop as she passed by the Shuhara Life Church holistic healing retreat. The church consisted of a shingled house with a large sign hanging from the living-room window that proclaimed: Spiritual Ointment for Cracked and Damaged Souls. On the three-step walkup were two potted plants that took up most of the stairway. The top step had a folded beach chair that leaned against the house. On the front door there was a lighted ornament of two hands clasped together in prayer.

"That's me," Jacinta said to Desmond. "Cracked and damaged soul."

Desmond turned his head and studied the building as they passed. He turned back, facing Jacinta. "You got a booboo, baby?"

Jacinta's eyes were on the road but you could have passed a hand across them and she wouldn't have blinked. A vision of her onstage, swiveling her hips, danced through her head. She considered her other work at the Berkeley Carteret; the sweaty men with receding hairlines and hairy bellies. Men who checked in to the Berkeley using an alias.

She thought about herself, down on her knees, crawling across thick, lush hotel carpet wearing a thong and a fake-diamond neck choker. The sound of heavy panting filling the room, the rhythmic slapping of flesh, stuttered phrases like, "Oh, brown sugar, brown sugar. Keep moving like that, brown sugar." That pervert, Jeffries, masturbating to her moves and then wanting Jacinta to lick the life milk off his thighs.

"Are you zoning out on me?" Desmond asked.

Jacinta forced a smile but didn't give him her eyes. "Thinking."

"Care to share with the rest of the class?"

Jacinta continued to drive in her trance. "Tell me about your girlfriend, Desmond. The woman that had you all shook up the other day."

"What?"

"Is she pretty? Smart? What does she do?" Jacinta tapped her hand on the steering wheel, softly at first, then increasingly harder. "I bet she's in the financial industry—a broker, an accountant, something classy." Jacinta nodded, conversing with herself, not even waiting for a reply from Desmond. "She has got to be a classy woman. I bet she's all into the Donna Karan and Liz Claiborne suits. Ooh, and designer eyeglasses—carries a briefcase..." Jacinta made a wild turn around a corner, all gas and no brakes. The front end of her sports car veered into the other lane. Desmond sat up in his seat but said nothing. "What college did she go to?" Jacinta continued. "Ivy league or private I bet."

Jacinta took her right hand off the gearshift and held to the steering wheel with both hands. The transmission made a jarring sound as her speed and the gear she drove in didn't quite fit each other. Her eyes flooded with tears. Desmond reached over and downshifted as she steered and braked. She brought the car to a stop and plopped her head down on the steering column. The horn wailed but she didn't seem to notice. Desmond took her by the shoulders and eased her back into her seat.

"What's going on?" he asked as she wiped away the tears with her fingers.

"I'm sorry."

"That still doesn't answer my question."

"Just wishing I was in a different place," she said. She took a breath, leaned her head back with her eyes closed and then took a second breath. "I went to college, Desmond, did you know that?"

"I figured as much," Desmond said. "You're very intelligent. What happened?"

Jacinta laughed. "That's always the next question. What happened? How did a fairly intelligent woman like you end up as a whore?"

"I didn't say that," Desmond interjected.

Jacinta looked over to him, her eyes reddened, the runny mascara painted in a ghoulish-looking circle around her eyes. "Sure you did." She swallowed, turned off the engine. "I didn't graduate for one. I stopped a few semesters short."

"You can always go back."

Jacinta laughed and shook her head. "Not me."

"So what got you dancing?"

Jacinta shrugged. "A girl in one of my classes did it, was open and proud of it. She turned me out. And I found that I'm good at it. The money made it a no-brainer for me."

Desmond pinched his lips. "Oh."

"Disappointed are you," Jacinta said. "You were hoping I had some tale of woe, that some abusive boyfriend pushed me, I had a terrible childhood, something like that. I didn't."

"Why are you crying then, Jacinta?"

"Because I'm still a victim of my circumstances, Desmond," she said, emphasizing each word.

"Which are?"

"I love sex. I love the power my body and my movements have over men. On the other hand, I feel demeaned, cheated by my natural impulses. I wish I was the kind of woman that deserved a man like you. I wish I were normal. It would be so much easier if I were a man with these desires…"

Desmond nodded. "Men do get off easy."

Jacinta turned to Desmond. "God, how I wish I deserved a man like you. I think I would stop dancing and make you a bunch of little babies, attend to your every need."

Desmond crinkled his nose. "Deserved? Don't you think you're shortchanging yourself? You're making me out as some kind of saint. I come into Hot Tails to watch you when I should be tending to my business, or working to build on this relationship with my woman. I'm no different than any of the other men that come in to watch you. You're a special woman, don't shortchange that. And, by the way, I think you've got a lot more to offer than making somebody's babies and attending to their every need."

Jacinta wiped away her tears and leaned in closer to Desmond. "I'm done analyzing myself for the day. Can you do something for me?"

"Anything," Desmond said.

Jacinta touched his arm. "The thing about you, Desmond, that struck me right away was that I could see a certain appreciation in your eyes when you came to the club. Fear, too. You enjoy women, you enjoy sex. I gathered something about you, as if you thought it would be easier to enjoy us from afar. You're fighting demons."

Desmond's mouth dropped open. "How could you gather that?"

Jacinta smiled. "I have the same fight, but like I said, it's different when a woman has a large sexual appetite. I'm never going to own my own business and walk through society with my head held high."

"And why not, Jacinta?" Desmond wondered. "You're beautiful, intelligent—"

"A slut," she said.

"Stop it."

Jacinta reached for Desmond's hands. "It doesn't matter. I just want you to do one thing for me."

"Anything," he said for the second time.

"I know this is crazy but I want you to have sex me, Desmond, right here, just this once. I promise I won't cause you any problems with your girlfriend. I just want to feel you inside of me. We're two of a kind, you know."

Desmond frowned. "After all you just said, now you want to sex me, Jacinta? This is screwed up."

"Please, Desmond," she cooed. "I need this. I know it's screwed up. I'm screwed up, but I need you so much right now." She pulled her sweater up above her breasts so they'd be on display. "Please! Don't you want some of my stuff?"

Desmond's jaws tightened and he could feel himself hardening with erotic desire. The street was devoid of people, a ghost town. Jacinta reached down and grabbed a hold of that manly part of Desmond through his pants, a twinkle forming in her eye as she examined his girth. "Sure you want this. This is the evidence."

"I have a lady. I'm trying to build something special with her."

"I'm not looking to tear down that house," Jacinta said. "Just looking to rent it for a brief moment."

"This isn't right."

"Our little secret," Jacinta assured him.

Desmond hung his head and closed his eyes.

Jacinta worked open his zipper.

Slay paused at the sight of his mother's apartment door cracked halfway open. He looked both ways up the hallway before inching forward. He never carried a weapon, knowing he'd never use one if he did carry it. He made a couple of baby steps and pushed in on the door. The darkness of the apartment met him. His mother's radio was playing as usual. He stepped inside and looked around for something to grab. The closest thing at hand was a single broken-heeled shoe. He picked it up and walked toward his mother's bedroom. He paused for a moment and then kicked in the door.

"Waaaaa," a voice yelled out in surprise.

Slay dropped the hand he held the shoe with to his side. "Kenya, damn, you almost got yourself hurt, girl. I thought somebody broke in, the front door is open."

Kenya touched her chest, looked to the shoe in Slay's hand. "Them Payless shoes is hard as hell but I don't think it would have done much if I was in here boosting."

Slay smiled, dropped the shoe on the floor. "You got jokes." He moved over to the bed where Kenya was wiping his mother down with a bath cloth. His mother was covered in sweat, rocking back and forth, her eyes concentrated on the ceiling. "How she doing?" Slay asked Kenya.

"Look, see there," Nancy said, grabbing Kenya strongly by the wrist. "Them buggers are huge, huge, huge, huge..."

Kenya shook her head. "I don't see anything, Ms. Nancy."

"What's going on, Mama?" Slay said.

Nancy looked toward the sound of his voice, recognizing him for the first time. "This stupid-ass girl of yours don't care that my place is getting overrun by roaches. I keep telling her to kill 'em, kill 'em, kill 'em, kill 'em!" She jumped up suddenly and grabbed a magazine off the nightstand. "Bunk it, I'll kill 'em myself."

Slay moved quickly to her side, took the magazine from her hand, sat her down. Nancy shot back up just as quickly. He sat her down again and she took a swing at him that he dodged.

"She's suffering," Kenya told him.

"I thought she was pulling herself up. She started taking

better care of herself lately." Slay put his arm on Kenya's shoulder, looking down on his mother who'd commenced to rocking again, her eyes still trained on the ceiling as an angry scowl darted across her face.

Kenya turned to him, leaned in, sniffed. "Where you been?"

"Had to handle some business with a couple dudes from around the way," Slay lied.

"Them dudes must be some real faggots," Kenya said, " 'cause that's some strong perfume I smell on you."

"I hope you ain't getting jealous on me, Kenya."

Kenya turned away, shook her head.

"Good," Slay said. "Because I ain't yours and you ain't mine."

Kenya nodded.

Slay clasped his hands together. "Finish washing her if you would and we can go ahead and get her somewhere." He shook his head. "I didn't want to have to do this. Have them looking at my mother like she's a junkie."

"She is, though, Slay."

He shook his head. "I know she is," he said softly. "We'll take her to the hospital and act like we don't know what's wrong with her..." His voice trailed off. He shook his head.

Kenya moved closer to his mother and resumed wiping the sleep and mucus from around her eyes and mouth. Slay watched Kenya dabbing at his mother with a nurse's care. His stomach churned because with each passing day it was becoming more and more painful to realize this was what his mother had become...and Kenya wasn't his.

"Those buggers are huge, huge, huge, huge," Nancy called out.

Jacinta curbed her car just outside Cush and let the engine idle. "Back to the lab," she said.

Desmond looked away from her, to his restaurant. He was paralyzed by what they'd done. The new depths he'd sunk to.

In a few hours Cydney would be calling him and he'd be up on his stage, performing, pretending that everything was business as usual.

"Don't beat yourself up," Jacinta said. "I forced your hand."

Desmond put his hand on the door handle and let it rest there.

"I wish you and your girlfriend the best," Jacinta said.

Desmond opened his door and exited without a word. He shut the door and the sports car immediately pulled from the curb and moved up the street in a whir. He walked slowly to Cush and moved inside with strength he didn't know he possessed. Karen looked up, her eyes like his mother's that day when he told her he was calling off the wedding to Nora. Desmond looked away and moved past Karen. She didn't attempt to stop him. He walked into his office and closed the door behind him. He felt his way to his desk, pulled out the chair and sat down at his desk in the dark. He could hear the voice of his father, sucking his teeth, shaking his head, the word *failure* on Frank Rucker's breath like a mint. He could see Cydney's eyes through the darkness, refusing to look away from him, refusing to let him off the hook. Nora was next to Cydney, whispering in her ear, telling her all about the exploits of Desmond Rucker.

"What is wrong with me?" he wondered out loud as the tears began to fall from his eyes.

"Yoohoo."

Cydney turned to the voice behind her as Professor Greenwood scribbled his almost indecipherable script on the blackboard. Victoria was all smiles. Faith had her head down, trying to suppress a giggle.

"What?" Cydney asked through clenched teeth, one eye on her friends and the other eye on Professor Greenwood.

Victoria handed Cydney a sheet of paper and then made a

quick gesture for Cydney to turn around. Cydney took the paper and turned just as Greenwood began to address the class again.

Greenwood was fond of wearing turtleneck sweaters and dress jackets. Tonight he had on a black shirt with a gray jacket. His hair was brownish-gray and cut close, his skin was tanned, pock-marked, and clung so close to his skull he looked ghoulish. He wore a pair of glasses that always hung on a chain around his neck, yet no one had ever actually seen them covering his eyes. His voice was three-packs-of-Viceroys-a-day scratchy and he used it to intimidate and humiliate his students at every opportunity.

Greenwood took a hold of his glasses as if he was about to place them on his face, then stopped to speak, with them in his hand. "I'd like you geniuses to read over what I've written on the chalkboard and then jot it down in your notes. I have to make a quick run to the lavatory. When I get back I'll hand out last week's exams and then we'll go over this new material. Can you geniuses handle that?" No one answered him. He shook his head and rushed from the room.

Cydney looked down at the paper Victoria had handed her. She could hear her friends giggling again from behind her. The paper was a crude note with two boxes in the margins and a sentence next to each box. At the top was the instruction *Check the one that applies*. Cydney looked to the first box. It said: *I got my freaky deaky on with you know who since I last spoke to you beautiful divas*. The second box said: *I plan on getting my freaky deaky on but haven't yet. You beautiful divas will be the first to know, the moment I do*. Cydney smiled and shook her head. She was about to ball the paper up when she noticed a line at the bottom of the page, written in smaller handwriting. It said: *If you ball this up without checking a box you ought to be ashamed of yourself with your fast ass*. Cydney's mouth dropped open. She turned and faced Faith and Victoria. The both of them turned away and hummed at the same time.

"Simple asses," Cydney said to them. She turned back to the chalkboard and started writing down Greenwood's notes as he returned to the room.

"Sorry for that interruption," Greenwood said, walking into the room and talking at the same time, "but the majority of you will be thankful for the delay when you receive your scores. I don't know whether to blame your parents, your high schools or your capacity for learning. This is a university course, ladies and gentlemen. I'll expect college-level work in the future."

Cydney's stomach muscles tightened. She glanced back at Faith and Victoria again; the playful energy had left both of them as well. Faith's and Victoria's shoulders slumped in the same manner as Cydney's did.

Greenwood pulled a pile of papers from his briefcase and tapped them on his desk into one neat stack. He started moving through the maze of desks. When he reached Cydney's desk it seemed as if he took a pause. He dropped her test, faceup, in front of her. She looked down at the exam.

C-

She'd hoped for a B at the least.

Felicia scooted across the linoleum floor in Desmond's kitchen. Her sock-covered feet allowed for a nice slide to the kitchen countertop. She grabbed the counter edge like a woman on ice skates, to stop herself and regain balance. She glanced at the caller ID as the phone continued to ring. A smile darted across her lips. She cupped a hand over her mouth and picked up.

"Rucker's Massage Parlor and Ecstasy Lounge…we massage shit," she said into the receiver. "Felicia speaking."

"Felicia?"

She let her voice rise and put a little crack in for good measure. "Oh my goodness, is that you, Daddy?"

"What was that you said when you answered?"

"No—nothing, just a little side business Desmond has going until things pick up at Cush," she said, her tone serious.

"I hope this is just part of your twisted sense of humor," Mr. Rucker said.

Felicia laughed. "You think I'm twisted, huh?"

"Among other things," Mr. Rucker admitted. "I didn't know you were visiting Desmond."

Felicia walked with the cordless to the sink area and jumped up on the counter for a seat. She looked out the window at Desmond's bare backyard. Desmond needed a pool and a nice flower garden arrangement when the weather warmed again, she thought. She closed the thin curtain and returned her thoughts to the call at hand. "Yeah, I ran down to spend a few days with Desmond. Things are good, though, Daddy. How are you and how's Mommy?"

"I'm fine. Your mother is off doing some of her charity work," Mr. Rucker said. "I figured I'd call and leave Desmond a message to call us. We haven't spoken in some time."

"That was nice of you," Felicia said.

"I left one on your machine in New York, too."

Felicia switched ears with the phone. Had she heard correctly? "You called me, too?"

"Yes," Mr. Rucker said. "I left you a message earlier."

"Man, that's…" Felicia didn't know how to respond. "That's nice."

"You sound surprised," Mr. Rucker said.

"I am."

"Why is that?"

"Let's not get into this, Daddy."

"I think we should. My youngest child acts all surprised because I called to check on her, something isn't right about that."

"I know I don't exactly measure up to your standards," Felicia conceded. "I know I disappoint you."

"You go out of your way to try and disappoint me, Felicia, but you don't."

"I'm not Desmond, bending over backward trying to get one word of approval from you. You thrive off that little dance you make Desmond do."

"That's how you see me?"

"I told you we didn't need to get into this. Your voice is changing, you're getting upset."

"I want to know how my children see me, I'm a big boy, I can take it. Go on."

"I've watched how desperate Desmond has always been to get your approval," Felicia said. "I've watched how broken he's been when he gave his best and still didn't get a nice word from you. I decided early on that I wouldn't even try."

Mr. Rucker was quiet on the line.

"I know you love us," Felicia continued, "but it's hard being your child."

"It was hard being my father's child," he replied. "The job of a parent is to push their child to be the best they can be."

"I couldn't have come up with a better word if I tried— pushed."

"It saddens me that you don't know my true intentions are always to help you reach your great potential," Mr. Rucker stated.

"Let me ask you one question," Felicia said.

"Go ahead and ask it."

"I always wondered what you said to Desmond the day he called it off with Nora. I saw you talking to him by the stairs and I'll never forget the look on his face."

Mr. Rucker cleared his voice, said nothing.

"Daddy?" Felicia prodded.

"I told him it takes a real man to hoist a real woman on his shoulders and not have them both fall down."

"And what did he say?"

Mr. Rucker hesitated. "He asked me if I thought he was that real man."

"And you said?"

"I told him the God's honest truth, Felicia."

"Which was?"

"Nora better have herself some strong bones, because he was sure to drop her."

Cydney walked in her door, dropped her backpack on the floor, slid out of her shoes and tossed her jacket on the arm of the couch. She moved to the kitchen and hung her keys on the key hook, opened the refrigerator and pulled out a carton of orange juice. There wasn't much juice in the container so she made an exception and turned it up to her lips, gulping down the drops inside, frowning the entire time as the taste of the juice was spoiled by the taste of carton. She took out her little billfold that held her license and one credit card and placed it on the counter next to her purse and the wallet she normally carried. Later, she would put everything back in her purse. Tomorrow was a workday and she'd have to carry her purse instead of a backpack.

She went into the bedroom and changed into her silk pajama bottoms, removed her bra and put on a simple white T-shirt. She noticed her nipples pressing through the material and went and turned up the heat.

She went into the bathroom and wiped away her touch of eye shadow and lipstick, brushed her teeth, gargled, sat on the toilet and squeezed out a drop. She rinsed her hands thoroughly and went back out to the living room and glanced at the clock on her digital cable box. Okay, she'd been home for thirteen minutes. That was time enough. She could call Desmond without feeling like some excited schoolgirl dealing with her first crush.

She grabbed the phone and settled in on the couch, her fingers tripping over each other as she dialed Desmond's number.

"Desmond Rucker."

"Guess who?" she said, her voice high.

"Cydney," he said. "Hey."

There was no sound in the background, as if he were inside a vacuum. "Are you still at work?"

"On the road driving home," he said.

"It's awful quiet. What, no Eddie Murphy playing?" She was hoping to hear the smile in his voice.

"Not tonight."

"How was work today?"

"Good."

She waited for him to say more but the line sat silent. "I didn't do as well on that exam from last week as I'd hoped," she offered as a conversation starter.

"You passed, though?"

"Yes, I passed—barely."

"That's all that counts."

"I don't like just squeaking by."

"Hmm."

"You're not too talkative tonight," Cydney said. "You sure everything went okay at work today?"

"Yes, Cydney, I'm sure."

Usually the sound of him saying her name sent a shiver down her spine. This time, however, it made her want to end the conversation. "You want me to give you a call, or you can call me, when you get home?"

"Whatever you want," he said.

"I want you to come spend the night with me," Cydney said.

"I'm halfway home."

"I didn't expect you to cartwheel or skate here, Desmond. You are in a car. It wouldn't take you long. I want to hold you, make love to you and give you a backrub."

"Okay," he said halfheartedly.

"You don't have to."

Desmond sighed. "I'm on my way."

He didn't give her a chance to respond. Cold silence hit her ear. Cydney dropped the phone on the sofa cushion and hugged a pillow.

Something wasn't right.

A short while later Cydney got up to answer the door. Desmond stepped in without giving her a hug. He took off his shoes and dropped them in a pile by the door. She frowned but kept silent.

"I need to use the bathroom real quick," he said to her.

Cydney stood in the doorway with the door still propped open. She nodded her head. Desmond walked down the hall and went in the bathroom, shutting the door loudly behind him. Cydney closed the front door, latched the lock and took a seat on the sofa. She sat there thinking and then picked a magazine off the coffee table when she heard the toilet flushing, the bathroom door click open and Desmond's footsteps. He came over and kissed her forehead, took a seat in the chair next to the couch. Cydney didn't look up but she saw his hand reach for a magazine. She closed the magazine she'd been pretending to read and tossed it back on the coffee table.

"What's the deal, Desmond?"

He looked up. "What do you mean?"

"Something is wrong. You're in a real crabby mood. You're here but it's like you're avoiding me."

Desmond smiled, closed his magazine, tossed it on the coffee table just as Cydney had done. "I lied to you. This business is kicking my ass right now. You feel neglected, baby?"

The tension left Cydney's shoulders. She'd thought Desmond's bad mood was probably related to work stress. "Yes, I suppose I do feel neglected, but that's okay."

"No, it isn't, baby." Desmond moved closer to Cydney, bent to his knee and took her hands from where they were crossed on her lap. He wrapped Cydney's arms around his neck, lay his head on her warm lap. "I'm sorry," he said. "I had a long day and I'm tired and I'm taking it out on you."

Cydney rubbed his head. "You could have told me so and went on home."

Desmond smiled. "I tried, but you were sounding like Elvira the vampire, like you were ready to draw blood if I didn't get over here."

"Everybody is a comedian today."

Desmond leaned up. "Who else tickled my baby's funny bone?"

"Victoria and Faith," Cydney said, "trying to get all up in my business."

Desmond dropped his head again. "Oh, okay. I thought it might be some smooth operator trying to put moves on my baby."

"Do I detect a bit of jealousy?" Cydney asked.

"Let's just say I've been thinking all day about how good you are, how lucky I am. I appreciate you, Cydney." Desmond meant it, too. He'd actually vomited when he got back from the ride with Jacinta, after he had time to consider his terrible betrayal of Cydney. He was determined more than ever to get himself flying straight.

"You are so sweet. I think it's your tiredness talking."

Desmond shook his head. "I'm being real. But I am tired."

"I guess," Cydney said as she continued to rub his head, "that you're too tired for some loving then."

Desmond raised his head up. "Are you making me an offer?"

"I might be."

"Make it firm and I'll accept."

"Ooh, firm," Cydney said, biting the tip of a nail. "Isn't firm your department, though?"

"You are too good at this, Cydney."

Cydney smiled, pushed against his shoulders so he'd ease up. "Come on then and let Miss Wonderful make you forget all about your day. That's what couples do, you know...they give each other strength."

Desmond stood and Cydney took him by the wrist toward her bedroom. If she only knew how badly he wanted to forget about this day. If she only knew how badly he needed her to give him strength.

CHAPTER 18

A thin film of sweat covered Cydney's naked back. She was on her side, the ridges of her ribs, the profile of her flat stomach and the lay of her heavy breasts illuminated by the snake-armed lamp on her nightstand. Her eyes were closed and her chest rose in peaceful waves. A wheeze like a slow air leak from a tire passed through the small crack of her lips. She had her legs pulled up and a pillow lodged between her knees. When Desmond eased his arm from around her waist she made a face, twisted her head, but then fell back into a deep sleep. Desmond's heart stopped for that moment when it appeared she would awaken. He paused and then moved from the bed with a grimace on his face. He stood over the bedside watching her for a moment before putting on his boxers and tiptoeing to the living room.

He regained his normal step as he entered the living room, went to the Venetian blinds that led to the patio and peeked through the slats to outside. The black sky was dotted with stars and a swollen moon, the street lamps cast a bright light down on all the parked vehicles. Even in darkness there could be light. He turned from the window and looked around the living room. He went to sit on Cydney's couch, plopping down hard against the cool leather. His skin clamored to the material.

He looked up at the ceiling, noting for the first time that she'd had it done in popcorn texture. She had a nice place, a nice disposition, a good head on her shoulders, ambitions, smarts. Not to mention the kind of beauty that made you stop and take notice. What more was there? What more did he need? He dropped his head into his hands and kneaded his temples. He didn't have a headache, but his head felt as if it might explode. He jumped up before his thoughts pushed him further and threatened to make him break down in tears. If Cydney caught him crying on her couch after what happened between them in the bedroom, he knew he'd be in for it. A smile and a shrug wouldn't move her from tossing a round of questions his way like a firing squad.

He moved over to the entertainment system and crouched to look over her selection of movies.

"There you are," Cydney's voice called to him a moment later.

He turned as the overhead light from the chandelier came on.

Cydney ran her fingers over her eyes, yawned and stretched. "Why did you leave me like that?"

Desmond stood up with a video in his hand, the case pressed against a muscular thigh. "I couldn't sleep with you calling those hogs," he said, attempting clumsily to lighten the mood. "Three of them called back and said they got your messages, loud and clear."

Cydney smiled. "Don't even try it. I don't snore." She moved closer to him and took his hand, examined the video.

"*Boomerang,*" Desmond said, "is one of my favorite movies."

Cydney looked up at him. "There you go with the Eddie Murphy again. Do you have something you need to get off your chest, Desmond? I'm starting to think things."

"What do you mean?" he asked, on edge.

"You got a closet fetish for him or something? Do I have to worry about you sneaking from the bed in the middle of the night to watch *48 Hours?*"

Desmond smiled, the tightness left his shoulders. "Ha, ha… Nah, I just like the movie." He started to feel a bit more like his usual self. "It's bugged though, because they made it seem like Eddie getting with Halle Berry was settling, as if Robin Givens was the greater prize. That's some shit."

"That was the pre-Oscar Halle, don't forget," Cydney reasoned.

"The Oscar didn't change how she looks."

"Poetic license, I guess, then," Cydney said.

Cydney turned to move but Desmond caught her shoulder and pulled her in. He held up the back of her hair and kissed the nape of her neck. Grabbed her by the waist and brought her buttocks in contact with the rock beneath his boxers. Cupped her breasts. Unfortunately, the rock shriveled, as it had done during their previous failed attempts in the bedroom.

Cydney shook from his grip. "See, now I'm starting to get self-conscious. Every time I come near it, it deflates."

"I don't know what's going on with me," Desmond said. His voice sounded as if it were straining against a torrent of wind and losing the battle.

Cydney faced him. "Have you ever had this happen before?"

Desmond avoided her eyes. "Never."

"Don't let it get you upset. I'm a determined sistah, we'll keep trying. You're just tired from your long stressful day."

"Yeah," Desmond offered. "It was a tough day."

"Well, you just remember that I'm here for you."

Desmond rubbed her head. "I'll do my best to remember."

Cydney looked into his eyes, his drifting eyes, and she knew that something wasn't right between them. Relationships were supposed to uplift, to bring you joy. Early in this relationship all she had experienced was a roller-coaster ride. It was as if Desmond were a critically ill loved one in the hospital; she didn't know what to expect from him from one day to the next. Shoot, from one hour to the next. She continued to look into his wandering eyes and he continued to stare across the room, oblivious to her glare. She pulled from him and moved to go to the bathroom.

"Where you going, babe?" he asked.

"Quick shower," she said.

"You want some company?"

She had hoped he'd ask.

But then she saw the light fade in his eyes, an understanding take hold of him. He looked scared and confused. "You know what," he said. "I think I'll just chill."

Cydney shrugged and turned to go shower alone. She heard the give of the couch behind her, Desmond's weight hitting it with a thud. "I'm going to check out *SportsCenter*," he said. She heard him pick up the remote and move through a few channels, then stop. "Hey, Cydney?"

She was at the bend leading to the hallway, which then led to the bathroom. She stopped and turned to him, hopeful he'd changed his mind and was going to join her for that hot shower after all. "Yes?"

"I think I'm going to just go, pop my head in at my house and make sure my sister hasn't wrecked the place. What's on the agenda for you today?"

She glanced at the clock; it was just after four in the morning. "I've got a paper I have to work on," she said, her voice a raspy whisper. "A kick-ass assignment if there ever was one."

He got up off the couch and moved toward her. "Let me get a hug then before I head out."

She raised her arms in formality as he crossed the carpet in her direction. They met at the bend and hugged.

"Good luck with your paper, Cydney."

Damn, why did he have to call her name? She could always tell his emotions by how he said it. This time there was no warmth in his tone. "Thanks," she said anyhow. She turned and went straight to the bathroom. She caught a glimpse of herself in the mirror as she moved past. Even with the quick glimpse she could tell that she lacked the glow that a woman headed for love was supposed to have.

In the shower stall, she mediated the hot and cold water and settled under the spray stream of her showerhead and let the water run down her face. That way she could pretend she wasn't crying.

Desmond was still on Cydney's mind hours later but she was determined to chase him away from her thoughts. She arranged the pillows on her bed into a neat pile and fluffed them until they were just right. She needed that soft dip in the middle that she could fall into, that dip that allowed the outer edge of pillow to wrap around her like the comforting arms of a lover, or a parent, or a sibling. More than the silken sheets, more than the sweet scent from her baskets of dried flowers, more than her bed itself, the pillows were what made her bedroom a safe haven, a place to fall back until you couldn't convince her life wasn't all honey.

She went into the kitchen and grabbed the plate of hot brownies and the flute glass filled with sparkling apple cider. She placed them on the nightstand next to her bed. Next, she went into the living room and dug through her collection of CDs. She settled on the one with Maxwell's soulful reworking of Kate Bush's "This Woman's Work." She grabbed her laptop case and took that and the CD back into the bedroom. She set the computer case down next to the bed and removed the CD from the jewel case and put it in her CD player. She adjusted the volume so it wouldn't drown out her thoughts as she worked. The music would serve as something to hum to as she periodically broke her thoughts from the paper she had to write for class.

She stood on the floor and surveyed everything: music playing softly, brownies, cider, pillows fluffed and arranged just right. She snapped her fingers and went to get her Bic SureStart to light the scented candle on the dresser. All of this preparation was foreplay that she hoped would lead to a smooth enjoyable ride once she opened her Microsoft Word file to start work on her paper. She needed this paper to be the home run Professor Greenwood didn't expect. She got the Bic and lit the candle. She was ready.

She opened her laptop case and pulled out the computer, plugged one cord in the electrical outlet to reserve her battery, placed another into the phone jack in case she decided to dial up to the Internet. She brushed a film of dust off the keyboard with her hand and eased into the bed, placing the laptop, aptly, on her lap. She fell back into her pillows as the computer started up. She paused at the icon screen before she went ahead and clicked on the AOL logo to go on the Internet. She wouldn't stay on for long; just long enough to check her e-mail and make sure her bank account was balanced.

Cydney didn't have any e-mail, but there in her buddy box— the grouping of online friends who she chatted with over the Net—was the name Rbanstyles. The screen name of one of the ghosts from Cydney's past. Stephon. Villa Moore had called and told her he was home, recovering, doing well, even in the midst of saving his marriage. They'd decided, Villa and Cydney, it was best if Cydney kept that relationship in the past, didn't try to contact him, let him heal.

But now Cydney glanced at her computer monitor, at Rbanstyles just sitting there, calling out for her.

Did Stephon know how much he'd meant to her?

Was he really happy?

Did he know the guilt that Cydney had carried with her since his...accident?

Cydney scrolled her mouse to send him a quick message. She'd keep it cryptic, nonemotive.

DreamGurl: Hey. Glad you made it through.

There was a long pause. Cydney sighed. She couldn't blame him for ignoring her.

Rbanstyles: Hey.

Cydney smiled, the slouch left her shoulders.

DreamGurl: You're not mad at me, I hope?

Rbanstyles: Should I be?

DreamGurl: You could be. I wasn't very supportive at the end.

Rbanstyles: No?

DreamGurl: I'm paying for it now. My life is so mixed up and confused.

Rbanstyles: How so?

DreamGurl: I don't know. Everything is muddy. You were always clear about how you felt about me. Your feelings didn't change from one day to the next.

Rbanstyles: Was I?

Cydney hesitated. She'd already taken this further than her original intent.

DreamGurl: Yes. I always felt your love…strong.

There was a long pause again. Cydney thought maybe the connection had been lost, but then a message came through.

Rbanstyles: Who are you?

Cydney's eyebrows knitted.

DreamGurl: What?

Rbanstyles: You obviously have me confused with my husband, right? This is Samantha James, Stephon's wife. Who are you?

Cydney's mouth dropped open into an O. She quickly clicked out of the program and pushed her laptop off her. She fell back into the dip of her pillows, took their comforting embrace. Nothing was going right.

* * *

"Slay—who this?" There was a hitch in his tone because of the blocked number that came through to his cell. He thought it might be the doctors from the hospital where he'd dropped off his mother calling to tell him that she'd scratched some nurse's eyes out and that they couldn't keep her. Or that he needed to rush back because it didn't appear she would last much longer.

"Yes, I'm interested in getting my hands on some street pharmaceuticals," a woman's voice bellowed into the receiver of Slay's cell. "Something potent enough to chase away the monotony of life in the boonies."

Slay smirked, his heart rate moved back in the direction of normal. "Felicia Rucker."

She sucked her teeth. "Dang, I blocked the number and even changed my voice. I'm that recognizable?"

"How you been, girl?"

"Good today," Felicia said. "I just got a call from my agency. They've got a gang of shoots lined up for me next week. I'm going to be heading back to the city."

"You ain't leaving before my little thing on Saturday, I hope?"

"I might be," she said. "I wanted to know if you could get together with me before then. Maybe you could come hang here. My brother was here for a hot minute but he's gone off to work now. We'd have the place to ourselves."

Slay grumbled. "I've been thinking about Saturday since we first hooked up, girl. You're breaking my heart here."

"So that's a no for you coming over then?"

"I'm busy. I wish I could, though."

"Brokering?" Felicia said, putting emphasis on the word.

Slay looked up through the windshield of his car toward Kenya. Kenya was on line inside the fast-food joint with her neck craned to the overhead menu. "Right, right…brokering."

Felicia sighed. "If I stay, and I come to your party, you really better show me a good time, Slay."

"You got that," he said.

"What time is the party?"

"Party starts at eleven but I thought we could hang out earlier. Listen, take a taxi over to the Berkeley and then tell them my name at the front desk so they can give you a key to my suite. My boy Barkley will be working that night, he'll take care of you. You can come, like, around seven o'clock."

"Taxi?"

"Yeah," Slay said. "But I'll pay you back. I'd come give you a ride myself but I'm gonna be running late, got some—"

"Brokering to do?"

Slay laughed into the receiver, his voice a tonic to Felicia's ears. "Who are you, Miss Cleo?"

"You know that chick isn't Jamaican or psychic?"

"I heard that," Slay said, "shame."

"Three dollars a minute for a scam," Felicia said, sucking her teeth.

"Buyer beware, right?"

Felicia smiled. "Right, right."

Slay cupped a fist to his mouth. "Oh, you're taking my shit, now?"

"What's yours is mine," Felicia said, pausing before adding, "And what's mine...is yours. All yours."

Slay let out a puff of air.

"On that note," Felicia said, "I think I've gotten your attention. See you Saturday."

"I'll be there as soon as I can. Remember you come around seven, and wear something sexy."

Felicia harrumphed. "Judon'tknow. I could make MC Hammer pants sexy."

"I don't doubt it," Slay said, "but don't prove it to me on

Saturday. I want to send you back to the big city with a smile on your face. I'm not sure Hammer pants can get me inspired."

"Oh, behave," Felicia said.

"Sexy, Felicia," Slay said with the sternness of a father.

"Saturday, Slay."

They hung up and Slay closed his flip, tapped his cell phone like a pack of cigarettes and put it in the inside pocket of his jacket. He scanned his watch and blared down on his car horn. Through the glass of the KFC he could see Kenya still on line. Kenya, so beautiful and so sweet. She deserved so much more than what he'd given her, what he still gave her. She deserved so much better than to be mixed up with a guy like him.

CHAPTER 19

Shake what your mama gave you
  Back that thing up
  Shake your ass and show me what you workin' wit'
  She's a brickhouse

Jacinta ripped the sheet she'd been scribbling on out of her personal journal, balled it and tossed it in the garbage container across from her. She took her pencil in a fist, holding it like a stake, and ground the lead tip into black crumbs on her makeup counter. The mirror in front of her, with the high-wattage bulbs running down the side, pulled her in. She studied her reflection. Her eyes were shaped like a slit heart, her lashes were long and vibrant, she had a nice even skin tone, straight teeth, full lips, a nice linear nose. She was beautiful. She also was a performer on a stage that no longer felt good under the sharp point of her pumps. A stage that felt as if it might collapse from the weight she carried on her back. She hung her head to avoid the mirror.

Beside her chair, on the floor, was the forgotten one-liter bottle of ginger ale she'd picked up on her way in to Hot Tails this morning. She reached down, grabbed the bottle, twisted off the cap and swallowed the lukewarm soda. It stung her raw throat as it went down. Her chest burned. On top of everything else she appeared to be getting a cold or the flu. She took another swallow anyhow, put the cap back on tight and set the bottle on the counter next to her makeup bag.

Her set was fast approaching and all she'd done in the

twenty minutes she'd been backstage was remove her socks and sneakers and scribble in her journal. She couldn't seem to muster the energy or care to remove her Clark Atlanta University jogging suit or put on her makeup. She sat back in the fake-leather swivel chair and closed her eyes. Phyllis Hyman's angelic voice sang out from the speakers of Jacinta's little cassette recorder. Jacinta had pulled the cassette with the faded lettering from the door console of her car and brought it inside with her today. She hadn't even known who or what it was. The choice ended up being perfect, for Phyllis spoke to Jacinta's soul like few others did. Phyllis's music touched the deepest layers of the soul, leaving smudgy fingerprints behind as evidence.

Two taps came in quick succession against the wooden door. Jacinta gritted her teeth. She knew the distinctive knock. The last thing she wanted to do was deal with this fool today.

Tap. Tap.

Pesky bastard wasn't going away.

"S'open," she said, relenting.

The door cracked and the heavy bass music from outside poured in. Then the door closed after he'd come inside, and the heavy bass subsided. He didn't have his usual grin, Jacinta noticed, and his eyes looked almost as haunted as her own.

"Ha-seen-ta," he said, subdued.

Where he normally emphasized the "seen" part of her name, today he said all three syllables with the same lack of enthusiasm. Jacinta wondered what crawled up in him and died. She hadn't kneed any more clients in the balls recently.

Jacinta turned her chair sideways as he slowly moved to his usual seat on the table below the mirror. He hunched his shoulders in and rubbed his hands together as he sat on the table.

"It's getting cold as shit out," he said.

Jacinta recognized it as small talk. He seldom if ever engaged in small talk. She nodded at Slay. "I woke up with a scratchy throat. I think I might be getting a cold or something. My stomach is kind of queasy, too. Could be the flu coming on."

"I been thinking about getting one of those flu shots," he said, "someone told me about." Kenya, his something borrowed.

"Yeah," Jacinta said. "They're good to get." Now she was volleying small talk back at him.

Slay jutted his chin at her. "You dressed up warm, that's smart. For some reason I pictured you coming in here wearing one of your outfits, a big trench on to cover up."

Jacinta laughed. She was actually comfortable in his presence today. "Only in the movies would you see that."

Slay turned to her little radio, rocked it back on its haunches like a chair, looked at the spinning cassette through the clear window. "What's this you listening to?"

"Phyllis Hyman."

He set the radio back down, chewed his lips up in approval. "She's tight."

"As a drum," Jacinta agreed.

Slay turned back to Jacinta and wove his fingers together, squeezing his knuckles until they cracked. "I got a little something coming up for you."

Jacinta shook her head. "I don't think so. I'm reevaluating that part of my life." She looked around at the plain concrete walls of the dressing room. "This place, too."

Slay nodded his head, jut his lips out. "I can understand that."

Jacinta crinkled her forehead. This wasn't the Slay she knew. "You got a fever or something?"

He smiled. "Nah. Just finished tearing up some KFC, I think it weighed me down."

"You're taking this mighty calm."

"What I'm gonna do, bitch-slap you? Pardon the word."

"Oh, hell no," Jacinta said. "But what's up with you? You're acting like someone bitch slapped you. Pardon the word."

Cracks, like thunderbolts, formed in the skin around Slay's eyes. He blinked a few times. "Going through some things, is all."

Jacinta wasn't about to let him leave it at that. "Like?"

"It don't matter," he said. He looked away from her. Studied the walls, the crude comments someone had spray painted on an entire section of one of the walls. When he returned his gaze to Jacinta she was still watching him, waiting for him to open up. He sighed. "I'm having a little situation with my mama. I had to put her in the hospital. She's, she's got a bit of a problem…"

Jacinta's eyes widened with understanding. Dollars to donuts his mother's problem wasn't a urinary tract infection or even something decidedly more serious, such as high blood pressure. No, it was drugs or alcohol he spoke of—the abuse of drugs or alcohol. She recognized that uncertain look in Slay's eyes that people got when dealing with a loved one fighting the substance abuse demons. "Sorry to hear that," Jacinta said.

Slay nodded, pursed his lips. There was more he needed to unleash. "And this dude I grew up with, Boom, he's been locked up for a minute. It looks like he's coming home sooner than originally thought." Kenya had discussed it with him while they ate their honey-barbecued wings. Slay laughed to himself. "Probably get out in time for Christmas."

"That's good news, isn't it?"

"It's one love for him. But dude ain't handling his shit right." Slay's eyes drifted. "He's got shit dudes would die for."

"You should let him know that," Jacinta offered.

Slay's eyes moved to her again. A smile teetered from his mouth. "I don't think so. Some things you just can't tell someone. Plus, I ain't exactly the right dude to be telling him." How many times had he himself been told by his mama, the only person that knew the realities of his relationship with Kenya, only to shrug it off?

Jacinta leaned back in her chair and took a deep breath that seemed to never end.

"Damn," Slay said. "What was that for?"

"Drama," Jacinta told him, shaking her head. She had her demons as well. "Life is drama."

"Tell me about your drama."

She shook her head.

"Come on now, Ha-seen-ta. You had me all up in here like this is Oprah or Montel. Bring it on."

Jacinta couldn't help but smile. Slay had returned to emphasizing the "seen" part of her name again. Just talking to her had done him a world of good. Maybe that trick would work for her. She took another breath. "I've been doing a lot of thinking about my life lately. I want more than what I have. I want to be able to feel good about myself when I lay my head on the pillow at night, and when I move from it in the morning. I need to start treating myself with love. I've been disrespecting myself for a long time for a dollar. And the dollar just isn't enough anymore. I keep telling myself I'm just a big ol' sex freak and there isn't anything wrong with that, but I know I want more in my life." She shook her head again as the words poured from her, her voice rising. "I had sex with that guy that owns that restaurant the other day thinking that—"

"Whoa, whoa, whoa, whoa," Slay said, easing off the counter. "You fucked Desmond Rucker?"

Jacinta dropped her eyes, nodded her head. "I knew it was wrong, but I was hoping he'd see something in me, something of value, and want to give me a chance." She snickered. "Foolish. He hasn't even given me a second thought. No call. He hasn't even stopped in."

Slay stood in the middle of the floor, shaking his head.

"I played myself," Jacinta said. "Bad." She looked up at Slay. He was somewhere far off from her. She tried to call him back. "Slay. Slay. Slay…"

Desmond had just finished a meeting with his staff, a meeting in which he'd acquiesced to every want and whim his workers wanted. Not at all like the typical hard-business Desmond that usually conducted these meetings.

Everyone pulled from the table, stood and left; everyone except Desmond and Karen.

"Have you lost your mind?" she asked.

"What?"

"You're giving Jacoby carte blanche to add menu items?"

"He is the head chef," Desmond defended. "I have to trust his judgment. He's been doing his homework, talked over most of what he wants to do with my father."

"Mrs. Green will have your payroll through the roof," Karen added. "You're gonna let her hire three more people, for what?"

"We get busier with each passing day."

Karen shook her head. "It's not right. This isn't how you run your business. What gives?"

"I need to take some chances," Desmond said.

Karen ran her gaze over him. "You take plenty of chances, Desmond." She propped her elbows on the table. "Are you planning on any more wild rides in a certain red sports car with a certain wild lady anytime soon?"

"It was just that, Karen," Desmond said, "A wild ride and nothing more."

"I hope you don't crash, Desmond. I really do." Karen smirked, pushed from the table and left him to his thoughts.

Desmond sat back in his chair. He hoped for the same thing. He was alone, buried in his thoughts, and didn't immediately realize that Karen was standing over his shoulder a few minutes later.

"Desmond," she called to him.

Desmond turned. Karen was flanked by an Asbury Park policeman. Desmond's heart started to race. "Yes?"

"It looks like you crashed after all," Karen said.

Desmond stood. "What do you mean?" he asked, looking at Karen and then the cop.

"Somebody took what looks like a sledgehammer to the front grille and window of your truck, Mr. Rucker," the officer announced.

Desmond squinted and looked at Karen. She shook her head and moved away, back toward the front.

"Something you should see," the officer added. He handed Desmond a slip of paper. "This was lodged under your windshield-wiper blade."

Desmond looked down at the slip.

Keep your dick in your pants was scribbled on the paper in black Magic Marker.

"Have any idea who would send you this message, Mr. Rucker?"

Desmond looked at the officer. "No idea whatsoever."

Cydney had just filled the tub with water for a hot bath and was in the living room picking through her CD collection for mood music when the doorbell chimed. She turned and looked at the door in surprise. No one ever rang her bell. She hardly ever had visitors. She walked across the floor, slow enough for a second chime to break out. She stood on tiptoe and looked through the peephole. Desmond was in the hall, his arms busy with a large brown bag, his head down. Cydney unbolted the latches and opened the door. He looked up as she stood before him with a hand on her hip.

Desmond lifted the large bag. "I brought some food over." He waited for her to scoot to the side or say something. She did neither.

"I wasn't sure what you'd want," he said. "I know you have your cravings. So I picked up a pint of shrimp fried rice and spring rolls from the Chinese place."

Cydney just stared at him.

"And," he continued, "just in case you didn't want Chinese, I picked up a ham, salami and cheese sub from the Italian place."

Cydney sucked her teeth.

Desmond smiled weakly. "I also got you a meatball sub in case you wanted a hot sub instead."

"I kind of have a taste for some of that honey-fried chicken from your place," were Cydney's first words.

Desmond's shoulders sagged. "Damn...I was there, too. That would have been easy." He grimaced, bit into his lip. The devastation looked as if it might topple him.

Men.

Cydney shook her head. "Come on in. I'll eat the fried rice, you can eat one of the subs."

Desmond looked up, his eyes immediately brightening. "I can come in?"

Cydney gave him some neck action. "Oh, you don't have to, now. I know you're wishy-washy."

Desmond struggled to raise a hand. "No, no, no. I want to come in."

Cydney took her hand off the door, turned and walked back toward the kitchen. Desmond stepped in, slipped out of his shoes and closed the door behind him. He placed the bag on the carpet and fastened the locks, picked the bag up and joined her in the kitchen. She had two paper plates and two glasses on the table by the time he got there.

"I was about to take a bath, but I don't want that food to

get cold. Shrimp fried rice doesn't go over so well in the microwave," Cydney said.

"How are you coming along with your paper?"

"Shitty."

"I'm sorry."

"You should be." Cydney poured soda into the two cups and turned away from him.

"I was acting kind of strange this morning, yes?"

"Yes." She dropped a cube of ice in Desmond's cup and the soda shot up like a spray from a water fountain. He jumped. Cydney turned from him and placed the ice tray back in the freezer.

Desmond cleared his throat. "I have different issues from time to time, and instead of—"

Cydney sat down, bowed her head and closed her eyes. Desmond did the same. "Lord, we thank you for the food we are about to receive. Bless the hands that prepared it. For Christ's sake. Amen."

"What I was trying to say," Desmond continued, "was…" His voice lowered. "Something you should know about me. I have a habit of running away when someone gets close to my heart."

Cydney looked down and twirled through her rice with a fork.

Desmond reached across the table and grabbed her wrist. Cydney looked up. "I'm falling in love with you, Cydney, honestly. And I'm scared to death. Can you understand that?"

Cydney dropped her fork in the heap of shrimp and rice. "Yes."

"So how do I handle this?"

Cydney shrugged. "I don't know."

"I was hoping for more insight than that," Desmond said.

"One thing I can tell you," Cydney offered. "Running solves nothing. You have to stand down your problems."

"I bet you're an expert on standing down problems, Cydney. That's not really one of my strong points."

A sad smile crossed Cydney's face. "No, actually, I'm with you, Desmond. I'm an expert on running."

"Isn't that tiring?" he asked for corroboration.

"Yes," she acknowledged.

"So how about the both of us stop running?"

"I'm not running from you, Desmond—other things, yes, but never you."

"I'm not running away from you either, Cydney. Not anymore." He thought about his damaged truck. "You know, someone took a sledgehammer to my truck today."

Cydney's eyebrows crested. "What happened?"

"Some kids doing vandalism most likely," Desmond said. "At first the cops thought someone had it in for me, but they found another vehicle smashed in the same manner up the road." Desmond didn't mention that the other car didn't have a note neatly tucked under its wiper blades, or that his did.

Cydney's shoulders eased. For a moment she'd thought it might be the work of Slay. "It's drivable?"

"She ain't as pretty," Desmond said, smiling easily. "The windshield is cracked and the front grille is busted up, but she's drivable. She has an operation from a motor medic due to come in her near future."

Cydney shook her head. "Crazy."

Desmond took her hand. "Crazy would be you and me not putting our best foot forward to make something special." He sighed. "I have to make an admission, Cydney."

"Oh boy, here we go."

"Hear me out before you cut me off," Desmond said. Cydney nodded. Desmond sighed again, his sigh tally rising with each passing second. "I was engaged to be married last year." Cydney took a deep breath. "I backed out of it with Nora," he finished.

"Nora?"

"My intended," Desmond offered.

"Are you still in love with her?"

Desmond shook his head.

Cydney gave Desmond her hardest look. "You two still...?"

Desmond shook his head.

"Well, this is quite an admission."

"Actually," Desmond said. "That isn't the full admission."

"There's more?" Cydney asked.

"I want to tell you something that I've never told anyone, not even Nora."

"I guess I want to hear it," she said. "Go ahead."

Desmond smiled. This was the first step in a major breakthrough for him. "Cydney Williams...I'm committed to loving you the way you deserve to be loved."

"Thanks," Tuffy said as Slay handed him a wad of bills.

"No problem," Slay said. "And do something with that sledgehammer. You can't be walking around with that thing over your shoulder."

Tuffy dropped the sledgehammer by his feet. "That cat had a nice truck."

"Had?"

Tuffy smiled. "Yeah, had. I fucked his shit up."

"You left the note?"

Tuffy nodded. "Under his wipers. I wrote it with my left hand like you said."

Slay touched the youngster's shoulder. "Keep your ears open and yourself ready, little partner."

"Aiight."

"Peace."

"Peace."

Tuffy walked off and Slay jumped in his car.

* * *

Cydney sat up as soon as Desmond rolled away from her. Their exchange had been more like what she expected—tender, passionate. He didn't have any problem performing this time— these times—for they'd done the do thrice since Desmond showed up at Cydney's door. Desmond seemed intent on proving that he was a caring, concerned lover, that he wanted Cydney forever in his arms.

Sweat, cologne, sex enveloped the air of Cydney's bedroom.

"Thirsty?" Cydney asked as Desmond's chest rose like an asthmatic in desperate need of Primatene Mist.

He touched her wrist and indicated yes with a nod of his head.

"I've got some sparkling apple cider or some Coke. What's your poison?"

He nodded his head, smiled.

"Either-or, I take it," she said. "I guess that's what you're saying."

He nodded again.

"I worked you good," she bragged.

Desmond ran his finger over the outline of her breast, circled her dark nipple. Cydney shooed his hand away as if it were a pesky fly. "Don't start anything you can't finish," she teased.

Desmond laughed, his breathing returning to normal. "I can—I can finish."

Cydney smirked. "Let me get those drinks."

She caught herself half skipping toward the kitchen, stopped, and leaned against the hallway wall and laughed. Slow your roll, girl.

She moved straight to the cupboard and pulled down two glasses, moved to the refrigerator and took out the cold two-liter Coke. She turned and was headed back to the bedroom when she remembered she'd gotten a call while Desmond was arching her back and curling her toes. She placed the two-liter soda bottle and the glasses on the counter and picked up the phone, dialed the access number to retrieve her voice mail messages.

"Hey, Cydney," Slay said. "*I need to speak with you, sis. No bullshit. Call me. That GQ Smooth cat is no good, trust me. He—*"

Cydney erased the message. She wasn't about to let Slay, and his craziness, mess with her high.

CHAPTER 20

Desmond noticed the bright red sports car with plumes of white smoke rising from the back as soon as he neared his restaurant. The car was parked just up the road from Cush, facing the restaurant but on the other side of the street. The headlights flashed as Desmond slowed his truck. Just got my truck fixed and now she's showing up here, Desmond thought. He sighed and drove on past Cush. He crossed over the center line of the road and pulled next to the car. Jacinta powered down her windows. Desmond did the same.

"Can we talk?" she asked.

Desmond looked over his shoulder. "I'm kind of busy."

"I won't take up much of your time, I promise."

Desmond pointed up the road behind her. "Meet me up by that weeping willow." He moved immediately in that direction. Jacinta did a U-turn and followed.

He was waiting, standing outside his truck with the engine running, when she arrived. She eased her car close to his bumper, wiped her eyes and got out to meet him. Just as Desmond had done, Jacinta left her engine running. Desmond's face seemed to tighten as Jacinta neared him and she lowered her head to avoid the glare of his eyes.

"Thanks for having a moment with me," she said as she reached him. She kept her head lowered.

"No problem at all," he answered, all business, as if he were talking with one of his vendors. His tone almost made her get in her car and drive off, but she didn't.

"I wanted to let you know that I quit Hot Tails, quit dancing," she said.

"Good for you," he offered. "I'm glad you told me. Not that I was planning on coming in there anymore. It took what we did for me to realize how much I was jeopardizing—"

She looked up, her eyes rimmed with red. "Running around after whores," she finished for him.

Desmond shook his head. "Don't be dramatic, Mona."

"Keep it real—I'm Jacinta to you. Never could be anything but Jacinta to you."

He nodded. "Jacinta, don't be dramatic. All I'm saying is I've got a good lady in my life and I messed up."

"You tell her about us?"

"Hell no, what are you crazy!"

"Are you ever going to?"

"No, and I hope you aren't either."

"Your secret's safe with me."

Desmond sighed. "If things were different maybe you and I could have worked out."

Jacinta looked at him again, hard. He turned his eyes away from her. "What would have had to be different?" she pressed. "If I wasn't a slut, is that it?"

"If I wasn't falling in love with someone else," he countered.

Jacinta wrung her hands together. "I guess this is for the best," she said. "If you call how you operate love, then I hope never to find love."

Desmond was clearly angered by the cut of judgment in her voice. "What was the point of this? Did you even have a point in waiting outside my place of business?"

Jacinta snickered. "I did," she said sadly, "but it would be wasted on you."

Desmond rubbed his hands together. "Cool. Are we done here then?"

Jacinta nodded.

Desmond touched her shoulder. "You take care of yourself. I'll be praying for you. And be thankful I didn't press charges for what you did to my truck."

Jacinta shrugged her shoulder away from his touch. "What are you talking about, your truck?"

Desmond looked at her for a moment, then shook his head and got in his truck. His tires wailed as he sped off toward Cush.

Jacinta moved to her car and sat staring at the bent tree off to the side of her. For as long as she could remember it had been bent out of shape like that, looking as if it might fall, and yet it didn't. It didn't fall, it didn't collapse. It wasn't straight and perfect, but it didn't fall, it didn't collapse. She had to remember that.

Desmond looked back at the shiny red car as he drove up the block. Something in his gut told him that Jacinta, despite what she proclaimed, wouldn't be moving so easily from his life. He tapped his steering wheel in disgust. Having sex with her was the stupidest thing he'd ever done in the name of lust. He prayed that God was merciful enough to pass him through this, unharmed. He prayed that she'd gotten all the anger out of her system by banging up his truck, and that was the end of her. He pulled out his cell phone as he parked outside his restaurant and dialed a number.

"Hey," he said when Cydney's voice mail picked up on the third ring. "I'm right outside my restaurant preparing to go in for what I'm sure will be a hectic, hardworking day, and the only thing sustaining me is the thought of you. I just want to let you know that I'm so looking forward to Saturday night, and hopefully the rest of our lives. All right, I've got to go." He hung up, a flush of happiness chasing away the blues of a moment prior. This was what love was supposed to feel like. Finally, he was ready to embrace it fully.

* * *

"You no-good sorry nigga, I dread the day I birthed you."

Slay looked at his mother, her hospital gown falling off her bony shoulders, her arms and feet shackled to the metal bed rail, food caked in the corners of her mouth. "You don't mean that," he said, unsure.

"I mean it," she said. "You're a piece of shit."

"I'm trying to help you," he defended. "The doctors said this program can get you cleaned up."

"Where's my Cydney?" she cried. "Lord, I miss my George."

Slay gritted his teeth. "Neither one of them ever really gave two shits about you. I'm the one that has stuck by you."

She churned her lips and tried to spit at him. Her attempt failed, no spittle forming in her dry mouth. Slay's feelings hurt just the same as if a stream of nasty mucus ran down his cheeks.

"You're hurting, I know," he said.

"Fuck you, nigga. I want out of here."

"You signed the papers, Mama."

"I didn't know what I was doing," Nancy said. "You tricked me. You've been fooling me your whole life."

"What are you talking about, Mama?" Slay said. "I've always kept it real with you."

"I should have listened to George," she whined.

"Leave that be, Mama," Slay cautioned her.

"Touching your sister with sex on your mind," she continued.

"Shut up!"

"Shut me up, you nasty nigga! Why, boy? Why'd you do that nasty thing?"

Slay refused to revisit that dead issue. "Aiight, then," he said, backing away and stumbling for the door. "I'm gonna head on out, but I'll be back to check on you soon."

"Get out!"

Slay's back banged the door; he turned, surprised to see himself up against it, and struggled with the handle.

"Get out of here, nigga!"

He moved through the doorway and up the hall. One of the doctor's he'd been speaking with earlier approached him, a clipboard in his hand, smile on his face. The doctor stopped in his tracks.

"As you can probably see, your mother's already making progress. At least now she's communicat—"

Slay pushed his hand into the doctor's chest and trotted past. He pushed through the double doors at the end of the hallway, and as they closed behind him he bent over and squeezed his eyes shut. He gasped for air. She was so wrong, his mother was, and Cydney, too. He was the only one who'd ever cared about them. Why didn't they see that?

Cydney placed the telephone back in the cradle, a smile threatening to crack her face into a thousand pieces. *The only thing sustaining me is the thought of you,* Desmond had said. There was pure poetry in his words and the imminence of love in his heartfelt tone. Love, proper love, was indeed sustenance. The thought of a lover was indeed shelter from the harshness of this cold world. Cydney's worries from just a few days prior dissipated like a puddle on a hot June day. She stared off into the living room, the laundry basket of clothes on the counter in front of her at risk of turning to a pile of wrinkled cottons and polyesters. The extra hours she'd have to take on at Macy's, the overload of schoolwork, none of it seemed to matter anymore. She'd found her Mr. Wonderful. She shook off her daydreaming, grabbed the phone and moved to the living room where she settled on the couch.

She muted the volume on the television at first, and then picked up the remote a second time and just shut the television off completely. She punched in some numbers on the phone and waited as the rings cycled. A sleepy voice picked up after a few rings.

"Hello," the voice said.

"The only thing sustaining me is the thought of you," Cydney said into the phone.

"Cydney, do you know I'm trying to get some darn rest?" Faith asked, still groggy.

"Yes."

"And I can see that doesn't matter to you. I was up all night working on Greenwood's paper. You finish yours?"

"Not yet."

"You better step to it."

"I will."

"Now, what was that you were saying about staining me?" Faith asked after a long yawn.

Cydney laughed. "Desmond called and left me a message. He said, 'The only thing sustaining me is the thought of you.'"

Faith perked up. "He said that? Why?"

"He just called me on his way in to work and told me he wanted me to know that."

"Darn."

"What do you think?" Cydney said.

"I think you answered the question V and I wondered about," Faith said.

"Oh, yeah?"

"Yep. You gave up the booty."

"Maybe."

"No maybe. Hold on, I'm going to get to Victoria on three-way."

Cydney smiled. News travels fast.

CHAPTER 21

Saturday.

Nighttime.

An opportunity for some much-desired thug love.

Felicia stood in the middle of the floor looking at the outfit she had laid out across the bed. Silk-and-wool patchworks wrap skirt with embroidered flowers along the hemline. A blouse made of fine lace. And a new pair of suede knee-length boots with side laces and tassels that she hadn't broken in yet. All the items were designer, all expensive.

Felicia stared at the items on the bed. She thought of Slay. Remembered that animal look in his eyes. Instinctively her hand rubbed over her stomach as she thought about his rippling muscles, as she imagined the faces he'd make as he pumped in her like an engine piston. The faces and sounds she'd make as that piston moved through her. Thug love.

Felicia shook off the fantasy and walked over to the floor-length mirror and checked herself out. She wore only a black bra-and-panties set. Her legs were long and cut with precision, her stomach flat; her breasts bulged from her bra enough to make men lick their lips but not so much as to make clothes designers give her the thumbs down. She was sinewy and shapely to the fashion folks. *Gat damn!* to the brothas. She wasn't quite sure of what she was to herself. She continued to study her reflection, her skin glistening from body oil like a Thanksgiving bird painted with its moist juices. She smiled at the reflection, took a deep breath and wheeled from the mirror. She was a beautiful and sophisticated young woman and she needed to remember it. Plus, this was going to be the most special night of her young life. She was prepared to give away the most precious gift she had; prepared to give it to the charming thug lover that showed up on her doorstep as if directed there by God.

But then that outfit greeted Felicia again. She turned away from it quickly then caught herself. "Get a grip on yourself, girl," she said aloud. "You are most definitely tripping."

Determined, she marched over to the bed and picked up the wrap skirt, and without further thought fit her hips inside the clingy warmth of it. She eased the lace blouse over her head, slowly, so as not to disrupt her carefully done, beautifully coiffed hair. She adjusted the skirt so the material didn't bunch around her hips. She pulled the blouse up so the line of cleavage and the plumpness of her breasts were less prominently displayed. She moved to the mirror again and clucked her tongue in approval, giving herself a finger snap. She needn't worry. Bring on some of that much desired thug love.

Felicia called for a taxi and sat in the living room lacing up her boots as she waited. Within half an hour an old blue car with white lettering on the side door pulled into the circular driveway out front. Felicia could see plumes of black smoke trailing the bumper and the hood vibrating. It wasn't the horse and carriage that she dreamed about, that was for sure.

She got up in a hurry. Even though she'd been sitting doing nothing for a good ten minutes, she wasn't prepared for the cab's arrival. She grabbed her coat and hung it over her arm. She looked around for her purse, found it on the couch. Made sure she had the spare key Desmond cut for her, and headed for the door as the horn sounded a third time for her outside. Desmond was out on his own jaunt, so she didn't have to bother leaving him a note. She'd probably be home before him, unless her thug lover put it on her as she dreamed he would. She shook her head and smiled at the thought of the dreams she'd been having for the past week. She'd had more than enough opportunities to give her greatest gift to a young man, but the time had never felt right. Today, though, and with Slay, it felt right. She couldn't explain why, and hadn't even tried to analyze why. All she knew, finally, she was headed for her thug love. She hoped he appreciated what she was about to give him.

She walked outside, scooted in through the back door of the taxi. The driver turned around, his arm up on the seat, and looked her up and down. He had a Yankees cap, two sizes too small, squeezed on his head, but Felicia could see that his black hair was graying throughout. The skin on his cheeks was pink and peeling. He had a thick wide nose with hair protruding from his nostrils and bushy eyebrows that carelessly connected in the middle.

Felicia could smell the mix of coffee and cigarettes on his breath. She noticed the Yankees pennant banner and the nude-model deodorizer hanging from his rearview mirror. Great, she'd hit the cabdriver jackpot. She had to be sure to thank her thug lover for subjecting her to this.

"Thought you weren't coming out, sweetness," the driver said. "I'm glad I waited, tho'. Where you headed looking so—" he stopped and kissed his fingertips "—divine?"

Felicia rolled her eyes. This guy was the cover boy for *Stereotypes* magazine. The Guido issue. "Berkeley Carteret, along the boardwalk in Asbury Park," she said.

"Ooh, a nice little ride so we can get acquainted," the driver said. He smiled and his eyes continued to soak up the whole of her. "By the way, my friends call me Mondesi."

"What do the people who can't stand you call you?" Felicia said.

He smiled. His teeth were both yellow and brown. He shrugged. "Sonovabitch, I guess."

Felicia tapped her watch and pointed to his steering wheel. "I'm on a tight schedule...sonovabitch."

Mondesi smiled again, pointed his finger at her and narrowed his eyes. "Ha, I get it. You're a little firecracker, aren't you? I shouldn't say little, though. Geez, your legs are longer than my Joey Nightstick."

"Joey Nightstick?"

Mondesi smiled, a habit for him, it seemed. "Yeah, you want to meet him?"

Felicia shook her head. "Some other time." What was it about her that brought out the crassness in men? Other than her thug lover she couldn't think of the last guy that showed any sexual restraint in her presence.

Mondesi turned around and pulled the transmission handle down to drive. "Suit yourself."

It wasn't much longer after that exchange before he pulled up in front of the Berkeley.

"The royal Berkeley Carteret, sweetness," he said.

Felicia unzipped her carry purse. "How much do I owe you?"

"Twenty-one," Mondesi told her.

"Dollars?" Felicia's voice rose and her eyes were threatening to bulge from the sockets.

Mondesi licked his lips. "We can do some other type of exchange if you like."

Only one person she wanted to barter with, thug lover; her wit and wisdom in exchange for his street smarts and rugged sex appeal. Her wet tunnel for his hard shaft. Felicia pulled the money from her purse and handed it to Mondesi. "It's been real, sonovabitch." She stepped from the cab and switched inside.

The lobby was an ultrachic blend of fall colors—mustards, tans and various browns. There were several large paintings hanging on the walls and a soft-playing classical piece emanating from some small, wall-mounted speakers. The bellhop, dressed in burgundy, smiled as Felicia passed. An old white couple boarded the elevator, their arms interlocked, with the husband singing some old tune to his blushing wife as the doors closed.

Felicia rang the bell at the main desk and a young black gentleman emerged from the back. He had on a simple dress shirt and slacks, a gold-plated nametag—Barkley inscribed on it—and a deep black beard that looked as if it had just been trimmed that day.

"Hello," Felicia said. "Shammond Slay told me I should stop and have you give me the key to his suite. You're Barkley, right?"

He nodded. "Felicia Rucker?"

"Yes."

"Yes, Slay told me to expect you. He's not in as of yet."

Felicia nodded.

Barkley swiped a plastic key through a machine and handed it to Felicia. "His suite is on the third floor. We're having a problem with the elevator, but you can take those stairs right over there." He pointed to a door in the far corner of the lobby.

"I just saw someone ride up the elevator," Felicia said.

"It chooses when it wants to break down. I've called maintenance three times today," Barkley said. "Management wants me to pretend there's no problem, but I wouldn't want to see a sistah get stuck. You know?"

Felicia gripped the key and smiled at Barkley. "Thanks."

He picked up the phone and half smiled. "Glad to be of service. I hope you enjoy your stay."

Felicia walked through the stairwell door; it slammed hard behind her. She stopped and looked at the stairs before her. Don't dwell on the glitches so far—the cabdriver from hell and three flights of stairs—think about the thug love, she thought to herself. The music from the lobby was piped through to the stairwell also. Felicia wrapped her little carry purse in her coat and placed it under her arm, started the climb upward.

As she rounded the turn for the next landing she heard a heavy door above her slam shut. Some low voices and snickers echoed down to her. She climbed on.

Halfway up the set of steps that led to her floor she paused. A group of four young black males surrounded the door. They were facsimiles of one another, all wearing big goose-down jackets and oversize jeans and unlaced boots. All with baseball caps on, the caps pulled so low you couldn't clearly see their faces. They looked as if they were waiting for her. Didn't Slay say something about renting a string of suites? They were probably here for the party that would begin later. Felicia swallowed and regained her strut up the stairs. The four stood, watching her move to them. Felicia glanced down at her feet as she climbed, as her heart rate climbed as well.

"Open the door for the lady," one of them said as she neared the top. He was dressed in all FUBU.

Felicia relaxed. She'd been worried for nothing. She smiled in appreciation to the FUBU-clad boy and went to move through the door. The young guy holding the door shut it just before she could clear the entrance.

"Not so fast, chicken," he said to Felicia.

Felicia looked to FUBU, hoping his earlier courtesy continued. He shrugged his shoulders and smiled wickedly. "Excuse me," Felicia said, raising her arm to take the handle herself.

One of the other two, who'd moved behind her, took hold of her wrist.

Felicia turned to the owner of the ashy, rough hands. "What are you doing?"

He didn't say a word. She wrestled her wrist free and

reached for the door handle again. One of them took hold of her shoulders, pulled her back to the corner of the landing.

"No," Felicia said. She felt herself falling back into their arms. She felt sandpaper fingertips gripping her ankles. Sandpaper fingertips running up her thighs, hiking up her beautiful and fashionable skirt. Sandpaper fingertips tugging at her panties. "No," she said again. Sandpaper fingertips touched her waist and poked at her breasts. Her voice left her, and tears came, sudden and warm against her cheeks, as those sandpaper fingertips whittled away her dignity. This certainly wasn't the thug love she had had in mind.

Saturday.

Nighttime.

An opportunity for some much-desired love.

Desmond stood in Cydney's kitchen sipping on a flute glass of sparkling cider as Cydney prepared a bowl of popcorn. He wore only his boxers and a smile. Cydney wore only his dress shirt, the buttons unfastened, her breasts stable beneath the material. The back of the shirt stuck to her moist shoulders, the shirttail hung low but jutted out slightly as it passed her round ass. Desmond was content just watching her, she could be his movie.

"Why are you staring at me?" Cydney said after a while.

Desmond moved his lips from the flute glass and licked the moist cider from them. "You're beautiful. I could see it becoming a habit of mine."

"I'm determined that we watch this movie before we do anything else," Cydney told him. "We've been going at it like two horny little rabbits."

Desmond moved to her, wrapped his arms around her waist as she removed the dish of melted butter from the microwave. "Can we snuggle while we watch the movie?"

Cydney moved to the counter with her lover draped over her like a shawl. His arms wrapped around her, making her task difficult and awkward, but she dare not tell him to release his hold, it felt too good. "Snuggling, that's a must," she answered him. She poured the butter on the large bowl of popcorn, sprinkled salt, picked up the sugar bowl and dipped out a spoonful of the sweet stuff. Desmond's weight eased off her back.

"What are you doing with that sugar?" he asked her.

Cydney looked at him. "I'm going to sprinkle it on the popcorn."

"Wait a minute," Desmond said as he moved beside her and leaned an arm on the counter. "Salt and butter, I understand. But sugar?"

"Not a lot of sugar, just a few pinches."

"That's odd."

"Trust me on this, it gives the popcorn a special bite. The salt and sugar contrast nicely."

Desmond waved his hand. "Do your thing."

Cydney pinched off some of the sugar and sprinkled it on the popcorn. "So you really want me to come with you and meet your family for Thanksgiving?"

"That's right."

"Should I be looking into that gesture for something more? I mean, does it signify something about our relationship? Or is it just a dinner?"

Desmond took hold of her shoulders, turned her to him and fingered her chin. "It most definitely signifies something about our relationship, Miss Wonderful."

Cydney's cheeks bubbled like hot chocolate. "You haven't called me that in a while."

"Miss Wonderful."

Cydney could feel that familiar warmth coming to her midsection, that tingle of desire. She turned away from him, did something useless with her hands, moving things on the counter that didn't need moving. "We've got to watch this movie first."

"Miss Wonderful," Desmond whispered, moving directly into her view. Cydney turned away again.

"*Ruby's Bucket of Blood,*" she said. "D-didn't you, um, say you loved Angela Bassett?"

Again he chased her gaze. "Not as much as you, Miss Wonderful." Desmond licked his lips.

Cydney stopped running. "You're killing me, Desmond."

He took the bowl of popcorn and Cydney's wrist. "Let's go in the other room... To the couch."

Saturday.
Nighttime.
Guilt.

Slay tapped on the front door of Knocking Beats Records. He could see a small army of men in the back of the record store gathered around two turntables. Rafael, who owned the store with his brother, Ramon, indicated the place was closed by pointing to the sign. Slay made a gesture with his shoulders, moved closer to the door. Rafael squinted his eyes, smiled and moved to open the locks.

"Damn, dawg, my bad," Rafael said as he opened the door. "I didn't see it was you. I'm not wearing my contacts today."

"I was about to say," Slay said as he stepped in, "as many dollars I done put in your pocket and you dissing me like that."

They clasped hands and pressed shoulders in a ghetto hug.

"What's the word?" Rafael asked.

"Chilling. You?"

Rafael looked around the store with pride. "Trying to get those ends, B."

Slay nodded. "Right, right."

"That new Nas *Godson* joint isn't in yet," Rafael said. "I know I said November but it isn't coming to December. The seventeenth I think."

Slay shook his head. "I wasn't coming for Nas, actually."

Rafael made a playful gesture as if the ground was coming out from under him.

Slay smiled. "You heard of Phyllis Hyman?"

Rafael hunched his eyes, nodded his head. "Yeah, man. She was beautiful, dawg. Underrated but mad talented. Her shit was deep. She did herself on a night she was supposed to perform at the Apollo."

Slay was taken aback. "Did herself? She killed herself?"

Rafael nodded. "Yeah. Tragic shit, B."

"You have any of her CDs?"

Rafael smiled. "You're trying to get some ass tonight or what, B?"

Slay threw a weak jab at Rafael's shoulder.

Rafael turned and walked toward the CD bins. Slay followed. "We got *Prime of My Life* and *I Refuse to be Lonely.*"

"Give 'em both to me," Slay said.

Rafael snickered. "You really want the panties, dawg. Play your chick 'What Ever Happened To Our Love' off this CD—" he flipped the second CD over "—and 'Why Not Me' off of this one. I'm not sure which one of those songs, but I know I busted the hardest nut of my life off one of 'em."

Slay crinkled his nose. "You had to go and ruin them for me before I even listened. I'm gonna be thinking about your gorilla face when I hear them shits now."

Rafael laughed. "That's twenty-five beans, B."

Slay handed him a fifty and Rafael went to the register to get change. He stopped, tapped his head. The drawer was empty. He pulled the money for change from his pocket. "And yo, Rafael," Slay said, "can I get a receipt?"

Rafael looked at Slay. "What, you filing taxes now? You buy so many CDs it's a tax write-off or something?" He smiled, rung up the sale on the cash register and ripped the receipt from the paper roll. "For your accountant," Rafael said as he handed Slay the receipt. Rafael balled a fist to give Slay dap. Slay balled his fist and they tapped hands.

Rafael walked Slay to the front door so he could lock up behind him. Slay nodded his head at the group in the back surrounding the turntables. "What's up with that?"

Rafael turned to the group. "Something I do after closing. Teach some of these little knuckleheads how to DJ. Keep 'em off the streets and out of trouble. So much shit out there for them to get sidetracked by, or killed by."

Slay nodded, gave Rafael dap for a second time, and walked through the door.

Cydney rolled over onto her back and accidentally bumped her head against the leg of the coffee table. "Shoot!"

"You okay?" Desmond asked. He sat up, supporting himself on the floor with his arms. His boxers draped on one shoulder, a used condom hung on his flaccid penis.

"I'm fine," Cydney said, rubbing her head nonetheless. "Okay, I mean it this time. We're watching the movie now."

Desmond rolled off the condom, pinched the open end and tied it in a knot so his life juice wouldn't leak out. He took the boxers and pulled them on. "Think of that as the previews before the movie. Or pretend you were in line waiting for soda and popcorn."

"You owe me another ten minutes then," Cydney said. "The previews, or standing on line, they never go that fast."

"What!" Desmond reached for her, started tickling her rib cage. "You think you're a comedian, huh?"

A gasp left Cydney's throat as she tried to move away but

found herself pinned by the coffee table. "Stop! Please, I'm sorry! Stop! You're going to make me pee!"

"Good."

"Please, I'm sorry!" she begged.

Desmond stopped tickling her and touched his mouth to hers. He could feel passion, energy in her kisses that he'd never experienced before in life. In fact, Desmond hadn't particularly liked kissing until Cydney came along. Now he could kiss the night away. He stopped short, though. "We can't. We've got to watch this movie."

"In a minute," Cydney said. She pulled him back to her, found his lips again.

"Welcome to Cush. How many in your party?"

Slay eyed the beautiful black woman greeting him. He remembered her from last time. He scanned the restaurant to see if he spotted Desmond anywhere. He didn't. He looked to the woman. "Actually, I wanted to know if I could get something to go?"

Karen smiled. "Sure, we can handle takeout. Do you know what you want?"

Slay twirled his hand, looked toward the ceiling. "That dessert thing...with the apples and the pudding, bread crumbs."

"Apple brown betty?"

Slay pointed at Karen. "That's it."

"We can do that, but I hope you aren't traveling far. It's best served hot."

"I'm going to see my girl, Kenya. She doesn't live too far from here."

Karen smiled. "Kenya. That's a beautiful name."

"She's a beautiful girl."

Karen stopped one of the passing waitresses and told her to bring out an apple brown betty dessert to go. Karen told Slay he could wait right where he was but she'd appreciate it if he stepped aside if anyone came in. Slay nodded.

Slay scanned the restaurant again. "You guys sure are busy."

"It's a Saturday night," Karen acknowledged. "Probably our best night for business."

Slay turned back to her. "What time is it—" he squinted to read her tag "—Karen?"

She turned up her watch. "Seven thirteen. I get a quick break at seven thirty."

Slay nodded. "Thanks. I brought Kenya here once. She loved the place. I remember you…and the owner, he came over and talked with us. He's not in tonight?"

Karen shook her head. "No, he was in earlier." She crinkled her mouth. "He's off spending some quality time with this new love in his life."

"That's good. That's important."

Karen smiled halfheartedly. "Yes, it is."

Slay extended his hand. "By the way, my name's Shammond Slay, my friends call me Slay. You can call me Slay."

Karen reached forward and took his outstretched hand. "Nice meeting you…Slay."

Felicia's nipples were sore from the young thug's unkind hands and the teeth of one of the most brutish of the four. She struggled to catch her breath. She looked down at herself, her clothes all wrinkled and hanging off of her, one of her breasts bulging out of her bra as a reminder of the violation she'd endured. Her panties lay in a puddle by the door. She crawled the few feet and snatched them up, held them in a fist. Her vagina ached. They hadn't entered her but they'd done nasty things down there with their rough fingers. She wondered if she could still be considered a virgin. The insides of her thighs were badly bruised and the majority of her nails chipped and broken. She touched her throat and grimaced as she swallowed saliva. One of the four had pressed down on her throat as they attacked her. She wished he would have squeezed harder. She closed her eyes and sat back against the concrete wall. She wanted her mother, her father, her brother.

What she didn't want was thug love.

Slay killed his BMW's engine just outside the apartment tower. He ripped the plastic wrap off the two Phyllis Hyman CDs and tossed it out of his propped-open door. He grabbed the white bag that held the container of nicely packed apple brown betty and exited the vehicle. He closed the door, engaged his alarm and walked toward the building. As he walked through the unsecured lobby he noticed the black clock on the wall. In spite of himself he frowned as he thought about what had happened not too far from here in the past hour.

He moved to Kenya's first-floor apartment and did his little two-knock tap-on-the-door thing. He waited a moment and no one answered. He could hear the television playing loudly, so he knocked a second time.

The door opened to Kenya, looking sleepy-eyed and haggard. Slay smiled at her but she didn't return it. She had on big fluffy slippers and one of those long pajama shirts that women wear. Sweat stains darkened the aqua-colored shirt under her arms and across her chest. Her hair looked as if she'd run her fingers through it chasing after some elusive scalp itch.

Slay held up the white bag. "I got some of that apple brown—"

"Who dat, Kenya?" a deep and unmistakable voice called from behind her.

Slay's shoulders sagged and he looked at Kenya. She had her gaze on the ground. He could feel his heart start to race in his chest.

The voice moved closer and soon was right behind Kenya. "Sham, what's going on, son?"

Slay forced a smile to the only person who called him Sham. Boom.

"What's up, yo," Slay said. "When did you get home?"

Boom brushed Kenya aside, took her place in the door. "Today, Sham. They had a nigga sweatin' this time, son. I didn't think I was getting out. My lawyer, though, she was on point with hers. I wasn't supposed to get sprung until, like, December but this chick went all out to get me home for the Thanksgiving holidays. Made me feel like I had Johnnie Cochran instead of PD reppin' me. Bitch had some nice green eyes, too. I tried to talk her into hooking a brother up during his conjugal visits."

Slay looked at Kenya, cowering behind Boom. "Yeah, Kenya told me the other day you might get out before the end of the year."

"I didn't tell her about this latest shit," Boom said, "in case it didn't work out. Have me on some ol' Denzel Washington, Hurricane vibe, up in that piece pressing my fingers to the glass, telling Kenya to go on with her life without me and shit."

Slay forced out a laugh that hurt his sides and made him feel as if he would vomit any minute. "You crazy, Boom."

"Until they put dirt on me," Boom said, agreeing.

"You doing aiight, though?" Slay asked. He had to force himself to speak. His head swam like Greg Louganis.

Boom patted his own chest and then pulled Kenya close to his side. "I'm cool, Sham."

Slay looked at Kenya, her head still down, and then back at Boom. A lump filled Slay's throat but he managed to speak through it. "I was just checking in, making sure everything was cool with your fam."

Boom nodded. "Kenya said you looked her and her kids out while I was down. I appreciate that, Sham."

Slay shrugged. "We soldiers in the same war, Boom. You know I got nothing but love for you all." He looked behind him, signaling his own exit. "Aiight, then, I'm gonna let you all do your thing. It's good to have you back."

Boom initiated a hug. Slay moved to him without hesitation, looking over Boom's shoulder at Kenya walking down the hall into the apartment on shaky legs. Her boys were at the end of the hall, too, grouped together like children waiting at a bus stop. Slay turned his eyes away from them and bit his lip.

"You need anything, hit me off," Slay said as they broke their embrace.

"Aiight, Sham."

The door shut on Slay. He turned and walked back through the lobby. Once outside he looked for the nearest trash container. It was at the end of the bare grassy lawn. He walked over to the receptacle and dropped the white bag that carried the apple brown betty dessert inside. He stuffed the Phyllis Hyman CDs in the side pocket of his jacket and started the slow walk back to his car, refusing to look in the direction of the apartment tower as he stepped through the cold, dark, lonely night.

Doomp doomp doomp doomp…doom da da doom doom
Doomp doomp doomp doomp…doom da da doom doom

"Damn!" Desmond eased Cydney off his chest. "I've got to get that, it could be the restaurant. Pause the tape, baby."

Cydney took up the remote and hit pause as Desmond scrambled toward her kitchen counter. "What ring tone is that?" she asked him.

"Cumparasita," he said as he extended his arm to the ringing cell. He didn't have time to catch his breath. "Desmond Rucker."

Cydney didn't want to listen in, but the silence of the apartment gave her no choice. She sat back against the cushions of the couch, with her legs crossed underneath her, Angela Bassett's body on the television screen blurred and cut in half by jagged white lines. Tape on pause.

"Yes," Desmond said, his voice sounding odd. "When? Where is she? No, I wouldn't suspect that I would. Yes, I have someone here that can drive me." He took a deep breath that reverberated throughout the apartment. "Man oh man. Okay, thanks."

Cydney knew something was wrong but she didn't know how to respond. When Desmond flipped his cell phone closed and fell in a heap on the floor, tears coming to him sudden and violently, she jumped up and ran across the living room to him. He took another one of those deep breaths and held his arms up and opened for Cydney to embrace him.

"What's wrong, Desmond?" she asked, her voice as odd to her ears as his had just been.

He took a third deep breath to settle himself down. "Oh God, Cydney!"

"Desmond?"

"My sister's in the hospital. She was sexually assaulted."

Cydney's hand moved to her mouth. "Raped?"

Desmond's head dropped.

"Where's she at? We have to go?"

"Jersey Shore Medical Center," he managed to say.

"How did this happen, did someone break in to your place? I thought you said she stayed sequestered there all the time."

"She left and went somewhere. I don't know the details."

Cydney rose and reached for his hands. "We've got to go."

"You can drive?" Desmond asked.

"Of course," Cydney told him.

Desmond reached his hand up and let Cydney struggle to pull his weight from the floor. His vacant eyes were glazed with moisture. The VCR Pause function ran its course and the movie automatically started playing again. The sound made Desmond jump. Cydney patted his arm and led him to the bedroom, where his clothes sat in a wrinkled pile by the foot of the bed.

They dressed without speaking. It was urgent that they get to the hospital quickly, but neither Desmond nor Cydney seemed to have the strength to move fast. Desmond, in particular, moved in a crawl. Cydney slid on her shoes and moved to help him fasten the buttons of his shirt that were giving him such problems.

"Thanks," he said as Cydney did the last button and pulled him down to fix his collar.

"Your shoes are by the door," she said, "and your jacket is on the coat tree. I need to use the bathroom before we go."

Desmond was waiting for her by the front door when she emerged from the bathroom. She grabbed her keys and purse, slid on her own coat and opened the door for him. He walked out with his head bowed and waited for her as she locked up. He couldn't seem to move himself more than a few feet without her close by.

Cydney walked with him, arm in arm. The cold wind stabbed Desmond's face. He walked on with Cydney, nonetheless, dark visions of his sister's violation haunting his imagination.

"Trees are damn near bare," Desmond said, to chase away the dark visions.

Cydney understood fully what he was doing. "Yeah, they're awful, but the pine trees they planted are nice. The condo association sent all of us letters asking if we wanted to volunteer to decorate the pine trees for Christmas. You think you might want to come out on that Saturday and put up bulbs and ornaments with me?"

"That would be nice."

"Great," Cydney said. "I'll send in the letter and let them know I'll volunteer."

They reached Cydney's car and she moved to unlock the passenger-side door for Desmond.

"She's only eighteen," he said as Cydney held the door open for him.

"I know" was all she could manage in return.

Silence sat heavy between them again during the ride to the hospital. Desmond fingered the rubber padding at the base of the passenger-side window, looking blankly out the window at the moving landscape as Cydney drove on. Cydney had attempted to turn on the stereo when they first got in, but Desmond asked if she wouldn't—his head ached. Cydney respected his wish.

As they finally neared the approach for Jersey Shore Medical Center, Cydney turned to Desmond. "Where do we go?"

"Follow the signs for the E.R. She's there."

"You want me to let you off at the door and park, or do you want me to park and we'll walk in together?"

"Park," Desmond told her. He put his hand on her knee and squeezed. Cydney nodded and blinked back tears. Seeing Desmond hurting so much challenged her emotions. And what of poor Felicia? Cydney had expected the day she met the young girl to be so much different than this.

Cydney found a spot not too far from the entrance. She and Desmond hugged close and walked inside.

Desmond went to the information desk centered in the bright room. A flurry of activity went on around him but all he saw, all his vision would allow him to see, was that one desk. "I received a call a short while ago from an Officer Jackson," Desmond said. "My sister was assaulted, she's here."

The lady behind the desk, spectacles on her forehead, rolls of fat where her neck should have been, pointed to an officer standing off in a corner of the waiting area, looking out the window. "That's Officer Jackson over there. You can have a word with him and then we'll let you see your sister."

"How's she doing?" Desmond asked the woman.

"I'm not at liberty to—" Something in Desmond's eyes made the woman stop. "This is the most traumatic of experiences, but she's tough."

Desmond nodded. "Thanks." He looked behind him for Cydney. She stepped forward and met his arm.

"You want me to go in with you?" she asked.

"I have to speak with that officer over there first," Desmond said. "And yes, if Felicia doesn't mind. I'd like you to come in with me."

Desmond took Cydney's hand and they walked to Officer Jackson.

"Officer Jackson?" Desmond said.

"Yes." The officer turned sudden, his preoccupation with his thoughts broken. He had deep chocolate tones and weathered skin. His eyelids slanted down and made him appear sad even as he smiled at them.

Desmond extended his hand. "I'm Desmond Rucker. We spoke on the phone."

Jackson took his hand. "Mr. Rucker. I'm so sorry about the circumstances." He turned and indicated the window he'd been looking out of. "I was standing here thinking about how ugly the night is. Not just this one, every night. I think I've just about seen enough over these twenty-some-odd years I been on the force." He sighed. "But that's neither here nor there."

Desmond nodded to Cydney. "This is my special, special lady. Cydney Williams."

Jackson smiled at Cydney. "Nice meeting you, Ms. Williams."

"So what happened?" Desmond asked, surprised by his strength.

"Let's walk," Jackson said. Desmond and Cydney moved with him. "Your sister took a cab over to the Berkeley Carteret for a party just a little before seven this evening. She told me the party wasn't due to start until later, but she was planning on spending some time with a gentleman she met."

Desmond's voice cracked. "Alone with some guy? Who?"

"Now, don't get too upset with her," Jackson said. "She's at the age when young women start thinking all their feelings somehow spell out love."

"She didn't tell me about any guy."

Jackson smiled. "She said you'd say something to that effect."

"So this guy," Desmond said, "he did this to her?"

Jackson shook his head. "No, she was accosted in the stairwell on her way up to the guy's suite."

"No one heard anything?" Desmond's voice rose. Cydney clutched his arm.

Jackson shook his head, pursed his lips. "Not a thing."

"What about this guy she was meeting, what's he saying?"

"We have someone trying to contact him."

"I want to talk with him," Desmond said.

"You should let us handle that, son," Jackson said.

"Handle it right and I will."

Jackson nodded in understanding, pulled out a little notepad. "I'm sorry," he said. "I'm bad with names, which is crazy in this case because this guy is a local celebrity of sorts. It pains me to call his kind a celebrity but that's what he is. He was a high-school football star in Asbury and now he donates a lot of money to the municipality—dirty money, which I don't particularly like, but I guess I can't fault them for taking it, because it is put to good use. They bought computers for the middle-school kids last year, I remember."

Desmond nodded, not that he cared.

"Okay," Officer Jackson said as he came across the name. "One of them funny names...Shammond Slay."

Cydney's arm dropped from Desmond's grip, she stopped walking.

Desmond turned to her. "What's wrong, baby?"

She shook her head and started walking, backward, away from Desmond. Desmond turned to Jackson. "Excuse me a moment, Officer." Jackson nodded.

Desmond moved to Cydney, but she kept walking. She turned and hastened her step. Desmond ran and grabbed ahold of her arm. "Baby, what's the matter?"

"I'm sorry, Desmond, I have to go."

"What!"

"I hate to leave you without a ride, but I can't stay with you."

"Baby, I need you here. Now, what's the matter?"

"I have to go," Cydney repeated.

"Don't do this to me."

"You wouldn't want me here," she said.

"What, are you crazy? I do want you here. I need you now more than ever."

She shook her head. "You wouldn't. You don't know."

"Don't know what?"

She shook her head again. "You don't know."

Desmond took her face in his hands. "You're scaring me, Cydney. Don't know what?"

"Shammond Slay," Cydney said.

"What about him?" Desmond asked. "You heard of him?"

"I have to go."

"Have you heard of him?" Desmond said.

Cydney nodded. "He's bad news, Desmond. He's also my brother."

Desmond's mouth dropped open and his hands fell to his sides. He shook his head. "He can't be. You're an only. You told me so yourself."

Cydney shook her head as her eyes began to tear.

Desmond backed away from her the same way she'd backed away from him. "You lied to me?"

"I'm sorry I got you mixed up in this, I always seem to do this sort of thing," Cydney said, and she turned and hurried off.

Desmond watched Cydney move through the door and disappear into the black of the night.

SLAY

"Whatchu doing, George?" I say.

He turns to me, 'bout to shit on his self, his face looking all guilty and shit. I walked in on him, placing my cell phone back on Mama's kitchen counter where I left it while I went to piss.

"Phone was ringing," he lies. "I tried to answer it, shut it off, do something."

I nod at the pencil and folded piece of paper in his hand. "You need that stuff to shut off a phone, George?"

He looks down at his hand but can't say shit.

"Talking to you, nigga," I say.

His back straightens and he clears his throat. "This is some…never mind," he says. "We need to get back to what we were talking about, boy. Your mama's a stone-cold junkie. We gotta deal with that."

I've got my fists balled tight. I straight up hate this motherfucker. My mama. Your wife, I feel like telling him.

Eff it, why am I sparing this nigga's feelings? "My mama is your wife now, George? Remember, you stole her away while my daddy was still cooling to death?"

"What do you even remember of your daddy, boy? You were only five when he passed."

"I remember he was my daddy," I tell George.

George shakes his head. "You don't remember nothing in particular then?"

This fool is trying to play me, always has, always will. "Aiight then," I say. "I do remember him taking me to a Sixers game. We got a flat in that old beat-up car he had and he changed it and still got to the game on time. I thought for a long time I wanted to be an auto mechanic."

"Versus the Celtics," George says, smiling. "I remember that. I gave him those tickets."

My shoulders fall for a second but I quickly raise them back proud so George won't notice and consider it a victory. *This motherfucker always got to get one up on me.* "You'll be waiting the rest of your life if you expect me to thank you, George," I tell him in my most menacing tone.

George shakes his head and turns extra serious. "Don't worry about that," he says, stammering like a bitch. *I like this, with George looking all small before me and shit.* "You know people. I need you to help me with your mama," he continues.

"The people I know ain't no help to Mama."

"She's gotten beat up a few times going out there for that stuff," George says. "It ain't safe out there for a woman. I'm at the end of my rope."

That's when it all comes clear to me. Why George was going through my phone and acting all suspicious and shit when I straight up caught him. Looking for a drug connection in my address book and shit.

"You ain't asking me to set you up with a drug source, is you, George?" I ask.

George's eyes droop. *I know this motherfucker ain't trying to get me into that shit.* "You are most definitely top-notch, George."

"Don't judge me, you not carrying around this burden, boy."

"Ain't I though? I know you think you're the only one in Mama's world, but I came before you, George. Who you think tries to keep an eye on her during the days while you at work?

I know you don't think calling her on all your breaks is gonna keep her from pounding that pavement. You see for yourself that hasn't worked. She's slippery like an eel. A junk—what you said she is." It was still too difficult to admit it out loud. Junkie.

George softens. *"I don't want to fight you, Shammond. I need your help. She's not gonna give rehab another shot, not now at least. I know you don't want her out there any more than I do. Give me a name and a number. This is a short-term solution, believe me."*

Name and number, damn, I was right. I ain't giving him shit, though. And dollars to donuts, as my mama would say, he came across some numbers already in my celly.

"What you always had against me, George?" I ask him. I want to what they call "humanize" this motherfucker before I walk him straight into a wasps' nest.

George crinkles his nose as his eyes and mind head somewhere else. *"You remind me so much of Dare. I think of your daddy and the word* waste *comes to mind first thing."*

I smirk. I gave him his chance and he fucked it up. *"I'm wasting my time here, George. I'm out."* I can't contain my smile as I put together a plan in my head.

"Go, boy," he says.

Sure he don't care if I goes, 'cause just like I thought he got a few numbers from my celly and he's just itching to try them, see if he hit the jackpot.

"You're foul, George," I say before I leave. *"Always was, always will be."*

He goes over by the couch and plops down right next to the table with the phone on it. His hand rests on the table, inches from the phone. That makes me smile. I'm gonna definitely walk this motherfucker into the wasps' nest. Definitely.

Out in the hall, I pull my cell phone and check it for

missed calls. None. Smiling, I start dialing numbers, out to alert my peoples that if they hear from George they should humor him...then hit me so we can plan just how to sting this motherfucker.

CHAPTER 22

"My mother is a black woman," Slay fumed. "My sister is a black woman. I wouldn't ever bring harm to a woman with the same brown skin as my mother and sister." He ended his short outburst with a slam of his fist on the table in front of him.

Officer Jackson smiled warmly. "Young Ms. Rucker mentioned she was meeting you for a party you were throwing, but the hotel staff we talked with said no party took place. Can you explain that?"

"I canceled it," Slay said.

"You didn't tell young Ms. Rucker that the party was canceled?"

Slay smiled. "I was planning on still having that little private party."

"But you didn't?"

Slay shook his head. "I've got a conscience, Officer. I've got a good woman by my side. I couldn't go through with cheating on her with young Ms. Rucker."

Jackson nodded thoughtfully. "We'll check with the owner of that record shop to corroborate your presence there."

"Rafael," Slay offered.

"Yes, Rafael."

"And I also stopped by Cush for those desserts," Slay added.

"Can't get enough of the Ruckers?" Officer Jackson asked.

"A sweet tooth for them," Slay said. "If you ever tasted that apple brown betty, or got a look at young Ms. Rucker in one of her sexy outfits…you'd understand."

"I'll be checking into all of this," Officer Jackson said.

Slay touched his chest. "I'm free to go, Officer?"

Jackson nodded.

Slay smiled and rose from his seat. "I hope you catch up with whoever did that to young Ms. Rucker. She was a nice girl, didn't deserve no shit like that to happen."

"You keep close," Jackson said. "I might have some more questions for you at some time."

Slay said, "Right, right," a smile inappropriately wide for this terrible situation plastered on his face.

Outside in the hall, he took a deep breath. His head throbbed. Damn, this had gotten seriously out of control.

Desmond clutched his keys in one hand, Felicia's arm in the other, as he led her from the hospital to his truck. Away from probing law enforcement and medical staff. Soon he'd be alone with Felicia, traveling home. He'd have to talk with her. He'd have to offer her comfort. Unfortunately, he didn't believe himself up to the task. It made his stomach churn. His thoughts went to Cydney and her deception, her brother's certain role in this situation. Those thoughts made his mind churn.

"You okay?" he said as Felicia groaned with a step.

"No," she said softly. "I'm not okay."

Desmond rubbed her arm. "Couple more steps and we're there."

They reached the open passenger side door of Desmond's Range Rover. Felicia stopped and considered the climb into her seat. "Couldn't buy a Honda Civic or a Toyota, could you?"

Desmond smiled. It was important she kept a somewhat lighthearted outlook on things. He helped her inside and closed the door behind her. Desmond looked up at the lowering clouds as he moved behind the truck. His mind flashed again on

Cydney's admission. He hadn't told Officer Jackson about Shammond Slay being Cydney's brother and Officer Jackson hadn't seemed to know. Desmond wasn't sure if he'd tell Felicia, either.

"Where did you disappear to earlier today?" Felicia asked as Desmond drove from the parking lot.

"I had Officer Jackson take me to pick up my truck. I didn't have any ride home."

"How did you get to the hospital?"

Desmond hesitated. "Cydney dropped me off."

Felicia lowered her eyes. "She knows about what happened to me?"

Desmond nodded.

"She left, huh? I guess she didn't want to meet your soiled sister."

Desmond found himself defending Cydney. "No, it's not like that. She couldn't stay."

"I can't say I blame her."

Desmond tapped his fingers on the steering wheel as he made a turn. "I don't think me and her are going to continue seeing each other anyway."

Felicia turned to him. "What! You really liked her, Desmond. I thought things were going so well."

"Romance is tricky," Desmond said.

Felicia looked away. "I'll say."

Desmond looked over at Felicia, staring absentmindedly out her window. "Tell me about this guy, Shammond Slay."

"Sort of a thug," Felicia said, talking slowly. "He's the guy I told you about that came to our door wanting to use the place for a rap video."

Desmond gritted his teeth. He vaguely remembered Felicia mentioning that. This meant Cydney's brother had made a calculating play on Desmond's life, had come into his inner circle looking for a weakness. What did that all mean? What kind of relationship did this Slay have with his sister, Cydney? "I remember that," Desmond said. He wondered if he could have saved Felicia from this ordeal if he'd paid more attention to her that day when she first mentioned Shammond Slay. Felicia had told Desmond about the situation with an air of nonchalance, but as Desmond now remembered it there was definitely a gleam in her eye.

"He was cute," Felicia continued. "Hard acting, but it was like a role he played more than the real him. He took me out for Italian hot dogs."

"Why did you never mention any of this?" Desmond asked. "You never told me you two went out. You just said some guy came by like it was nothing. No hint that something might be blossoming."

Felicia shrugged, her back still to Desmond. "You were busy living your own life. Plus, you bug out over stuff like that. I didn't want you fitting me with a chastity belt."

"I don't like the sound of this Shammond Slay guy, Felicia."

Felicia rubbed her arm. Desmond turned up the heat.

"You hear me, Felicia?" Desmond said after the blowers started to release hot air into the cool interior of the truck.

Felicia frowned. "The police questioned him. He wasn't there. He didn't have anything to do with it."

"I don't buy it."

Felicia looked at Desmond. "Why? Why are you so gung ho about him being involved? It was a random…thing."

Desmond watched the road. "Just doesn't add up. Have you talked with him since the…" Desmond gritted his teeth.

"Rape," Felicia said. "I struggle to say it myself, but neither one of us can continue pretending it didn't happen."

"Have you?"

Felicia shook her head. "Officer Jackson said Slay wanted

to call me but they suggested he didn't until they finished their investigation."

"Why don't you give me his number, Felicia. I'd like to have a word with him."

"No."

"I'm a little bothered by the whole thing. I just want to have a few words with the guy."

Felicia put her hand up in protest. "Just leave it alone, Desmond."

Desmond sighed. "How are we going to tell Mom and Dad?"

"We're not," Felicia said.

"What?"

She grabbed his arm. "I don't want to tell them, you hear? I want to deal with this in my own way, under my own terms. I don't want you talking to Slay, either." Desmond thought about Shammond Slay. He could understand his sister wanting to handle things her own way. Desmond was prepared to handle this situation with Shammond Slay his own way. "You hear me, Desmond?" Felicia asked more forcefully.

"Yes."

"Promise me you won't say anything to them, that you'll let me handle this my own way."

Desmond gripped her hand. "I promise."

After a moment, Felicia settled back into the leather seat. She sighed. "Why, Desmond?"

"Why what?" Desmond asked.

"Why would those guys do this to me?" she said. "Men are such sick animals. You would never have four girls gang up on a guy and do such foul things to him."

Desmond didn't have any reasonable response. Men were sick animals at times, and Desmond, he was a man. Sick at times just like the rest.

* * *

It was an ugly day. The sky had a hint of blue and a dusting of gray, but those colors could do nothing to make up for the missing sun's colorful orange smile. Moments before, large drops of rain had fallen, widening into clear splotches as they collided against Slay's windshield with the thud of heavy mud-caked boots. The raindrops had come in a flash, and disappeared just as suddenly, but still held the sky hostage with the threat of a return. The to-and-fro swiping of Slay's windshield wipers broke through the otherwise silence in his car. The hum of rubber kissing glass served as the perfect hypnotic backdrop for Slay's wandering thoughts. Slay looked out his window at the quiet boardwalk, thinking of Kenya, his mother, the father he never really knew, Cydney, Felicia...

Meet me down at the boardwalk in Long Branch around ten.

Cydney's words echoed in Slay's ear, the angry tone, the directive. She hadn't given him time to reply. They were the only words she said before the dial tone chased the venom in her voice. Slay frowned and ran his hands over the sloping curve of his steering wheel.

Directly in front of Slay was the slice of boardwalk where the seasonal vendors conducted their business: the ice-cream parlor, the pizza shop, the psychic, the gaming center. No one was in sight now though, except for a woman with black roots streaking through her blond hair. The woman wore a purple jogging suit, and judging by the puffiness of her form, probably a full set of clothes on under that. She ran by, stopped after about fifty feet and walked a stretch before breaking off into a trot a second time. Before she disappeared from Slay's range of view he saw her stop and walk, then break off into a run again, then repeat the process. He shook his head, wondering why she couldn't decide if she was a jogger or a walker.

Ten minutes later, Cydney's car pulled up in a spot next to

Slay. Her appearance beside him was quieter than those NJ Transit electrical trains. Cydney sat in her car, trying to look composed and strong, but the crumpled Kleenex tissues on her dashboard and the dark sunglasses she wore exposed her—she'd been crying. Slay sighed, cut the engine of his BMW and slid outside. He walked around to Cydney's car and gripped the door handle. The door wouldn't budge; the locks on. He waited a beat and tried again. It was still locked. He leaned down and made a gesture to Cydney. She didn't look in his direction. He tapped against the glass. After a moment she clicked the locks and he opened the door and sat inside.

"I wasn't sure if I was going to have to jimmy your door, Cydney," Slay said in an attempt at levity.

Cydney turned to Slay at that point and started beating her fists violently against his chest and face. Slay let Cydney get off a few shots before putting his hands up to deflect her punches. Cydney tired and fell against her door, crying. Her sunglasses fell off and landed in the jamb between the door and seat. Slay touched Cydney's shoulder and she shrugged away from him. He bit into his lip, nodded his head in understanding.

"You're a son of a bitch," Cydney said after a while. "I hate your ass."

Slay didn't respond.

"Desmond's sister is eighteen," Cydney cried. "Eighteen! Did you have to get her involved in this?"

"I was sorry to hear about what happened to her," Slay said. "But I wasn't there."

"How convenient that was."

"You think I had something to do with her getting raped?" Slay tried to sound shocked, but even to himself it sounded like a soap opera actor putting too much histrionics into a simple line of dialogue.

Cydney shook her head and looked at Slay with contempt.

Red veins, like tree roots, shot from her dark pupils and ruined the whites of her eyes. Her eyelids twitched as if she had some kind of nervous condition.

Slay couldn't bear to look at Cydney so visibly upset. He turned away. "I didn't have anything to do with what happened to that girl."

"I've always made excuses for you, Slay," Cydney said. "When you got sent to juvie the first time I tried to pretend you weren't snatching women's purses and that you didn't beat that boy to near death with that rusty hubcap. When you came out the second time with all of that anger in you I explained it away. Who wouldn't be angry at having most of their childhood stolen? Who wouldn't be angry at living a prison existence when they should be at football practice or lip synching to Michael Jackson records in their bedroom? Who wouldn't—?"

"Be angry about coming home and finding out the man who claims he was going to be a father to you—" Slay spat the words out "—adopts your sister but not you. Tells you pretty much that you an unwanted bastard."

"Put that to rest," Cydney said.

"Who wouldn't be angry," Slay continued, "about getting in a fight and stabbing your fast-assed sister's maniac boyfriend, just to have her take the crazy fucker back like he was Denzel fucking Washington? *How convenient it is of you,* Cydney, to leave that situation out. You and I both know that was the final straw that got me sent to juvie a third time—protecting you. I know I was doing a lot of messing up, but with football going so well and all those college scouts paying me some attention, I was trying to get my shit together. Then I go and take on Byron because I was sick of him beating the shit out of you and..."

"I—"

Slay ignored Cydney. He was on too much of a roll. "...you

taking it like a dumb ass. I always been your protector and you've always wanted me to be when it was convenient for you.

"Who wouldn't be angry about being the only one to care two shits about their crackhead mama, just to have that same mother go and call you all kinds of nigga 'cause you won't go get her some rocks to finish the job the last rocks didn't? You judge me when you want, Cydney. Funny though, I don't remember you judging me when I gave you money to buy your condo and pay your tuition."

"There's a part of you that is noble and gallant," Cydney agreed, a hitch in her voice, her nose runny. "But you choose to let that other side dominate, that nasty, ugly side that rapes unsuspecting girls in stairwells."

"I wasn't there," Slay said. "I spoke with the cops and they let me go."

Cydney shook her head. "I bet they were part of your gang, too."

"Oh, now I'm a gang leader?"

"You said it, not me." She twisted her mouth into a smirk of a smile. "Tell me exactly how it is you earn such a nice living for yourself without any signs of a real job that I can see?"

Slay huffed and waved her off. "At least I didn't run from my own family like they had the fucking plague. At least I ain't some stuffy-ass wannabe that forgot where I came from."

"No," Cydney said, "you sure didn't forget where you came from, Slay. And I know where you're headed, too. Facedown in the gutter, probably with a bullet hole in your head. I came today to let you know that I look forward to that day. It pains me to realize it, and even more to say it, but you're of no worth to anyone here on earth. You've been hurting me for longer than I want to admit. I'll be glad when the world is rid of you." The words were harsher than she'd meant for them to be, but she took a special pride nonetheless in having the strength to say them, for having the strength to stand up to Slay. And, truth be told, it was exactly how she felt at the moment.

Slay turned to his sister, his mouth half-open, words stuck somewhere in him that he couldn't seem to find. The hate in Cydney's voice surprised him. This time it was more authentic than in any of their past arguments and disagreements. Cydney held her glare on Slay as he processed what she'd said, as his mouth finally closed, as he gasped for air to clear his head, as the hardness of his shell cracked under the weight of one simple tear falling in a trail from each eye. Cydney was the only person in his life he'd let see him cry.

"You think your boy, GQ Smooth, is the be-all and end-all," Slay said after he composed himself. "But he ain't. Only thing I've ever done is tried to be there for you and you toss me aside like this, like I'm some piece of trash." The tears of a moment prior were replaced on Slay's face by a smirk and the smirk's hateful cousin scowl. "Ask your boy, GQ Smooth, about Hot Tails. Ask him about the dancer that works there, Ha-seen-ta. I dare you, Cydney. Your boy ain't all you think he is, and neither am I. He's not all good and I ain't all bad."

Slay opened the door. He got out and closed it behind him with a child's gentle touch. Moved around the back of Cydney's car and went to his BMW. Started the engine, backed from the slanted space and slowly drove up the block, no music playing, alone with his thoughts.

He was getting used to being in this place.

Getting used to being alone.

Changing Lanes Bowling Alley held down one of the darkest streets of Asbury Park. The bowling lane's location was fitting, seeing that no matter how much track lighting was installed and lit in the building the place was darker than the tomb that couldn't hold Jesus. The establishment was also one of the few in town that welcomed the graffiti sprawled in contrasting colors along its brick facade. The graffiti gave it that gritty quality, a spice that kept the place packed with the city's lowest common denominator from midday to late night. Drunks saw a trip to the alley as an opportunity to work off some barley calories and an excuse for chugging beers at a breakneck pace. Teens fed the arcade games an endless stream of quarters, danced to the music from the jukebox and flirted members of the opposite sex into bathroom stalls for their quick expressions of love. Unlike the suburban bowling alleys, this one didn't cotton much to families. Fights broke out at Changing Lanes on an almost daily occasion. For the owners the place was a perfect business, they didn't have to worry about the expensive price of upkeep and they kept a packed house.

Slay had called Tuffy early this morning and set up a meeting at Changing Lanes.

Now Slay spotted Tuffy in the arcade section as soon as he walked through the door. Slay walked over, his conversation with Cydney still burdening his heart. "Peace."

Tuffy bent down as he wiggled the joystick, a grimace on his face, intensity in his eyes as he challenged the game. He didn't look in Slay's direction but acknowledged him after he made his move. "Peace."

Slay nodded at the throwback game of Pac-Man across from the Mortal Kombat game Tuffy played. "Pac-Man. I ain't seen one of those in a minute. I used to be nice."

Tuffy continued maneuvering the joystick. "Yeah, that's an old-school joint there."

Slay leaned in closer to Tuffy so he could see the screen on the Mortal Kombat. "My other shit was Double Dribble. Remember that joint?"

"Nah," Tuffy said.

"How old you now, Tuff?"

"Seventeen."

Slay thought back on where he was in his own life at the age of seventeen—tossing footballs to social counselors and fellow juvenile delinquents instead of preparing for a Division I football scholarship. "That's a tough age."

Tuffy shrugged. "You say so."

"You gonna get together with your family for Thanksgiving?"

Tuffy got his head ripped off in the game. He slammed his fist against the machine in disgust. He turned to Slay. "What's that?"

"Thanksgiving... You got folks to spend it with?"

Tuffy narrowed his eyes. "What? You writing a book on me or something? You askin' a lot of questions."

Slay smiled. "Nah, just curious, I guess. I like to know a little of what's up with my top dawgs."

Tuffy smiled at the compliment. It made his day. Tuffy shook his head, turned with his back facing the game and leaned against it. "Nah, I ain't got no family besides my nana. Pops ran out before I was born and my moms, she died from leukemia or some shit, I ain't really sure."

"Your nana takes care of you?"

Tuffy cracked his knuckles. "I take care of myself."

Slay nodded. "I hear you."

Tuffy paused. He cleared his throat. "I appreciate what you done for me, too. You been like the father I never had."

Slay frowned, gritted his teeth. He couldn't reconcile himself as a father figure.

"But, check it out, yo," Tuffy said. "That model girl was off the hook like you said. She came up in that stairwell like she owned the motherfucker. Had on some nice-ass shit. Titties hanging out. My boys held her down and I jammed my fingers up—"

Slay turned away from Tuffy. "Where's the bathroom up

in here?" The mention of Felicia made his mouth salt over with nausea.

Tuffy pointed to a far corner.

"Aiight," Slay said. He reached in his pocket and pulled out a wad of bills, handed them to Tuffy. "My stomach is bubbling from this chicken I ate. I better go handle this. I'll get up."

Tuffy took the money and clumped it into his side pocket. "I did good on this last job? 'Cause you know I want some more work."

Slay managed, "You took it a little far…"

"How it goes sometimes," Tuffy said.

Slay nodded, though he didn't believe it. "Yeah, you did a good job, Tuffy." He tapped the young boy on the shoulder and headed for the bathroom, his stomach a mess of nerves and guilt. The vision he had in his head of Felicia Rucker on that stairwell made his insides feel as if they would spill out at any minute. He was getting soft. Soft was a dangerous thing to be where he came from.

SLAY

"Need to keep your hands off my sister," I say.

Byron looks at me, an amused look on his face, then turns that look on the girl on his arm. "You believe this little fake gangsta nigga, baby?" he says to the girl. She looks me up and down, smiles her own self.

"This fake gangsta nigga will fuck you up," I say to Byron.

His head turns to me real quick. His eyes narrow. He reaches in his pocket and pulls out some crumpled bills, hands them to the girl, eyes on me the entire time. "Tomalika," he says to the girl, "baby, go on ahead and get your outfit. I'll catch up."

The mall isn't crowded yet, which is good, 'cause there is no telling what I might do to this nigga.

"Yo, Tomalika," I say, "see if they selling new names or tits in the store. You need both." I look her up and down. "I'd probably try for the tits." I don't need to be tossing stones at her name like my name is William or Michael or someshit.

She gives me the finger, hugs Byron and jets.

"Her tits is just fine, Slay. They don't slap me in the face like Cydney's big-ass tits do when I'm banging that ho like nobody's business, but they make do."

I ignore that jab. "Let's step outside, Byron."

He does a fake shiver. "What, little fake gangsta nigga, you watched Scarface on television or something today?"

I start walking and he follows.

Outside, I wheel on him. Grab his collar. "Keep. Your. Hands. Off. My. Sister."

The fear is in his eyes. He attempts to remove my hands. I move one my own self, slap his face with it. Hard. His eyes water. Then I let him go and push him back.

"You done fucked up now," he says, rubbing his face.

I take a step forward, he shadows it, but backward. I smile and stop. "I wish you'd put your hands on me the way you do Cydney," I taunt.

"Oh, you like taking it in the ass. In the mouth. In the—"

I lunge forward again, pounce on this nigga. Push him against the building. Slap him a couple more times. I'm bouncing on my feet, like I'm jumping rope, hands balled in fists, ready to do more damage. "Say something else, pussy. Say something else."

"I ain't studying Cydney," he says, breathing heavy, bent over but with his eyes on me. "I'll leave her stank ass be. The only one thinks that pussy is worth anything…is you."

My knife is out of my pocket and in Byron's stomach before I know what happens. I leave him there and walk to my car without a worry in the world.

CHAPTER 23

Officer Raymond Jackson parked his unmarked patrol car outside Cush and walked inside. He was dressed in dark blue slacks and a thick brown sweater. Despite the nip outside, he wore no jacket, keeping himself warm throughout the day by drinking steaming-hot cups of coffee at the rate a heavy smoker puffed on cigarettes. All about business, Jackson didn't stop to admire the fancy awning outside the restaurant, or the elegant setup once he was inside. The pretty woman at the podium reminded him of his wife, going back some years, of course, before the accumulation of late-night worry started lining her face with wrinkles that makeup couldn't conquer and Jackson's proclamations of "I'll be okay" couldn't slow. The streets and the random crime on them had taken so much of Jackson's life. Where once he considered himself a hero, and his greatest goal was to make the streets safe for everyone, he now considered himself a victim, and his greatest goal was to make it through the day without becoming any more embittered than he was when it started.

"Welcome to Cush." Karen beamed at Jackson as he walked in.

Jackson looked past Karen instead of at her. "Is Desmond Rucker in?"

Karen's smile faded. This guy was like the scent of nail-polish remover, harsh. "Yes, he's in his office."

"May I speak with him?"

"Is it anything I might be able to—"

Officer Jackson looked at her like a parent looks at an unruly child. "Tell him it's Officer Jackson waiting to talk with him."

Karen shook Jackson off with a roll of her eyes. "I'll see if he's busy."

"You do that," Jackson said. He stepped back and took a seat on the leather chairs they had on either side of the aisle. He crossed his legs and sat back, whistling some long-ago song that hadn't even been popular when it first came out.

Karen returned to the podium in short order. "He'll see you in his office," she said tersely.

Jackson stood. "And his office is…?"

Karen turned, pointed. "Right down that path, to the right. The door marked Office."

Jackson tapped the podium as he passed. "Thank you, dear."

Karen smiled a closedmouthed little ditty. "You're quite welcome, sir."

Jackson moved to Desmond's office door and knocked once. He opened it and stuck his head in without being invited to.

Desmond wheeled his chair to face Jackson. "Officer," he said in a monotone.

"Mr. Rucker."

Neither of them offered a hand to shake.

Desmond did extend his hand toward a chair, though. "Have a seat."

Jackson shook his head. "I'll stand." Jackson turned and made sure the door was closed behind him. "I called your house and spoke to your sister. She seems to be coming along. She told me you were here working. Nice little spread you got here."

Desmond leaned to the side, eyes on Jackson. "Thanks."

"Your sister said an investigative officer informed you both at the hospital that the Shammond Slay guy checked out."

"Yes."

"He had a receipt showing that he was at a record shop

about the time the crime was committed, and the record store owner, Rafael, he confirmed it."

"Right," Desmond said.

Jackson scratched the side of his scalp. "Also, curiously enough, he stopped in here and got two desserts to go. Apple brown betty, he says. He told our investigators 'it's the bomb,' and that he got the desserts and went over to his girl's place."

Desperately as Desmond tried, he couldn't hide the surprise in his eyes.

"You weren't aware that he came by here, Mr. Rucker?"

Desmond shifted his weight in the seat. "No, I wasn't."

Jackson looked up and around the perimeter of the ceiling. "You have surveillance cameras here, Mr. Rucker?"

Desmond shook his head.

"Would you mind if I have a word with the woman out front?" Jackson asked. "She matches the description of the woman Slay says took care of him."

"That's fine," Desmond said, "but please don't mention what happened to my sister."

Jackson nodded, put his hand on the doorknob, but didn't leave. "All quite suspicious about this Shammond Slay, don't you think, Mr. Rucker? And you say you never met him?"

"No, I've never met him I don't believe."

"I'm as sure as I think you are, though," Jackson added, "that he's somehow involved with what happened to your sister. It's difficult, though, because people around here don't like to talk too much against him. That guy has some serious pull in underground Asbury, as I told you. Nothing but a hoodlum, but he has major league connections. Word is he had something on some pharmaceutical executive that summers down here on the shore and he used whatever he had to black-mail the guy, get himself some money, start up his own little enterprise." Jackson nodded to himself. "He's involved. I just have to figure out how and why."

Desmond shook his head. "Yes, it all seems fishy, doesn't it?"

Jackson smiled. "I was meaning to ask you the other night why your special lady friend left so fast, and what seemed to upset her so."

Desmond eyed Jackson. "She was shocked, traumatized. She didn't need to be there."

"What was her name again?"

"Why does that matter?" Desmond asked.

Jackson shrugged and looked around the office. "I've always wanted my own business, but I wouldn't know a thing about handling a business. Say, running a restaurant like this," he said. "And I'd make a big mess of it if I ever tried." He looked at Desmond. "You should leave that kind of stuff to the professionals. You know what I mean?"

"Sometimes you just follow your heart," Desmond said. "If it's something you feel you must do, you do it and let it work itself out however it does."

"Many of lives negatively impacted by folks following their heart," Jackson shot back.

Desmond tapped his watch. "I don't mean to be rude but I have quite a few things I need to attend to."

Jackson smiled again. "Of course," he said. "I'll be talking to you again, I'm sure."

Cydney looked across the table at her two friends. They both looked stunned by what she'd told them. Victoria's hair peeked from under an expensive-looking burgundy scarf. She sipped her Starbucks coffee slowly, leaving a smudge of auburn-colored lipstick along the foam lip of her cup. She had a pastry on a napkin in front of her that she kept twisting like a chess piece but didn't bite into. Faith was dressed down, in a Reebok jumpsuit with a hood, and purple mittens that she hadn't removed yet. She had a cup of coffee, too, but had only sipped it once.

"I don't understand why you didn't tell us about your brother and mother before," Faith said, breaking the silence of the table. "Why you had to make it seem you grew up differently than you did."

"She was embarrassed," Victoria said. "I can understand that."

Cydney looked at Victoria with a frown. "Thanks."

"I don't mean that you should have been," Victoria said. "Just that I can understand that you were."

"And you think your brother had something to do with what happened to Desmond's sister?" Faith said.

Cydney nodded. "I'm pretty sure. Slay has a problem, he's overprotective, and he's a hoodlum."

"How did he get into that life, get this power you say he has?" Victoria asked.

"Slay's resourceful," Cydney admitted. "He was approached by a lot of people when it looked as if he might do something with his football talents. He befriended a lot of different people, from different walks of life, some of them very respected. Slay's smart in his own way…he chipped in on those alliances later, I guess. He just started living this lavish lifestyle a few years back with no visible means of support. Whenever I've asked him about it he just smiles at me or ignores me."

"And you took money from him?" Victoria asked. She turned her mouth up.

"For my place and school," Cydney said. "Yes, I did." She gave Victoria a hard look, waiting for her friend to impart her high-principled judgment. Cydney had done it to better herself, to change her station in life. She wouldn't let anyone make her feel bad about the decision. She'd still be catching the back of Byron's hand and probably be the mother of two or three of his children if she hadn't chased her dreams.

"Have you said anything to the police?" Faith asked, noticing the tension between Cydney and Victoria.

Cydney shook her head. "I told Desmond. I'm sure he'll let them know. I got out of there as quickly as I could when the officer said my brother's name. It was like my life was coming to an end, my heart started racing, my legs tightened, my stomach doing backflips."

"Desmond must be devastated," Victoria said.

Cydney sighed. "I haven't spoken with him since then. I don't know what to say to him. Obviously, he doesn't have anything to say to me."

"You're not going to let him get away?" Faith said.

Cydney looked down at her own full cup of café con leche. "I can't imagine why he'd want to stay with me. I lied to him."

"Because," Faith said. Her voice was loud and strong across the divide of the table. "You're beautiful, intelligent, ambitious and you two were building something really strong. It's not like you cheated on him. Practically everyone embellishes their past to some degree."

Cydney didn't seem too convinced. "Our foundation is based on lies, though. That poor girl, she's just a baby really. I can barely sleep thinking about what my brother did to her. I never thought he'd mess with Desmond this way. I can't shake the look of hurt and surprise in Desmond's eyes when I told him Slay was my brother."

"Are you falling in love with Desmond, Cydney?" Victoria asked.

Cydney looked to her friend. Victoria seemed to have come down off her high horse. "Falling hard and fast," Cydney admitted.

"And he with you?" Victoria pressed.

Cydney nodded. "I believe so. At least, I thought so."

"Then you got to go clear the air, explain yourself, and see what you two can do about fixing that foundation." Victoria picked up the pastry and took her first bite, licking her lips to get a sliver of apple filling from the corner of her mouth.

"You make everything sound so easy," Cydney said.

"Has getting where you are been easy?" Faith chimed in.

Cydney smirked, rolled her neck and eyes. "Hell no. Girls where I'm from don't often go to college, don't better themselves…"

"Was all the hard work worth it?" Victoria asked.

Cydney gripped her coffee cup with both hands. Her head was bowed. "Yes."

"Then you have to decide if Desmond is worth the hard effort it'll take to make your relationship survive," Victoria offered.

Faith looked at Victoria. "Darn. That was well said."

Victoria licked her fingers. "Besides food, the other thing I know well is relationships. I've had plenty of practice."

Cydney looked up, reached forward and touched both of her friends' hands. "Thank you, both of you. Thank you."

She hadn't told them the other thing that was caressing her brain into doubt.

The thing Slay told her.

About Hot Tails and some dancer named Jacinta.

A turn for the worse.

Slay stood outside his mother's room looking through the door's window. Nancy was wrapped in three thin sweaters, but Slay could still see her shivering. The nurse he spoke with earlier informed him that his mother was suffering from withdrawal and that even though the hospital normally handled addiction recovery on an outpatient basis, because of Nancy's years of abuse, the drugs had wracked her body and left her with serious ailments in addition to the addiction. The nurse lowered her voice as she neared the end and said in an even tone, "She's really taken a turn for the worse. We'll do our best to extend her life." Those words were even more painful to Slay than the words Cydney had said to him.

"Why don't you walk on inside, son?"

Slay turned to the foreign voice. A white man, dressed very conservatively, with fat red cheeks and a generous smile, stood next to him. Slay looked down at the man's feet. He wore a clunky pair of black shoes with scuff marks on the front and laces with the ends frayed and missing the plastic tips. Despite the clunky shoes it was as if the man walked across a thick carpet, his footsteps were so quiet.

Slay moved his eyes to the man's face. "What was that?"

"I'm Reverend Jameson Pinckney, the head of Pastoral Services here at the hospital. I've stopped in on your mother a few times and prayed for her. The nurses told me that her son comes in all the time and I asked them to let me know the next time you came." He smiled at Slay and put his hand on his shoulder.

"You Catholic?" Slay asked. "Because my mama, she a Baptist." He looked back into the room. "Was a Baptist."

"Presbyterian," the reverend said. "But I'm under the same umbrella of God's graciousness that your mother's under."

Slay smirked and nodded to the room. "You call that in there graciousness?"

The reverend nodded in acknowledgment. "Sometimes it is hard to see. Yesterday I performed my first marriage ceremony here in the hospital. Twelve years, and yesterday was my first wedding. Beautiful couple." The reverend sighed, looking off beyond Slay. The reverend's face held his smile like a child holds his protective blanket or toy. "Young man, terminally ill, couldn't change himself, couldn't eat on his own, but he held his fiancée's hand tight, tight." The reverend's grip tightened on Slay's shoulder and Slay turned and looked at it.

"And the young woman," the reverend continued, his grip

still firm on Slay's shoulder. "You couldn't have pried the joy off her face with a crowbar. So I married them yesterday afternoon." The reverend shook his head as if to brush off flecks of rain or flakes of snow. "That young husband died this morning. I just left from praying with his wife."

Slay smirked again. "Graciousness you called it?"

"You're standing here loaded to bear, filled with hurt, son," the reverend said. "I can see the care and love in you though, under that hard exterior you're presenting. The graciousness is that God brought someone into your life that created enough happy memories, thoughtful interchanges and loving experiences with you so that you could hurt when you see them slipping away. The graciousness is that God chose to share her with you in the first place."

Slay thought about the heartbreak on his mother's face when he was sent to juvenile detention, the times she'd come out in the street, down alleys and avenues she shouldn't have been on, looking for him. He thought about her in the stands at his football games, braving the cold, carrying those big signs she wrote on poster board. Number 13 Is My Son, the signs read. She loved Slay. Slay loved her. He turned to the reverend, a lump in his throat. His love for her hadn't kept him from letting her down, though, hadn't kept him from breaking her heart. Her love, likewise, hadn't kept her from breaking Slay's heart. That's all love was—heartbreak.

"She wasn't always a junkie, Reverend. She was a good mother. Things just twisted her up and she didn't know how to handle them."

"I'm sure she wasn't, son."

Slay looked at the reverend. "There's this real thick sweater my mama has at home, I'm thinking it might keep her warmer."

The reverend smiled. "You need to go on and get your

mother that sweater, son. And when you put it on her, give her a kiss, tell her you love her and thank God."

Slay felt the urge to do something he never would have imagined himself wanting to do. He struggled with his emotions for a moment and then just decided to do it.

Slay leaned over and hugged the reverend.

Sometimes life has you run smack-dab into the walls that imprison you, the hurdles that confound you and the obstacles that challenge you. Cydney was moving through the doors of Cush when Desmond came hurtling out, his head down. They collided in the pass-through.

"Oh, man," Desmond said, "I'm so—" The sight of Cydney halted him in his tracks and forced his apology to the background. He rolled his eyes with disgust and looked up at the dim light fixture flickering on its last legs in the lobby. He had to remember to change the bulb later.

Cydney hadn't prepared enough for this quick meeting. "Hi, Desmond," she said. She cringed at the simplicity of her words as she thought about those movies she loved on Lifetime, how different the line would have come out in one of those dramas, how something clever and enlightening would have been delivered by the actress.

"Excuse me," Desmond said, and he moved to past as if they'd never shared more than this head-on collision.

Cydney stepped to the side, blocking his exit. "We need to talk."

"I've got to get to the bank," Desmond said, raising his arm to show her the leather pouch gripped tightly in his hands.

"I don't mind riding with you," Cydney said. "In fact, I kind of wanted to talk to you away from here anyway."

"Okay," was Desmond's reply, delivered quicker than he meant it to come and than Cydney expected.

Cydney stepped aside and allowed him to move through the door. She followed close behind as he stepped with purpose to his truck. That one small word, *okay,* was a big step toward Desmond and Cydney recovering what they'd built. Cydney swallowed the word with delight, her heartbeat returning to normal as she eased inside Desmond's truck. The leather seat welcomed her unconditionally, molding itself to her instead of her having to mold herself to it.

"How's your sister doing?" Cydney asked as Desmond started the engine.

The words set something off in Desmond. His forehead bunched tighter than a fist. "How's your brother doing?" he shot back. He moved the transmission gear from park to drive and pulled from his spot with reckless energy propelling him.

"I made a huge mistake not telling you about him," Cydney admitted. She wanted to tell Desmond to slow down but decided against it.

"And why was that?" Desmond asked. His voice was high and it cracked as easily as model-airplane wood.

"I don't come from the same kind of place as you, Desmond. I guess I just thought you wouldn't understand where I come from, who I come from."

"We all have black sheep in our families," Desmond reasoned as he made a turn. He seemed to settle down, the odometer needle dropping like the temperature.

Cydney sat back in her seat, the tension in her upper body settling. "Do we all have a family of black sheep?" she asked him.

"Come again?"

"My mother isn't in a home, she's addicted to crack cocaine and my brother is a street thug, a hustler. I don't have anyone besides the two of them. My stepfather, the only good in the family, was murdered down on the beach not too long ago. I grew up in a neighborhood where the biggest ambition was to hit the numbers. My first real boyfriend was a creep with three other girlfriends. He beat me less than the other two because I was prettier. My brother got in a fight with him, protecting me, and ended up stabbing him. I took the boyfriend back even after all that because I thought he could get me something better in life. He's in jail now for shaking the baby of one of his other girlfriends to death." Cydney stopped to catch her breath. "I've got a shoplifting offense in my past because I didn't have a dress to wear to the prom and I took matters into my own hands." She smiled and shook her head at the memory. "I couldn't boost for shit…"

"So you grew up rough," Desmond said. "I would have just respected all that you are now even more."

Cydney shook her head. "You ever have a bad dream when you were younger and your mother came in the room to quiet your screams?"

"Sure."

"What did she do?"

"She'd rub my head, tell me it was a dream and that I should try and forget it."

Cydney nodded, smiled a smile that was more pain than joy. "Try and forget it. That's what we all do with bad dreams."

"Your brother has been on my trail for a while, Cydney. I just know it. I'm sure you knew it, too. You should have warned me."

"I know Slay has his ways," Cydney said, "but I never suspected he'd take it this far. I would have told you if I did, you've got to believe that."

Desmond rolled into the bank's parking lot. He parked the truck and turned to Cydney. "So you believe he had something to do with what happened to Felicia?"

Cydney dropped her gaze. "He said he didn't, but I don't believe him. I'd told him—shortly after I began with you—that I didn't want him in my life anymore. He knew about you, he blamed you. My brother has always felt it was his job to protect me. He means well but he doesn't have any concept of walking right. Everything with him is thug rule."

Desmond shook his head, sighed. "You should have told me, Cydney. You should have told me." He banged the steering wheel in frustration.

Cydney reached over and touched his hand. He didn't pull from her. "I know," she said. "I'm so sorry."

"My sister is coming along," Desmond said. "Slowly." He looked away for a moment and turned his intense glare on Cydney. "I needed you with me these past few days. I've been trying to figure this out and all I know is…I missed you, Cydney."

Cydney gripped his hand. "I missed you, too. I swear I did. I want to make everything right. I want to be there for you. No more secrets."

"I hope not," Desmond said.

"If it means anything to you, I've been lying to myself about Slay, too."

"I don't understand," Desmond said.

Cydney sighed. "When we were younger, he did a few things to me, things brothers shouldn't do to their sisters. It was a weird situation. It started innocently, and he took it places it didn't need to go."

Understanding registered in Desmond's eyes. "You've never told anyone that?"

Cydney shook her head. "My stepfather confronted me about it and I denied, denied, denied. My mother tried to ask me about it once, but she could barely get the words out."

"So why are you telling me?" Desmond asked.

"Like I said," Cydney told him, "no more secrets."

Desmond nodded, gripped her hand.

Cydney hesitated. "Desmond?"

"Yes?"

"My brother mentioned that club around the corner from your restaurant where they have the go-go dancing—Hot Tails—and a dancer named Jacinta." She looked at the new wrinkles that formed on Desmond's forehead, how his eyes stayed on her but seemed to want to run for cover. "No more secrets," she said to Desmond.

Desmond pursed his lips. He didn't have to say anything; his eyes, his lips, they said it all. Cydney squeezed her eyes shut for a moment and dropped her head back against the plush leather headrest. "Okay," she said as she reopened her eyes. She increased the strength of her grip on Desmond's hand and said "okay" a second time, but much softer than the first.

It didn't escape her that a short while before, the word *okay* held such a different meaning for her.

Slay stepped off the elevator in his mother's apartment tower with her thick sweater under his arm. The door to the right of the elevator, Kenya's door, was opening and for a moment he considered getting on the elevator and heading back up. He didn't though. Kenya stepped outside her apartment, a large green bag of laundry at her feet. She locked her door and turned to find Slay standing there staring at her. She dragged the bag of laundry with her and stopped about ten feet from Slay, with the plump bag resting against her leg.

Kenya spoke first. "Hey."

Slay nodded at her the same way he nodded at his people in the streets.

Kenya looked down at her green bag. "Heading off to get these clothes washed," she said.

"Bag looks heavy."

Kenya squeezed her lips together, shook her head. "I can manage it all right. I'm not going to carry it over my back or nothing crazy like that."

Slay fidgeted in place. "Things good?"

"Damon got his report card," Kenya said, speaking of her youngest son. "He made the honor roll."

Slay seemed warmed by the news; he stopped moving and listened to her.

"Shamar," Kenya said of the oldest, "got a D in Social Studies that messed him up." She smiled. "He has Mrs. Wakefield."

Slay smiled, too. "Damn, is she still teaching? What was that she used to always say to me?"

"You lie like a rug," Kenya answered.

Slay threw his head back. "Right, right. Mrs. Wakefield couldn't stand my ass."

Kenya nodded. "Maybe she's taking that out on Shamar now."

A breeze cut through the lobby, one of the local winos walked in and searched the garbage can by the front door. Slay looked over his shoulder, gritted his teeth at the sight of the wino. He turned back to Kenya with a new look in his eyes. "Mama isn't doing so well. I was taking her this sweater."

Kenya pocketed her keys and moved forward another few steps, dragging the overstuffed green bag of dirty laundry. "Sorry to hear that. They still got her at the hospital?"

Slay nodded. "Yeah."

Kenya stayed a decent distance from Slay so she wouldn't mess up and take him in her arms. "I've missed you."

Slay smirked. "Boom wouldn't want to hear that shit. You know that dude jealous than a mug."

Kenya shook her head. "Boom ain't about much, he's gone all day, comes in late every night smelling like Strawberry Hill and CK One—the woman's one."

"You still his lady, though," Slay said. "At least that's how he sees it."

"I was the happiest I ever been while he was locked up," Kenya said. "When it was just you and me, you know?"

Slay nodded. "It didn't last long enough."

"It could be different, you know that."

Slay shook his head. "You know me and Boom have our understanding. Plus, me and Boom go back a long ways."

"Me and you go back further," Kenya said.

Slay thought about the letters Kenya sent him when he was in juvie. They were still up in his mother's apartment, filed away in a rusty old Maxwell House coffee can. He gripped his mother's sweater. "I got to get this over to the hospital." He offered Kenya one last smile and turned to leave.

"I'd tell him about us if you let me," Kenya called to Slay. Her voice had risen at the beginning of the sentence and then settled into an almost whisper at the end. She stood in place, her body tense from the can of worms she'd opened, the can she'd wanted to open for so long.

Slay stopped, his back to Kenya, and looked down at the sweater. "Go ahead," he said. "And, yo...those letters you sent me when I was in juvie, they kept me going. Even now I think about them and they keep me going." Slay walked on, through the doors and out to his car. When he got inside the car he placed his mother's sweater on the driver's seat, patted it like you fluff a pillow and drove off.

Inside the apartment tower, Kenya looked down at her bag of laundry. She gripped the tie strings in her hand and pulled the bag down the hall toward the community laundry room, her pockets jingling with the required quarters. All of a sudden the load didn't seem quite as large anymore.

CHAPTER 24

"Why did you do it?" Cydney asked Desmond.

"I don't know."

"How often did you go there?"

Desmond shrugged. "I went there a few times."

"You care for this girl?"

"No."

"The truth," Cydney said. Her voice was soft and tender whereas her demeanor was hard and forceful.

"The truth is, I did it and I'm ashamed. Jacinta's a decent soul and all but she isn't you. I'd like to say it happened because I was concerned you were going to go running back to Stephon, but I can't. I mean, that was in my head, but I knew what I was doing and at the time I wanted it."

"So, you have a problem with monogamy?"

Desmond looked at Cydney. "Yes, in the past I always have."

Cydney sighed. "Okay."

"But," Desmond said, "I can also honestly say I've never dealt with anyone that made me want to conquer that problem like you do. I never thought too much about it until you came along. I'm feeling so good just being honest with you. I've never done that before."

"Honestly, Desmond," Cydney said. "Do you want to be with me?"

Desmond reached over and took her hands. "I want to be with you more than anything in the world."

"I think we should both get HIV tests done."

Desmond nodded. "I get one every year, but yes, I think we should."

Cydney sighed. "I'm scared."

"You think I'm not?"

Cydney shook her head. "You know if I hadn't lied to you and messed up myself, I wouldn't give you a second chance, Desmond."

Desmond smiled. "Yes, I figured as much."

"We moved too fast, didn't we?"

Desmond nodded again. "Probably," he said.

"Why do people do that, knowing the consequences?"

Desmond shrugged. "I was just afraid you'd get away. I wasn't sure if you were what I needed or if I was what you needed. But I knew I wanted you."

Cydney's eyes were lit with a new understanding. "You were dictated by lust then?"

"Yeah," Desmond acknowledged. "Part of it was lust."

"What was the other part?"

Desmond leaned back against the leather of his seat. "Your playfulness... How you teased me about my Eddie Murphy tape. The way you made me feel... You were so complimentary and so impressed that first time you came by the restaurant. You made me so proud to be the owner. I didn't even feel that good when my parents came on opening night. And then when you told me what you were looking for in a man—someone you'd look at in forty years and wonder how the years went by so fast and how it was you enjoyed them so much. That was the answer I've needed to hear from a woman my whole life. That's what I want and I didn't know it until you said it." Desmond stopped and smiled at a memory. "The first time I kissed you. I never was much of a kisser but your lips pulled me in. I appreciate a beautiful body, Cydney, and you have one, but not every woman has a spirit that you can see as clearly as her body. You have the kind of spirit that just is out there in the open, in plain view. I love that about you. It's contagious."

"And yet you still did this thing with the dancer?" Cydney asked. There was no bitterness or anger in her voice, just a question.

"Yes, I did."

Cydney shuddered. "God, this is so scary to me."

"I think that's a good thing," Desmond said, "because everything I've ever done that really meant something to me caused me some anguish and nervousness at the beginning, and yet I knew it meant something because I did it anyway."

"We're pretty much starting all over," Cydney said.

"I think we're awful lucky to get that chance," Desmond added.

"No matter if you stumble or not, I want you to always be truthful with me," Cydney told him.

"And you with me," Desmond answered.

"So how do we start again?"

Desmond took her chin in his hand. "How about we start with a kiss?"

Cydney nodded. Desmond kissed her...

It was the type of conversation that embedded itself in one's mind like a video recording, to be played over and over again. Desmond turned his truck off and removed his keys from the ignition—his way of stopping the recording of his earlier episode with Cydney. He moved from his truck and crossed the street to see about handling the other issue that held his mind captive. There was still the unsettled issue of Shammond Slay. Desmond owed Slay for his involvement in Felicia's attack.

Desmond gripped the familiar door handle and moved inside.

The heavy voice and disinterested drone hadn't changed from the first time Desmond visited Hot Tails. "Two-drink minimum. Make sure you get the first drink before you get a permanent seat," the bouncer said. He didn't appear to recognize Desmond.

Desmond frowned as he walked into the darkened building. He noticed for the first time just how cheesy the place was. The strobe lights that circled the walls was a drab bluish-purple, the speakers that cranked out the excessive bass of the DJ-spun records cracked with static, and the air ducts blew out warm air that smelled stale and mildewy. The place was like the bouncer, no personality whatsoever, just concrete walls painted white, horny men, and women doing sexual gymnastics with the air. It was hard for Desmond to imagine how the place once held such a spell over him.

Most of the same faces from the other times he'd been here were here now and Desmond hoped one of them would lead him to Jacinta. He was desperate to get in touch with Shammond Slay and he hoped Jacinta would shade in the blank areas of the thug enigma for him.

Wendy, the bartender, was on a stool on the customer side of the bar, nuzzling noses with a ruddy-looking man wearing a wrinkled dress shirt. Desmond walked up to her and tapped her on the shoulder. The man Wendy sat with took the opportunity to sip from his drink.

Wendy turned, a tight red shirt with Boys Lie inscribed on the front, the shirt tied in a knot under her store-bought breasts. "Hey there, Mr. Screwdriver," she said. She leaned in and gave Desmond a hug that he didn't reciprocate. She didn't seem to pick up on his discomfort. "I'm going on in an hour, are you here to check out my show?"

"Oh, I was wondering why you weren't behind the bar," Desmond said. It was his way of avoiding her question.

Wendy smiled. "Yeah, I'm done with that. So you gonna check out my show?"

"Actually," Desmond admitted, "I'm trying to get in touch with Jacinta. I know she quit this place but I was hoping you might be able to tell me how to get in touch with her. Or maybe you can get in touch with her and let her know I've been looking for her."

Wendy furrowed her brows. "What do you mean she quit? She's on right now."

Desmond left Wendy without a further word and went to the room where the main stage was. Sure enough, Jacinta was on her knees on the platform, her back to Desmond, slow grinding some imaginary lover. Desmond moved closer and took a seat by the front.

Jacinta worked the crowd on the other side of the room, jiggling her breasts and playing coy with her nipples at the same time. As the staccato rhythm of the drums pulsated, Jacinta rose to her feet, turned and wiggled her hips as if she were balancing a Hula-Hoop. The DJ spurred her on, his voice cutting in over the music. "*Chachachachacha.*"

Jacinta easily bent into a split, cupped her breasts and kissed the plumpest part of each one. Three college-age boys stood, their arms around each other, their mouths wide with pleasure, and flashed her fistfuls of money. Jacinta obediently moved in their direction. Desmond shook his head. For the first time he felt sorry for Jacinta—for Mona. For the first time he felt sorry for himself—and for Cydney.

A hand gripped hard into Desmond's shoulder. He turned to face the wall that had greeted him at the door.

"You must not have heard me, my man," the wall said. "I told you to get yourself a drink before you got comfortable."

"Okay, okay," Desmond said. "I'll go get one now."

The wall ushered him back to the bar.

"Let me have a cola," Desmond said to the new bartender.

"A rum and Coke?"

Desmond shook his head. "Just a Coke."

Desmond took the drink and walked back to Jacinta's performance. She was on Desmond's side of the room now. Their eyes met as soon as Desmond took his place at the front. The smile left Jacinta's face but she kept up her erotic grind and dollars continued to pass her way. Desmond reached into his pocket and pulled out a dollar. He held it up for Jacinta to see, and she did, but she moved away from him. Desmond reached deeper in his pockets and then flashed a bit more money. Jacinta continued to ignore him, dancing on the other side of the stage again. Her set came to a close and she quickly disappeared through a door at the back of the stage.

Desmond got up and went to Wendy. Wendy was sitting on some guy's lap, a different guy than the one she was nuzzling noses with when Desmond walked in.

"Wendy," Desmond called to her.

"What?"

"Can you go in the back and ask Jacinta to come out and have a word with me?"

"I'm busy, Screwdriver," she said. "I'm promoting my upcoming set."

Desmond handed her the money Jacinta had ignored. "What can I do with five dollars?" Wendy said, crinkling her nose.

Desmond pulled out another five and handed it to Wendy. Wendy kissed the guy—whose lap supported her—on the cheek and hopped off to go get Jacinta.

Desmond took a seat at the bar. After a few moments he could feel a presence behind him. He turned.

"Hey," he said to Jacinta.

"Thought you were staying away," she said as she took a seat next to him.

"Thought you were quitting," Desmond shot back.

"I decided to finish out the year," Jacinta said.

"Can I get you a drink?" Desmond asked.

Jacinta shook her head. "No. I don't plan on being here long enough to finish a whole drink."

"I need to ask you something?" Desmond said.

"Ask away."

"You know a guy named Shammond Slay?"

"No," Jacinta said. She looked away.

"Please...Mona."

"Jacinta—and I said no."

"You're lying."

"What!" Jacinta moved to leave. Desmond took hold of her wrist. She looked to the wall that guarded the front door and made eye contact with him. Desmond turned to see the bouncer taking long hard strides toward him.

"Mona...Jacinta...whatever... Please. My sister was raped. I believe this Slay character had something to do with it."

Jacinta looked at Desmond, studied his eyes. "It's okay," she said to the bouncer just as he prepared to rip Desmond from his bar stool.

"You sure, Jacinta?" the bouncer asked. She nodded. The bouncer gave Desmond a hard stare and then walked back to his post at the front.

"Thanks," Desmond said to Jacinta.

Jacinta took a seat next to Desmond. "What were you saying about your sister?"

Desmond dropped his eyes. "She was raped by a bunch of guys at the Berkeley Carteret. She was going to meet this Slay guy."

"He was one of them that raped her?"

"No."

"I don't understand."

"I'm dating Slay's sister and he's not taking too kindly to it."

Jacinta's eyes registered something. "Slay has a sister...and you're dating her?"

"Yes." Desmond looked at Jacinta. "I know I hurt you and for that I'm sorry, but I need to know what you know about this Slay. He's been watching me or something. He mentioned me coming to this place—and you—to his sister."

"This is the woman that had you all shook up?"

"Yes."

"So she knows all about us now?"

"Yes."

Jacinta nodded several times to herself. "And she's Slay's sister?"

"Yes," Desmond said. "You obviously know the guy."

Jacinta sighed. "Yeah, I know him. He's not that bad, unless you cross him."

"Apparently I have."

"And you think he had something to do with what happened to your sister?"

"Either that, or it is one huge coincidence. You know where he lives, or do you have a number for him?"

"I usually just contact him through his cell," Jacinta said.

"Could you give me the number? My sister wouldn't and neither will my lady. The police interviewed him and have cleared him...they say it's a privacy issue and they can't give me his contact info."

"What are you planning on doing?"

Desmond smiled. "Why is everyone so worried?" Jacinta held her eyes on him. "Just having a word with him," Desmond told her.

"Don't go writing a check your ass can't cash."

"That sounds like a line from one of those seventies blaxploitation movies."

Jacinta smiled. "I am foxy...and brown."

Desmond nodded. "I just want to have a word with Slay, see if he knows anything."

Jacinta processed it all for a moment, staring at the determination in Desmond's posture and on his face. She was glad in a way to see him. Disappointed that things didn't work out between them, but that was to be expected, she'd set it up for failure from the get-go, she'd given herself to him with a promise of no strings attached. He'd done what most weak-willed men would do in that situation. Jacinta motioned to the bartender and asked him for a slip of paper and a pen. She wrote the number down and handed the slip of paper to Desmond.

Desmond took the paper and held it in his hand. "Can I ask what dealings you had with Slay?"

Jacinta rose to her feet. Her eyes were sad and her lips held several secrets. The work she did for Slay, and the baby, Desmond's, she'd aborted after that fateful day by the weeping willow. She smiled weakly and patted Desmond's hand. "Take care of yourself, Desmond."

Jacinta walked off through the side door to the back of the building. Desmond watched her stride away. He finished off his Coke, rose, and left for what he knew would be the last time. Hot Tails had been good while it lasted, but it was time he moved on to something else. Cydney Williams.

But first, he had a call to make.

The traffic light was still a shade of orange as Slay approached it, but he pressed down on his brakes and came to a stop rather than ride through. Despite his mother's worsening condition, seeing Kenya had put him in a relaxed state of calm. He had his music turned down low and rode with the exaggerated lean that marked young black males for profile targeting of racist cops. In his world, though, cops were the least of his concerns.

At the same time as the light turned green his cell phone

chirped for an incoming call. Slay turned his stereo even lower
and picked up the line.

"This is Slay."

"Shammond Slay," a foreign voice said, dragging it out.

Slay gave his car some gas, moved through the intersection
with the phone pressed to his ear. "Yeah, who is this?"

"You know who this is," the voice said.

"No, I fucking don't. Who is this?"

"Desmond Rucker."

A smile crept across Slay's lips. "The mighty, infamous
GQ Smooth."

"See," Desmond said. "I knew you knew me."

"Look," Slay said, "if this is about your sister—"

"This *is* about my sister. It's about your sister, too, right?
What you mad because I'm hitting it and you aren't."

"What did you say?"

"You're a sick guy, Slay."

"Whatever," Slay said. "I told Cydney and I told the cops,
I didn't have anything to do with what happened to Felicia.
I'm sorry about what happened."

"You got to do better than that."

"Look, B, I was planning on fucking your sister, just how
you fucking mine, but that's it. I wanted to show you how that
feels, but I wasn't there when Felicia got raped and I didn't have
anything to do with it."

"You're a liar."

"What's that saying?" Slay said. "Pot calling the kettle
black, someshit like that. You got nerve calling me a liar, Mr.
GQ Smooth. Running around with your nose up in the air like
you the shit. Meanwhile, you be tossing your dollars at hoes
on the side. Bet your family would love to see that side of you,
Rucker. I told Cydney about your little fascination with Hot
Tails and a certain Latina we both know."

"You don't worry about that, Slay. I talked it over with Cydney. We're all clear on that. Now, you and I got to get clear on what you did to Felicia. Me dating your sister—who's a grown woman—is a heck of a lot different than you messing with an eighteen-year-old girl, setting her up to get raped."

Slay pulled his car over to the side of the road. The only thing Desmond said that registered was that Cydney and Desmond were going to be okay in their relationship. "Cydney let you off the hook on that shit with Jacinta?"

"Cydney cares a whole lot about me, like it or not. Now, about my sister—"

Slay growled like a wounded animal. "This is someshit. Cydney let you off the hook on that?"

"We need to focus, Slay."

Slay slammed his fist on the dashboard. "I ain't have nothing to do with Felicia, motherfucker! And she's a grown woman, too. She came on to me, yo. She's a little fast ass just like these girls in the street. Still, though, I didn't do anything to her. Like I said, I was going to, but I changed my mind. I didn't even go to the hotel. I went to see my girl instead."

"I don't believe you, Slay."

"Believe it," Slay said. He slapped the flip of his cell phone closed and tossed the phone on the seat next to him, on top of his mother's sweater.

It rang back in less than a minute. Slay picked it up, anger flashing through him that he couldn't control. "I didn't have anything to do with what happened to Felicia, man!"

Dead silence.

"You heard me!" Slay hollered.

"How many dudes' girls you messing with, Sham?"

Slay lowered his voice; the anger left him. "Boom?"

"Yeah, nigga."

"Kenya spoke with you already?"

"Yeah, she couldn't wait to tell me you were running up in her while I was locked down."

"Yo, look, Boom, I—"

"Nah, Sham, I ain't trying to hear it. You broke your word, Sham. That's some foul shit you did."

"You know me and Kenya go back like—"

"I know your word ain't your bond," Boom said. "You got her taking care of *your* seeds by herself, me pitching in like I'm they real daddy and you off doing your thing. I go down in the belly and you run over there and play daddy, and hit off my girl. Our understanding was since you left her hanging with those boys you were to stay gone—on the motherfucking periphery. That's some foul shit you did, Sham."

"It's complicated, Boom, I know. I always thought those boys were better off not having me in their life as a father. I don't know nothing about being nobody's father. And I admit I haven't always appreciated what Kenya is to me. But look, I'm going through some stuff, I can't deal with all this right now."

"You got no choice, Sham. I don't care how big these shook-ass niggas around here think you are. I'm making you deal with it. Ain't nobody ever pulled your card before... I'm fiddin' to test you and I think your ass is gonna fold. You think I'm some bitch nigga gonna let you disrespect me like this. Nah, Sham, I'm on you."

"Boom, come on, man..." Slay's voice trailed off as the other line went to static. "Shit!"

Once again Slay slammed his phone down and immediately it rung back. Slay let it ring, gritted his teeth and looked out the window at a couple of kids horsing around on the sidewalk outside the 1 Hour Photo shop. The bigger of the two kids held the smaller one in a headlock that the smallest couldn't break from and that the bigger kid refused to release. Life was nothing but a big fight. Life beat, punched, kicked and bit at you until you either fell in defeat or closed your eyes for that eternal sleep. Life was a pesky son of a gun that refused to lose.

The bigger boy finally let his grip around the other boy's head loose. The smaller boy fell to his knees, rubbed at his neck, and then, on the sly, jumped up and swung wildly at the bigger boy. His punch missed by a country mile and he quickly found himself locked in the wrestling hold again.

Slay was sick of it all. Everything was coming to a head, quick fast and in a hurry, and he was struggling to keep up, struggling to even care about the outcome of the fight any longer.

NANCY

"I'm gonna see to getting you something, Nan," George says to me.

He leans down and kisses me on the cheek. I'm sitting on the couch watching television, pretending that I'm keeping up with the story, picking at the bowl of soup George had placed in front of me an hour before.

"I'm just waiting on a callback," George says to me. "I left a message with the guy a short while ago."

I look up at him. He is serious about this. He is serious about holding me up. I smile even though I know the missing teeth in my mouth take away from the love and warmth I desperately want to show him.

"We not gonna stay this route forever, mind you," George continues. "I want you to start preparing yourself for a better fight, you hear?"

I nod. My head feels as if it's too big for my neck, as if nodding would make me break apart. George pats my head, closes his eyes, prays out loud for God to understand that "right on time" is approaching like a bullet.

"How?" I force myself to ask after George's prayer. I rarely talk nowadays because I hate how distorted my voice sounds. Swollen lips, rotted-out teeth and a mangled brain capacity wreak havoc on the voice.

"How what?" George asks me.

I lick my lips and close my eyes, swallowing as if my throat was sore.

"Oh," George says, realizing. "I asked around."

I'm glad he did.

"Much better than going out there willy-nilly, hoping for lightning to strike," George says to me. I want to say it wouldn't be so hard for me if you gave me money, but I don't.

"I'm gonna draw you a hot bath, Nan. You want a bath, baby?" George asks me.

I nod. A bath would be good.

George kisses my cheek again, rises and goes to prepare my bath just the way I like it—plenty hot. I try to focus on the love I have for this man and the love he has for me but I can't. All I can think about is sucking. Sucking some more life back into my system.

CHAPTER 25

The nurse at the ARU floor's main desk straightened her posture and gestured to a passing nurse as Slay made his burdened lope in their direction. The nurse who'd been walking stopped, looked over her shoulder and put her hands in her pockets as she waited for Slay to reach her. She tapped her feet and kept stealing glances at the other nurse behind the desk.

Reverend Jameson Pinckney sat at the end of the hallway on a flowery couch that sat next to the pay phones. It was as if the reverend could feel the air leaving the hallway, could feel a change in the corridor, for he looked up from the newspaper he was reading and caught the eye of Slay moving down the hall. The reverend folded the newspaper and placed it on his lap, his high-riding pants showing off the pasty skin of his shins and those clunky black shoes. His fat red cheeks contrasted with his downcast eyes and the always smiling reverend had his mouth closed for a change as he watched Slay approaching the nurse.

"Mr. Slay?" the nurse called to Slay as he moved to pass.

Slay turned to her. "Yeah?"

"I need to have a word with you."

"Let me go put this sweater on my mama," Slay told her. "And I'll come right out."

"I need to speak with you first," the nurse insisted.

Slay looked at the nurse closely. She turned away. He turned and noticed the reverend, down at the end of the hall, looking up with concern. The reverend tapped the folded newspaper against his leg, twice, and rose slowly and began walking in Slay's direction. Slay turned back to the nurse. He shook his head. "No, no, no, no."

"It was a peaceful surrender," the nurse told him.

Slay rocked on the balls of his feet. He could feel a horrible, indescribable type of pain rising up through him. His breathing became a labor. "Peaceful?"

The nurse nodded. "We attempted to reach you but your cell phone—"

Slay wheeled and started walking toward his mother's room. The nurse followed on his heels. Reverend Pinckney was waiting by the door as Slay neared it.

"God in his infinite wisdom has called her home," the reverend said as Slay stopped and looked through the window of the door.

Slay brushed the reverend aside and walked into the room. He stopped a few feet in, the nurse and reverend at his shoulders. "Why ain't she covered or something?"

"She expired just a few minutes ago," the nurse told him. "The doctor has to come and make it official. Do you have a funeral home in mind? We can call and ask them to pick up the body later."

"I waited for you so we could say a prayer over her," the reverend said.

"Will y'all shut the fuck up?" Slay barked. "I can't hear myself think over y'all." He took another step forward and stopped. This was a one-step-at-a-time process.

"I'll be at the front desk if you need me," the nurse said.

Slay took another baby step forward. "Damn, man. I brought your sweater." He groaned. The sweater was balled in his fist. "I brought your sweater. I brought your sweater…"

"I'll let you have a moment with your mother. I'll be right out in the hall," Reverend Pinckney said, backing from the room.

Slay took the last step that put him up next to the bed. His mother looked peaceful, happy. He hesitated as he reached forward to touch her. She was still warm. He blinked his eyes as it looked as if her chest was still rising. He turned his head and let out the breath it seemed he'd been holding for the past few minutes.

R.I.P.

Pour out a little liquor.

This kind of hurt couldn't be extinguished with a cute phrase or some ghetto tradition. He'd seen senseless deaths and murders since he was a little boy but this was the first time it touched him this close. "Damn, man. I brought your sweater." He couldn't come up with any other words. He couldn't release the sweater from his clamp-tight grip either.

Alone.

He moved over by the window and pulled out his cell phone. Hospital regulations forbid the use of cell phones but he was beyond caring about hospital regulations.

He dialed the number to Kenya's apartment. She picked up on the third ring.

"Kenya," he said. "Is Boom there? Anywhere around there?"

"No, he left," she said. "I told him."

"I know."

"He was angry but—"

"My mama died."

"What?"

"Yeah…she's gone. You're my heart now, Kenya. Always was. You all I have left. I'm gonna do right by you and the boys. I'm gonna fix things."

Kenya was too concerned with Slay's well-being to bask in the wonderfulness of the things he was saying. "Where you at?"

"The hospital. I need you to do me a favor."

"Anything," Kenya said.

"Call my sister. Call Cydney—"

"Slay, I can't be telling her your moms died."

"No," Slay said. "I want you to see if she'll let me come see her. I'll tell her this myself."

"Okay," Kenya said, relaxing. "You're at the hospital, you said. You want me to get a cab over there?"

Slay shook his head as if Kenya could see the gesture. "Nah, I'm coming to you."

"That ain't a good idea, Slay. Boom was crazy mad, he might—"

Slay flipped his cell phone closed.

He turned and looked at his mother's lifeless body. "I'll see you again."

Officer Jackson was sitting on the steps that led to Cydney's second-floor apartment as she walked up. In one hand he held a disposable cup, in the other a pink rubber ball that captivated his attention as he squeezed it. Cydney started to turn and head in the other direction, but what was the use of that, Jackson looked determined, as if he'd sit here waiting for her until the sun set and rose again if he had to.

Jackson wore dark blue slacks and a disgusting shade of brown sweater covered in lint balls that looked like flakes of snow. As Cydney crossed over from the grass to the sidewalk, the clack of her heels made Jackson look up from that pink rubber ball. He pocketed it and stood.

Jackson flexed his hand as Cydney stood before him. "Carpal tunnel syndrome," he said. He pulled the ball he'd just deposited in his pocket back out and showed it to her. "My doctor suggested this might help with my wrist strength. If not, then I have no choice but the knife." He put the ball back in his pocket again. "So, how are you doing, Ms. Williams?" he said in an effort to pull some words from her. His breath, a heavy mixture of coffee and mints, touched her at the same time as his voice.

"I'm good, Officer...?"

"Jackson."

She nodded.

"I've been sitting here waiting for you for a good hour, hour and a half. You're the first soul I've seen the entire time."

Cydney looked around. "It's quiet here."

Jackson sucked his teeth, picked at them with a ragged fingernail. "Ominously quiet, you ask me. You know they identified that body they found on that construction site up the street?"

Cydney nodded, but her eyes showed she didn't know anything about a found body.

Jackson, great observer that he is, picked up on the admission in her eyes. "You didn't hear about that? Some construction worker came up with a body part while working his backhoe. Turned out to be a fifteen-year-old girl from Nicaragua that had only been in the States a couple of months. She went from Nicaragua to Mexico, and walked across to Texas. The INS released her into the custody of her aunt who was already here. The girl got mixed up with the wrong crowd apparently. The last anyone saw of her, she was coming from some seedy little bar in Asbury Park." Jackson shook his head. "Arbitrary violence, it's a shame. And then whoever did it to her goes and buries her in a construction site. A couple more months, if she wasn't found, her cemetery headstone would have been a Home Depot, Target, maybe she gets lucky and it's a Wal-Mart." Jackson shook his head. "Crime is everywhere, dear. It's disheartening."

Cydney agreed by way of raising her eyebrows into a rainbow arc and pursing her lips. "That it is."

"Which brings me to why I'm here," Jackson said.

"You mind if we take this discussion upstairs to my apartment?"

Jackson stepped to the side, extended his arm. Cydney passed and climbed the stairs. Jackson crumpled his cup and tossed it in the trash receptacle next to the stairway, and then he tackled those stairs.

Inside, Cydney asked, "Would you care for something to drink?"

"No, I better not," Jackson said, patting his stomach. "That coffee will be running through me soon, as it is."

Cydney nodded. "So what can I do for you, Officer Jackson? I take it you want to talk to me about Felicia Rucker's attack?"

Jackson took the liberty of finding a seat for himself on the couch. Cydney sat in the chair across from him. "Your boyfriend didn't want to give me your name when I spoke with him. I'm bad with names, you know. But then, as I was going through our investigation file something clicked as I kept looking over the name we had for Shammond Slay's sister—Cydney Williams, Cydney Williams. And then I remembered the night at the hospital. I wasn't sure, but something told me that's what Desmond had told me your name was. I knew something was wrong anyway by the way you hightailed it out of there." Jackson massaged his bad hand and frowned. "I'm glad my sixth sense hasn't left me."

"What's your sense telling you?" Cydney asked.

"Shammond Slay is your brother."

Cydney nodded. "Yes, he is, unfortunately. You knew that from your file. That's fact, not some kind of sixth-sense hoodoo."

"Your brother's a charismatic young man," Jackson said, smiling, "Why the disdain for him, Ms. Williams?"

"I don't approve of the life he's chosen," Cydney answered.

Jackson's eyes crested. "Oh, really, what life would that be?"

Cydney simply smiled.

"Other than the problems he had as a juvenile your brother has a perfectly clean adult record," Jackson noted.

"Wonders never cease."

"And a rock-solid alibi for his whereabouts the night of Felicia's attack."

Cydney sat silent.

"Let me venture a guess if I might," Jackson said. Cydney didn't object, so he went on. "Shammond was completely cool when we talked to him except for one moment. I asked him point-blank how he felt about young women being raped and he went off on a tangent talking about his love for black women. He mentioned your mother and he mentioned you. He kept going on about how you two were his heart and soul and that he'd never harm a black woman because of that. He was quite strong in his opinion about the topic. So strong I decided to check and see what you and your mother had to say about his character." Jackson stopped and cleared his throat. "Now, as I'm sure you're aware, your mother wasn't in any condition to tell us anything. And then when I had you looked up...and I remembered the name. It all began to make sense why Mr. Rucker was so evasive when I asked about you. I knew something was wrong from the night at the hospital, like I said, but I wasn't expecting it to be that you were Shammond Slay's sister. I also wasn't expecting to find that years ago you had a restraining order against your brother."

Cydney shrugged. "So?"

Jackson forced a smile. "Your brother wasn't too fond of your seeing Desmond Rucker, was he? In fact, my guess is he's not too fond of you seeing anybody."

"Shammond can be overprotective," Cydney admitted.

Jackson nodded. He could tell it was best he leave this alone. "Do you think he'd harm Felicia Rucker to get back at Desmond?"

Cydney looked off around her apartment. "I'm not sure what he'd do."

"Let me put it a different way," Jackson said. He moved

forward on the couch, his backside barely in contact with the leather, and leaned in to Cydney. He looked like a man apologizing for wronging his woman; she looked like a woman scorned and milking the apology for all she could. "Would you put it past him to harm Felicia Rucker to get back at Desmond?"

Cydney thought about innocent Felicia Rucker and Desmond's despondency the night of the incident. She thought about the poor acting job her brother had put forth when she questioned him about Felicia. She looked at Officer Jackson. "No, I wouldn't put it past him."

Jackson settled back into the couch. "I thank you for your truthfulness."

"Are we done here?" Cydney asked him.

"Yes."

Cydney stood. "I hate to be rude but I desperately need to take a hot bath and get myself some rest."

"Oh, of course," Jackson said, rising to leave.

Cydney followed him to the door. Jackson stopped before crossing out into the hall and turned back to Cydney. "Your brother is responsible for his own actions. Don't believe for one minute that you could change him, or by telling me what you have that you've done him an injustice."

Cydney placed her arm on the door and inched it forward a tad. "Good day, Officer Jackson."

The door closed and Cydney took a deep breath. The phone started to ring but she paused by the door, in reflection.

Breaking up was so hard to do, especially when it's someone you truly love, someone who truly loves you.

There was no doubt left. She'd broken up with Slay for good.

She went to answer her phone.

Felicia trembled as she dialed the numbers and waited for a pickup. Each ring in her ear brought with it the painful memories. Stubborn stains and odors stuck in the fabric of her mind that couldn't be dissolved with elbow grease, Heloise's hints or Felicia's own sheer will.

Slay, her supposed thug lover.

The cab ride over with that annoying driver.

The couple she encountered in the lobby, smiling, arms entwined in love, riding up the elevator together. The supposedly broken elevator.

The cold stairwell.

The climb up those three flights of stairs.

The voices, giddy and high-strung, up above her head.

Her initial hesitation—and then her shaking off that hesitation, strutting up those stairs as if she didn't have a care in the world, looking for love in all the wrong places.

Those rough fingers gripping her by the ankles and then...

"Hello."

And then...

"Hello, who is this?"

Felicia licked her dry lips. "Hi there, Daddy."

"Felicia? Hey yourself. We were just talking about you and your brother. What—your nose itched?"

Felicia laughed at the old wive's tale.

"The Karnegys stopped in," Frank Rucker continued. "You remember them, don't you? They used to get Desmond a different oil company toy tanker truck every Christmas, and you they got a different Barbie. All of those little outfits. You would spend hours mixing and matching them." Frank Rucker laughed to himself. "Coordinating them, you said. I think the Karnegys set you up for this modeling thing."

"Yeah, I remember," Felicia acknowledged.

Felicia always had a fascination with clothes, but since the stairwell she was like a cruise traveler, seasick. She was nauseated by just the sight and feel of clothes, as the seasick traveler would be by the sight and smell of food. She felt as if the way she dressed had brought about the way she was treated on that cold stairwell.

Over the past few days, Felicia had bagged up the short skirts she'd brought down from New York and placed them on the curb outside for garbage pickup. Then she remembered that she'd been wearing a long skirt that night. She immediately bagged up all her other skirts and curbed them as well. Next, she bagged all her cleavage-revealing tops, all her other tops, and curbed them for garbage pickup as well.

She was left with only a pair of blue jeans fading to yellow and an oversize Penn State sweatshirt that she'd taken from Desmond years back.

"So how are things going?" her father called through the line.

"Fine, I suppose," Felicia lied. For now, that would be her stance. Later, she didn't even know when, she'd confront the truth with her parents.

"What's going on with Desmond?"

"Running that restaurant," Felicia answered.

"Yeah," her father mused. "That's a gift and a curse."

"You've been mighty down on the culinary business lately," Felicia said.

"Like I told you, your mother and I didn't get nearly enough time with your brother and you because of those restaurants," Frank Rucker responded. His voice was easy but there was bitterness in his words. "That's the curse part. I've been thinking about that endlessly these past few months. That and the stuff you said about me being so hard on you two, putting so much pressure on you, never being satisfied."

"Have you?"

"Yes indeedy. The older you get the more you start to reflect on things. I hope you two learn earlier than I did. Particularly Desmond."

"Desmond?" Felicia chuckled. "You're worried about Mr. Perfect?"

"Mr. Perfect?"

"Despite what you think," Felicia said, "Desmond is squeaky clean. The wedding fiasco is probably his only real slipup, and you're partly the blame for that."

"You don't know?"

"Don't know what?"

"Why I was so hard on him during that time. Why I insisted he rethink the wedding."

"Because that's how you are and—"

"Caught him having sex with one of our waitresses," Frank Rucker said. "They were out in the parking lot like some teenagers. She happened to be a married woman, two children."

"Oh?" was all Felicia could say.

"Told Desmond he needed to do some reflecting," Frank Rucker said.

Felicia cleared her throat, chased away her surprise, moved on. "I've been doing some reflecting of my own."

Frank Rucker hesitated. "Oh?"

"I don't think the modeling is for me. If you guys haven't spent that tuition money, I think I want to give college a try." Felicia thought about the knowledge she sought about herself and the world at large. What better learning ground was there than college?

"A try?"

"I want a degree," Felicia added. "Criminal psychology, something along those lines."

"What brought about this change?" Her father's voice cracked with excitement. It made Felicia feel good that she was the source of his awakening joy. She needed that.

"That's a long story," Felicia told her father. "One day I plan on sharing it with you and Mommy."

"Hold on," Frank Rucker said. "Your mother just finished showing the Karnegys out. She's coming now. I want you to tell her."

"Okay."

Felicia could hear her father in the background as her mother walked up. "Felicia's on the phone. She wants to give up the modeling and go to college."

Felicia smiled and shook her head. Her father never was one for keeping secrets.

Barbara Rucker's voice came on the line. "Felicia, hey there, baby."

The sound of her mother's voice was like arms wrapped around her, providing her with warmth and security. This was going to be a long struggle, no doubt, but just as Felicia thought, she could make it through it. "Hi, Mommy," she said.

"You got something to tell me?"

Felicia smiled, the stairwell forgotten for the moment. "Yes, Mommy, I do. I want to go to college."

The drive from the hospital to Kenya's apartment was when it finally hit Slay that his mother, his precious mother, was gone. He kept his Nas pumping through the stereo speakers but the clacking of drums and the vibration of bass didn't comfort him as it normally did. He turned the CD off completely when it came to Nas's song, "Fetus," a tribute from the rapper to his own mother.

Slay had just gotten his windows tinted last week and outside he could see people staring as he drove down the block. Normally, he would have cranked his music loud and slowed his driving, but today wasn't a normal day. He looked over at the passenger seat. The sweater he was too late in bringing to his mother lay in a crumpled mess. On top of the sweater was a pamphlet the reverend had given him at the hospital about grieving. Slay took the pamphlet out of courtesy, but he was sure as death and taxes that nothing written on those scant pages could come close to helping him deal with his loss.

At Kenya's, no longer his mom's as far as he was concerned, he parked and slowly strode down the cracked sidewalk path to the building's lobby. His hand was on the door handle when he felt a presence behind him. A shadow. He wheeled quickly, his hand balled in a fist, ready. Expecting to see Boom.

"Cydney?"

"Slay," she said, soft, but all business.

"Shammond."

"Slay," she repeated.

Slay nodded, not about to press the issue. "Kenya called you?"

"You know she did."

"I was gonna come by your place."

"Don't want you there," Cydney said. She looked around, couldn't fight the wrinkling of her nose. "As much as I despise this place, I'd rather come out here and see you than have you in my domain again."

"It's that serious?"

She mimicked his question with an answer. "It's that serious."

Slay eyed his sister, looking so odd in an oversize blue jacket. Blue—his mother's favorite color. A color Cydney had sworn off the minute Nancy Williams became a slave to the crack pipe. And yet, today, Cydney was covered with the tattered, oversize, blue jacket. Fitting she'd break her ban on the day her mother broke the plane between this world and the next.

"Did you call me to tell me the truth about the girl… Felicia?" Cydney asked.

Slay didn't answer; instead, he continued eyeing Cydney, studying her even more intently. His appraisal seemed to unnerve her, as she hunched her shoulders together, pulled the blue jacket tight around her frame. Having trouble meeting him, eye to eye.

"I know you were involved," Cydney managed to say. "Might as well go ahead and—"

"Mama's gone," Slay said, heading Cydney off.

She sniffed. "Gone where? On another binge, running the streets, chasing down—"

"Passed on today," Slay said in a shaky whisper of a voice. "I'd had her over at Jersey Shore."

Cydney gasped, raised a trembling hand to her mouth; her tattered, oversize, blue jacket fell open. Slay eyed her chest briefly. She recovered, pulled the coat tight around her body again.

"But you wanted to talk about Felicia," Slay said. "So, shoot away, ask your questions."

Cydney shook her head. "Mama…"

"Forget Mama. Felicia Rucker. GQ Smooth's little sister. Was I involved in what happened to her?"

"Shammond, don't."

"Slay," he barked. "Slay. Was I involved…yes."

Cydney's eyes drooped, a slow but strong sadness taking hold.

"George, too," Slay continued.

Cydney stood mute, shaking.

"Sicced my dogs on the both of 'em," Slay said. A weight came off his shoulders. His throat tightened but he continued, "Mama's gone. You *been* gone. I don't have anything to lose," he choked out. "I'm a bad guy. Always have been."

"Shammond," Cydney said, trying to move forward and touch his sleeve, his wrist, something. But Slay shrank away. Turned back and looked toward the building.

"All I got is Kenya and them boys," he said. "They're mine, you know. Both of Kenya's boys."

Cydney shook her head.

"Mama knew," Slay said, shaking his head now too. "Told me to settle that situation. Walk right. I'd be happy. I never listened. Until it was too late."

"It's never too late," Cydney said.

A strange smile graced Slay's face. "Ain't it though, sister?" He gritted his teeth, then settled his jaw, proud, strong. "I ain't any good, Cydney, you called it right. Of no worth. Kenya and the boys been managing without me for all this time. They'll continue to." He looked expectantly in the distance, searched the grove of bushes by the building, the parking-lot area.

Finding nothing, he turned his gaze back on Cydney. "I've loved...wrong. But I've loved. I wish I'd done better. Tell you the honest to God truth, I don't have the stomach for the tough-and-rough shit. George. Felicia. The both of them situations just ain't sat right with me. I fucked up. I sicced my dogs on 'em and, damn, messed up. My dogs did what I set them out to do. They innocent in all this, under my thumb and shit. I'll never give 'em up. But me, I gotta pay."

There was a quiet rustling in the distance. Four men made their way in Slay's direction. One lone man, so different in demeanor from the other four, loped along sadly behind them.

Slay looked up, grinned. "Here they are, Cydney. You can take off the coat."

A rookie officer reached Slay first, grabbed him strongly by the wrist. "You have the right to remain silent..." The words were lost on Slay's ears. Instead, he looked at Cydney, smiled, turned and looked at Kenya's apartment tower, allowing a stream of tears to run down his face unabated.

Officer Jackson reached Cydney as the others shuffled Slay to a waiting, unmarked car. Jackson reached out his hand and Cydney removed the blue coat, Jackson's wife's, and handed it to him. She reached under her shirt and pulled out the mess of wires. Dropped them hard and unpleasantly in Jackson's hand. "You did the right thing," he said.

Cydney turned without a reply. Desmond stood back a distance, leaning against the building for support. Their gazes met. Desmond nodded. Cydney moved to him, slowly. Desmond wrapped her in his arms.

"He knew," she whispered. "He knew I was setting him up. He turned himself in."

"Tired of running," Desmond replied.

Cydney nodded. She knew the feeling. She let the tears fall. For George and Nancy. For Slay, Shammond. For...her own self.

DESSERT (EPILOGUE)

"I named it after an ancient city in Africa," Desmond said. "Cush. I liked the ring of it from the first moment."

Mary Roberts, a correspondent from the *Today Show* smiled and then placed the microphone in front of Cydney. The *Today Show* was filming a special segment in Asbury Park, mirroring Bruce Springsteen as he toured his adopted hometown, a hometown quickly rising from the ashes. "Your boyfriend has taken the city by storm with this restaurant," Roberts said to Cydney. "What's your favorite dish?"

"Actually," Cydney said, "I've been looking forward to a certain dessert that Desmond has been promising to share with me for some time."

"Ooh, you've got my attention," Mary said. "What dessert would that be?"

"Apple brown betty," Cydney told her.

Mary Roberts looked at Desmond. "Are you going to make sure this stunning young woman gets her apple brown betty today, Mr. Rucker?"

Desmond nodded. "I most definitely am."

Bruce Springsteen's folksy voice could be heard in the background, blending in perfectly with the house band. Cush was filled, even more than usual, with patrons eager to get a good meal and possibly a quick run on television.

"I'm going to allow you two to continue with your meal," Mary said, "and meanwhile, for you folks out there in TV land enjoy this impromptu performance from the one and only Bruce Springsteen as we head toward the commercial break."

Mary politely thanked Desmond and moved with her camera crew to the back of the restaurant, where the performance pit was.

"Are you feeling like a celebrity?" Desmond asked Cydney.

"Going to hold on to my fifteen minutes as long as I can," she told him.

"My folks wanted Thanksgiving to be the first they saw of you," Desmond said, "but I figured you'd get a kick out of being on camera with me."

Cydney smiled, nodded, her thoughts drifting.

"What are you thinking about?" Desmond said.

Cydney sighed. "Thanksgiving," she said softly.

"What about it?"

"I didn't care over the past few years that I wasn't sharing it with my mother and my brother, but this year…"

"It's going to take some time," Desmond said.

Cydney nodded her head. "I'm trying to move forward. It's hard, though. I feel so guilty."

"You have nothing to feel guilty about, Cydney."

"My mother needed me. I didn't even know she was in the hospital. I should have at least been there to hold her hand as her life slipped away." Cydney's eyes drifted. "Shammond, in all of his craziness, he was always there for her, always there for me, too, in his own way."

Desmond sighed, thinking of his own sister and the rough road ahead for her. Luckily, Felicia seemed to have had the courage for the good fight. She'd been feverish in her planning for college, collecting brochures, visiting campuses. "It's a sad situation," Desmond said.

"My brother made his bed," Cydney said unconvincingly.

"Yes, he did."

Cydney's eyes squinted; she looked off behind Desmond. "There's a woman and man over there staring us down."

Desmond turned. He fought like hell to keep his mouth from dropping open. "She's...she's coming over," he stammered.

Jacinta approached their table. She wore tan pants and a plush cashmere top. Her eyes were alive like the atmosphere, the music and the mill of voices. Her stroll was strong and assured. She had a beauty about her now that greatly surpassed the beauty she possessed half-naked onstage. She looked happy.

"Mr. Rucker," she said, extending her hand as she reached the table. "My boyfriend and I've been standing there for a few minutes trying to figure out if I should approach your table. Your restaurant is just fabulous." She turned to Cydney, smiling. "You must be so proud of your husband."

"Boyfriend," Cydney said. "And yes, I'm very proud of him."

"Boyfriend, that's it?" Jacinta frowned. "Work on him, girl." She turned and looked at the man she'd just left. He smiled and nodded. She turned back to Cydney. "I'm working on mine, too. It's still very early, but so far, so good. Think he might be the one. Pray for a sistah, please."

"I will," Cydney said.

"Thanks for your compliments," Desmond cut in.

Jacinta nodded. "You're quite welcome. And, oh, by the way—"

Desmond flinched. Here it came.

"My name is Mona," Jacinta said. "I didn't mean to be rude."

Desmond's shoulders eased back against his chair. He started to breathe freely again. "Well, thanks, Mona."

Jacinta nodded. "You two enjoy your meal—" she looked to Cydney "—and, sister, you work on getting that ring like I said."

Cydney smiled, nodded. "Same to you, Mona."

Jacinta walked off.

"What a nice woman," Cydney said. "You're touching so many people with this place."

Desmond shook his head, watched Jacinta move toward the front of the restaurant. "So you want a ring?" he asked Cydney.

Cydney was in the process of sipping her lemonade. "Hmm... Yes, when the time is right, with the right guy."

"You think I can be the right guy someday?"

Cydney smiled. "I like your chances."

Desmond patted the table. "What do you say we order our dessert now?"

Cydney rubbed her hand over her stomach. "Let's do it. I saved some space, hoping you'd ask."

Desmond gestured for one of his waitresses. When the waitress arrived, he smiled at her warmly. "We'll have an apple brown betty, one plate, two spoons." When the waitress walked off Desmond turned that warm smile onto Cydney.

"Why the wide smile?" Cydney asked.

"I've been waiting for this for a long time, to share an apple brown betty with you."

"You just have a sweet tooth."

Desmond's eyes narrowed and he studied Cydney closely. "I sure do, *sweet* Miss Wonderful. I sure do."

"Ms. Hudson-Smith is well-known for her romance novels, but she will soon be well-known for her inspirational fiction as well."
—*Rawsistaz Reviewers*

Essence bestselling author

Linda Hudson Smith

FIELDS *of* FIRE

A novel

Newly engaged and working in professions dedicated to saving lives, Stephen Trudeaux and Darcella Coleman differ on one important decision—whether to start a family. Then tragedy strikes and they know it will take much reflection, faith and soul-searching for their relationship to survive.

Coming the first week of April, wherever books are sold.

NEW SPIRIT

Visit us at
www.kimanipress.com

KPLHS0270407TR

Celebrating life every step of the way.

YOU ONLY GET *Better*

New York Times bestselling author
CONNIE BRISCOE
and
Essence bestselling authors
LOLITA FILES
ANITA BUNKLEY

Three fortysomething women discover that life, men and
everything else get better with age in this entertaining
three-in-one anthology from three award-winning authors!

Available the first week of March wherever books are sold.

KIMANI PRESS™
www.kimanipress.com

KPYOGB0590307TR

Pleasure SEEKERS

Part of the Hideaway Legacy

A sizzling, sensuous story about Ilene, Faye and Alana—
three young African-American women whose lives are
forever changed when they are invited to join the
exclusive world of the Pleasure Seekers.

Rochelle Alers

NATIONAL BESTSELLING AUTHOR

"Fans of the romantic suspense of Iris Johansen,
Linda Howard and Catherine Coulter
will enjoy [*Pleasure Seekers*]."
—Library Journal

Available the first week of January wherever books are sold.

sepia™

A special Collector's Edition from
Essence bestselling author

KAYLA PERRIN

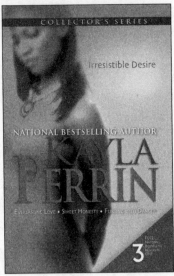

Three full-length novels

From one of the most popular authors for the
Arabesque series comes this trade paperback volume
containing three classic romances. Enjoy warmth, drama
and mystery with EVERLASTING LOVE, SWEET HONESTY
and FLIRTING WITH DANGER.

"The more [Kayla Perrin] writes, the better she gets."
—*Rawsistaz Reviewers* on *Gimme an O!*

Available the first week of January wherever books are sold.

KIMANI PRESS™
www.kimanipress.com

Enjoy the early *Hideaway* stories
with a special Kimani Press release...

HIDEAWAY LEGACY

Two full-length novels

ROCHELLE
ALERS

Essence Bestselling Author

A collectors-size trade volume containing
HEAVEN SENT and HARVEST MOON—
two emotional novels from the author's
acclaimed *Hideaway Legacy*.

"Fans of the romantic suspense of Iris Johansen,
Linda Howard and Catherine Coulter will enjoy the first
installment of the *Hideaway Sons and Brothers* trilogy,
part of the continuing saga of the *Hideaway Legacy*."
—*Library Journal* on *No Compromise*

Available the first week of March
wherever books are sold.

KIMANI PRESS™
www.kimanipress.com   KORA0650307TR